The Sweet *Redemption*

An Inspector Korg Mystery

For Laurie,
Tom Stienstra

Thomas F. Stienstra

The Sweet Redemption
Published by Wild Earth Press

Cover concept and design: Kerima Furniss
Book design: the eBook Artisans
Edited by Steven Griffin
Proofread by Suzanne Finney
Advance readers of draft: Stephani Cruickshank Stienstra, John Beath, Jim McDaniel, Shelly and Lance Lewis, Kerima Furniss, Robert Stienstra, Jr., David Zimmer, Ed Rice, Doug Laughlin, Tom Hedtke, Il Ling New

ISBN (Print Version): 978-0-9839844-8-1
ISBN (eBook): 978-0-9839844-7-4

Wild Earth Press
P.O. Box 15
Arcata, CA 95518
www.wildearthpress.com
E-mail: wildearthpress@gmail.com

For Stephani

A vagabond dreamer, a rhymer and singer of songs.
Singing to no one and nowhere to really belong.

—Waylon Jennings, 1977

One ship sails East, and another West.
By the self-same winds that blow.
'Tis the set of the sails, and not the gales
That tells the way we go.

Like the winds of the sea are the waves of time,
As we journey along through life.
'Tis the set of the soul that determines the goal,
And not the calm or the strife.

—Ella Wheeler Wilcox, 1916

1

SATURDAY

Inspector Korg heard the shot the same instant it blazed past his left ear. Another quickly followed and clipped the tip of his shoulder. It burned instantly.

Korg grabbed his shoulder with his left hand. His palm filled with sticky red liquid. On instinct now, heart pounding, he ducked behind a juniper thicket and dropped to a knee.

He raised his gun, peered over the top of the junipers and launched three rounds, trying to hold off his attacker. All his years of training sparked to life. Another shot came from behind him. He felt a piercing sting in his left side. He looked down and saw more red, dripping down in a stream.

Korg then caught movement on his far right. He turned and glimpsed a second gunman sneaking in from the rear, pivoted and fired. 'Maybe got a piece of him,' but the shooter then darted behind a low wood fence.

Both gunmen wore masks. Korg, stung and flooded in red, was desperate to avoid crossfire. He crawled forward into the cover of the junipers. With open space surrounding the junipers, there was no escape. This was as good a spot as any to make his stand, he figured.

"So this is how it will end," the inspector said to himself. "A week from retirement, and I'm about to get gunned down." Two more shots sizzled over his head.

Kristopher Korg was an inspector for the San Mateo County District Attorney's office, specialty homicide. For an entire career, he'd defined a sense of detached force. With his pal and best man, Deputy District Attorney Joseph Roper, he'd arrested and convicted 161 straight perps in murder cases over 25 years. Sure, there were many homicides where no arrests were made; mostly two-fers, gang killings where suspects were whacked in revenge shootings. When they brought a case, it stuck.

Korg and Roper worked out of San Francisco for 20 years, but bailed as a team for San Mateo County down on the Peninsula when a newly elected D.A. announced that San Francisco wouldn't prosecute any death penalty cases. More than 1,000 unsolved murders and 900 unsolved rapes were on the books, and for some felonies, entire investigations by other detectives consisted of phone calls to the victims. So, the local thugs getting away with murder, Korg and Roper jumped ship and headed south 15 miles to Redwood City on the San Francisco Peninsula. All that had earned him was a request for early retirement — getting fired — and now caught in crossfire.

From his concealed location in the juniper shrub, Korg rose a few inches to fire. Four shots, dispatched from his left, burned over his head in rapid succession. Then from behind and to the right, three more whistled past. "Semi-automatics, lots of ammo," Korg muttered to himself; outgunned and trapped. Just moments before, Korg thought he'd snared a shooter in the backyard of this Redwood City home. But it turned out to be the other way around.

His cell phone intoned "Sweet Dream Woman." Emma. His wife.

Two more shots went flying past. One nearly grazed his graying fluff of black hair.

On his phone, there was no time for hello.

"I'm in trouble, sweetheart," he whispered. "Gun battle. Been hit twice. I ducked down in a big juniper, but they've got me pinned down now. The two of them have me in crossfire. I'll try to hold them off as long as I can. But when I run out of ammunition, they'll move in for the kill. Just always remember this: I love you."

Emma's voice was urgent. "I love you, too."

Korg whispered again. "I might have nicked both of them. Not enough to stop anything."

More volleys of automatic fire erupted and whizzed overhead from each side of the trapped inspector.

"Well, after they get you," Emma responded, "come on in, I heated up chile verde burritos for lunch."

"It won't be long now."

"And then call Joe. He called the home line, said he tried calling you on your cell but you didn't answer."

"Yeah, I heard his ring tone."

Korg stood. Directly ahead, a masked gunman was sneaking up like a burglar through an unlocked window. Korg fired three times, striking the masked gunman in the chest with all three.

"Die," Korg shouted.

But seconds later, Korg was hit from behind, not once, but five times, drilled over and over. His gun slipped from his right hand as he fell to the ground.

Korg, still conscious, rolled over to get a glimpse of his attacker standing over him, gun pointed at his chest.

"Got you," said Korg's 14-year-old daughter, Rebecca.

"Yeah, but I got your brother Zack first, so the score is 1-1."

"No, I won," Rebecca insisted. "Zack lost and you lost."

"Didn't I hit you in the arm?"

"That doesn't count."

"Let's discuss it over lunch."

At the table in the Korg breakfast room, Zack, who had just turned 16, and his younger sister, Rebecca, described how they had trapped their dad in the paintball game.

"You never seem to win," Emma noted with a smile thrown to her husband.

"There's a lesson there," Korg said. "You ever notice how everybody gets shot up whenever we play paintball? Remember that. The general idea is to leave this world with the same number of holes you came into it with. Look what happened to me, a trained expert, when the shots started flying."

"Trained expert?" Zack howled. "Dad, you're the easiest guy to kill of all time." Zack wore a black T-shirt with the message, "To err is human. To blame someone else is good skills management."

Zack's cell chimed. "Hey," he mumbled into the phone, and then rocketed away from the table, off on another mission.

Rebecca's blue eyes glowed. Korg noticed again that his daughter had inherited his mother's radiance. "Dad, I don't think you've like ever won against us, like even once."

"Well don't tell any of the criminals I'm chasing."

"Like you're going to catch any criminals with one week to go."

"Ouch," Emma interjected.

Korg shook his head with a baleful grin. "Man, they're hard on me. Almost as hard on me as our illustrious new chief deputy district attorney, Ms. Roberta Pritchett."

"Now don't start in on her again."

Korg's phone rang, and this time the ring tone was "Good 'ol Boys," and that could mean only one thing: it was his old friend, Joe Roper. Korg stood and walked into the living room, talking.

"They got me again," he lamented into the phone.

"When are you going to learn to stay out of gun battles?" Roper asked.

"As long as my kids learn that, we'll be OK," Korg said. "You want to come over for a burrito? Chile verde. Emma's best. Lots of cilantro."

"You want a case?"

Korg stopped breathing for two seconds. One. Two.

"You there?" Roper asked.

"What do you mean, 'Do I want a case?' A case of Pacifico? Or Cabernet?"

"No, a case kind of a case."

"A week to go and I'm out. Pritchett has me on the next train out of Dodge, or don't you remember? And isn't this a Saturday, a day off?"

They both chuckled. When investigations are hot, there is no such thing as a day off. Sometimes no such thing as an hour off.

"This one comes straight from the top."

"Why don't they put Sager on it? Isn't he their guy now?"

"C'mon."

"Then why's he taking my job?"

"You know the answer to that."

Yes, he did. Roberta Pritchett.

Korg's official job title was Inspector with the Bureau of Investigation, which was under the jurisdiction of the district attorney's office. That gave Pritchett the hammer over the stable of inspectors on the 3rd floor at the Hall of Justice.

Roper broke the uncomfortable bubble of silence.

"This could be one of those real easy ones, where the guy shows up this afternoon. Or maybe complicated, the kind you like, one that would give you a chance to go out on top."

Roper heard a crack in the silence.

"Hell, you solved a lot of these in a day, sometimes two. C'mon, remind everybody what a genius bulldog you are."

Silence again.

From 25 years of interrogations, Roper knew that silence from Korg meant invisible compliance. Korg knew it too.

Roper pounced on the opening. "I'll pick you up in an hour. Wear your uniform."

Korg muttered as he folded shut his phone, and headed to the bedroom for a quick shower and a dark suit.

"Who cares?"

But the answer was obvious.

Roper picked up Korg in the county-issued dark green Ford Crown Victoria and worked their way ahead on U.S. 101 in fast, thick traffic, heading north.

"Why me? Why now?" Korg asked.

Roper ignored the question. "What's that red shit all over your hand?"

"Zack shot me in the shoulder with a paintball. Stung like hell. I grabbed it, and got a hand full of paint. But don't go sideways on me. Why me?"

"Because we both know you're the best. And I'm getting heat from up top to get something done fast."

"If I'm the best, why am I getting railroaded?"

"Because Roberta Pritchett does not like you."

"Besides that."

"There isn't any besides that."

"Just who does she think she is?"

"She thinks she's your boss."

Korg's embarrassed laugh told his friend he'd hit the mark.

Korg and Roper worked San Mateo County five years with fourteen straight successful murder arrests and homicide convictions. Then Roberta Pritchett shows up, appointed as chief deputy D.A.

Some might call this déjà vu, but Korg called it "vujà dé," an experience he didn't want to live all over again. At 55, he had plenty of good years left. But like five years earlier in San Francisco, at 50 he was considered an old white guy. Pritchett too considered Korg a dinosaur, a corroded penny in a tray of new silver dollars. She bulldozed him out, called it early retirement with benefits, versus getting booted. So another week and he was gone.

"OK, what's going on, Mr. Deputy District Attorney?"

Roper explained.

"This guy, Stephen Griffin, manager of a rock star, disappeared last week. He's a high-profile guy and a lot of people miss him."

With the tips of his fingers, Korg smoothed out his eyebrows, from the bridge of his nose outward, then pressed his temples. That was a good sign, Roper knew: The brain gears had engaged in the mind of the great Korg.

"Body?" Korg asked, looking straight ahead.

"No body," Roper answered.

"Crime scene?"

"No crime scene."

Korg turned to his old friend with a subtle hint of scorn.

"How long has this guy been gone?"

"A week."

"A week," Korg echoed in a derisive chortle. "A successful white male gone a week is hardly a missing person. There must be politics behind this, Joe."

Korg laughed and then muttered: "Just don't tell me Pritchett is pushing this."

Before he could answer, Roper had to brake as the traffic slowed for a BMW cutting across three lanes to reach the exit for San Francisco International.

"The guy was first reported missing by a rock star,

called us from New York," Roper said. "Actually, the chief roadie made the call. He's a biker who once killed a guy in a bar fight. Then the missing guy's sister calls every day, sometimes two, three times. When she didn't get any response from us, she went to the papers. Everybody's had the story, or at least something about it."

"Yeah, I saw it," Korg noted. "My wife pointed it out."

"That put some heat on us. Then yesterday, Jesse James Johnson, this rock star guy, called Roberta Pritchett and wanted details on the progress of our investigation, which by the way, hasn't started yet. Pritchett says People Magazine is going to have something, and we need to show that 'We're on the trail.'"

"You mean like, 'Hot on the trail?'"

They guffawed at the ludicrous vision of Pritchett doing the dirty work and tracking down a criminal. After the Sheriffs Department had arrested so many gang members in East Palo Alto and Ravenswood, Pritchett had been appointed chief deputy D.A. in an elaborate public relations scheme for TV sound bites and photo ops, not investigations and litigating. She was smart, Korg admitted, good looking, too, even charismatic, but he preferred litigators who were part detective, not politicians like most.

"What's the missing guy's name again?"

"Stephen Griffin. A great guy, apparently. Everybody loves him. So we're going straight to AT&T Park, track down this roadie, Winovitch, and sniff out the principals. They're setting up for a big concert. The case is yours."

"Mine for a whole week."

Korg grinned at the thought of Pritchett's absurd sense of urgency whenever the press showed up.

"OK. Just as long as Sager isn't involved."

2

BADGES OPEN DOORS. So it didn't take long for Korg and Roper to weave their way inside San Francisco's AT&T Park to the pitcher's mound, where crews were setting up a sweeping outdoor stage, sound system, video and lighting, for the biggest late-summer gig of the year. Jesse James Johnson was one of several acts lined up ahead of Tenaya, the superstar rock headliner who would close the show.

Roper and Korg gaped at a massive biker who appeared to be running this setup. He had to be 6-5, 300, maybe bigger. He wore a leather vest over tanned bare skin. With a slick of sweat, he looked even bigger and more menacing up close. Tattoos everywhere. Still, Korg spotted a cell phone hitched to his jeans; even an outlaw had to answer to somebody.

With a nod at Korg that said, "This is our guy," Roper led the way. Korg pulled his badge.

The big guy didn't wait for a question.

"What the hell do you want with me?" he said with a growl. "I had nothing to do with those guys and that hot bike ring. I'm clean, on parole, everything by the book. I like being out of prison and plan to stay out."

"We never said anything about a hot bike ring," Korg countered with a grin. "Let's start with something easy. What's your name?"

"Klondike." The words rumbled like Sierra thunder. On his right forearm, in gothic lettering, Korg saw that the letters, printed diagonally, read F-u-c-k, and on his left forearm, in matching style, Y-o-u. "I run this place."

Klondike appeared to be descended directly from Cro-Magnon Man, Korg thought, but perhaps that was too kind; maybe he was linked rather to the woolly mammoth.

"Listen guys," Klondike countered, with all the respect he could muster. "Now does not work, isn't that obvious? We're setting up for the show."

But Korg stood his ground. "You're the head guy for Johnson's crew, right?"

"I run this fuckin' place."

"What's your real name?"

"Klondike."

"Well, I can see we're not going to get anywhere. Guess we'll just take you in and do it official-style."

Klondike halted. "Wait. I don't have time for this. I got a goddamn show to run. OK. Wait." He turned to see no one was eavesdropping. "Fred."

Roper laughed at the surrender. He wasn't accustomed to seeing the detectives do their thing, but this was a special treat, on a Saturday to hang with his buddy Korg, and he couldn't resist his own needle. "The same Fred Winovitch who murdered a guy by bashing his head into a brick wall."

Klondike offered no apologies. "They said I only

manslaughtered him. It was the buffalo that did it."

Roper had quickly reviewed the case late the night before when he ran a computer background check on all those close to Griffin.

"Except that you are the buffalo, right," Roper responded.

"I don't have time for this. OK. This is it: The buffalo is the only range animal that refuses to turn tail to a winter wind. The guy kept coming. I wasn't going to back up. No real man would ever back up. Just like a buffalo. The buffalo does not back up."

Korg was amused. I made a mistake, he calculated; this guy isn't part woolly mammoth, but bison, at least half.

Klondike's victim was a crankster with felony warrants who was mixing Tequila with meth, and also a member of a rival biker gang. When they crossed paths, neither would back down. But Klondike killed a wanted felon, got five-to-life and was out of prison in three. Now on parole, he had three years to stay in the clear.

"OK Fred, let's try something easy. What does that tattoo mean on the base of your skull? FTW."

Klondike scanned the surroundings again to make certain no one overhead.

"OK, it's my initials. Fred Theodore Winovitch. But since I'm a wrench, build choppers, some guys called me Fred The Wrench. That was before I got tagged Klondike."

Roper grunted a muted laugh. "Perhaps there is another explanation," he said, "like 'Fuck The World'."

Korg was enjoying the interplay. Actually, he respected Klondike, who lived by an honor code, just not one that others might comprehend. He also realized how the big man was connected to Jesse James Johnson and the missing guy, Griffin.

"OK," Korg said, taking over, "What do you know about Griffin's disappearance."

"Fuckin' nothing. I was in New York. As far as I know he went to Las Vegas to check out some talent and disappeared."

Korg looked at Roper like he had antlers growing out of his head.

"Las Vegas? He went to Las Vegas?"

Roper lowered his head in acquiescence.

"You didn't know that?" Klondike said in amazement.

"I just brought Inspector Korg in on the case this morning," Roper explained.

Korg pocketed his notebook. But Roper pressed on, and in minutes, acquired the itinerary of Johnson and the band, the location of Johnson's Woodside estate and recording studio, and a contact, Rosemary Yamani, who ran Johnson's office.

Klondike's gaze drifted to the stage. He saw that a roadie from Tenaya's crew, Spoogs, was making time with a sweet-looking young blond.

"Get to work," Klondike shouted.

Roper drew the big fellow back in. "You didn't much like Stephen Griffin, did you?"

"What you really mean, is "Did I do him?'"

That response drew Korg in. "Well, did you?"

Klondike turned away, an arm flexed. On a bicep, the knife-in-heart tattoo with drops of blood was alive with a waxen coating of sweat and dirt. A spider web tattoo extended from his elbow. By the glare, it looked as if beads of blood might start forming on his forehead.

"There was a time when I squished anybody who questioned anything I did."

Korg was unfazed. He actually grinned.

"Same here, Fred."

Klondike gritted his teeth into a contorted grin. That was the one answer he respected.

"A missing person isn't exactly my style."

"What do you mean by that," Korg asked.

"If it was me, you'd have a body, not a missing person," Klondike said. "I'm more like, 'Take care of it all at once.'"

Korg was stone. "You mean like bashing a guy's head into a brick wall." Now it was Roper who was amused.

The big guy paused, then said, "Yeah something like that. I figure somebody wasted Stephen Griffin in Vegas, then buried him out in the desert. Hell, I wasn't even in Vegas. We were all in New York. I told you that."

The senior agent stroked his chin and tried to lighten his stance.

"Think back. The night before you flew out to New York to set up for the opening show. Tell us where you were that evening and the next day."

"That's easy. I was at my place at Johnson's that evening. I live in the caretaker's cottage. I was there that night. And we haven't been to Las Vegas yet this year."

Klondike almost cracked his face into a smile, the corners of his mouth lifting almost imperceptibly, then spoke slowly to make sure the agents got it.

"You got it? I was at Johnson's that night, all night."

"Can anybody verify that for you?"

Roper was still silent and peered in, shoulders hunched.

"Yeah. I was with Jesse most of that night, getting our shit together."

Korg noted it.

"We flew out to New York the next day," Klondike added.

"When?"

"Around 1 o'clock. Arrived in New York that night."

At the stage, Spoogs, the young roadie for Tenaya, practically gave himself whiplash when the pretty blond approached him from the side.

"Hi, I'm Kristina," she started, light and innocent.

Her eyes were set off by subtle touches of eye shadow. She had clean, soft cheeks and a hint of a desperado smile set on her thin lips. Sandy blond hair fell about her shoulders, carefree and beautiful. In contrast to her blond hair and tanned skin, she wore a black tank top, twin points standing high, and low jeans so tight it was like they were a part of her.

To Spoogs, she had a way of tilting her head and smiling that made her seem defenseless; the gaze of a face you could trust.

The roadies were scurrying about, orders being shouted this way and that, setting up for the big show. Few even noticed the interaction along the back edge of the scaffolding. Not the other roadies. Not Klondike.

Kristina eyed him. Spoogs was smallish, slender, and adorable, your basic skinny kid who yearned for even a small piece of show business. Below the stage, he was running a 32-line Snake to the Mackie soundboard, 30 rows deep from the stage.

She pointed a single finger at him.

Spoogs just about stepped on his tongue. God, she was gorgeous. Her eyes danced with fireworks. "Me?"

She smiled and swung her blond hair across a shoulder. "I've seen you around. I'm working here, too, this weekend."

"I've got some blow," he said. "The best. Maybe we could share it."

"Here," she said, handing Spoogs a folded piece of paper. Then with a wink and a wave, she was gone.

Spoogs, the boy-man roadie, his pants torn at a knee, T-shirt hanging out, slinked off to a corner of the stage and read the note.

"Meet me in a half hour at the Upper Deck arcade, right behind Section 307, to share a great view."

He checked his watch. He'd heard about miracles like this. Once in a lifetime. Twenty minutes later, after hooking up the stage monitors for the rhythm section, he bailed.

"Stomach bothering me. Got to hit the bathroom."

And off he went.

"Where is that kid?" growled Klondike. It was a demand, not a question.

He knew Spoogs. Hired him for Johnson's road crew the year before. Then the kid jumped ship to crew for Tenaya. That little shit's been hanging out with Tenaya for a couple weeks, Klondike thought, and now he skips the stage like he's on a free-for-all vacation, not a job.

Through a stroke of management idiocy, road crews for several acts were forced to work as one. It wasn't exactly what roadies called "a finely tuned machine," and Klondike, no glad-hander when it came to accommodating strangers, but nevertheless in charge, was on knife edge to get the job done right.

Another Tenaya roadie, The Gator, spoke up. "He said he had stomach problems, had to hit the can."

Klondike exploded.

"I'm fuckin' allergic to bullshit. Which way did he go?"

"Thataway," and a single finger pointed toward the upper deck on the south bay side of the stadium.

"You done with me?" Klondike bellowed at Korg and Roper. He didn't wait for an answer.

"You guys get these guitar monitors wired," he ordered across the stage." Then he glanced at Korg. "I'll be back in 15 minutes."

"We'll catch you later," Korg answered, but Klondike had already stomped off. FTW, tattooed at the base of his skull, glared at the world behind him.

On the walk out of the stadium, Roper glanced at his watch, then eyed his old friend.

"We need to take a look at Griffin's beach house, like pronto. We're meeting Griffin's sister there, the one who called the press."

"Las Vegas?" Korg muttered at his friend. "Las Vegas?"

A light wind and the sun's low angle created wall-to-wall reflected silvers across the surface of South San

Francisco Bay. Spoogs scanned across miles of emerald water and absorbed the scenery. Visibility was crystal. Spoogs felt that he could take a running start and sail right across the bay and land on the Oakland hills.

McCovey Cove was quiet. Third Street was practically vacated. In the distance to the west, traffic was light in and out of the train station. In six hours, Spoogs figured, there would be 40,000 people jammed in here. The arcade, so peaceful where he was standing, would be chaos.

Spoogs, as Kristina had requested in her note, was waiting. He read the note again to make sure. It was signed with a heart.

Spoogs checked his shirt pocket. The packet of coke was ready. He'd love to get buzzed with her, and then, who knows? He turned and rested his slight forearms on the belt-high concrete wall and peered out to the south. She was right. You do get a great view from here.

Then Spoogs looked straight down, a free-fall drop of 165 feet to the asphalt below. He grinned as he felt a slight dizziness from spatial disorientation. Wait 'til he broke out his prize stash. He'd saved it for a moment like this.

Spoogs daydreamed a bit as he watched a lone sailboat pushing its way south on the bay at a slow crawl. She'll show eventually. Let Klondike cool his jets. Too bad the big guy is on parole, getting checked all the time for drugs; he could use getting stoned. It was like the big guy was born with his pants too tight.

A gull sailed past, gliding without a wing beat, from right to left, just above Spoogs' gaze. I'd love to be a bird, he thought. I wish I knew what it felt like to fly.

At that moment, Spoogs heard a crack as if somebody had slapped a pair of 2-by-4s together, and felt a hot jab pierce his back. Dizziness and weakness overwhelmed him, and he sprawled atop the concrete railing. Before he could turn and right himself, Spoogs felt a push from behind.

"What the..."

In one motion, his waist, thighs and ankles cleared the cement wall. He plunged head first, then tumbled.

As Spoogs somersaulted in free-fall, the world freeze-framed. He looked up at the arcade and the concrete rim. There, peering down, watching him, was the smiling face of his attacker.

'Why?' he wondered.

That person alone heard the scream. The thunk. The silence of death.

3

Roper took one look, dropped to his knees, coughed and spasmed.

Korg put a palm on his old friend's shoulder.

"It's tough to see something like this," Korg offered. "You never get used to it."

Roper retreated to the edge of the sidewalk, his right hand covering his forehead and eyes. He looked up at his old friend. "No wonder you're retiring. I'm not used to being out here."

Korg waited for SFPD to arrive, and in the meantime, kept gawkers clear of the area.

"What do we have here, Korg?"

It was Leroy Anders, one of Korg's old stable mates from San Francisco Homicide.

"A shooting and some sidewalk pizza," Korg answered. "Looks like the guy was tossed off the deck from up there." He pointed to the park's arcade level.

"But what are you doing here, Anders?" Korg asked his old friend. "Even if you catch the perp and get a signed confession with video, your D.A.'s not real hot on convicting murderers."

Anders winced. "Ya think?"

"How's the prisoner rehabilitation program going?"

"You mean for us in Homicide? Man, we're all beyond help."

Anders shook his head at his old running mate and added, "Say, aren't they retiring you down there on the Peninsula?"

Korg twisted his head in a contorted grin. "Touché, detective, touché."

"What do we have here? Is this as bad as it looks?"

Blood spatter was splotched on the concrete around the covered body.

Anders turned to face Korg.

"Why are you here? You know anything about this?"

"Just chasing my tail, Leroy, but a good place to start is to go inside the stadium and track down a big guy out on parole. Name is Winovitch. Biker guy goes by Klondike. Runs the roadies. Bashed a guy's head into a brick wall a while back."

"Thanks ol' friend."

"Last we saw him, he was heading from the field up toward the arcade up there." Korg pointed straight up to the concrete overhang above the street.

"Thanks again. Now what do you want, ol' boy? I know it's something."

Korg grinned. "My old partner. Knows me so well."

After a pause Korg added: "Copy me your CSI file on this. Maybe there will be something there for me."

Korg then eyed the blanched Roper with a single raised eyebrow.

"Let's go, man, let's go. Before someone else gets it. The clock is burning."

4

"WHAT'S HE DOING here?" shouted Korg.

From a distance Korg had spotted the pair of them, Inspector Jeremy Sager and a woman, apparently Griffin's sister, Bonnie, standing in front of Stephen Griffin's Miramar beach house.

"Pritchett ordered it," Roper said softly, his head dropping a bit, chagrin on his face, as he guided the car towards them. "She figured you would need a hand. Sager's here to support you, to do whatever you want him to."

"Anything I want him to?"

"C'mon, inspector, you need someone to chase down all the loose-ends and crap you won't have time for, you know that."

"That sounds an awful lot like a partner. He's not my partner. He's the asshole who's taking my job."

Roper turned public defender. "It's not his fault. You know that. He's a good kid."

Korg was not giving in, even to his best friend.

"And what about you? You picked me up and delivered me here, as what, my chaperone?"

"They thought I'd help you get used to the idea. Hey, you're my best friend."

Korg slapped the dashboard with a palm. Then he smiled.

"Why do only best friends screw with you?"

After a pause, Korg added: "I'm not going to work with Sager and that's all there is to it."

As they pulled up to the curb, Roper punched his buddy lightly in the shoulder. "Just have him interview the sister, keep him busy and out of your way, and then do your thing. He only does what you tell him to."

"How about he takes a nap on some train tracks?"

As Korg exited the car, he did not acknowledge Sager's presence. He walked with purpose up to Bonnie Griffin. Her mouth engaged instantly without an introduction.

"I know my brother better than anybody. He'd call. He'd always call. Something bad happened."

She stopped with a confused look.

"What's that red stuff all over your hands?" she asked.

"Paintball. I lost."

Bonnie Griffin was 5-8, with dark hair, brown skin, and dark eyebrows with light blue eye shadow setting off deep brown eyes. She was wearing khakis and a button-down stone canvas shirt; well built, if a little thick when viewed from the side.

Bonnie pressed on.

"When we were kids, our mom was gone and dad was in the dumper," Bonnie said. "So we were always there for each other. It was automatic. It's how we survived."

As they entered the beach house, Korg was transfixed by the ocean view. A large picture window provided a perfect vista not only of the sea, but the entrance of Pillar Point Harbor. From here, a fisherman could track the comings and goings of all the boats, listen in on the marine radio and always know where the fish were. Sea conditions would be no mystery; he'd just look out the window. Maybe this is where I should retire, he thought, here at the harbor at Miramar. But then again, his wife hated the fog and his kids would shoot him for real if he made them switch schools.

"You touch anything in here?" Korg quizzed.

Bonnie stiffened. "Nothing. Just stacked the mail."

Korg finally turned to Sager. "Get her story," he ordered, and with a nod at Roper, started inspecting the premises.

KORG FOUND HIS way to Griffin's office, Roper trailing close behind. On an expanded counter top, even from a few feet, Korg recognized the logo for Expedia.com on a computer print-out that sat on top of a loose jumble of office papers. With a pair of long tweezers, he picked up the document and inspected it.

"Look at this. The guy flew to Las Vegas," Korg muttered. "Here's his itinerary. Give me a break. A big-time guy in the music business goes to Las Vegas, is gone a week, and his sister is in crisis? You've got to be kidding. I've got a week to go and I'm wasting my Saturday afternoon doing this? With Sager?"

Korg continued to mock his pal. "No body. No crime scene. All you've got is a worried sister whose grown-up brother went to Las Vegas and didn't tell her about it? This is the D.A.'s idea of a missing person?"

Roper grimaced in another awkward moment.

Korg inserted the document into a plastic Zip-Loc, standard procedure when starting a case and dealing with unknowns.

Roper was a bit deflated. "At least check if there's anything suspicious here at all."

"Hey, the guy went to Vegas. What else do you need to know?"

Sager waved Bonnie Griffin aside.

"Come with me and tell me about your brother."

Sager, black, razor thin and with the piercing dark eyes of a Doberman, considered her in silence. He liked how she talked, her effortless style, like there was a direct connection from her mind to her mouth. She was everything he was not. He unconsciously massaged the front of his gold tooth with the tip of his tongue. His shoulders hunched, eyes narrowed, and hovered like a vulture in search of dead meat.

"Stephen and I didn't even look related because we had different mothers," she started, "but we always looked out for each other…"

Amid a galaxy of lookie-lous, her brother could find the one star, she explained. Stephen Griffin would become the catalyst for that talent, the engine to run a powerful machine where every gear interlocked with little wasted energy. He didn't cast much of a physical presence — a bit overweight, high forehead, balding, glasses. But he had a fast mind, quick gentle wit, and was well loved. He was good with money and details, and women felt safe with him. Most all who knew him, loved him.

Griffin discovered Jesse James Johnson on a hot night at Biscuit & Blues, the club on Mason in San Francisco. Even with a raw back-up band, in which each player seemed to be on a different song, Griffin saw something special in the guy, a charismatic force that connected with the audience. Griffin signed him to a management deal, fronted him money, built a new band around him and set up the theatrical backdrop. Griffin even renamed Jimmy Johnson to Jesse James Johnson. He co-wrote songs with Johnson, including the new song "Straight Ahead," a potential rock anthem.

Griffin paid for the demos that got Johnson in the game, and negotiated Johnson's five-CD deal with Diogenes Sound. Johnson retained primary artistic influence over the music and the label supplied a producer to keep tabs on things.

"He is the kind of guy who could take a million free-floating atoms and get them aligned to create a force," Bonnie said.

Sager was thinking money. "Any financial problems?"

"His cut was 15 percent of everything Johnson made, plus his cut from songwriting royalties, so he was probably stacking it up. He just bought a new Corvette and paid cash."

Sager took a deep breath and said: "Guys like that just don't up and disappear."

The young inspector sized her up. He liked what he saw. They were about the same age, he figured; maybe she had a few years on him. "What about you?"

Bonnie loved a captive audience.

"We had a lot of family problems, you know, and I basically raised him. That's why we're so close. Even now, we check in with each other all the time. That's why I reported him missing. Something is wrong." Then she added with a wink: "He always wants the details about any guys I see, I guess to make sure they're good enough for me. He's that kind of brother."

"Walk with me," Sager instructed.

They caught up with Korg and Roper at the bathroom counter.

"That's kind of weird," Korg said.

"What?" Bonnie asked. "Did you find something?"

Korg ignored her.

"Well, that's weird all right," Korg muttered again. "It's not what's here. It's what is not here."

Roper immediately took note. He knew how Korg worked when his mind engaged the complex. They both knew that every detail had to make sense and that the verified facts must follow a logical sequence. This chain of events would establish someone's guilt, no matter how unlikely — or how obvious — it might seem at the start.

Ignoring his onlookers, the stocky Korg charged into the walk-in closet and then froze to survey the contents. The closet was like a small room, about 15 feet deep, six feet wide. On one side were rows of hangers and shelves, with a scattered pile of worn clothes on the floor at the far end on a shelf. On the other side was a series of file cabinets.

Bonnie was transfixed. "What's he looking for?"

Sager, too, watched from the background, and he

nodded wisely at her, as if he was in on Korg's secret. Truth was, he didn't have a clue what Korg was up to, either.

Korg pulled out his pocket digital camera and snapped several photos of the closet, and then turned to his audience.

"Nobody touch anything in the beach house. I might bring Forensics in here."

"Why?" Bonnie said. "What's wrong? What did you find?"

"Let the man work," Sager suggested.

Piece by piece, Korg scanned the shelves and then peered behind the row of shirts on hangers to make sure he missed nothing. When he reached the back of the closet, he picked up each article of clothing that had been tossed in the corner.

"Bingo!" Korg erupted.

"What?" asked Bonnie.

Korg held up a forest-green toiletries travel bag in the air, and with a pixie grin, he peered at it as if it was a crystal ball.

"If Stephen Griffin was going to Las Vegas, then why..."

"Then why," responded Roper, completing the thought, "wouldn't Mr. Griffin take his travel bag with him?"

Korg nodded at the old school prosecutor. "Of course."

Korg then made another note.

"Yet did you notice what we did not find?"

Sager remained silent.

"I did not find his toothbrush or toothpaste on the bathroom counter, or anyplace else in the bathroom. No shampoo in the shower or anywhere else. Why would he take his toothbrush, toothpaste and shampoo from the bathroom for a trip when he has another set packed in his travel bag?"

"Everybody out. I want Forensics in this place before anything gets disturbed."

Then he turned to Bonnie. "You mind if I take Stephen's computer? It could help."

"Will he get it back?"

The old Korg massaged the worried sister with his kind words. "Of course, Bonnie. For all we know, Stephen could walk back in here in the next five minutes. There's no real evidence that anything is wrong."

On the way out, Korg came to an abrupt stop when he spotted a large stack of mail placed on a small table near the front door.

"How'd that get here," the inspector asked.

"When I didn't hear from Stephen, I'd drop in from time to time to check in on things."

"You touch anything else?"

"Nothing. Nothing at all. Just stacked up the mail."

To the side of the stack, there was a brown envelope with the return address, "Cantara Pharmaceutical, Inc."

Korg, deadly serious now, opened it. He found a filled insulin prescription and a packet of syringes.

The inspector turned to Bonnie as if there wasn't another person in the world. "Is Stephen a diabetic?"

"Yes, yes," she said frantically. "He's a Type 2 diabetic. Why do you think I've been so worried?"

Korg's gaze lowered to the toiletries bag in his right hand. He set it down on the small table, next to the stack of mail, and opened it. In a zipped middle compartment, he found more insulin and syringes.

Sager nodded at Bonnie.

"A diabetic doesn't go off to Las Vegas or anywhere else without his medicine."

On the west flank of Montara Mountain, Deego DeGenaro took a seat on a rock outcrop that overlooked the Pacific Ocean. It was a rare sparkling late afternoon on the coast, just north of Miramar and Half Moon Bay, 15 miles south of San Francisco. Deego scanned for miles across the old sea and could make out the jagged tops of the Farallon Islands on the horizon 30 miles away. The air tasted clean and fresh, and he took a deep breath and held it in, and marveled at his recent fortune.

A short way below his lookout were the remains of an old concrete army bunker, dug into the mountain during the Cold War. Back in the day, it was a military outpost for a radar station built to track incoming attacks across the Pacific Ocean. It had been decommissioned and stripped years before, as with more than 20 such outposts on the Bay Area coast.

"Life is great," he thought. He'd been out of prison for three years — involuntary manslaughter was all they could pin on him — and like the weather, was clean and clear: off parole, a good job with Jesse James Johnson as the band's road manager and back-up muscle to Klondike, all with decent pay. He was getting these young starlet babes now and then, a side benefit from all the girls who hung around the band hoping to get a glimpse of Johnson. Back in his days at San Quentin, these were the kind of girls he'd imagined in his wildest fantasies. They helped dissipate the imprint of all those lonely, fear-ridden nights in his pod, surrounded by the violent, both inmates and guards alike, where you tried to sleep with a towel over your eyes to block out the light and the world.

Deego was built like a brick barbecue, jet black hair greased back, and though just 5-9, with his muscle and mob connections, nobody messed with him at San Quentin. Out in the Rec Yard, even the El Nortes, Bloods and Aryans would pass without a nod or a word.

"Let's stay here a bit," Deego said from his perch, as he watched a tanker cruise 20 miles out to sea. "The way things are in this crazy world, you never know if you'll ever see such a beautiful sight again. Let's enjoy it. Take in the moment."

In the next second, a titanium .38 Smith & Wesson revolver was placed at the base of Deego's skull, the trigger pulled. The lead slug rocketed into his brain. From a distance, the pop in the air sounded like a muted firecracker, then blew away with the wind and into the surrounding silence.

His body, still seated, stayed erect for a second, his motor functions operating on autopilot. Then, as if knocked over by a coastal breeze, he toppled over to his right.

He was then dragged 15 feet to a chaparral thicket. A hand swept back the branches and revealed a 10-foot hole, and in the next motion, Deego's body was poured into the hole. With a boot, the killer caved in the sides of the hole, covering the body with a layer of dirt. The branches of the chaparral sprung back into position. They provided cover and camouflage. Later, the killer could return and cave in the sides of the hole with a shovel.

Because of the hardpan surface near the bunker,

packed like concrete by eons of sunlight and wind from a western coastal exposure, there were no drag marks anywhere. Anybody who surveyed the scene from this exact spot would notice only the remnants of the old concrete bunker and the adjacent rock crag that provided an ideal perch for an ocean lookout on a rare clear day on the San Mateo County coast.

Across the vast western slopes of Montara Mountain, amid nature's grand scheme in a wild land, nothing appeared out of place.

5

KORG PLACED HIS business card in the locked front door, and then turned to the group. "Conference," he ordered, and with a wave, pointed across the street to the Miramar Beach House Restaurant & Bar. The senior inspector detoured a short distance to the car and set Griffin's computer in the back seat. Roper placed the printer next to it.

As they walked into the Miramar, a guitar player with the stage name Johnny Capo sat on a bar stool, tuning up a Martin, sipping a Corona and getting ready for a sound check for his solo set. Capo looked up, sensed the collective ominous mood of the bunch, and with a bit of angst muttered, "The cops are here. So much for good crowd and tips." He nodded at Bonnie, though, always hoping for one more fan to sing to.

Before a waitress could take their order, Korg opened court.

"This case is like a game of chess," he said. "We have to figure out who is what piece. The timer's clock is running. Our move."

Roper glowed. He could sense the old Korg magic

starting to stir. He and Sager pulled out notebooks. Bonnie was transfixed, as if watching a drama.

"First," Korg announced, "we have a timeline."

The senior inspector unfolded and studied Griffin's flight itinerary.

"According to this, Stephen Griffin flew out of San Francisco to Las Vegas on September 26, a Thursday, at 1:18 p.m. on AirWest Flight 3547. Got it?"

Sager nodded.

"Find out if he was on that flight," Korg barked. "Do that tonight. If he was, put a tracer with the parking authority for his car at all the lots. A Corvette, black, no plates. Brand new. Should be an easy find."

A waitress served drinks. Korg squeezed a lemon wedge into his iced tea, and then turned to Bonnie, sipping a Long Island.

"Bonnie, tell me, where does Stephen usually stay when he goes to Las Vegas?"

"That's easy," Bonnie replied with a smile; from the corner of an eye, she noticed Sager staring at her body. "Stephen always stays at The Mirage. If he is with an act, he always gets comped. If he is scouting, he still gets a big discount. He knows everybody at The Mirage. They like him."

"Then start with The Mirage," Korg said, nodding at Sager. "Check the computer records of all the nearby major hotels, too. Then call Las Vegas PD and have them put out a missing persons alert for him."

Korg rolled on.

"Track everything. Credit cards, ATMs, cell phone."

Then he turned again to Bonnie.

"Do you have a few good photos of Stephen, digital?"

"Sure. Lots."

"Get a few to Inspector Sager," Korg instructed, then turned to Sager: "E-mail a shot to Las Vegas PD and The Mirage."

Korg held his hand up to explain.

"If Stephen Griffin was on that flight, track down who was sitting next to him, show them the pictures and verify it was him. Go door-to-door around here, too. See if anybody saw anything, like anybody coming and going from his place."

After a pause, Korg lightened up.

"Call his major act, Jesse James Johnson. See if you can find out who was the last person to see him. Call me every time you learn anything, no matter how small the detail might seem."

Sager bristled slightly at the barrage of orders. "While I'm doing all of this," he finally said, "Can you tell me what you are going to be doing?"

Korg appeared pained and glowered at the young inspector as if he were a juvenile delinquent.

Roper interceded. "I think Inspector Korg has plenty to do," he countered lightly.

"Maybe I can get a few hours sleep tonight," Korg said with a grin. "Maybe not. We'd better go."

"I'll stay here a bit longer," Sager answered, a hint of a smile, "might as well start with Bonnie here."

As Korg and Roper stood to leave, Korg added to his old friend, "Let's have Forensics work over Griffin's place right away. I don't care if it's the weekend and it's a missing person. Get 'em in there."

"Dinner?" Sager asked.

"I'd like that." After a pause, she added, "What did

he mean, 'Get Forensics in here.' Is there something I should know?"

Sager, not much of a talker, tried to imagine what was going on inside of Korg's head, then thought better of it. That was a place he did not care to venture.

"The old guy's out in a week," Sager said. "Retiring. I guess he's looking at this as his last big case. So he's taking it real serious-like."

"I guess that's good," Bonnie said.

"Couldn't your brother just have gone to Las Vegas anyway, you know, forgot to pack his little travel kit. Maybe he has a separate insulin kit?"

Bonnie squinted at the young inspector. "It's possible. Not likely because he always had his special bag. But possible."

Sager relaxed his Doberman's eyes a bit, and then tried to coax out more information about Stephen Griffin, and maybe learn a little more about Bonnie as well. Her lightning verbal abilities continued to captivate him, he discovered, and he enjoyed the sound of her voice. Her eyes seemed to sparkle.

She appreciated this absorbed listener. "If you understand where he came from, his childhood, it will help explain the kind of man Stephen is, how he turned out so great."

Sager provided rapt attention. His eyes dropped to her shirt. He liked what he saw. The buttons strained at the fabric.

Bonnie glowed from the attention. She explained that Stephen Griffin's mother had been a police dispatcher. At age 38, after sending a police unit to a family disturbance, she complained of headache, removed her headset and then fell out of her chair. She was dead by the time she hit the floor. Brain aneurism. Stephen was 7. So Bonnie, at 11, took over the task of raising Stephen.

"My mom was a Guatemalan immigrant who showed up once a week to clean house. I'm told she was beautiful. A court-ordered blood test proved that my dad was the father. So he paid off the housekeeper, who left me in bed, wrapped in a blanket, and then disappeared in Los Angeles."

"I'm sorry," Sager interjected.

"That's nice of you," Bonnie answered, eyeing him. "It seems maybe because she didn't want me, that's why I talk too much, always looking for approval."

"You've got mine. I approve. I like."

Bonnie smiled. Her talking motor was warmed up and she shifted into overdrive.

They started trading personal information almost as if this was a date. Maybe, Bonnie thought, it was a date. It felt like it. The young inspector didn't say much, but she could tell by his intense dark eyes that he was riveted.

In clipped sentences, Sager explained that he graduated from San Jose State with a major in Administration of Justice, then added a Masters. After an internship with the San Mateo County Sheriff's Department, had been hired as entry level beat cop. He'd set himself up to climb the career ladder. "I've always been a little ambitious," he admitted, "and with a Masters, I was on the fast track to move up." After five years, he'd just made Inspector, one of the fastest rising young stars in the department.

"I'd like to see more of you," he said. Sager let his

gaze trace over her chest, as if mentally undressing her.

"I'd like to see more of you, too," came the answer. It had been a long time since a man had been so mesmerized with her.

Sager realized he'd wandered off his investigation. He reviewed his notes. He had work to do.

"Here's my e-mail address. Shoot me a couple of pictures of Stephen, close ups." He reached over and gave her shoulder a non-regulation gentle squeeze.

That evening at home, Korg stared into the computer screen as the home page for Expedia.com loaded up. It had only taken Korg a few minutes to hook up Stephen Griffin's computer to a monitor. In a few seconds, he had a support supervisor of Expedia.com on the line; she identified herself as Janey.

Korg detailed his credentials and the urgency of the investigation.

The response was less than encouraging.

"That's personal account information that I cannot provide you," said the woman, all business.

"That's fine," Korg said. "I'm not going to ask you for passwords, credit card numbers or anything like that."

"That's good because we wouldn't provide that without a subpoena."

"What I need to know is this: Was the password on this account changed before Stephen Griffin booked a trip on Thursday, September 26 to Las Vegas?"

"Let me see if that information is available and if it's in bounds."

Korg, on hold, scanned his desk. Emma smiled at him

from a photo of the two of them, his arm around her and his hand resting on her shoulder, on a vacation they'd taken in Belize. He was so lucky to have found her, that day in the real estate office some 20 years ago, when he'd been looking to buy his first home. He cherished the memory; the instant attraction. Over the years, he had relished the intellectual match, the spiritual alignment, the shared ethical and parental values. In their kids, Zack and Rebecca, he could see a little of the best of both of them, and prayed every night they wouldn't get mixed up in the tempting sucker bets of youth, the instant gratification of drugs, alcohol abuse and sex.

Another framed photo, taken on Splash Mountain at Disneyland, caught the Korg family in terror, in mid-scream as the "log" they were riding in cascaded down a waterfall. Staring into that picture was like looking through a window and seeing his life on the other side. He'd always wanted to be a steady, solid man, provider and parent, but instead, life had turned into the log ride on that roller coaster. Sometimes you just had to hold on for the landing. His bizarre work hours, and her perpetual cash droughts and watersheds, had made for peaks and valleys.

The phone clicked.

"This is Sheila, I am a senior supervisor, now who are you and what is it you want?"

Korg repeated the spiel, starting with his credentials.

"We cannot give out confidential account information," she told him.

Korg wouldn't go away.

"That's not what I'm asking. I don't want the password. Just tell me if the password was changed that night."

There was a long pause.

Korg waited.

Finally, she spoke.

"Yes," she said. "New password. Set up that night."

Korg didn't have a search warrant for Griffin's computer, but that didn't stop him. He scrolled through Griffin's e-mail. Other than the details of the flight ticket purchased from Expedia.com, there wasn't much juice; a ton of unopened spam, a few pleading letters from musicians, and a series of short, intense memos sent back and forth between somebody named Rock Winston at Diogenes Sound. Korg printed everything of interest and stashed it in a file folder for later review.

Griffin's computer desktop was littered with icons. Where to start? He clicked on one: Songs. Inside the folder were dozens of files, titled with apparent song names. He opened one titled, "Straight Ahead" and read one of the verses:

I looked at you and we seemed to share
A cry in the wind, like a lost prayer.
I know you've opened your heart and bled.
Time has come for you to look straight ahead.

Lookin', lookin' straight ahead.

Korg moved on. At random, he opened a folder titled, "Archives." Nothing much in there; just old itineraries of concert tours. "Contact List." Korg opened it: It had more than a thousand names. At least it had phone numbers; that would somewhat short-cut the process of tracking down people in Griffin's world. Still at random, he clicked on a folder titled "Bahamas."

An Excel document was inside the folder. He clicked again. A homemade spreadsheet appeared on the screen. In the left column were the names Prychene, Synchro, Zagorski, Morkul and Smythwyck.

Korg's eyes homed in on Prychene at the top of the list. He traced out the figures to the far right. His eyes narrowed: "$12,748,021."

He looked closer at the document. It appeared to be from an offshore account based in the Bahamas. Korg ran a palm across his forehead. What could this mean?

Synchro was on the next line. Same thing: "$7,121,238."

Nearly $20 million was stashed in these two offshore accounts.

Korg's heart pounded like a subwoofer. He started to sweat. He felt as if he had been lifted off the ground by the scruffy graying hair on his head.

He scanned the rest of the page: Zagorski: $241,234. Morkul of Reno and Smythwick of Las Vegas were comparatively empty of money. Korg printed the page and pressed on.

At the bottom of the folder he found a sub-folder titled Transactions. Dozens of more documents were inside the folder. He clicked on Zagorski and found an address: Zagorski, Inc., 714 State Street, Carson City, Nevada.

He then opened the folder for "September." Korg saw how money had been transferred from Morkul to Smythwyck, and then from Smythwyck to Zagorski. Zagorski had then purchased a property in Redwood City; in fact, Korg was astounded to find it was a house located less than a quarter mile from his home in Brittany Canyon.

It was getting late now, but Korg had no sense of time. Only the chime of his phone, the one that defined a restricted number, that is, no ID, snapped him out of the blur. That was likely only one person.

"Yeah," Korg answered.

"You still up?" Sager asked.

"Hard at it. Getting deep into Griffin's computer."

"Do you have a search warrant?"

"You've got to learn, young man. Don't let little things like a search warrant get in the way of an investigation."

Sager's shock was followed by silence, after which his curiosity got the better of him. "Found anything?"

"A lot of young women sent him songs," Korg said with a laugh. "Maybe you should be in the music business."

Sager stayed on task. "I wish I could paint you a clear picture."

"Explain."

"The ticket to Las Vegas was used," Sager explained. "Like everybody who goes through the airport, he had to show a photo ID with his ticket, so I guess the guy flew to Vegas."

Sager paused for effect.

"His new Corvette? Found untouched in Long Term Parking at San Francisco International."

Korg kept listening and making notes.

"That's where the trail ends," Sager said. "He booked a reservation for three nights at The Mirage, but never showed. Credit card purchases stopped. No cash withdrawals at any ATMs. No more phone calls logged."

"Who was the last person to see him?"

"Far as I can tell, it was Jesse James Johnson."

"The rock star?"

"Like you have to ask, man?"

"Hey, easy on me, I'm Old School. Where was this?"

"Johnson's. He's got a big place in the Woodside hills."

"So nobody saw Stephen Griffin in Las Vegas?"

Sager noted a new lightness in Korg's voice, then interjected: "For all we know, he's playing poker at the Bellagio as we speak or he's buried out there in the desert. What do we do now, chief?"

Korg took a deep, appreciative breath. He liked being called "chief." Korg had thought the pup had patronized him for the past month, but maybe not. Maybe Roper was right. It wasn't Sager's fault. It was Roberta Pritchett's.

"Young man, this is what we do now: First thing tomorrow morning, we go to airport security and dig up the surveillance tapes. Then we track down Johnson. You might want to see Forensics in action at the beach house. Then while you're over there, hit the neighbors."

Korg paused for a moment.

"You get a Griffin photo off to Las Vegas yet?"

"Two hours ago."

"I'll pick up you up at 7:30 a.m. You live in San Mateo, right?"

"How do you know that?"

"You've got to be kidding."

At 1 a.m., Korg finally slipped into bed.

Emma gave him a squeeze. "Up late."

"This guy disappeared," Korg said. "A big-time music agent, a brilliant, nice, sensitive guy that everybody loves. Missing person. But watch, he'll probably just show up tomorrow."

"Go to sleep, honey."

As Korg drifted off, a gut-level thought welled up and wrenched him back awake: What if the guy is dead? My last case and somebody is going to get away with murder? Hell no!

6
SUNDAY

KORG AND SAGER marched into Airport Security at San Francisco International looking for the big dog, Sherman Bender. The room was full of TV video screens where the pictures changed constantly. A master control board let security forces focus on any part of the airport, inside or out. Bender ran the place.

"Homicide," Korg said as he flashed his badge to a melancholy woman at the controls. Here it was early Sunday morning, Sager noted, and yet even now, it was clear how much Korg relished announcing his arrival. This was different from what Pritchett had told him about Korg, Sager thought: the guy clearly loved his job.

Sager made a sweeping gesture at the video equipment. "So you film everything?"

"Of course," answered the woman at the control center. "Standard."

When Korg spotted Bender, his eyes glowed with recognition. They went way back, first meeting on a case nearly 15 years ago, back when Bender helped run private security for football games at Candlestick Park.

In a drug buy gone bad, a local gang member from Hunter's Point had shot a guy in the Candlestick parking lot before a game. Korg had been assigned the case. They hit it off from the first moment.

"We want to look into your archives."

Bender's eyes widened. "Terrorists?"

Korg shook his head. "Nothing like that. A missing person."

A bit disappointed, Bender walked over to the master console and explained how the video system operated. Embezzlers, tax cheats, divorced dads kidnapping their kids, they'd all been filmed either trying to flee or when arriving, with cameras set up at the check-in counters and other strategic spots throughout the airport.

Bender smiled.

"What day? What airline? What flight number? What counter? What time?"

"Perfect," Korg answered. "September 26th, a Thursday, AirWest flight to Las Vegas, departing at 1:18 p.m. Flight 3547."

Bender broke into an even wider grin.

"What?" he asked in sarcasm, then added: "You guys aren't exactly on top of this one."

Sager soured. "What do you mean by that?"

"That's more than a week ago" Bender admonished. "We don't keep video around that long."

"Why not?" Korg pleaded.

Bender grinned yet again.

"Do you realize how much computer space you'd need for all these cameras to archive 24/7 indefinitely?"

"Are you telling me you don't have the video?"

Bender laughed again. "Man, you've got to be kidding.

We use the space on the computer hard drives over and over again."

"What?" Sager asked.

"Sure, we record on the same hard drives over and over again."

"How'd you catch all those other guys?" Korg asked.

"Oh, we keep it around for awhile, a week max, usually less than that. It's always been long enough. We get alerted to a case and we just pull the video out. You didn't do that. So neither did we."

Korg's face drooped in disappointment.

IN THE CAR, Sager gazed straight ahead, his ferret eyes small and black, a machine-gun gaze.

Korg was also silent. Soon enough, he'd be fishing, put out to pasture. Sager would be chasing the drug gangs again. This case would be filed and forgotten. He just needed a little more time. That was the one thing he did not have.

"This isn't how I want to go out," Korg grumbled. "If I don't break the case, it'll turn to the polar ice cap."

Sager shook his head. "Well, maybe there's some hope, because they say it's melting."

Korg made his speech.

"You know what the problem is with our Sheriff's Department? We have no computer file of our handwritten field notes that could be shared by agents or other agencies. What we do is in the scrawl of our pocket notebooks and the ideas in our heads. So if we don't break the case, nobody else can figure out what we have."

"I thought they spent a couple million to overhaul the computer system," Sager said.

"That doesn't change the fact that the details are in our cryptic, incomplete handwritten notes, and in our heads. Nobody is going to type those up for someone else to read or even try to decipher them."

Sager gazed into the sky, watching a departing jet burn a hole over San Bruno Mountain.

"So you're saying we either nail this in the next week, or it doesn't get nailed."

"What you've got to do, Inspector Sager, is track down who sat next to the alleged Mr. Griffin on that flight to Las Vegas, show them a photo of the alleged Mr. Griffin, and make sure that person sitting there was indeed the alleged Mr. Griffin."

"Where we going, chief?"

Korg smiled as he guided the county-issue Ford north on Bayshore Freeway to Highway 84. He was trying not to like Sager, but was finding it impossible. "Jesse James Johnson."

Sager glowed. "Going straight for the big fish."

After a short silence, Sager quizzed the senior inspector.

"Korg, you intrigue me," Sager said. "What happened to you? I've heard the stories. But what really happened?"

"You really want to know?"

"Entertain me."

"At one time," Korg started, "I was considered a pretty damn good investigator…"

Korg was promoted to Homicide at San Francisco Police Department after nine fast years. In his first test, tossed to him as a cold-case throwaway, he broke the big Jacoby case. "That was a front-page murder investigation." Back when forensic work was in its relative infant stages, Korg tied millionaire Richard Jacoby to the murder of his wife, Camellia, by linking four strands of hair found in the trunk of Jacoby's Cadillac to six strands of hair he found on a bush in Golden Gate Park where Jacoby said they'd been on a picnic. From this he discovered a nearby burial site hidden beneath vegetation and linked Jacoby to the murder.

As Korg talked, Sager daydreamed about Bonnie. He fantasized what it would be like to unbutton that stone canvas shirt and reach inside. He'd had a built-in excuse to call her at any moment, he realized. Meanwhile, Korg kept going.

At SFPD, Korg explained, he'd emerged as a relentless investigator. "In the early years, they called me The Bulldog," Korg said, almost embarrassed. On the Booker case, when nobody bought his theory that Booker had a direct tie to an international Asian heroin ring that linked San Francisco to L.A. and Vietnam, Korg staked out Booker's Sunset District hideout. "I hid in a bush for three days, and then through a back window, filmed him executing an Asian mob underling. Big stuff. I had lots of big cases."

The truth was, Sager already knew about Korg. When he was first partnered with him, he had done his own background check. But Sager wanted to know if Korg would play it straight with him; that's why he'd asked him a personal question. Meanwhile, he wondered what Bonnie smelled like; clean with a touch of perfume, he figured.

For 15 years, from his early 30s to late 40s, Korg was a testament to the SFPD way. Korg had the right look, the right attitude, and when he walked into a room, you knew you were in the presence of a heavy. Just the right amount of emotional distance and quiet force. He could inject short, pointed questions followed by utter silence when others talked. Like all homicide detectives, there was something about him that said, "Don't come too close."

Korg had married lovely Emma, manager of a restaurant in the Presidio and a part-time real estate agent. Emma combined an innate sense of business with book-learned know-how to get a Broker's License, and then opened a small sales business. She converted restaurant earnings into real estate buys. In the meantime, they raised two fine kids, Zack and Rebecca, who put up with them most of the time.

Sager daydreamed whether Bonnie was shaved, trimmed or ran a wild jungle that would take a weed eater to get through.

In the new millennium, Korg noticed that the zeal of the District Attorney's office waned. Then Korg got peeved when two of his homicide arrests were tossed out when the D.A. said his evidence was "circumstantial and coincidental."

In the meantime, he saw other detectives let cases slip through their fingers; in one rape case, the investigating officer didn't even interview the victim or try to get prints off the car in which the rape occurred. The "investigation" consisted of a phone interview with the victim, and in turn, another violent criminal walked the streets. It became so difficult to get witnesses of gang crimes to talk that arrests became the exception, and

Korg and his pal, Deputy D.A. Roper, started hoping the gang perps would erase each other in two-fers. It was better than making an arrest and watching a criminal slip through the porous San Francisco criminal justice system.

Sager let Korg go on without interruption. To talk would have snapped his continuing fantasy. That Bonnie, she had a little desperado in her. Maybe a little ride-em cowgirl, too.

Korg kept on, driving into the Woodside hills, timing his speech to end at Johnson's estate. Together, he explained, Korg and Roper bailed on San Francisco for San Mateo County, and went back to work prosecuting violent crimes. But when he hit 50, Korg noticed that the young guns were getting many of the high profile cases and he was being left behind like an old wooden bridge coming apart board by board. He considered himself Old School, but some in the office viewed him as just old.

Then Roberta Pritchett, a hoity-toity mover-shaker, with connections in politics and skill in front of the TV cameras, showed up. Korg found himself shut out of the high-profile cases. He was assigned to some cold cases, mostly missing persons, and then found himself "tapped on the shoulder," as they called it, wired for early retirement.

"So I escape to the one place where I feel free, the open water of San Francisco Bay and Pacific Ocean on my boat," Korg explained to Sager, "fishing, smoking cigars, watching the pelicans, murres and grebes, hoping for a bite now and then."

A burning glow, like a 250-watt bulb in the back of a dark cave, lit the notion in the back of his mind that he was being railroaded because of his age.

"But the truth is," Korg added with a pause, "I really want to solve this case, go out on top."

"We need a body," Sager pointed out. "We need a crime scene."

"It's one of two things," Korg responded. "Either the guy really did disappear, or he got berked."

"What does that mean?"

"You don't know, Inspector Sager? Berked? That's means snuffed."

Sager's face was a blank.

"It's from Son of Sam, Dave Berkowitz," Korg said. "That's how the word berked got invented."

Korg laughed, then added, "Man, you are green."

"No, I'm black."

Korg glimpsed a sliver of grin from the young man.

"Is that a smile I'm detecting from you, Inspector? That would be a first."

"No, just a nervous twitch I get every week or so."

Korg shook his head and provided a snapshot analysis of the case.

"You consider Stephen Griffin a missing person? At any one time, there are 100,000 missing persons in America. Less than 1 percent involves a successful adult male. Of that 1 percent, just about all of them turn out to be homicides."

Korg smiled gently at his young partner.

"The worst-case scenario is a murder where there is no body, just a disappearance. With no apparent crime scene, there's virtually no physical evidence."

"What percentage of cases gets solved?" Sager asked.

"After two days, the odds of an arrest are cut in half.

On a cold case, with no lucky tips from the public, no physical evidence, no body, no crime scene, it can be damn near impossible to break a case."

Korg paused. "But sometimes there's still a way to figure it out."

Korg guided his car up Johnson's driveway. It led to a black wrought iron gate framed by brick columns. A remote camera, with a speaker box and numbered panel, was mounted on a black, iron arm, set adjacent to Korg's driver-side window. A black iron fence, covered by ivy and topped with arrow-like spikes, traced the expansive perimeter of the property.

7

SAGER FLICKED HIS gold front tooth with his tongue, then pointed at the speaker box. "Button." Korg was starting to notice that for Sager, knife sharp and glowering, anything more than a one-word sentence was considered a filibuster.

Korg, a bit irritated at the obvious, held his badge to the camera, pushed the button, and announced the presence of homicide inspectors. He heard a buzz and the gate opened.

As they drove in, Korg and Sager scanned the property. The driveway circled a small island with a manicured lawn, set off by red maples and dozens of freshly planted flowers. It fed into a curving entry walkway, edged by brick. Near the house, an expansive lawn was lush yet cropped, and sprinkled with weeping willow, liquid ambar and a few red maples, with exotic tall, thin evergreens positioned like Roman columns along a far edge. Windows down on the car, they picked up the scent of fresh-cut grass.

Sager motioned at a 10-foot picture window near the

entrance to the house. Inside, two men were engaged in what appeared to be a bitter discussion.

"I READ IN Rolling Stone about all this money I'm supposed to be making," said the rock star. "Well, where is it? Sure not in the quarterly royalty payment you sent me last week. Where's all the money?"

Music executive Rock Winston, even some 30 years after his training in Special Forces, still projected authority and strength.

"The industry is down 75 percent over the last 20 years," Winston answered. "The top-selling CD last week sold 50,000 copies. Hell, 10 years ago that figure wouldn't have made the top 20. The No. 1 CD would sell 250,000, 300,000 a week. But the CD, as you know it, is dying. The big money days are gone. Kids are downloading songs, burning and sharing, ripping us all off."

The rock star flamed. "You've got to prosecute these people who are stealing from me."

Winston paused a moment for effect.

"We go after the worst, but when you look at the scope of the problem around the world, it's like trying to bail water out of the Titanic. The whole industry is in free-fall. Tower Records, Borders, dead, long gone."

The rock star didn't buy it.

"What about distribution? My staff called Walmart, Target, Best Buy and like a half dozen independents, and nobody has any of my CDs. None. How are people supposed to buy them if they're not in the stores?"

"They want 60 percent discount. Why should we

subsidize their profits? We're doing the best we can with the real market, electronic sales. Nobody under 40 buys CDs. Plus, you haven't put out any new product in two years."

That did not pacify Johnson. "What about my catalog? It's always sold when it's in the stores."

"You need a new hit. You know that. Plus these kids don't have to buy the whole album like the old days. They can pick one song off the CD on their computer and we get like 10 percent of the income compared to selling the whole album."

A rap on the door cut the conflict short.

As the rock star stomped to the door, he shouted over his shoulder. "We start recording later this week, but I'm not convinced you can get the thing out and sell it." He paused before opening the custom 8-foot door, all mahogany and beveled antique glass. "To be continued."

The two inspectors were dressed in dark suits. The older one, Korg, a big, swarthy type, seemed affable enough during his entrance; the other, young, slim and dark, seemed like a cobra ready to strike.

"We're here for one reason," Korg explained with an elf-like smile. "The disappearance of Stephen Griffin."

Sager watched every move. Fans called rock star Jesse James Johnson "Wolf Eyes," and Sager noticed that the guy did look kind of like a wolf. More like a work of art, sculptured, the classic edged jaw, flawless skin, deep brown eyes, and dark hair with a touch of wave. But those eyes. Lasers.

With a wave of his right hand, Johnson whisked his

luxuriant dark hair back over his right ear, and walked the inspectors into his living room, then introduced them to Rock Winston, president of Diogenes Sound. Johnson directed them to seats, and then buried himself in the corner of an Italian leather couch done in luxuriant green, the color of money. He took a sip from an ice-cold Corona with lime.

"Beer?" Johnson asked, holding up his bottle.

Korg declined the offer; he'd go out the last week by the book, well, pretty much. For Mexican beer, he preferred Pacifico or Bohemia, anyway. He scanned the spacious room: high ceilings, wall-to-wall Karastan carpet in pristine white, and a wall of glass exposing the grounds.

Sager also took in the details. He noticed that each item in the room appeared to be a one-of-a-kind, from the bronze eagle on the fireplace mantle, which was hand-finished, to the ornate trim on the door frames; everywhere he looked, he saw nothing but the best, most of it stellar handwork, styled and precious. Beyond the foyer was a curving staircase with a smooth railing supported by spars with ornate oak carvings, each identical. A lit blackberry candle scented the air.

Korg raised his hand and smiled like an old, warm friend.

"Tell us what you know about Stephen Griffin."

It was an investigator's trick to ask such a general question. The length of answer would reveal how important the respondent believed the subject was.

"Griffin isn't the only person missing around here," Johnson answered. "My road manager was supposed to be here. Deego. Nowhere to be found."

"Is that significant?" Korg pressed.

"He's probably at Applejack's sitting at the bar. But usually I can count on him showing up. He just didn't today."

"Tell me about Griffin."

It took Johnson a second Corona to eulogize his former manager, while the three onlookers listened intently to every word.

As Johnson talked, Sager noted an unusual pin clipped on Winston's lapel. It was a roundish silver-black pin, about the size of a dime; in the center of it were two arrows, with the words *De Opresso Liber* set in a half ring beneath them.

"Everybody loves Stephen Griffin," Johnson concluded. "Without Stephen Griffin, I'd probably still be playing clubs at $250 a night."

Korg crossed his arms. In the background, Sager and Winston seemed to be having a contest as to who could go the longest without uttering a sound audible to the human ear.

"Are you missing any money?" Korg asked. "Could he have embezzled a fortune and disappeared?"

"No way." Johnson settled back, embedded in the leather seat, and drained the final half inch of his Corona. "Despite the downturn in CD sales, he was making a fortune with me from our live shows. But if we don't have a new hit, that will dry up."

"When was the last time you saw him?"

"That's easy. He was over the day before we, you know, the band, took off for New York to open an East Coast swing."

"Can you verify the exact time and date?"

Johnson nodded. A pocket calendar was sitting on the coffee table in front of him. He picked it up and thumbed to September.

"Stephen Griffin was here, actually out back at our recording studio, on the afternoon of Wednesday, September 25th."

Sager noted that Johnson had anticipated the question to the point of having his calendar within an arm's reach.

Korg bored in.

"What was his mood?"

"Euphoric. Said he had a date with somebody special that evening."

"Name?"

"Didn't mention any. Just that she was special."

Korg cast a quick glance at Sager, his right eyebrow twitching, and then continued.

"What time did he leave here?"

"About 4 o'clock or so."

"P.M.?"

"Yep."

Korg squared his broad shoulders directly at Johnson.

"Where were you that evening and the next day?"

"That's easy. Here at my place. Packing for the trip. Then we flew out of SFO around noon for New York."

Korg pressed his fingertips together. "When exactly?"

"About 1 p.m. or so. I spent the morning packing."

"By yourself?"

"Of course. I'm not married."

"You should try it," Korg said. "Can be the best thing on earth," and then added: "Anybody with you the night before you left?"

Johnson was quick to answer.

"Sure, my chief roadie and head of security, Klondike. We always go over everything before a trip. He lives here on the property. And before you look him up, I'll tell you straight out, he killed a guy once, and roughed up some others." Johnson paused to grin. "Didn't mean to kill him. Big guy, biker guy, got in a bar fight, and wouldn't back down."

Johnson paused for moment, and then added, "I used to have a security problem. Had some equipment stolen. Since I hired him, no more security problem."

"I think we met Mr. Klondike," Korg noted.

"I hear you took him in for questioning yesterday."

Korg lurched. "Not us."

Sager piped in. "Must have been SFPD."

Korg pressed on.

"So according to his flight plans, Griffin was going to Las Vegas on the 26th, a Thursday?"

Johnson picked up the lead.

"He didn't mention that to me, but guess he was going to check some talent, and yes, fly to Las Vegas. That's what I was told."

"By who?"

"Maybe I read it in the paper."

"You never heard from Stephen Griffin in any way after that 4 p.m. meeting here on Wednesday, September 25th?"

"Nothing. It's as if he vanished. The next day, I flew

out to New York. I became alarmed when I didn't hear from him when I was in New York. I'm the one who reported him missing."

"Have the flight number?"

Johnson smiled. "I took my private jet."

Korg responded with a sheepish grin — his own jet? — and then raised a finger, as if to make a request.

"What?" Johnson asked.

"You mind if I use a bathroom?"

"Sure, I've got six of them. Right through there, turn left, then straight, then right, and it will be on your left."

Meanwhile, Sager and Winston eyed each other, sizing each other up, each figuring he could take the other in a fight.

Amid the mosaic of hallways and rooms, Korg managed to get lost in the giant house. At one point, he turned left instead of right, and then looking for the bathroom on the right, he instead found himself staring into what appeared a den, a small office with bookshelves and plenty of counter space, all of it upscale. A Tiffany lamp illuminated several documents on a desk, with open envelopes scattered alongside.

Korg, always curious to a fault, sauntered in. Instantly, he spotted a document that looked like a computer print-out of a bank statement: "Prychene Corporation." It sounded familiar. Next to that he spotted another, "Zagorski." It had a Carson City, Nevada address. Korg searched for his notebook, but each pocket was empty. Damn! He'd left it out in the living room. But he still had a pen.

Korg pushed back his sleeve, and on the inside of his

left forearm, wrote the names of the corporations and the Carson City address for Zagorski, scrawling with a fever, sweating.

Behind him, there was a subtle noise and Korg froze. He turned, half expecting a gun to be pointed at him, and instead saw a small Siamese cat walking into the room, looking up at the window, eyeing a small bird on the windowsill. Korg exhaled like an empty paper bag being compressed by two strong hands.

He quickly turned to the open door, and then decided to head back to the living room. But as he tried to retrace his steps in the mansion, he simply became more confused than ever. Finally, he called out.

"Hey, I'm lost in this giant place."

With no response, he called again, this time louder.

Off in the distance, through the corridors, he could hear Johnson laughing.

AT THE DOOR, Korg stopped midway upon his exit and turned to the rock star.

"Say, you ever heard of a roadie kid named Spoogs?"

Sager studied Johnson's face as his gaze dropped to the floor.

"Yeah, heard about what happened to him. Damn terrible. Used to work for our crew. Klondike hired him. Never actually met him. Think he worked over the summer, then he quit to crew for Tenaya."

Sager discerned no crack to Johnson's facade. The words came out evenly, not too slow, not too fast.

Johnson turned to Winston. "I wonder where the hell Deego is?"

Sager went for his phone. Bonnie Griffin was calling.

8

"We'd like to meet with you again at Stephen's beach house," Sager said into his phone.

"Both of you or just you?" Bonnie asked.

"Both this time. Maybe later, just me."

"I'd like that."

"So would I."

As Sager listened to Bonnie, his phone beeped and buzzed. Incoming. He looked down at the screen. It was the call he'd been waiting for.

"See you soon," and with a click he was on it.

Korg, eavesdropping, could discern nothing from his partner's Sphinx-like lack of nuance and clipped monotone answers.

"OK. Yep. Figured. Uh huh. Anything else? Bye." That was the extent of replies sprinkled over two minutes.

"What?" Korg inquired, as he guided the emerald Ford west on Highway 92, heading toward Griffin's Miramar beach house.

"I need pictures of all the people of interest," Sager said.

"Why?"

"A neighbor and the hostess at the Miramar said they saw some people around the time we're looking at."

"Why didn't you tell me?" Korg asked.

Sager looked straight ahead and raised his eyebrows at the upcoming hairpin turn on 92. "Could you slow it down a little?"

"Sorry. I'm eager to get there. Explain that phone call."

Korg slowed the car and Sager turned his head to address the senior inspector.

"Everything stopped with Griffin. Cell phone. Credit cards. ATMs. Nothing. Everything."

"Figures," Korg responded. "It's good, by the way, to hear you talk."

"It's like the guy fell off the edge of the world," Sager said.

"In my experience," Korg answered with a smile, "when guys fall off the edge of the world, they're usually given a pretty good push."

Sager smiled back. To his surprise, he was starting to like Korg and his unusual perspectives.

"Was that a smile I just detected, Inspector Sager?"

"Just trying to stifle a yawn."

"Right."

The surf reverberated in the background. To the north, a few cumulus clouds hovered over Pillar Point Head. Out to sea, Korg could just make out the distant silhouette of a commercial salmon boat, its outriggers set. He felt that familiar pang. That's where I should be. On my boat. Out to sea.

Bonnie greeted Sager with a gleaming smile, and immediately started in, describing everything that crossed her mind in graphic and extended detail.

Korg opened the gated walkway, fumbled with his keys, and then turned to Bonnie Griffin. He tried to appear as comforting as possible as he interrupted her speech.

"Bonnie, does Stephen have any enemies?"

"Well, he works in the music business. What else do you need to know?"

"What do you mean by that?"

Bonnie stopped and tried to size up the senior inspector. A bit of a swashbuckler perhaps, but otherwise he was a hard one to read.

"Stephen said it was a terrible business to be in. Everybody cheats."

"How do you mean?"

"There's a lot of cash and it's hard to trace, so everybody working on percentages is worried about getting cheated. There's this chain of money on the live gate, a lot of cash floating around. On the recording end, the songwriters get ripped off all the time for their royalty and publishing money. A lot of people get screwed. Most get mad. Some get even."

"She's just getting warmed up", Korg thought, so he kept quiet, trying to trim the meat from the fat.

"Bonnie, who was mad at Stephen?"

Terror gripped her face.

"Are you saying something bad happened?

As Korg and Sager entered the beach house, they looked as curious as kittens getting a whiff of catnip.

Korg, as usual, took the lead. "Any idea of where Stephen keeps his photographs?"

Bonnie was on a mission. "He had photo albums, and more recently, a digital library, but he was printing out quite a few of those shots, too. It was a hobby of his."

As Korg pawed through hundreds of photographs, Bonnie filled the air with relentless chatter.

Sager found every word fascinating: The grinding rock of life reduced her father to an amorphous blob addicted to Lancers straight from the jug and watching the nightly re-runs on ESPN Sports Classic. But that same grinding rock of life had polished Bonnie and Stephen to a brilliant luster. They were made of tougher stuff and discovered that hard work provided the escape route from the household dysfunction.

After college, Stephen meandered through a succession of jobs in the entertainment industry — as co-manager of a club, free-lance booking agent and promoter of small shows, and in time, manager of several small acts. He'd finally struck gold with Jesse James Johnson. He always credited Bonnie with his success. When troubled, he often felt her shadow and support.

"Because of our screwed-up family, Stephen and me had to rely on each other to survive," she explained. "That's why I kept calling about him being gone, why I'm so worried. It makes no sense that he's gone."

She wore a tight-fitting, thin cotton shirt. She had a good body, she knew, and she liked that she had met a man that actually liked listening to her talk, at times even seemed to hang on every word, and wanted to make sure he noticed her attributes.

Sager felt the spark.

Bonnie, looking over Korg's shoulder, interrupted the senior inspector's search. She grabbed one of the photo albums, not for Korg's benefit, but rather to show her admirer, Jeremy Sager, a picture of her and Stephen, together on her last birthday.

"That's nice," Sager said. Unlike Bonnie, he couldn't think of anything to say.

In the photo, Stephen and Bonnie Griffin stood side by side in the beach house. MaryLou Dietz, a back-up singer, had taken the shot.

"We were just getting ready to go out to dinner with the whole gang and…"

Korg suddenly snatched the photo album from her hands. His eyes clicked on high beam. He studied the photograph.

"That's it," he shouted. "Can I have this?"

"Sure, but I'd like to get it back."

"Oh, we'll get it back right away. We'll just make a copy."

Bonnie was grateful for the audience. Before her extended outpouring with Sager, she hadn't had anybody to talk to for three days. She had phoned eight friends, but she had instead connected to eight answering machines.

"Anything else, you call me," she said to Korg.

But it was Sager who shook her hand. "Anything else, you call me."

"I might have something else."

Back in the county-issue Ford, Korg whistled.

"Man, that woman can talk."

Sager was chuffed.

"I like her." She had all the qualities he did not. Then he added, "What'd you see in that photograph?"

"Maybe nothing. Maybe everything."

Korg's phone chimed the song, "I'm Just a Working Man," the coded ring tone for Mel Sturgeon at county forensics and CSI.

"The report is on your desk," Sturgeon said.

"I still have a desk?" Korg said in jest.

"Remember, Korg, for coming in on my day off, you promised to take me fishing on San Pablo Bay. I've never caught a fish or even seen a sturgeon."

"We can do that, Mr. Sturgy. But stick around. I've got an emergency job for you. We'll be there in a flash."

"What? More work?"

Korg rubbed a palm over his gray-flecked scruff of hair, the BlueTooth ear piece glowing.

"I'll make it worth it for you. You not only can see a sturgeon, but you might actually catch one. And eat one."

"How about throwing in a bottle of my favorite malt beverage?"

As he closed his phone, Korg smiled at his understudy Sager.

"Come along, lad, Mr. Sturgy might teach us something."

At county headquarters, Korg charged Sturgeon with his request and then opened the lab's forensic report on Griffin's beach house. Sager stood alongside Korg's massive desk, The Aircraft Carrier.

Korg quickly scanned through the report, searching for keys to unresolved issues. The forensic team had found a piece of cheap glass under a sofa, with glass bits in the rug next to it. Above, in the wall, was a small dent as well as blank spot from where there seemed a missing piece of framed art or photograph.

The glass was the kind used in picture frames. They had checked the contents of the vacuum cleaner bag. More glass crystals, the same kind of glass.

"You know what's wrong?" Korg asked. "Suppose the glass is from a picture frame. Where's the rest of the glass for it?"

The wheels were turning a little too fast for Sager.

"What do you mean?"

"I mean, let's say the picture frame broke into a bunch of pieces. Where are they?"

"Obviously somebody picked them up and threw them out."

"But who? And when?"

Sager finally thought he'd wrapped his head around the question.

"Why Griffin, of course, whenever, maybe long ago."

Korg's words were crisp.

"Nope. The vacuum cleaner bag was packed full, like it hadn't been emptied for months, how most guys keep house. The glass crystals were lodged right on top of the lint, right near the entry hole, so no, this just happened recently. But the rest of the glass isn't anywhere, not in the trash. The picture it came from is gone from the wall. Where'd it go? Who cleaned it up? Who disposed of the big pieces of glass?"

"There's the dent in the wall," Korg continued. "Maybe

somebody was angry enough to throw that picture into the wall."

"Or it could be a gouge from the moving guys?"

Korg waved his hand.

"Nope," Korg said. "Wrong place. Too high. Forensics checked that out. Look here," he continued, pointing to a page in the report. "That dent in the wall?"

"What about it?"

Korg beamed.

"It fits the corner of a picture frame."

Sager scowled.

"Well I wouldn't get stuck on any of this if I was you."

Korg admonished the younger agent with another wave of the hand.

"You highly-educated, well-trained youngsters should know better than us old guys that there must be an explanation for every question."

KORG AND SAGER waited outside the lab. Forever, it seemed.

Korg's thoughts drifted to his boat, 4-Play, and how he felt on the water: beyond the reach of his problems.

He suddenly realized that this case provided relief, similar to time on his boat. He was losing himself in the work, like the old days in Homicide with SFPD, those first cases with the rich-guy murders where he made his mark. Every waking moment he was rolling it over in his mind. In bed, the faces of suspects appeared in his dreams. As he drove, he navigated theories. In the office, he tried to distill the complex down to essentials, based solely on the evidence. Well, there wasn't much of that, but what there was compelled him forward.

Sitting outside the lab, Korg knew he'd like nothing better than to crack this case in his final days, arrest the guilty, and upstage Pritchett. Hell, retirement was just ahead. Solve this case and maybe he'd piss on her desk on the way out. He was snapped out of the fantasy by the voice of the Forensic chief.

"Korg, we found what you want." It was Sturgeon. "Take a look."

Korg's face filled with contentment. Sager appeared little more than a blank, subtly amused by Korg's reaction.

"You're the best, Mr. Sturgy."

"You know, Korg, I'm the only guy around who'll let you get away with this stuff, you know, calling me that. Pritchett might say it's disrespectful."

Korg laughed, a winner's laugh.

"Oh, you mean, Roberta? Hah! Hell, she'll come around."

"What, by the end of the week?"

As Korg analyzed the picture, Sturgeon and Sager peered over his shoulder

"Got a magnifying glass?"

"Just like Sherlock Holmes. You came to the right place. I did my best to enhance the details. I scanned the print as a computer image. Cropped out everything but what you wanted, then cleaned it up, worked the colors to enhance it."

"You done good, Mr. Sturgy."

At first glance, the original photograph appeared to be a shot of Bonnie and Stephen Griffin, standing in his beach house. Smiling. It was birthday night, as she had explained.

In this picture, just to the right of Stephen, on the back wall of the beach house, about shoulder high, was a large, framed photograph, the missing photograph from the wall of Griffin's beach house. Sturgeon had cropped out everything in the original picture but this photograph in the background, then enlarged and enhanced it.

It was a group standing in a row, smiling. With a magnifying glass, the clarity was sufficient for Korg to identify each individual. Jesse James Johnson, Klondike and Rock Winston. But there were many others in the shot, 11 in all.

"Why's this so important?" Sturgeon asked.

"I think it goes straight to who murdered my guy and how the timing works out."

"How's that?" Sager asked.

Korg glowed.

"This is the missing picture from the open space on the wall at Griffin's. It's the picture that I think somebody threw in anger and then destroyed."

After a pause, Korg added: "If so, there's two ways to look at it."

"Explain," Sturgeon urged. Sager listened intently.

Korg complied.

"One way is that my victim, Stephen Griffin, threw the photograph against the wall. If so, somebody in this picture inspired his full wrath."

"Keep going."

"The other way to look at it is that the perp threw it. If so, the sight of this happy group collected in one spot set off flashpoint anger."

Sturgeon recalled the forensic work. "For my money, I like what's behind Door Number 2."

"So do I," Korg replied. "You guys found only a few

glass shards under a chair, with the rest disposed of. Yet it's unlikely Griffin had cleaned up the mess because there was no sign of the larger glass shards anywhere or the missing photograph."

"We saw this before, like 10 years ago," Sturgeon said. "The killer vacuums the rug and then disposes of the large glass pieces, frame and photograph elsewhere."

"Right," Korg agreed. "It is the best way to explain how glass bits could be found at the top of the inside of the vacuum cleaner bags — picked up the last time the vacuum cleaner had been used, and yet there was no sign of the rest of the glass."

Korg gawked again at the picture.

Sager scratched his chin.

"Who do you think did it?"

SAGER PUNCHED HIS cell phone, a text to Bonnie Griffin: "See U 2night?"

9

MONDAY

THE TWO INSPECTORS tried to slink through the door, hoping to infiltrate a gathering of young women to reach their target. It was early, but a throng had already gathered. But Korg and Sager were square pegs, and the Neanderthal confronted them at the entrance.

"I don't think you're on the list," Klondike deadpanned, raising a clipboard in his right paw. From too many hard nights, Klondike's tiny eyes beneath heavy eyebrows and shaved skull looked like the spinning wheels of a slot machine.

"You look like you just emerged from your cave," Korg noted, pixie smile.

The monster glared at the inspectors as if they were an invading force from a remote foreign land.

The big man held up his clipboard. "Like I said, you're not on the list to get in."

Korg flashed his badge, and said, "This puts me on the list. And where's the guitarist, Storm Clearwater?"

This was the Sound Factory, Korg learned, a recording studio with a side room built as a sound stage for rehearsals, along with an adjoining business office. It was set in redwoods in the back of Johnson's sprawling property.

Korg couldn't resist needling the big man.

"You sure you didn't make Stephen Griffin disappear?"

"That would violate my parole," Klondike answered as he rose up to his full height.

"What about Spoogs? That sounds like more your style."

"I wouldn't have had to shoot him. I would have just thrown him over the wall." Klondike glowered down at the inspector. "Was it you who had the SF cops pick me up?"

Korg's face pled innocent.

Klondike's eyes shot bullets. "Well, the cop who fucking hauled me in for questioning said he was a buddy of yours."

"When was this?" Korg asked.

"Right after they found the kid. Cops came inside the park like a posse and rounded me up. Screwed up my life for the day. Cops have a way of doing that."

Klondike turned toward the stage, towering over a small swarm of heads, and pointed to a wiry 6-footer up on the left side, tuning a guitar. "You want Clearwater, the guitarist? That's him. But you'll have to wait. We're having tryouts, to pick a couple of back-up singers. Stay out of the way."

"Fine." Korg then did the opposite and headed straight for the stage.

"STORM CLEARWATER?" HE asked the guitarist while

flashing the badge in one sweep of the hand. "We need to talk."

The guitarist, taken aback, stammered his answer: "What's going on?"

Korg measured the musician: a typical young maverick who thought he was beholden to no one. He preferred to grill young upstarts like this in the confines of an interview room at headquarters, a controlled environment, but given that Clearwater, at this point, was just a "person of interest," this could do right here. Plus who knew what else they might see?

"We have a few questions," Korg explained. Sager, quiet and watching, lurked in the background.

Clearwater fiddled with an electronic tuner while answering. "You'll have to wait. Try-outs for two new back-up singers." He never looked up from his task.

The band needed two new female vocalists, Clearwater explained, rapid-fire style. Johnson's band always opened the shows, but to make it work, he needed female vocalists to front the act. Plus, recording sessions were imminent for a new CD. The previous week, on the verge of the big show at AT&T and recording sessions, two female singers thought they had the leverage for a power play to extract more money out of Johnson. He canned them on the spot. The word had gone out, in L.A., San Francisco and Las Vegas, about the try-outs. In the music business, life fortunes could turn on a moment.

Korg tried a different approach. "I'm investigating the disappearance of Stephen Griffin. According to the phone records, you were the last person to talk to him."

That caught Clearwater's attention. He broke into a

nervous, crooked smile. "Fine, we'll talk. But first we have work to do here."

Both Korg and Sager caught the charged reaction.

Johnson was still absent, but Clearwater, by default, the bandleader and the dynamic force in the room, took charge.

"Let's get started," he announced.

KORG TURNED TO Sager and handed him a 9x11 envelope. Inside was the image that Sturgeon had created at the lab, a rough duplicate of the missing photograph from the wall of Griffin's beach house.

"Find out who runs Johnson's operation. They'll know everybody in this shot. ID all of them."

As Korg took a seat in the back right corner, off to his right, Johnson entered the room like he owned the place, which, of course, he did. The vocalists stirred, and some twitched nervously at the sight of the star. Johnson leered at the young women, then nodded with a frown at Korg, and sat nearby, within easy range, but out of his bubble.

"What are you doing here?" Johnson asked.

"Checking loose ends." Korg relaxed his inspector form, and confided, "You know, back in college, I was in a band myself. Wrote a few songs. This kind of brings it all back."

Johnson grimaced. "Everybody's got a damn song." But he pointed a finger at Korg.

"We've got somebody else turned up missing, I already told you once," Johnson said. "My road manager. Deego DeGenaro. Didn't show up. Won't answer his phone." Maybe that would get Korg out of his hair, Johnson thought. Then he turned to the stage to address the matter at hand.

First up was a dirty blond, wearing a red, cling-to top, and she wiggled at Johnson like a professional cheerleader gyrating at the little red light of a TV camera. Up close, it looked like she'd spent too many miles on the back of a Harley. She sang well enough. But no way, Johnson thought. He required vocal quality, but also the right look on stage, the right energy, someone who would mesh with the band's performance.

Next was a heavy-set brunette with sensational pipes, but hey, this is show business. Half the job is theatrics, out there in front of thousands, and she was big enough to wear a tent. Then came a young black woman, very small, thin and loud; once they toned it down on the soundboard, she started scoring with a big voice with range, a definite possibility.

After a half dozen more, Clearwater called out, "Lorelei Aicona."

"That's me."

Standing there in front of Clearwater, a few feet away, waiting quietly, was a young woman with a serene aura, soft almond skin and azure eyes full of mystery. Clearwater appeared stupefied. Her hair was soft and jet black, swept down across her shoulders, framing her face. She was just standing there, self-contained, content. Her gaze seemed to glow. Clearwater felt a rush, the upwelling of a strange sensation, and smiled back at her, his eyes firing like arrows.

"Are you ready?" he asked.

She nodded, demure.

Clearwater signaled at the bass player, and they launched into the chorus of Straight Ahead, the song that Jesse James Johnson was planning to turn into an anthem, a million-seller, on the new CD.

To start the tryout, all Lorelei had to do was sing the simple chorus:

Lookin', lookin' straight ahead!
Lookin', lookin' straight ahead!

Her voice was like an instrument with sweet, penetrating tones. Within seconds, it was as if Lorelei took those sparse lines inside and made them her own. She had a natural sense of ease and instant familiarity with the pull of the melody, taking the words up and then taking them down.

Clearwater handed her a lyric sheet.

"Try this."

Lorelei questioned the request. "No rehearsal? No melody check?"

"Let's just see how you do cold."

Clearwater fired up his skeleton band, and Lorelei took over.

I looked at you and we seemed to share.
A cry in the wind, like a lost prayer.
I know you've opened your heart and bled.
Time has come for you to look straight ahead.

Lookin', lookin' straight ahead!
Lookin', lookin' straight ahead!

She hit it perfectly. No hesitation. No wallowing or searching for a melody. By mid-verse, she even dropped the lyric sheet to her side, and with the words already memorized, put her soul into her unique inflection. 'An extraordinary talent,' Clearwater concluded to himself. 'She must be brilliant to memorize the lines so quickly.'

He tried to scan her body without her noticing. Slim but curvy. 'The perfect mix of sultry and sophisticated,' he thought.

In the back of the room, Johnson raised a hand.

"Try'er with her," he ordered, pointing at Talia.

Clearwater motioned for the thin, confident black woman to return to the stage. Lorelei and Talia approached their microphones, where over and over, they repeated the chorus.

"The right look," Johnson said to himself, then thought: Pretty, but not flashy. Elegant, not cheap. Smart, clean and cool kind of sensuality. Beautiful, yet reserved.

Johnson listened and watched. By the way the band moved to the swelling rhythms, he could tell that it was working for them, too.

"The right sound," Johnson said. Unusual voices. Nice blend between them. There was an effortless style with that one, clear and hitting everything just right, with a little sense of a cry at the end of the notes.

Johnson's wolf eyes bored in. Lorelei, moving gently to the music, had a natural grace, a way of swaying that blended with Clearwater's double-timed rhythms. Not audacious. Not too out-front. Maybe Lorelei could help create a fabric of sound, and be content to stay there, woven in that fabric.

As the chorus repeated in a loop, Johnson flashed the

thumbs-up to Clearwater. Johnson hopped up on stage to share Lorelei's microphone. As he blended his voice with theirs, Johnson picked up on a sweet but subtle scent of perfume.

Korg, watching from his corner seat, was impressed at how fast the two had been selected. The real thing was nothing like American Idol.

As the applicants filed out, Korg tried to corner Clearwater. Meanwhile, Clearwater was trying to corner Lorelei. And Johnson was putting a corral around all of them.

"You're in, if you'll have us," Johnson said warmly to Lorelei and Talia. "Welcome to the band."

Lorelei's smile was shy. Appreciative, yes, but pandering, no.

Clearwater beamed. Perhaps meeting Lorelei was his destiny.

Korg pulled Clearwater over to the side and back to earth.

"Phone records show you called Stephen Griffin the day before you left for New York." It was a statement more than a question, which required Clearwater to fill in the blanks. Korg stood there in silence, awaiting a response.

"That was no big thing," Clearwater started. Korg had learned long ago that the words 'no big thing' often meant just the opposite.

"Real simple. I was calling him about the band getting

our own deal, and checking on the progress on that."

Korg flinched. Even with his limited background of the workings of the music industry, where little wheels spin to make the big wheels turn, Korg knew that it was unlikely that Griffin, as Johnson's manager, would have allowed the band to create a spin-off act.

"Let's go outside and talk."

Under the shade of a black oak, Korg pressed.

"You want your own deal, then?"

Clearwater folded his arms. He was 6-1, 165, sinewy strong, driven and still a bit wounded from a recent motorcycle accident that had messed up his left shoulder and knee. His hair was a bit longer than it should have been, chestnut brown, and since the hospital time, when he decided not to shave, he had grown a beard and mustache, but with sharp, shaped edges, trimmed short. His eyes were blue, full of life, clear and strong, with curved eyebrows that came together at the bridge of the nose like the horns of a ram.

"Not just me, all of us, you know, the band, would like to take a shot with our own CD."

"Tell me more."

Clearwater dropped his eyes, the gears spinning, and then looked straight Korg.

"OK, here's the deal. We in the band create the sound for Johnson, but we're not making any money. Everywhere you look, every place we go with him, all you see is that we're doing all the work and he's just stacking it up, making millions, buying all kinds of stuff."

Clearwater gazed off at Johnson's estate home, then continued. "Since we've developed the sound as a unit, we'd like our own label deal, get paid a percentage of the live gate for opening shows, and if we hit it with a single on our CD, even break out on a tour of our own, or at least get paid separately at each show as the opening act."

Korg stared ahead, silent.

Clearwater filled in the vacuum. "That's what I called Stephen Griffin about. He'd said he'd get back to me on our East Coast swing, but he never did. Instead, the guy ran off to Las Vegas."

"How would you describe your relationship with Griffin, adversarial or partners?"

"Plenty of both," Clearwater said. "He needed me, and to be honest, I needed him."

Like an owl rotating its head to eye prey from a distance, Clearwater turned and scanned Lorelei as she left the Sound Factory with Talia and Johnson. He liked what he saw. She was about 5-7, slim, almost delicate, and when she walked, she seemed to glide, so smooth, with a built-in sensuality. No extra pushing was needed. She seemed filled with secrets that only a special few could unlock.

"You know," Clearwater said to the now quizzical Korg, "for years I've been looking for someone special. Maybe she could be it."

His shoulder and knee didn't seem to hurt so bad anymore, but there was more. He felt like he was healing inside.

Korg waived a hand. "Where were you Saturday afternoon during the band set-up?"

"At the baseball park, of course, getting ready."

"Where were you when Spoogs went over the rail?"

"In the park somewhere."

"Were you ever by yourself?"

Clearwater paused for effect, as if trying to remember. Sager jotted in his notebook: "Faking it."

"Hell, I don't remember. We were doing our set-up, just like we always do before a show."

JUST 50 YARDS away, inside Johnson's living room, the rock star popped the cork on a $500 bottle of Two-Star Dom Perignon.

"Hah!" Johnson exclaimed at the sound of sizzling bubbles, as if he had never done this before. He poured the sparkling wine into $400 diamond-cut crystal flutes, tilting the glass carefully so the liquid would slide across the side of the flute and retain its brilliant radiance.

As Johnson handed her a glass, Lorelei smiled, that sweet demure smile he'd first seen from across the room at the sound stage. He couldn't help but think he'd found himself an angel, and then in the next thought, wondered what kind of lover she would turn out to be. He knew lots of good girls have a naughty, devilish shadow side.

KORG FOUND SAGER at the car, on his phone. Snapping the phone shut, the young inspector's eyes flickered with excitement.

"You know that flight that Griffin took to Las Vegas? I've got a line on who sat next to him."

"Local?" Korg asked.

"Menlo Park."

"Yes."

Korg took a deep breath. "What about the photo?"

Sager nodded with assurance. "Got an ID on everybody." He explained that Rosemary Yamani, Johnson's do-it-all office manager, was a fountain of information.

Sager pulled out the photo, and one by one, identified each person.

There were those whom Korg was already familiar: Stephen Griffin, the missing person; Jesse James Johnson, rock star; Storm Clearwater, band leader, Rock Winston, president of Diogenes Sound.

Then there were the others: A fired back-up singer, MaryLou Dietz, road manager Deego DeGenaro, lawyer Justin Goldberg, guitarist Ryan Landru, bass guitarist Poochy McNabb, drummer T-Bone Robertson.

Korg rubbed his chin and eyed his assistant.

"You know what to do next, right?"

10

STEPHEN GRIFFIN, THE manager of a big-time rock star, was missing, Korg thought. A roadie, Spoogs, gets shot and thrown off the arcade before the rock star's big show. The rock star's road manager, Deego DeGenaro, suddenly also appears to be missing.

That's too much coincidence, Korg thought. Somebody's doing some killing.

Korg was propelled forward by his investigation. He was eager now, ready to dig, and dig fast, and he almost hopped out of his car as he arrived at Redwood City. He carried the quickly-expanding case folder in his right hand. Meanwhile, Sager had leads of his own and was off chasing them down.

It had been years since Korg had visited the San Mateo County Clerk-Recorder, but he managed to work his way past a small assemblage of real estate folks. The county office felt antiseptic and insular, thanks to the stark light radiating from the long, narrow overhead fixtures and squared coverings, making them look like trays of ice cubes. He flashed his badge to get behind the counter and asked for an open computer terminal.

A middle-aged clerk, Madeline, a little thick in the middle but with a kind smile, led Korg to an office cubbyhole.

"You're from Homicide?" she asked, almost nonchalant, failing an attempt to appear at ease. "What would a homicide inspector want to do with the recorder's office?"

"It's where the trail leads, Maddy," Korg said.

"Maddy?" she answered, blushing. "When I was a little girl, my daddy used to call me Maddy."

Korg tried not to react. 'Daddy' was probably his age.

He found he could navigate the computer system in the San Mateo County Clerk-Recorders office as easily as he could head his boat out to the Farallon Islands on a calm, clear day. Technology, gadgets and electronics had always fascinated him. On his boat, he had wired and installed the GPS, radar, radios and fishfinder himself, and linked the GPS, radar and autopilot the same way he'd link evidence to solve cases. Just for fun, over the Christmas holidays at home on the kitchen table, he built Zack a computer, a PC clone with all the new goodies.

Here at the county assessor's office, Korg stared into the computer monitor and typed "Zagorski" in the search box. He felt his heart pounding as the cursor blinked. That was amazing, he noted to himself: excited to be on the hunt. First time in ages.

A new page began to form on the computer screen, top-to-bottom. A moment later, listings of properties owned by Zagorski Inc., each with a Book Number and Parcel Number, appeared.

Korg's face contorted in shock.

In five minutes, Korg tallied 18 property listings. But Korg knew that the listings alone did not mean

Zagorski Inc. owned 18 properties. His wife, Emma, as a real estate broker, had taught him that each time a property was bought, sold or refinanced, it would show up as a document. So each property could be listed several times.

Korg pointed at the screen, his pulse dancing, and whispered to himself, "Let's connect the dots."

Each Zagorski property listed a Book Number and Parcel Number, and with that, Korg traced each parcel, its assessed land value, annual property tax, and sales price. One by one, the chips fell into place. All the properties had been purchased in the past five years for cash, no bank loans.

Korg conducted similar searches for four other corporations on his list. Morkul was listed with 7 properties, Smythwyck with 3, Prychene with 11, and Synchro with 6. My God, Korg thought, I'm hitting gold. These were the corporations Korg had discovered in Griffin's computer, then spotted paperwork for in Johnson's office. In the next few hours, he traced each property and then printed out every connected transaction.

Korg, with a detective's flame and smelling blood, typed "James Johnson," Jesse James Johnson's real name.

Several connects, Korg noted, but none in Woodside. The James Johnsons he had unearthed out of the computer, he figured, were not the star in question.

"You find anything, honey?" It was Madeline, the clerk, dying for information, anything, a little shred to add some buzz to the daily gossip. She handed him a large stack of print-outs.

"It might be everything," Korg answered. "Or it

might be nothing." She smiled politely and turned away, seeing there would be no additional dirt to spread today.

A stack of documents in front of him, Korg pulled out his cell phone, punched his auto dial to the FBI division in Carson City, Nevada, and in moments, was connected to Phil Rosenthal. Some 25 years ago, they had come up together at SFPD.

"Need a quick favor, Phil."

Rosenthal cringed. As much as he enjoyed Korg's long-time friendship, favors for his pal had a way of being nothing quick.

"Cruise over to 714 State Street in Carson City," Korg suggested, sweet-talking his friend. "Take a digital shot of what's there and e-mail me the jpeg."

"No problem," Rosenthal answered, knowing this was a job that he could assign to an underling. "What's it supposed to be?"

"Headquarters for a shell corporation called Zagorski Incorporated."

"Want to take me salmon fishing sometime?"

"Any time, 'ol buddy. Get your butt out of the desert and down here to paradise."

Korg ruffled through the stack of papers in his case folder with a fractured urgency — "Where is that thing?" — and eventually found what he wanted. It was the list of all employees and independent contractors that received pay-outs from the Jesse James Johnson Corporation.

There it was, near the bottom. He read the line slowly: "CPA/ATTORNEY, JUSTIN GOLDBERG."

"Thanks for everything, Maddy."

The clerk beamed. "Always look me up first," then she added, "Any suspects?"

Korg grinned, 'she never quits trying,' nodded and was out the door. In minutes, he was stuck in sluggish traffic on the 101, trying to head south to Palo Alto and Goldberg's office. He punched the center button of his Bluetooth, a fixture in his right ear when he drove alone, and rang up Sager.

"You got anything?"

"Lots." Sager answered. "How about you."

"Could be on to something big"

"Gotta go. I'm in Menlo Park. Trying to put Griffin on the plane."

"Hell, I'm going to Palo Alto, right next door. Let's compare notes in an hour."

Suddenly, Korg did not gloat as brightly at the prospects of retirement as he had for months. For nearly a year, all he could think about was retirement, not having to report to Pritchett and having a fish on his line. Now he found himself fully engaged in a case like few others in his long career; it had revived something in him that he thought had died. All he wanted was to ferret out truths and lies and nail the guilty. It was possible there were three connected murders, Griffin, Spoogs, DeGenaro.

He knew these lessons: Follow the money. Follow the passions. The power. Follow those close to the case. Look for those who might want revenge. And if something does not make sense, no matter how strange or subtle, get the answer to explain it. Korg had solved dozens of intricate crimes by doing exactly that. Money.

Passion. Sometimes power. Someone close. Sometimes the obvious. Sometimes the obscure. Connect the dots.

JOAN DAY LIKED playing the $1 slots, Sager learned, and to be amenable, he accepted the cup of coffee she had offered him. He hated coffee. Now he smelled it. The scent was rich. Then, just as before, when he tried a sip, it tasted nothing like it smelled; bitter and acrid. Sager quickly put the cup back on the small saucer, "Still a little hot," he explained.

For a "girls' holiday," as she called it, Joan and her best friend, Caryn, had caught a flight from San Francisco to Las Vegas. "AirWest," she confirmed.

Sager placed two photos of Stephen Griffin on the table before her.

"Was that the man sitting next to you," Sager said, "a kind, quiet type?" He watched her face closely.

Joan never twitched even an eyelid.

"Nope. I'd remember him. Nothing like that. This wasn't him."

IN DOWNTOWN PALO Alto, Korg bulls-eyed the office of Justin P. Goldberg, attorney-at-law, CPA and financial advisor for Jesse James Johnson, and sauntered in as if it were his living room. The Bulldog was out of his kennel. No Sager meant no leash.

The badge worked its magic on Goldberg's fortress-of-steel secretary, who typically fended off visitors. Korg flashed it again at Goldberg and smiled at what he called "The Schadenfreude Effect," when he would create discomfited moments for others and then enjoy watching their anxiety. He knew the badge could be petrifying.

Goldberg leaned back in his leather chair, simulating calm and comfort.

Korg engaged the lawyer.

"I hear Johnson is getting ready to record a new CD."

Goldberg listened and appeared mollified. He charged a minimum of $500 per hour, more on contract jobs. The inspector would be here, what, 15 minutes, and he'd bill Johnson the full hour.

Korg continued. "I have a song he might like."

Goldberg just stared, waiting for a bomb to drop.

"I play a little guitar myself," Korg explained, "worked my way through college back in the day."

Goldberg looked at his watch and forced a smile without showing any teeth. He was built like a sack of yams and had a butt the shape of his large desk chair. While nearly bald on top, Goldberg had grown out the hair on the sides and then greased it back to create a pair of strange-looking sidewalls. He wore bifocals with lenses as thick as the bottom of a wine bottle, and strutted around with the unmistakable presence of a super brain with money.

Korg furnished the lawyer with his best I'm-your-friend look.

"Hey, I'm trusting you here. This is in confidence, right? You're the first one I've been willing to share my songs with."

Goldberg nodded. "Oh, so there's more than one?"

"Oh yeah," Korg responded, encouraged. "I've got a bunch of songs."

"You give me your demo, I'll get it to the right place." Goldberg then stood. This was the invitation for Korg to depart.

"Thanks," Korg said, standing as well, as if accepting the offer.

"Oh, by the way," he continued, as if by now Goldberg really was his good friend, "was Stephen Griffin a member of the Jesse James Johnson Corporation, or did he get paid as an outsider."

Ah, so this is what the detective was here for, Goldberg presumed. The answer was quick and direct.

"Well, he got his 15 percent, but we paid him as an independent contractor. So I guess you would say he was outside the corporation but got paid on an insider's margin."

"Thanks," Korg smacked, handed Goldberg his card, and then headed for the door. Just as he touched the knob, Korg turned back halfway to Goldberg and added, "Say, you ever heard of Zagorski Incorporated?"

Goldberg could not hide the initial shock that jolted through him. But he gathered himself, rolled his eyes at the ceiling, and answered: "Maybe that's one of the boards I'm listed with as an honorary director, you know letterhead stuff to impress people. Other than that, can't say it rings a bell."

"That's funny, does it ring a bell that you're listed as Zagorski's treasurer?"

Goldberg tried his best to fake an easy smile.

"Wait a minute. Oh that? Zagorski? Yeah, that kind of rings a bell. That's just an honorary position. "

Korg nodded as he left.

"Well, that explains it."

The door clicked shut.

Goldberg was on the phone to Johnson.

"A homicide inspector looking into Griffin's disappearance was just in my office asking me if I'd ever heard of Zagorski Incorporated. I said no. Then he says he knows that I'm the treasurer."

"Oh shit!" Johnson reacted. "Move everything out of it. Close it down! Now!"

An ugly silence followed.

"It's not that simple to make it disappear. Especially with the properties."

Five minutes later, Korg was stopped in a gauntlet of red lights in Palo Alto, caught in the city's apparent mission to block all traffic flow. His cell phone chimed "Good 'ol Boys."

Korg's greeting was urgent. "You get it?"

"We got it." It was Roper, the deputy district attorney.

"Goldberg and Johnson?"

"Yep. They're going to try to close down Zagorski."

Korg guffawed.

"Wiretaps sure come in handy. Thanks, Joe."

"Don't thank me. Thank Judge Wharton, a wise man. He's signed off on it. I had to stretch the story a bit. I think he figured we're actually pretty lean on the facts, but he let me run with it. I told him there were three murders."

"There might be."

Korg's phone beeped. Call waiting. Sager.

"Gotta go," Korg barked to Roper.

Korg clicked his ear button on the BlueTooth to connect to the junior inspector. "Whatcha got?"

"You still in Palo Alto?"

Korg laughed. "Of course. It's impossible to leave Palo Alto. All you see in this town are red lights."

"Then make a U-turn and whip over to El Camino Real. Meet me at the Oasis, right next to a Beacon gas station. Storm Clearwater and his band are there. I've been tracking them. This is our chance to get 'em unawares. Plus I've got news."

"The lady who had the seat next to Griffin on the flight to Las Vegas?" The anticipation in Korg's voice was unmistakable.

"She said it wasn't Griffin. Somebody else used the ticket. I don't see how it's possible with all the security, but somehow it happened. At the Oasis, we could surprise Clearwater. He'd never see it coming."

"I'll be there," Korg said. "One more thing."

"What?" Sager asked.

"We're going to Vegas ourselves," Korg said.

"I don't want to go to Vegas. There are already detectives in Las Vegas. They can check things out."

"No they can't," Korg insisted.

"Pritchett clear this?"

Korg ignored the question and pressed ahead.

"You get everything else?"

"Just about."

"See you in 10."

Korg ended the discussion with a click of his thumb, and then punched it again. Information, he asked, San Francisco, AirWest, and then with direct connect, he was put through. Traffic, meanwhile, barely crawled. Korg pulled out his wallet and flashed open to his Cabela's VISA credit card.

Sager was right, Korg figured. Pritchett would never approve a trip to Las Vegas or even entertain a discussion to pay for it. So he made an end run around Pritchett and the bean counters and booked it himself.

At yet another red light, Korg swung his car around the stopped traffic and whipped into the right merge lane to hit El Camino at forty, which felt like Mach 10 after a crawling pace for 15 minutes. What else had Sager discovered?

11

IN 10 MINUTES, Korg strolled into the Oasis, a woodsy joint in Menlo Park frequented equally by Stanford students, Peninsula yuppies, construction workers, old hippies, softball teams and bikers. Peanut shells covered the floor. He spotted Sager, hidden in a high-walled, partially-enclosed private booth. In the adjacent booth, Storm Clearwater was holding court with his band. They were so passionate in discussion that none of them saw Korg, and once in a booth, he might have well been on another planet. Of course, Pritchett thought Korg *was* on another planet.

Over the course of 40 minutes, the band members had gorged on double cheeseburgers piled high with grilled onions, and two pitchers of beer, Sager said.

"That's some mighty fine detective work, young man," Korg chimed.

Sager ignored the friendly barb. "I ordered for you," he continued, keeping his voice so low that Korg could scarcely make out the words. "We can hear most everything they're saying. They're very angry, especially the main guy, Storm Clearwater. Just like I figured."

Korg grinned. For Sager, this was quite a few consecutive words, even multiple sentences. "Tell me what you got."

Sager, deadly serious, placed a close-up photo of Stephen Griffin on the wood table so it faced Korg.

"I showed this photo to one Joan Day of Menlo Park," Sager started. "She said she'd never seen this guy in her life."

"So it is possible, like you say, that Griffin never went to Las Vegas. More good work, inspector."

Korg, in thought, munched his cheeseburger. "Grilled onions," he said, "the best. Thanks. How'd you know I like them so much?"

"I overheard you one day."

"Nothing gets by you, eh?" Korg chuckled. "That's good." Then he added, "Guess there'll be no kissing my lovely Emma tonight," Korg laughed. Then he turned serious. "What else was it you were so excited to tell me?"

"Yes, there's more," Sager said.

"Go man."

Sager pressed his finger tips into the table so hard that the nails burned pink.

"I checked out alibis for our key 16 hours, starting the evening of Wednesday, September 26th, and interviewed anybody who lives or works close to Griffin's beach house."

Korg stopped eating, drinking, and for a moment, breathing. "Go, Man."

Sager opened up his notebook for review before he spoke.

"Well, we already know that Johnson and that big guy, Klondike, vouch for each other, so that could be bullshit.

They both said they last saw Griffin on the afternoon of Wednesday the 26th, at their place in Woodside."

"Of course, I remember that."

"In the band," Sager tilted his head, indicating they were right in the booth behind them, "Ryan Landru and Poochy McNabb were with their girlfriends. That's verifiable. And the drummer, T-Bone Robertson, get this, was not with one girl, but two. Man, the life these guys lead."

"It's all a facade, young man," Korg responded. "Heaven is having your true love in your arms. I feel that every night with my Emma. I wake up every morning in a nest. That's the life of love. Anything else is a mirage."

The corners of Sager's mouth appeared to lift in the hint of a grin. "Well, I wouldn't mind trying out a mirage. For one time, anyway."

Sager turned the page of his notebook.

"The road manager is this guy Deego DeGenaro. He disappeared. Gone since sometime late Saturday. The last call was from a disposable TracFone with minutes purchased from a WalMart. About 5 p.m. Saturday, incoming. Can't be traced."

Korg, still absorbed in his dinner, took mental notes.

"We still don't know about Rock Winston the music executive, Justin Goldberg the lawyer, and the two back-up singers who later got fired, MaryLou Dietz and Faye McFadden."

"What about that guitarist?"

Sager leaned forward and stared hard into the senior inspector's eyes.

"Storm Clearwater. That's his name."

Sager stopped to hold up his picture.

"I didn't want to act on Clearwater without your go-ahead."

"What?" Korg asked, "What?"

"I showed these pictures around to the neighbors and employees over at Miramar. A neighbor saw Clearwater at Griffin's house in the early evening on that Wednesday. She was sure of it. She and her husband were walking over to the Miramar Beach House Restaurant for dinner. She can verify the date because it was their anniversary. It gets better. Clearwater appeared irate."

Korg pulled out his notebook.

"So the last person to both phone and see Griffin, as far as we know, is Clearwater, and he was extremely agitated."

Sager confirmed. "And he lives way out in La Honda. That's why I tracked him to here and called you. It'd be easier to get him here, I figured, than try to get him in our office."

Korg shook his head.

"No, son, we'd never do it that way. I know you're eager, but don't be jumping out of your shoes. You only interrogate a person of interest when you can control the environment. Can't do that here, not even close. You don't want his friends around. And if you really think he did it, you'd want to film the interview."

Sager edged in another comment.

"Clearwater was at AT&T when Spoogs was shot and tossed over the arcade. He then left the park about the same time Deego DeGenaro got his last phone call and then disappeared."

"Where you'd say he lives?" Korg asked.

"Outside of La Honda, Santa Cruz Mountains, in the redwoods. Remote. Cabin. It would be easy to stash bodies out there."

RIGHT THEN, A voice familiar to Korg rose up above the din.

"I'm not just talking about how I feel about her, I'm talking about how Lorelei is our missing piece, the one who can give us our own label deal." It was Clearwater, talking in the next booth. The urgency in his voice was unmistakable.

"You're right, she's my missing piece," said Robertson, the drummer. "Man, she could fog up the windows of a bus."

"Stay clear of her," warned Clearwater.

Jeff Bridges, the bass player, who looked like he hadn't said anything for 10 years, still hadn't said anything. Next to Bridges, guitarist Poochy McNabb also watched and listened.

Ryan Landru could play any song, any style, with a dozen instruments, yet was a team player, in the studio and on stage, and was always looking out for others, how they felt, what made them tick, making sure they were on track.

"Take it slow, Storm," Landru said. "You actually don't know very much about her, do you?"

"I know how she makes me feel."

Landru shook his head gently at his best friend.

"The thing you have to ask, is 'Does she have an inside that is as beautiful as her outside?' Over time, her outer life will eventually match what is inside her."

Robertson laughed. "Like he cares. He just wants to get her shirt off."

After a pause, Robertson added to Storm. "I'll bet you a hundred bucks I get her shirt off before you do." He laughed. "I'd do anything to get a look at those baubles."

"Hey," McNabb countered to focus the group. "We've got bigger fish to catch. What about our own label deal?"

Clearwater broke into a grin at the thought. "Where is all the money? It seems to me that money is pouring in and we sure the hell aren't getting it. Without us, Johnson's got no sound."

Yet they all also knew the truth: Each of them was replaceable, a gear in a machine. Without Johnson, they were just another band without a front presence, having trouble getting gigs, being paid a pittance for playing the bars on the weekends, and having to get a real job during the week to support the illusion.

In the next second, two gunshots popped like firecrackers across the room near the bar. Shrieks flared. Some patrons hit the floor. Some dove under tables.

Two men, young, wired and angry, held up chrome-plated automatic pistols, and pointed them at the young attendants behind the two cash registers.

"Those are warnin' shots," shouted one. "Give us all the money. Both registers. I ain't asking again."

On instinct from training, Korg and Sager drew their firearms, .40 caliber Glocks. Still seated, they held them along their thighs, out of sight.

Off to the side, behind the bar, the bartender pulled

a handgun from under the rail. The robber on the right wheeled and fired in one motion. The bartender never got a round off. He was downed with a single shot to the shoulder. He fell with a scream.

"I want you all to watch what I do to heroes like this," shouted the robber. "I'm gonna make a dead hero out of him. Anybody wanna be next?"

The robber took two steps forward, leaned over the bar, and pointed his pistol at the wounded bartender, curled on the floor. "Good night, hero."

Someone in the room shouted "No!" A few women howled in terror.

Across the room, in the booth, Sager raised his firearm, his left hand cupping his right wrist, bracing his right elbow against the framed entry to the booth. He found the torso of the attacker and squeezed. The bullet entered the robber's left side and punctured a lung. Down he went, squealing like a pig.

The other robber turned toward Sager and fired wildly, popping off rounds anywhere in the general direction. Sager heard one bullet zing over his right shoulder.

Korg, a little slow on the draw, was still raising his pistol, when Sager, electric-fast, fired three times in 1.7 seconds. Two in the chest, one in the head. The attacker took one step forward, tried to raise his weapon, gurgled gibberish, and crumpled to the floor, dead.

The room filled with screams and shouts.

Sager dashed to the forefront and kicked the guns away from the downed bandits. He raised his badge to the room.

"Police!" he shouted. "Everything is under control."

On the other side of the room, Korg did the same.

After Sager checked the robbers — one dead, the other mortally wounded — he cleared the bar in a leap and checked on the bartender. No vital organs struck. The bullet had gone clean through flesh, missing bone and veins.

But all was not right.

Sager turned and saw that Korg was in the booth with the musicians, on his phone. The big bass player, Jeffrey Bridges, was in the back of the booth, slumped in a corner. The front of his shirt mushroomed in blood.

"Get me an ambulance," Korg commanded. "My 20, Oasis, El Camino, Menlo Park. I've got a civilian gunshot wound to the torso. Another civilian, gunshot wound to the shoulder, stabilized. Situation otherwise secure."

That night, Korg found sleep impossible. He draped his left arm over his wife and tried to submerge himself in her rhythmic breathing. But he was still too wired, replaying the scene, over and over, and finally, at about 1 a.m., he gave up and rolled out of bed.

"Is it the shooting?" Emma asked.

"Can't sleep. Too much on my mind. I keep replaying it. How Sager took 'em out."

He staggered into the kitchen, grabbed an ice cold Pacifico, and then headed into his office. He then surveyed five stacks of print-outs on his counter.

Each stack of paper represented the real estate transactions in San Mateo County that he had copied. Korg traced out each property, just as Emma had explained it was done, and lined out each listing that had been inventoried multiple times. He finally had a hard property list, that is, each property listed only once with its purchase price and property tax.

Korg then made a second list, categorizing the properties according to ownership. The work was logical and went quickly.

After three hours, he began to add the totals with a calculator, when he heard his wife at the door. He didn't have to look. He knew how her footsteps sounded on the hardwood floor.

"Honey, it's 3 a.m. You've got to sleep. I know what happened was bad, the shooting, but you need to sleep. You need rest."

"Sweetheart, the shooting is only part of it. You can't believe what I'm finding."

Through bleary eyes, Korg showed his totals to his wife:

ZAGORSKI INCORPORATED: 8 PROPERTIES, $27.4 MILLION
MORKUL: 3 PROPERTIES, $2.4 MILLION
SMYTHWYCK: 1 PROPERTY, $1.9 MILLION
PRYCHENE: 6 PROPERTIES, $28.9 MILLION
SYNCHRO: 4 PROPERTIES, $8.2 MILLION

"My God," Emma said. "Add them up."

He quickly punched in the numbers.

"In San Mateo County alone," he said, "these five corporations own 22 properties worth $68.8 million. What do you think?"

"I think you've got to do something about your breath," she said with a hand on her husband's shoulder. "Onions?"

"Sorry about that. But you have to wonder how it all

fits together. Where the money comes from? What other holdings the corporations must surely have, in other counties, other states, and likely in other countries. How does it all fit together?"

Korg walked over to his aquarium, fed his tropical fish, and as they darted about, nabbing the small flakes, he remembered that first day at Johnson's estate, when he had unearthed the corporate documents: There was another $20 million cash in offshore accounts.

Emma came up from behind her husband and wrapped her arms around him.

"If you face away from me, it's OK," she said.

"It was grilled onions, a whole stack of 'em on a double cheeseburger."

She laid her head on his back. "You really want this, don't you, Honey, to go out on top?"

"Yeah."

"Come to bed now."

In bed, he remembered how back in the day, the detectives at SFPD called him, "The Bulldog." When triggered, he was relentless. He'd chomp on to something and would not let go. He was nearly asleep when his body flexed and jerked.

He popped out of bed and headed straight back to his office. He started with the stack of print-outs of properties owned by Zagorski, Inc. "There it is," he cried with joy.

Korg held the document in his hand. The reason he could not locate Johnson as the owner of his Woodside house, recording studio and property was here, right in front of him.

The owner, he saw, was Zagorski Inc.

12
TUESDAY

THREE HOURS LATER, thoughts and questions caromed around his brain like a pinball. Korg stroked Emma on the shoulder, cast off the sheets, gargled some Listerine, threw on some clothes and drove in to headquarters. He sailed past a Mexican janitor, grabbed a handful of mail from his slot, and then zeroed in on his cubicle. He turned on his computer in a sweeping motion while simultaneously sitting down. He tapped his fingers on his desk, waiting for the PC to boot up, not bothering to take off his coat.

Korg pecked in his password, "4-Play," the name of his boat, and then opened his e-mail program. The computer quickly downloaded new messages.

At the same time, Korg sifted through the short stack of mail. One had his name and address printed out by computer, with no return address. He checked the postmark: Redwood City. Korg opened the envelope, and inside was a single folded sheet of paper. He took it out, unfolded it and read a single line, unsigned:

You only get so much rope.

What the hell was this? Korg wondered. He'd never received a note like that in his career. A computer printer had printed both the address and the note. So the writer had left no personal trail from handwriting that a graphoanalyst could trace. He placed the note quickly on his desk. He'd have Forensics check it for fingerprints.

He returned to the computer screen. The third message was from FBI, Carson City, with an attached file. Edgy with anticipation, Korg opened it.

"Are you sure you want to open an attached file," the computer asked.

"Yes," Korg shouted, goaded by the delay.

The janitor loading trash barrels stopped to check out the uproar in the quiet office.

Korg clicked yes again.

A digital photograph appeared on the computer screen: a small, cheap box-like house, probably two bedrooms, one bath, with an untended scrubby lawn, and an old beater, a Dodge RamCharger, parked in front of it.

This was 714 State Street in Carson City? Headquarters for Zagorski Incorporated? Owners of eight properties in San Mateo County alone that cost $27.4 million?

Korg ambled over to the coffee station, trying to distill what he had learned. In the first sip, he felt the familiar kick, as if the caffeine was running through his veins, trying to jump-start the brain… so much to do.

Back at his desk, Korg called up the Google search engine, typed in "Nevada corporate records" and clicked again. In seconds, he had the link to the State of Nevada website out of Carson City, with a search window titled "Search by corporation name."

He typed in Zagorski and clicked.

Korg was breathing hard now, inhaling and exhaling, sitting there at dawn, digging into computer records.

He clicked on "view selection."

The computer loaded the information and Korg stared at the screen, his eyes burning. Nevada records described Zagorski Incorporated as a "Limited Liability Company" and listed headquarters as "714 State Street, Carson City, Nevada." Korg was practically panting. He typed in the command to search for Zagorski's directors.

The cursor spun while Korg waited, tapping the fingers of his right hand on the desk. In a single flash, the information was presented on the computer screen: James F. Johnson was listed as president of Zagorski Incorporated, with the address: 4075 S. Western Avenue, Suite 1, Las Vegas, NV 89119.

It listed Stephen Griffin as vice president, same address. Justin Goldberg was listed as Secretary/ Treasurer.

Korg repeated the exercise while searching the records for each corporation on his list – Prychene, Synchro, Morkul and Smythwyck.

"Bingo!" Korg shouted with each selection. "Bingo! Bingo! Bingo!"

Goldberg, Johnson and Griffin were listed as officers and resident agents. Every time. All with the same Las Vegas address.

The janitor, confused, again turned to watch the agent's curious machinations.

For a half hour, Korg scarcely moved, sipping coffee, trying to digest the information.

As the day awakened, other inspectors filtered into the office, but Korg was oblivious. His mind was both fogged from so little sleep and buzzed from so much caffeine, and he headed back to the coffee station for another round.

"Heard about the gunplay," said fellow inspector Brett Nelson, who had a few years on Korg but had flown under Pritchett's radar and avoided the broom that was sweeping Korg out. "You and Sager OK?" Korg noticed that Nelson wore a small pin on his lapel that looked familiar, but he couldn't quite place it.

"Yeah, we're OK," Korg answered.

"You sure? You don't look it."

"Let me tell you, that kid Sager was amazing. Saved some lives. That room was about to revolt and these guys, they looked like tweakers, were going to blaze. In my career, I never did what Sager's already done."

"You look like you should go home, get some rest," Nelson countered.

Korg ignored the suggestion and again eyed the pin, small, but there was something about the two arrows that he couldn't place.

"Ah Brett, it's this case I'm on. Probably murder, and for sure money laundering, tax evasion, it's all here, but I don't know who did the dirty deed."

Korg grabbed a few discarded sections of a newspaper, while steadying a massive black coffee mug filled to the brim. On one side, in block yellow printing, were the words "Bite Me," and on the other, a painting of a salmon.

Korg took his seat, set the mug on his desk, popped on his reading glasses and opened the sports section. He was in luck. For once there was a story about fishing. The salmon were expected to gather and cruise the "Salmon Highway" along the Marin Coast from Double Point to Stinson Beach, he read. "Some of the biggest salmon of the year are now massing for their fall migratory journey through the Bay, Delta and up the Sacramento River."

He thought of Luther, the monster salmon that had eluded him for so many years, a fish that had become more a symbol than reality. Korg envisioned cruising his 24-footer up the coast at dawn, watching the rays of sunrise to the east turn the puffy cumulus clouds into pink cotton candy, with the Golden Gate Bridge aglow in the morning light. For a moment, reading that story, he was out there, the clean salt air in his face, filling his lungs with it, and then he was letting his bait down, the boat drifting in the currents.

In thought, he brushed his chin, hit stubble, and realized he had forgotten to shave. His hair was a mess. From lack of sleep and a 36-ounce caffeine injection, his eyes were rolling around like ball bearings. His suit didn't look much better.

I'll be outta here soon, Korg thought. I'll be on my boat and all I'll do is fish.

While reading, he unconsciously kicked his feet up on his desk, The Aircraft Carrier, and then stretched out full. His eyes half closed. Sleep seemed close.

Semi-conscious, he nudged his coffee mug with his right ankle and pushed it off the desk. The mug shattered into clay chunks, with 18 ounces of java splayed on the white tile floor.

Disheveled, rattled and desperate to be quick, Korg grabbed the newspaper and pounced on the spill, trying to swab up the liquid, hoping to get the mess cleaned up before anybody saw it. No such luck. He felt a shadow of presence cast over him. Korg looked up and saw Roberta Pritchett standing there, half disgusted, half amused.

Sad, so sad, thought Pritchett of an inspector who once had been a superstar talent, approaching even legend status.

"I'll just soak it up with the… " Korg tried to explain, still on all fours. But before he could complete even a sentence, the regal Pritchett departed, shaking her head as she walked, getting as much space possible between herself and Korg.

He reached down to pick up a sopping piece of Chronicle when a double-deck, single-column headline caught his eye. Korg read carefully:

DEATH PLUNGE AT AT&T PARK

A man identified as a member of the road crew for the rock star Tenaya was killed when he was shot and thrown off the arcade level of San Francisco's AT&T Park while crews prepared for a concert.

The victim was shot in the back and then thrown from the upper deck section concourse that

> overlooks China Basin, according to investigating officers with the San Francisco Police Department.
>
> A co-worker, Fred Winovitch, chief of the stage crew, told police the man had complained of stomach pains and nausea, and then left the stage area, according to a police report. The man instead went to the arcade level of the park.
>
> A small amount of cocaine was found at the scene, according to a police statement.
>
> His identity is being withheld pending notification of family.
>
> The concert went on as scheduled.

Korg was still on all fours, with two wide round circles of moisture growing at the knees of his slacks. He looked up. All in the office ignored his contortions.

A crazy thought flashed across his mind.

Could it be? Not likely, he answered to himself. He needed sleep, he realized. He was nearing the point where the coherent and incoherent could not be separated. He was thinking himself into the ridiculous. Sleep, I must get sleep.

He read the story again, and then gazed out a window. It could be, he thought again.

It felt like a hard rain after a dust storm.

LORELEI NIBBLED THE edges of a chicken tostada and chatted lightly about the band, the tours, singing back up and writing songs. Sitting across from her at the beach-side Mexican restaurant in San Francisco, Clearwater noticed how soft her face was, and he wished he could reach out and stroke a cheek. If he could just feel her cheek, he could imagine the softness of the curve of her waist, the inside of a thigh, the underside of a breast. If he could just touch her cheek, he would know.

She was wearing a very light thin shirt, arctic white, that showed off a gentle figure. Her black hair shined. It swept across her forehead and to her shoulders, like an ocean wave full of life.

"Killer margarita," she said with a tilt of her head.

Lorelei Aicona was the oldest of four kids in her family, he learned, and thus caught most of the flak and the pressure to a make a mark.

She had won the county talent show at age 8, singing and dancing, became a swimming champion at 13, topped the honor roll for years, and crowned her high school days as Homecoming Queen, Salutatorian at graduation, National Merit Scholar. With nearly a year's worth of college credits completed at 17, she nailed a full scholarship to UCLA and graduated Cum Laude, with double majors in public relations and pre-law.

"There were a lot of family arguments over what I was supposed to do," she recalled.

As Clearwater listened to her story, he noticed again that Lorelei's voice really did sound like a chord of music, like he'd first noticed at the tryout. He also noticed that something had changed in him since the motorcycle accident. No longer were the quick thrills enough. He wanted more. The chance for that was sitting three feet in front of him.

"I was thinking of going home to San Diego," Lorelei said. "Then this try-out thing happened. And suddenly here I am." She beamed. "It's funny how things work out."

Lorelei fretted over the family pressure.

"They wanted me to swim the Olympics and rammed it down my throat. I quit at 15 and got interested in boys instead."

More like they became interested in her, Clearwater figured.

"Then all I heard was how I would become a lawyer, all the work my parents had done to support me, to shape me, to create me to be a lawyer. I actually did the pre-law, and I was good at it. But I didn't go to law school just because they made it their dream, not mine."

Clearwater sat back, relaxed. She was a rebel.

As they walked out of the restaurant, Storm reached for her hand and felt it lock. "Little walk on the beach?"

"I'd like that," she answered.

Clearwater was radiant. Lorelei noticed how bright his eyes were, the black centers bright amid cobalt blue, clear and brilliant.

"Have you ever thought about leading your own band," Lorelei asked.

"All the time," Clearwater confided. "But I can't sing."

Good, she thought, plus, after all, I'm the singer. That meant he needed her.

"Well, you definitely have the stuff, Storm." The words were massaged with softness. "I've seen you work. We've only played a few times and you have a way of wrapping your guitar around my voice. It's so beautiful."

It was a cool day at Ocean Beach, north of Fort Funston on the San Francisco coast, and they fell into a comfortable silence, listening to dwarf waves lap at the beach, watching the light foam ease up toward them across the sand, and then fall back into the sea. It was low tide, with acres of tidal flats unveiled, and the faint scent of salt from the exposed flats.

Clearwater found a sand dollar and gave it to Lorelei. "This is for you." Now they were staring into each other's eyes, and Clearwater could feel his jaw and lips trembling from expectation, and he moved forward toward her. Their lips met perfectly. It was just the right match, Clearwater felt, the right touch, the right fit. The kiss was deep and sensuous, and Lorelei was surprised with the force of passion she was feeling from this strange young man. He pulled her to him, and she noticed that her body fit as perfectly to him as her lips. They broke softly, at the same moment.

Clearwater looked into her eyes.

"That was incredible."

Lorelei scolded him.

"Yes, nice. Now cut it out. Don't get so serious. Cool your jets."

But she said it with a quixotic smile.

Korg picked up the phone and punched the number for SFPD homicide. From the old days, he still knew it by heart, and he asked for Leroy Anders.

"Leroy, it's your old friend, Inspector Kristopher Korg," he started.

"Damn, Korg, I heard you damn near got your ass shot off last night," Anders retorted. "Are you going to make it to retirement?"

"Hopefully, and it should be in one piece."

"Heard your partner is quite the hero."

"Yeah, Leroy, this kid, Jeremy Sager, he's the real deal. Now if I can just get him to do everything I want him to."

Anders laughed. "That should be easy. Remember how I was putty in your hands in orientation?"

Korg cut loose a guffaw. At first, Anders resisted everything Korg had suggested when they met at SFPD. But over time, when they saw how alike they were, and how well their personalities meshed, they became lifetime friends.

"Listen, Leroy, can you shoot me the file on that case where the roadie was shot and thrown off the arcade at the ballpark."

"Why?"

"Hell, Leroy. I was there. I'm curious. Just want to know what you found."

"Retirement is not going to work for you, Inspector Korg," Anders noted, and then after a pause, asked his own question.

"What I want to know Korg, is what were you doing there at the ballpark?

"You know how it works. Just following a money trail. It all leads to this rock star Jesse James Johnson and his entourage."

"You think it connects to my case?"

"Hey Leroy, you brought in that big guy, Klondike, the ex-con who works for Johnson, for questioning. You think he's your guy?"

"He can't account for where he was when that kid got whacked," Anders said. "He was at AT&T setting up, but after the kid left the stage, he left too, to go after him. So the big guy's got no alibi. Throwing the kid off the arcade was a nice little add-on, you've got to admit. You know, a chance to admire his work. Not many people would do that."

"But why?"

"Yep. You're right. No motive. But the big guy could have exploded and just gone crazy. Done it before."

KORG LEFT HEADQUARTERS and rang Sager.

"I'm gonna get you outta here," Korg said.

"Can't," Sager argued. "Pritchett put me on psychological and administrative leave. I can't work until they finish the investigation on the shooting and I go through counseling."

"Counseling?"

"Yeah, as if I wasn't trained for what I did. I ran through thousands of rounds at the range, putting three shots in five seconds in a pie plate at 100 yards. Just reacted. Training kicked in. Just wish I'd got them faster. That one guy got off a wild shot and it clipped the band member. Really bothers me. I could have stopped that."

Korg was touched. He'd never heard Sager so effusive. The guy did need counseling. And even more, Sager needed to get away.

"Bring a toothbrush and a spare shirt. I'll be over in an hour."

As Korg hung up the phone, the words printed on that note suddenly haunted him: *"You only get so much rope."*

It was Tuesday. He was done for keeps Friday.

The clock was running fast.

13

"You OK?"

Sager ran a palm over his close-cropped head. "Had a rough one last night. Kept replaying it. Thanks for getting me out of town."

Korg and Sager were at San Francisco International Airport at the check-in counter for AirWest for a flight to Las Vegas.

Sager never said much when the paddling was smooth, but after traversing Class V rapids and emerging at a tail-out pool, he welcomed the sounding board of the seasoned Korg.

"How's the bartender and the other guy who got shot?" Sager asked.

By "the other guy," Sager was referring to the bystander, the musician, Jeffrey Bridges, not the perps, who both died. Sager already knew about them, of course.

Korg rubbed his right eyebrow.

"The bartender's gonna be fine. The shot went clean through his lower shoulder, nothing but meat. Just missed the artery and the bone. You never like to say he was lucky, but maybe he was, pulling a gun like that on a guy who had a bead on him. It'll sting like hell. You saved his life, you know."

"Hey, it's my job."

Korg was inquisitive. "How'd you ever learn to shoot like that?"

"After 10,000 rounds at the range, you learn what you can do."

After a pause as they moved up in the line, Korg injected a thought.

"A lot of guys are just like that bartender. They think they're going to rise to the occasion, but that's not what happens. They default to their level of training and they end up in trouble."

After another short advance in the line, Sager interjected, "So what about the other guy, the band member?"

"Not so good." Korg's voice, like a dirge, had the sound of death in it. "Got hit in the torso. Messed up his insides. He's in intensive care at Stanford, critical."

Sager scowled and Korg continued.

"I'm glad both the shooters went down. They'd just be let out of prison some day to do the same thing to somebody else. A violent criminal is just like a biting ant that crawls into your sleeping bag. Squish it or it will just bite you again."

"It's still rough when you're the one who pulls the trigger," Sager answered.

Korg's face softened, realizing the junior agent was trying to validate what he had done. He also knew that half of the police officers who killed in the line of duty quit their jobs within a year.

"Don't beat yourself up, inspector. You did the right

thing. You saved the bartender's life. You probably saved my life, too. And maybe a few others in the room, including your own. Who knows what those guys were going to do next?"

The black man reached out and shook the white man's hand, firmly, in silence, and locked eyes. The showdown at the Oasis had bonded them.

A moment later, their turn came for the check-in counter for AirWest.

"Driver's license or passport," commanded the ticket agent, officious and clean. Her name tag said "Eliza."

"Sure," Korg fumbled, producing his driver's license.

The woman matched Korg's face to the picture on his driver's license, and then handed his license back and rambled through the security protocol. With Sager, she frowned as she scanned the computer monitor's list of reservations, and then, after 10 seconds, perked up.

"There it is, I guess," she said. "Drivers license or passport."

Without a word, Sager complied with his driver's license. The ticket agent stared first at the driver's license, then again at Sager's face, and finally nodded.

"Well, they got your name wrong, but that happens." She paused for moment, and then explained. "On your ticket, it says Sater instead of Sager, but that's easy enough. Over the phone, a G could sound like a T."

Korg, standing in the shadows behind Sager, jumped to the forefront.

"Tell me, miss, we're homicide inspectors with San Mateo County," he started. "You always match up the ticket holder's driver's license with the person standing in front of you, without exception, right?"

"Homicide?" she asked with a flush of worry.

Out flashed the badges. "We're on a trip. Just a coincidence to ask you these questions."

After a momentary hesitation, the ticket agent answered: "Of course. Without exception. Driver's license or passport. Every person. Every airport. Every ticket. Several times. You know how it works."

The gears in Korg's mind tried to mesh and produce a coherent thought that would put his stamp on the significance of this moment, but nothing came.

"C'mon," Sager said with a poke to Korg's right arm and a nod to the attendant, "let's go."

"Just for the record," Korg said, "I saw you smile. But don't worry. Your secret is safe with me. I won't tell anybody."

"I liked the sound of her voice."

"I think it was a Portuguese accent."

Eventually they reached the next security checkpoint, where they produced their respective boarding passes and driver's licenses. The security officer halted for a moment with Sager, and then after examining his driver's license photograph, followed by a careful scan of the face of the black man standing in front of him, allowed him to pass without a word.

But Korg caught the moment, and flashed his badge. The security agent went mute.

"Don't be alarmed," said Korg, his voice a massage. "Explain to me why you hesitated just then, what you just saw."

"Well," came the abashed response. "These things happen."

"What things?"

"Well, it's him all right, that's what I have to make sure of. His name isn't quite right on his ticket."

Korg's expression begged for an explanation. He got one.

The security agent held up both Sager's boarding pass and his driver license.

"Look," she said, "the ticket says "Jeremy Sater." His driver's license says, "Jeremy Sager."

Korg acknowledged the point. The agent then pointed at Sager.

"Well, this gentleman standing in front of me is clearly the same as the one in this picture on his driver's license. That's my job."

Korg took it in and then fired a question.

"How often does this happen, where the name on the ticket and the name on the ID are slightly off?"

"Every day, all the time," she answered, no longer challenged. "You buy your tickets by phone?"

"Yes I did," Korg answered.

"The person taking the order heard a T instead of a G when you bought the ticket for Mr. Sager. Happens about once every 200 tickets or so, every 15 or 20 minutes."

Korg placed his forefingers on both temples, eyes turning to saucers, and laughed. The sudden joy both amused and confused Sager.

The air was dry, hot and stale at McCarran International in Las Vegas.

"Has to be 105," Korg said.

It took an hour for Korg and Sager to disembark the jet, trudge through the airport and get seated in a rental car, its engine running. Korg already had beads of sweat on his forehead.

"Get the air conditioner going," Korg pleaded, as Sager, sitting in the passenger seat, fiddled with the control panel.

"I'm not used to this heat," Sager responded.

"According to the assholes here," Korg said, "it's a 'dry heat.'"

Korg flipped open his notebook and punched the address, 4075 South Western Avenue, Las Vegas," into the car's GPS-powered moving map trip finder, and powered the car away from Hertz. In 20 minutes, the agents were standing in front of the building at that address.

Yet 4075 South Western Avenue was not a monolithic structure one might expect for a mega corporation. It was a minor, two-story building with seven small office spaces, whose occupants included an independent life insurance salesman, a tax specialist, and, up on the second floor, OutCorp Services.

Korg pointed the way. Sager, who didn't miss much, was fascinated by Korg's sudden jack-o-lantern smile. This was the address of OutCorp Services, Inc., Korg explained. According to Nevada records, it was the same address Johnson and Goldberg listed for Morkul, Smythwyck, Prychene and Synchro.

As they approached the door, every sensor alert in Korg's bullshit detector was firing.

Sager pointed. "This is it?"

Korg nodded and then snapped a digital picture.

Sager lightly rapped the senior agent on the shoulder. "You knew this was coming, didn't you?"

Korg smirked.

"This whole town is built on illusion. You've got whores acting like high-dollar ladies and high-dollar ladies acting like whores. Fish who are broke acting like they've got big money and the whales who are loaded acting like they've got none."

Inside, Korg's badge attracted an immediate audience with Benjamin Hernandez. He was direct. "Am I under investigation?"

Korg answered with a warm smile that said "No," while Sager, in the background, played Mr. Viper, whose presence said, "Yes."

"We're not here for a shakedown. We'll keep it simple and fast. I'll get right to it."

"Then go ahead."

Why the defensive insolence, Sager wondered.

Korg took a seat, smiled wide, turning on the charm. He tried to lighten the moment as he started the questions.

"So you set up shell corporations for people, eh?"

"Nothing illegal about that."

That confirmed the suspicion. Korg was one for one.

"They linked to offshore accounts?"

"I have no idea how the executive officers choose to run their corporations."

Korg next tried the silent act. Hernandez, as expected, then filled the awkward silent space with more information.

"Thousands and thousands of shell corporations are set up in Nevada. Nevada doesn't have state income tax, so if you base your business here, instead of say, California or New York, you save a lot of tax money. All the multi-national corporations do it, though not through me. I tend to get the mid-level businesses, a lot of national distributors and start-ups." He still seemed nervous.

"You're not a target," Korg said, trying to pacify him so the words would keep flowing. "We're gathering background."

Hernandez, sensing truth, managed a hint of friendliness.

"Nothing is illegal about any of this. If you are selling a product across America or around the world, then you set up a corporation in Nevada or Delaware. You save yourself thousands of dollars in taxes."

"But if you do not have anybody living in Nevada or Delaware, that is an IRS fraud case," Korg noted.

Hernandez hardened.

"That's not my problem. I just set up the structure, registered in the State of Nevada. Everything I do can be traced through Nevada records. It's all on the internet. Nothing is hidden."

Not as long as you know the names of the shell corporations to start your search, Korg thought; if you don't know the names of the shell corporations, nothing can be uncovered and traced.

"Right. That's how we found you. Your address is listed for a corporation we're interested in."

Hernandez clarified his point.

"I'm not linked in any way to the operational activities of any of the corporations."

The rest of the day went clean and fast, aided by several phone calls made in advance, and the badge, which, even out of jurisdiction, knocked down a few walls.

Sager had already done the ground work. There was

no record of Stephen Griffin staying at any hotel in town and nobody had seen him. Not even the manager of the Mirage, who had become a regular acquaintance from Griffin's many talent searches, plus the fact that Griffin always worked him for comp rooms, meals and a line pass for the buffet.

With the help of Las Vegas PD and the hotel executives, Sager found there was no record of Griffin staying at any of the major hotels. Computer checks revealed plenty of Giffins, Geffens, Griffiths, Griffith and Griffin, but no Stephen Griffin. Not one checked out.

"Clearly the guy was never here," Sager muttered.

Korg suddenly turned, his squinted eyes brightening. "Exactly."

"Well, then what?" Sager asked. "A clear paper trail shows the guy buying a ticket on a flight, parking his car at SFO, checking in at the AirWest desk, then flying here to Vegas."

"Yet somebody else was in his seat on the flight, right?"

Sager decided to play the devil's advocate. "Griffin could have switched seats. It wasn't a full flight."

Korg put his palm on the younger agent's shoulder. "Don't you think it's more likely that somebody else used his ticket?"

"Of course. I figured that when I talked to the lady who sat next to his seat with somebody else in it."

"Right."

"Then if you already knew that, why are we here?" Sager said.

"Tracking down a killer," Korg said. "All these people around Johnson are ending up missing or killed. That is not a coincidence. Where Johnson goes, we go."

14

After checking in at the MGM Grand, Korg and Sager were sauntering past a café en route to a pre-show dinner at the buffet, when Sager caught a glimpse of a familiar face.

"Look at that," Sager said.

Korg turned to take in the view: the young rocker, Storm Clearwater, in a booth, plus the profile of a formidable-looking executive type. By the look on Clearwater's face, it was a high-voltage exchange.

"Even from here, you can feel it, Clearwater's energy," Korg said. "He's supercharged or something."

Sager added: "Imagine him spinning out of control?"

"Man, light the fuse and stand back."

The agents turned, entered the café and approached the table.

The executive type, they could see, was Rock Winston, the president of Diogenes Sound; Korg remembered their first meeting at Johnson's home in Woodside. Even when taking a chomp out of a grilled chicken sandwich wrapped in ciabatta, Winston had the look of a guy who controlled fortunes. He wore a perfect-tailored light tweed suit set off by an emerald tie. He confronted the agents with insolence.

"You'll have to leave," said the executive. "If you want to see Storm, you can do it at tonight's show. After the show, sometimes the band members greet the audience in the auditorium lobby."

Clearwater, uncomfortable with the surprise appearance, made no move to connect with the inspectors.

Korg took care of that, pulling his badge, and addressed Winston.

"We met at Johnson's, I'm sure you remember."

"That's right," Winston muttered, exasperated at the interruption. "What do you want?"

Korg turned to Clearwater.

"We just want to know how your friend is." He then turned to Winston. "Jeffrey Bridges got hit in that shootout at the bar."

The executive type immediately stood, squared his shoulders to Korg, and with a warm smile and firm handshake that said, "I'm in charge here," formally greeted the senior inspector.

Clearwater also stood. "These are the guys who blew away those robbers in the shoot-out." After a pause of recognition, Clearwater continued. "That was our bass player, Jeffrey, who got hit by a stray shot. Missed me by a foot. He's at Stanford, intensive care, pretty much critical. He lost a kidney. There's some other damage to his intestines. He's day-to-day."

"I'm pretty much day-to-day myself," Korg said.

"Aren't we all," Winston answered, more of a statement rather than a question.

Clearwater was edgy and off center, tried to play the

part of host. "This is Rock Winston of Diogenes Sound. He runs the label."

Sager again noted the unusual pin on the executive's lapel.

Korg took over. "We've met." After a short pause, he added, "We're investigating the disappearance of Stephen Griffin. You may see us around."

Winston looked straight into Korg's eyes. "Well, I'm sure you know he was murdered." Winston made the comment as if it were a statement of fact, not opinion.

Korg was taken aback by the directness. "Why would you say that?"

"I shouldn't have to tell you, of all people, now should I, Inspector Korg? We both know that."

"We'll talk later," said Korg, who then nodded at Sager to depart.

Sager stared closer at Winston's unusual dime-sized lapel pin, the two arrows, with the words *De Opresso Liber* set in a curving arc beneath the arrows.

WINSTON, ALWAYS DIRECT, hammered Storm Clearwater with questions.

"Why are they interested in you?" The way Winston phrased it, several layers of questions seemed hidden in the request.

"They just wanted to know how Bridges was doing," Clearwater answered.

"You really think that? You think it was a coincidence they showed up? That younger one measured everything we did, taking in every word. The other was classic Old School, making small talk and collecting information."

Clearwater fidgeted as he sat down, stammered something unintelligible, took a short gulp of ice water, looked up and said, "Let's get back to business. We want our own label deal. The band, I mean."

Winston smiled like a parent to a child, scanned the room, and then focused on the guitarist sitting across from him.

"Let me ask you a question, Storm: 'What makes a star?'"

Clearwater squinted as if calculating an answer, but he was sizing up the kingmaker. Winston's once-dark hair was now mostly gray, but it smoothed out the former rough edges. He projected a natural sense of authority. Tufts of dark hair poked out his sleeves, and even though dressed immaculately, he still projected a rough-hewn edge. In the industry, everybody called Winston simply Rock. He was a man you did not cross; a man with know-how, power and secrets.

Clearwater decided not to take the bait. "You tell me," he answered. "What makes a star?"

Winston savored a long swallow of ice tea, and then cleared his throat.

"Five things make a star."

He noticed Clearwater's intense focus.

"Those five things are: 1. The Voice. 2. The Song. 3. The Look and showmanship. 4. The Musicianship. 5. The Ability to do whatever it takes for as long as it takes to make it work."

Winston again picked up his ice tea, this time with just a sip.

"You watch American Idol? How do you think they can go through dozens of people in a few hours and never miss?" Winston asked.

After another sip, he continued.

"So if the reason you asked me to lunch was to talk about signing you, well, it is not going to happen. You can't sing. You could practice all you want and it won't make any difference. You can run a donkey from dawn to dusk and it ain't gonna win the Kentucky Derby."

Clearwater laughed, a mix of embarrassment and chagrin that overshadowed his natural bravado.

"You also don't have the showmanship to carry a headline act," Rock concluded.

Clearwater took the assessment well.

"But what if I told you I found the missing piece of the puzzle?" asked Clearwater. "And that it comes with the rest of the package. All five pieces."

Rock set down his sandwich, clasped his hands, and stared straight into Clearwater's eyes.

"I get fed somebody every day who's supposed to be the next star. Usually it turns out to be a woman that some guy wants to screw."

Clearwater dropped his head. There was definitely some truth to that.

"Be at our show early tonight. See our opening act, before Jesse James takes the stage. You'll see."

Winston appeared to ignore the challenge. After a moment, he raised his fork like a pointer, and added, "They've also got to know how to tunnel. You know what I'm talking about?"

Clearwater looked up from his plate, puzzled.

"I only work with people who can tunnel. That is where you can submerge yourself into a project — into the tunnel — and not allow anything from the outside to deflect you from your path. Jesse Johnson can do that. Griffin could do that. You may have that ability. That's why I'm sitting here. But you may not. Most of the kids have no idea what it takes to succeed."

Clearwater didn't interrupt the speech.

"What happens out there," Rock said with an arrogant wave, indicating the world outside of the café, "is that people's brains get unplugged and they go zapping from thing to thing. Their mission gets compromised. Things don't get done. They don't know how to tunnel."

Winston manicured the edges of his coleslaw with a fork, then lightened and looked up.

"Hey, what happened to Stephen Griffin? That's what I thought the cops were here to talk about."

Clearwater was taken aback by the question.

"He's gone. Disappeared. Word is, he flew out to Las Vegas and vanished. Nobody knows anything."

"Vanished, eh?" Winston asked. The question again seemed symbolic, as if he already knew the answer to everything he questioned. "The guy was murdered," he told the musician. "No doubt in my mind. Otherwise the cops wouldn't be here. Somebody close is involved."

KORG AND SAGER were charmed by the scene. They were seated off to the right, well back in the crowd. The place was packed and humming. As the lights dimmed in the back of the auditorium, Jesse James Johnson crept in, his identity hidden behind a windbreaker and a leather cap pulled down low, and stole a seat in the back corner to watch his band open. His fascination focused on one thing: Lorelei.

Electricity was in the air. All the big shots were there,

including Rock Winston, along with a half dozen other executives from Diogenes, four men and two women, people who Johnson called "Masterminds of Nothing."

"Hit it!" Clearwater shouted to the band, with Lorelei opening the show out front. To cover for the loss of Bridges, Poochy McNabb had switched to bass.

The lights illuminated the band, and Lorelei, out front now, seemed to capture everybody in the house with charismatic aura.

Lorelei was wearing a black leather mini, black boots, a thin waist-high black lambskin jacket, unbuttoned, with a cobalt blue tank top showing through. Under blue, purple and red stage lights, her black hair was shining, long and flowing, framing her eyes. She showed just enough, a glimpse of the cling-to top under the leather jacket along with plenty of leg, to entice. Winston had seen thousands of pretty girls hoping for a label deal, but he was stunned by her simple beauty and sensual appeal. Perfect, he thought, attractive to men without scaring off women.

Clearwater doubled up his rhythm strokes while Landru hit cut time on his Stratocaster. Robertson filled and hammered the foot pedal on the big floor drum, in synch with the bass line pounded out by McNabb. It created a rolling wave of sound, an undercurrent of rhythm. It was irresistible to the crowd, and many rolled with the wave, shifting and moving as if dancing in their seats. Nobody could sit still. Even Korg, the dinosaur, found himself moving his shoulders around. Sager grinned at the sight of that. "Ridiculous."

Good, Korg thought. For the moment, Sager had forgotten all about the shoot-out.

Lorelei stepped out front and sailed her vocals right over the top, while Clearwater filled around her voice with licks on his Telecaster, phased and chorused.

It was a new song.

Hearts make their own rules.
Love's just one truth.
Hearts make their own rules.
Love's just one truth.

The room filled with Lorelei's haunting lyrics and Clearwater's cutting guitar licks, over the top of a layered rolling current of sound. People not only were rocking and shifting with the music, but as the song advanced, they zoned in on the fresh young vocalist as well. There was something special in her voice, something rare, almost like a cry from an aching heart, and it touched them.

Hearts make their own rules.
Love's just one truth.
Hearts make their own rules.
Love's just one truth.

The energy became a circle between the crowd and the band, and it kept turning, around and around between Lorelei and each member of the audience, back and forth, lifting them higher.

Except for Johnson. Sitting in the back row, he clenched his fists and his face turned purple. None of this had been cleared with him. How dare Clearwater try out a new song without first pitching it to him? How dare Lorelei front a new song? How could the band dare to act like they were creating their own act?

Johnson left his seat, hit the aisle, and then turned for one last look. There, in the fifth row, he spotted Rock Winston of Diogenes Sound, clearly transfixed by the scene unfolding on the stage.

"Shit!" Johnson said, agog at the collective shock of the moment.

ON THE THIRD song, Johnson cut short the band's opening set. He sauntered out on the stage, in command.

The stage crew flicked a switch. Towering crimson arcs lit up and framed him at the center of the stage. The lights were crafted in a half circle and a bright yellow-tinted spotlight beamed on Johnson. It was designed to appear as if Johnson was the sun dipping into the water of a sunset, with his brilliance illuminating everything in sight. He was the sun and the world revolved around him. Others could only be his moons.

The crew released smoke over the stage like a ground fog. Fireworks shot overhead. They seemed to blast as if Robertson, the drummer, detonated them with his kick drum. On each side, giant screens captured close-ups of Johnson. It was more than a music concert. This was a production. An event.

He opened with the rocker "No Dress Rehearsal" in straight 8s, double-timed, and blew the roof off. When the song ended he smiled, waved a hand across the crowd as if addressing each member of the audience.

"Great to be in Vegas, eh?"

The crowd hollered its approval.

"How many winners we got out there?"

A sprinkling of cheers shouted out.

"How many losers we got out there?"

Rolling shouts came from across the stepped auditorium.

"By the way, how you doin' with your gamblin'?"

They roared again.

Johnson had them in his palm and he kept them there for the entire 90-minute show. He closed with "Straight Ahead," encored with "What You Got I Need," and left the throng wired.

But then Johnson understood how crowds work. *Always leave them wanting more.* He was the one the babes wanted and the one the guys wanted to be like.

The after-show party was in a suite set high in the MGM Grand. Everybody munched on sushi and sipped drinks. About 50 insiders invited to the bash glowed at their status.

"How'd you get in?" It was Klondike, towering over the inspectors. "You need to get on the pass list to get in. You're not on the list. Seems to me you guys keep crashing the party."

Klondike was dressed in an immaculate suit, black pinstripes, with a gloss-black tie against arctic-white shirt. With his shaved head and gold earring, he still looked like a pirate, perhaps even more ominous than in his biker garb.

"We badged our way in," Korg countered, unsmiling and tough.

"You seen Deego?" Korg continued, still granite. "His last phone call was made right after you got out of your interview with the San Francisco cops. Then he disappeared. Where did you go after you left Detective Anders in San Francisco?"

"Fuck you. He was my best friend."

"Well, if you didn't do it. Watch out. You could be the next to disappear."

"Fuck you again. I can handle myself."

Without another word, Korg turned and led the way into the crowd. Spotting an opening, Korg and Sager entered a circle edged by Clearwater, Winston, and the attorney, Goldberg.

Winston spoke with a late-night touch of wisdom.

"I know how you're doing it, Clearwater. You're getting the same double-timed anchor rhythms that Bob Seger and Waylon Jennings used back in the day. But you can barely recognize it, with Jesse James' voice over the top, your guitar fill and the power rhythm section."

Goldberg looked on, confused. He had no idea what they were talking about.

"Nothing gets by you, does it?" Clearwater answered with a smile. "Yeah, there's a little John Fogerty back-beat in there sometimes, a little Kid Rock in there, too."

Clearwater then turned halfway away from Winston to include Goldberg in the conversation. It was as if the two inspectors were invisible, facing Clearwater's back.

"Did you see her? C'mon Rock. With her, you know we're ready for our own deal."

"Johnson could can your ass with a comment like that," Goldberg interjected. "Have you ever seen him get mad? Ask those two back-up singers who tried to leverage him for more money before the AT&T concert. He can make people disappear."

Korg felt every pore open as he soaked in the words.

Winston, too, listened closely, and pondered the vision of a spin-off act. Might sell, he thought, if they had a singer to launch with. That new one, Lorelei, was special... Clearwater had the band wired and tight... they could get exposure by opening for Johnson... maybe they could do it.

Clearwater sensed the advantage and Winston knew it.

"Let's talk serious back home. We're cutting Johnson's new CD. Everybody will be there."

Goldberg quickly cut himself into the conversation with a quick reversal of faith.

"I represent them," Goldberg interjected to Winston. "We'll talk. Maybe we could link the acts, increase the price of tickets as a two-for-one and double the gate."

Clearwater's heart thumped. Just like that, one show and a deal was possible. It was all about a front person and money. He would have to tell Lorelei immediately, that night. Was she at the party? He hadn't seen her. But then, what did Goldberg mean? 'I represent them.' How so? Goldberg was Johnson's lawyer. Clearwater had nothing to do with him.

Winston spoke again, even and firm.

"Storm, think about how you can put this together. I'll want a sound stage to see if she can carry a crowd for an hour. I've got to do some background on her. I'll think about what I need to make it work. We'll talk this week. Right now what I want is some hamachi, another Corona and lime, and to meet this girl."

As Winston left for the sushi bar, Clearwater turned

to Goldberg and took on the oafish lawyer.

"What do you mean, you represent us? We haven't signed a deal with you."

Korg and Sager, quiet, tuned into every word.

Before Goldberg could answer, well after midnight now, the door opened and Lorelei swept in. She wore a thin black cashmere sweater that stopped four inches above her stomach. As she entered, Clearwater noticed a slight wobble under the sweater. Tight black jeans were cut low. She was dripping with platinum, necklace, earrings, and a bracelet, punctuated with the diamond stud in her belly. What an entrance, Winston noted: her first Vegas show and she already looked like a star. Where had she come from? What was her past? He'd find out.

Clearwater's hard drive in his brain jammed and crashed on overload. He headed for the sushi bar, leaving the agents alone with Goldberg.

"What did you mean, when you said 'Johnson can make people disappear?'" Korg asked with a grin.

Goldberg rambled on endlessly, saying nothing. Korg's attention was drawn beyond over Goldberg's shoulder.

"We'll catch you later," Korg said, and moved in for a closer look himself.

Lorelei squeezed Johnson's left hand with just the right pressure. "Thanks for the opportunity," she said. "This is a long way from playing coffee houses with my acoustic guitar."

"I want to know all about you," he said.

"Maybe you'll get the chance."

Korg glanced askance at the pair, Johnson and Lorelei. They seemed plugged in to each other.

Johnson then bored in at the senior inspector.

"What are you guys doing here? You must have news about Stephen. Do you have something?"

Korg nodded at the rock star. "This may not be the best place."

Lorelei smiled, "I get the hint," and exited. That left Johnson, Korg and Sager in a triangle; Korg talking, Johnson listening, Sager watching.

Johnson's gaze swung past Korg, and off to the side of the room, spotted Clearwater engaged with Lorelei. She put her hand on his forearm, said something, and they both smiled and laughed.

Korg smiled like a fox, as if the proprietor of great knowledge, then frowned.

"It's murder, sir."

"What?"

Korg spoke the words with clear finality.

"Stephen Griffin was murdered."

"What? Did you find a body?"

"No body, but that's how we're proceeding," Korg explained. "It's the only way to answer all the questions we've developed."

"That is shocking. I'm flabbergasted. Devastated."

"We're also concerned about the sudden disappearance of Deego DeGenaro. Has he ever missed a road show?"

"No and I'm concerned too."

"People are disappearing around you. Your own safety could be in jeopardy."

"That's why I have Klondike. He's always around me."

"Always."

"Well almost."

Korg stared into Johnson's eyes. "I believe the killer is here at your party right now. We'd like to talk to you more. Actually, we'd like to meet with you first thing tomorrow morning, when you're first available."

"Of course. Anything I can do. That will be about 10. You can't believe how much I miss Stephen. Only today did I hire another manager. I miss Stephen so much. The poor guy. Murdered! I am shocked beyond comprehension. Now you're saying maybe Deego, too. I'll help you in any way you ask."

Johnson turned abruptly away from the two inspectors, and motioned to Klondike, standing alone in a corner surveying the room, and waved him over.

"I need you to have my back, all the time," Johnson instructed the big man. "I could be in danger." He nodded toward Korg and Sager. "You already know our detective friends. You may see them now and then. Anything these guys need, you get it for them."

"You're telling me I have to work for a couple of cops?" Klondike said in exasperation.

"Help them any way they say. And watch your back, too."

Johnson turned to Korg and clenched a fist of solidarity.

"What a fucking act," Sager wrote in his notebook.

Johnson, eyes roaming again, stretched his gaze across the room and scrutinized the scene. Clearwater acted as if confiding a secret of great magnitude to Lorelei. Lorelei first appeared to gawk at Clearwater in shock, and then squeezed his forearm. 'What the hell is going on?' thought Johnson. 'What are they planning?

Has Clearwater already bonked her?'

Korg brought Johnson back to the moment.

"We're glad that you'll help us solve the murder."

Sager jotted again in his notebook: "Gut feeling: Johnson's dirty."

15
WEDNESDAY

KORG AND SAGER were bleary-eyed and disheveled. Too much Vegas and not enough sleep made their squinted eyes look like sets of black peas. But the middle-of-the-night Texas Hold 'Em game had treated them well and that softened the wait at the front desk of the MGM Grand.

"I'm sorry," came the response from the clerk, "they checked out."

"Already checked out," Sager repeated to Korg. "Why so early? And to where?"

ON THE PLANE, Korg started to nod off, but woke with a start and rapped his partner on the shoulder.

"We don't have time to sleep, not now."

Sager refused to open his eyes. "Speak for yourself."

"How many people on your list don't have alibis?"

The master list consisted of potential suspects linked to Griffin by money, power or love. The two inspectors had split up the list between them.

Sager finally gave in and opened his pocket notebook. "Everybody on my list has an alibi except for Clearwater, Goldberg and MaryLou Dietz. What about you?"

Korg's notebook was already open.

"Johnson and Klondike vouched for each other, so that's probably bullshit. I haven't been able to check out Rock Winston, so he's a missing piece. Then there's a woman Griffin was supposed to have a date with, but she's a blank. And she's not named by anybody, just a remark Johnson claims Griffin made. So that could be bullshit, too, another try by Johnson to throw us off."

Korg waved in the air. "We've got Clearwater, Klondike, Johnson and Winston. We've got to move in on them, up close and personal."

Korg paused to scan out the window as the jet roared over the Sierra Nevada, and then he started in again.

"We both know what's wrong. There's no body, no crime scene and no murder weapon. So this is an elaborate scheme, carefully timed and tailored, not some random act of passion."

Korg turned to Sager. "What's your gut say?"

Sager's eyes closed as he spoke.

"Two theories make sense. Griffin discovers he's getting shorted in the money laundering real estate fraud scheme, maybe for millions. He wants more money, pressures Johnson, and when he gets nowhere, threatens to blackmail him. Johnson has Klondike send Griffin to the bottom of the ocean. End of story. It makes sense. Johnson is smart enough to set it up. Klondike has killed before."

"We keep getting back to the fraud case," Korg said. "All the money trails lead to Johnson, Griffin and

Goldberg, with Klondike the muscle behind them."

"Money," Korg said flatly. "One hundred dollar bills are like big fish. The supply never equals the demand."

Korg passed his hand over his bleary eyes, then continued his rant.

"At this point, we don't have one piece of physical evidence that ties any of those guys to Griffin's beach house at the right time. Deego's missing and hasn't even been officially listed yet."

Sager's heavy eyebrows furrowed in a notch over the center of his eyes. "We also got Clearwater."

"Tell me more."

"How about a misdemeanor assault conviction? A restraining order from a woman who claimed he was stalking her? Court-ordered anger management classes? He also seems to have trouble telling the truth."

"What? Storm Clearwater? I kind of like the guy."

"Except he's got flash-point anger that's like a nuclear bomb. You push his button and he blows up. It happens every year or two. I'm going over to his house today and put the screws on him."

Korg smiled. "Don't you remember? You're on psychological leave and recovery? You just shot a couple of guys."

"Well, Las Vegas is helping me get over that," Sager said. "Thanks for yanking me out of my world back there. But listen. I'd like to wire Clearwater up to our bullshit meter and see what happens."

"Whoever orchestrated this is one smart dude," Korg said. "It's a righteous murder and a skilled cover-up. We keep getting back to the fraud case. And we keep getting back to no body, no crime scene and no murder weapon."

"There's another possibility," Sager noted.

Korg tuned in. "What?"

"Maybe Griffin is in witness protection. You know, made a deal with the FBI, has already ratted out Johnson, then disappeared. For all we know, he's living in Kona with a new name."

"That's unlikely, since he just bought the new Corvette," Korg said. "He wouldn't buy a new Corvette and leave it at SFO, right? And if Griffin went into witness protection, we would never make him. The U.S. Marshall would never give that up. But maybe I can check with the IRS, see if they're already investigating Johnson's money scheme. If they are, that might be a tip-off that Griffin is a pipe."

After a quiet moment, Korg tapped the junior inspector on his forearm.

"Stay with me on this," Korg said. "I know you've been through a lot in a short time, but I need your help. I need you to squeeze Clearwater, plus maybe Klondike, and try to find out who used Griffin's plane ticket to Nevada. And I need you to do it today."

Sager put his palm over his eyes "Is that all?" But he felt a glow inside. He sensed Korg had accepted him, even needed him.

As the jet taxied to the gate, Korg's cell phone bleated the old Elton John song, "The Bitch Is Back." That could only mean one thing. "It's Pritchett."

Korg attempted to sound as professional as possible. "Inspector Kristopher Korg speaking."

Pritchett started howling.

"Where are you? Where's Sager?"

"We're having a meeting right now about the Griffin case."

"ATDQ Korg! Answer The Damn Question. I asked where, man, where."

It sounded like an order, not a question.

"We're going over our suspect list."

"I asked *where*. Got it? Where? Where? Where?"

Korg finally gave in.

"At SFO."

"Get your ass in here and report to me immediately. And what is Sager doing with you? He's been ordered on leave."

Click. She hadn't waited for an answer.

16

KORG AND SAGER hustled straight to headquarters in Redwood City.

"Sit down."

Pritchett was in no mood for chatter. Of course, with Korg, she never was.

Roberta Pritchett projected an air of accomplishment, not only from her trim, athletic frame, but from her clear dark eyes and steel glare, too. She dressed like a bank president, and said more with her flame-tempered eyes than words. Pritchett was brilliant, attractive and skilled. She believed that as long as she was in charge, things were under control. History showed that she was usually right about that.

The door closed. Pritchett's interrogation began as if Korg was a captured felon.

"You guys look terrible," she started. "Where were you yesterday?"

"Chasing down leads on the Griffin missing person case," Korg answered.

"Where?" she repeated. "I asked you *where*?"

Korg's words came out soft and thin. "Las Vegas."

"Las Vegas! You didn't have approval for Las Vegas! You know the protocol. Out-of-area trips require my signature in advance. It is just as easy to involve the FBI and LVPD."

Pritchett was in no mood to hear explanations.

Korg and Sager sat like second graders in the principal's office. Pritchett shot eye daggers at Sager, the silent conspirator. "You were ordered on leave."

"Yeah, and I left."

"Kill the attitude," Pritchett fired back. "Has Korg somehow corrupted you?"

Pritchett stood and walked to her window. She always did this when perplexed. The condition never lasted long.

"First, Inspector Korg, don't try to get reimbursed for your Vegas expenses. You didn't follow protocol."

Korg had to bite his lower lip and avoid Sager's face to keep from smirking. Korg had won $850 playing no-limit Hold 'Em. He managed to hold his face and say nothing.

"Now what do you mean about your case," Pritchett expanded. "You have something on Griffin? Anything I can tell the media?"

Sager gestured to the senior officer. Korg seemed to puff up his chest as he spoke.

"Well, it looks like we're on to a multi-million dollar money laundering scheme. Tax evasion, offshore accounts, shell corporations in Nevada, real estate fraud, all of it likely leading to murder."

Instead of offering congratulations, Pritchett scowled.

"You're on a missing person's case and you wander into white collar crime division stuff?"

"Just following the money trail. It might lead us to our murderer."

Pritchett eyed Sager. "Speak."

"Maybe he's got something." It was not exactly a ringing endorsement. Of course, under Pritchett's grilling, Sager wasn't about to give a speech.

Pritchett stood up. As if on cue, Korg and Sager left their seats as well. Then Pritchett turned to Sager.

"As for you, I shouldn't have to say anything. Get out of here. Go home. You're on paid leave. Report to Human Resources. See a counselor. I have something for Korg in private."

Sager disappeared as if Pritchett had waved a magic wand.

Korg was baffled. "What?"

"Did you interview a Palo Alto lawyer, Justin Goldberg?"

Korg relaxed.

"Oh yeah, him. Sure. He's the CPA-attorney for the rock star, Johnson. Goldberg looks like the guy who implemented the entire money-laundering and fraud scheme."

The black centers in Pritchett eyes looked like tiny bulls-eyes in pistol targets.

"This attorney said you flashed your badge to bully him and then tried to force him to take a song you wrote for Johnson's new CD. He says he recorded the conversation for his personal use, which is certainly legal, as you know."

Korg blanched. Pritchett wasn't done.

"That would be an ethics violation, using your leverage as an inspector, to negotiate a private deal for your financial advantage. Some might even say you tried to blackmail the lawyer. In fact, that is what Goldberg said. He's considering going after us, suing you and naming the county as co-defendant."

Korg smiled, then frowned, and then contorted, breathing hard, a crazy quilt, multi-fabric of emotions pounding through him. Damn lawyers.

Pritchett glowered. "This could threaten your retirement."

Korg, off balance, immediately thought of Emma. How had he screwed up again? Then he tried to explain.

"I brought that song thing up just to throw him off guard, soften him up, before I hit him with the real questions." The words were thin and high-pitched.

"He said you only asked one question about Griffin, and it had nothing to do with his disappearance."

Then Korg smiled.

"Hell, Roberta, it worked. Roper had a tap on his phone. You know that. You're the one who got Judge Lockhart to sign for it. As soon as I left, he made the call we were looking for. He fell right into the trap."

Pritchett stood as if nothing Korg said registered and then looked at her watch.

"Don't call me Roberta. This conversation is over. Now get outta here and find out what happened to Griffin before you're outta here for good. And please try to stay away from Goldberg."

"Do I need to call him and fix things?"

"No, no, no," Pritchett reiterated as if Korg was the village idiot. "I'll call him and tell him you'll never contact him again, and maybe he will go away from us, too."

Maybe it was a stigma from his childhood, when he had

always wanted a little more than what he had, but Korg always filled the county-issue Styrofoam coffee cups a little too high. Maybe he was afraid of missing out on something. That's why he eventually brought in his own huge mug, but he had not replaced it since it had broken to smithereens. He'd topped off two coffee cups and held one in each hand. He turned to return to his cubicle, but found himself in the path of Pritchett escorting a new hire on a walk-around. There was no way to avoid her. Pritchett, as usual, was in charge.

"Inspector Korg, this is our new assistant deputy district attorney, Regina McNally." She had flawless skin, big blue eyes and a smile that was as cute as a wagon full of puppies.

Korg nodded and raised both coffee cups. "I'd shake your hand but it'd make you very hot and wet."

Regina turned to Pritchett with a questioning look. "Yes, Inspector Korg is one of a kind," Pritchett explained. "His last day is Friday."

Korg, oblivious, sauntered down the aisle, passing agent Brett Nelson, another senior inspector.

"Stop!" Korg shouted.

Nelson, long accustomed to Korg's machinations, laughed. "What?"

"That button, that pin, the one on your lapel." Korg tried to point with a finger and spilled a few small pools of coffee on the linoleum floor. "I've seen this before. What is that?"

"This?" Nelson said as he touched the small pin.

In his cubicle, Nelson asked, "Do you want the short version or the long version?"

"Just go, man, go."

Nelson, a tall, thin man with a friendly face, an outdoorsy demeanor clad in a dark suit and tie, waved Korg into a seat.

"Can I grab your extra java?"

"It's black."

"It'll pass."

What had yanked Korg's attention was a round silver/ black pin with two arrows, and half-ringed at the bottom by the words *De Oppresso Liber*. It was identical to the pin that Rock Winston wore.

"Where'd you get that?"

"You have no idea?"

"None. But it could be important."

"Do you know what *De Oppresso Liber* means?"

"Not a clue."

Nelson put a finger on his pin.

"It's Latin for 'Liberate the Oppressed.'"

For Korg, there was still no connection. "Que pasa?"

Nelson leaned back in his chair, studying Korg's blank reaction. He took a moment, sipping his coffee. "When are they going to get the good stuff?" He leaned forward, elbows resting on the desk.

"This," Nelson explained, "is the miniature version of the badge I wore on my beret when I was in Special Forces, you know, Delta Force, Operation Phoenix."

Nelson again studied Korg to see if he was connecting the dots.

"Vietnam?" Korg asked.

"Yeah, I was a Cleaner."

Korg looked like a confused squirrel who couldn't find his nut.

Nelson gazed directly into Korg's eyes.

"We were the most effective killing force in U.S. military history."

Now it was Korg's turn to size up Nelson. The fellow inspector did not crack.

"More," Korg requested.

Nelson nodded. He spoke deliberately, in monotone.

"This was back in Vietnam. In dealing with the Viet Cong, there was Operation Phoenix."

"I remember the name, back in the old days."

"In the Phoenix program, I'd be given the name of a person in North Vietnam."

Nelson paused.

"And…" Korg continued, waiting for Nelson to complete the sentence.

"And that person became history."

"Assassinations?"

"All the Cleaners did a lot of them."

"How many for you?"

Nelson again paused, and then answered.

"63."

Korg's eyes widened.

Nelson paused. "You want to hear more?"

"More."

"It gets to the point where killing becomes instinctual. Some Delta guys were better at it than I was. They'd shoot a guy in the head, and 10 seconds later, be able to open a beer, take a drink and complain it wasn't cold enough. But there was no choice in the matter back then. You did it or you died."

Korg absorbed the words. Staying in school, keeping his credits up as a full-time student, he'd avoided being drafted into the Army.

"You ever hear of a guy named Rock Winston?"

Nelson's gaze turned incredulous. "The Rock?"

"Yeah, Rock Winston."

"There could only be one Rock Winston."

Now it was Korg's turn to appear stunned. "Speak."

Nelson put his hands on his desk, palms down, fingers pressed against the surface.

"Rock Winston was the baddest dude in Delta. I never met him. But word was he took something like 150, 200 assignments. Lived for them. He was in Project Omega in Cambodia, and he was in Phoenix in Vietnam, too.

"Word was that he got captured in Cambodia. We all knew that 6 out of 10 of us would get killed, and Rock knew that too. They tortured him for days, ugly stuff, terrible stuff, everything but cut his dick off, and they talked about doing that, too. So at sunset, the day before he's going to be executed, as a last request in his bamboo jail, he asks his jailer for a can of Coke."

"What?" Korg asked. "A can of Coke?"

Nelson stopped abruptly.

"I just realized this is the first time I've ever talked about this stuff. All these years have gone past and I've never told anybody what happened to me, to the others. What we did. The assignments."

"You're doing fine, Brett. I appreciate what you're telling me. Maybe we can go fishing some time. I think you'll like it. It's like a decompression chamber out there on the water. No cares."

"I'd like that."

"What happened to Winston?"

"Nobody called him Winston. It was Rock. Well, he drank that can of Coke, and as the legend goes, he then started working the can back and forth, using the center as a hinge, until the can cracked and broke in two. He used one of the pieces to cut the throat of his jailer that night, and escape into the jungle. Took him 12 days to get back to camp. The story was he killed five more guys, either with his Coke can or with his bare hands, to get out of that camp and back to our base. The next day, after being fed and getting one night of sleep, he got a few guys together and some choppers, and they went right back and wiped out the base where he'd been tortured. Killed everybody there. The guy's a legend."

Korg marveled at the story.

"Why do you want to know all this, anyway?" Nelson asked.

Korg took a deep breath.

"Rock Winston is involved in a case I'm working on. I just met him. He was wearing one of those pins, just like you have, on his lapel. He's now the head guy at a music label called Diogenes Sound. A guy he worked with disappeared."

"Diogenes? Oh yeah, that's good. He must have named it after himself. Looking for that one honest man."

Korg stood to leave, but Nelson stopped him.

"Be careful with this guy."

Pritchett glowered over Korg. She was standing just outside Korg's cubicle, leaning her arms, elbows out, on the chest-high divider wall. Her eyes had never seemed darker. "Tell me more what you got," she ordered.

"The mystery and the chase," Korg said. "That's what it's all about. It's complicated."

"Give me something."

"An elaborate scheme," Korg explained. "Somebody went to great lengths to make Griffin look like a disappearance. Griffin's new Corvette ended up in Long Term Parking at SFO. But somebody else used his ticket to Las Vegas."

Pritchett did not break her glare. "Anything firm?"

"A lot of loose ends."

"Keep me appraised. I'm getting media calls every day."

"Were you serious about Goldberg messing up my retirement funding? What would I tell my wife?"

"If we get Goldberg under control, you're OK."

"What if Goldberg is up to his ears in this?"

"Then it could get more complicated. In the meantime, Inspector Korg, don't pitch any more songs to these guys."

"Well, it could get a lot more complicated in the next 48 hours."

Pritchett departed and Korg turned to his computer, clicked on to the internet and Google Earth. A map of the Peninsula appeared. A miniature car was spotted on the map, in Woodside. Korg, the old techie, had placed a GPS tracking bug in Johnson's favorite car, a 1944 Cadillac Roadster that had been sitting out front of the Sound Factory.

"That's Johnson," Korg thought. "He's at his office, or

at least his car is." Just as advertised by the clerk at the MGM, Johnson and his entourage had apparently left Vegas early.

Korg quickly called Johnson's office, and his secretary confirmed the superstar rocker was in a meeting with his booking agent and Rock Winston.

What about the biker guy, he wondered. Korg clicked on his computer screen. "He's in La Honda!" Korg said aloud. "That's where Clearwater lives."

In minutes, Korg headed up Highway 84 for Woodside. Over and over again, he rewound the spool, the sight of that dime-sized pin on Winston's lapel. The guy was a killer. And advertised it.

In the Redwood City hills, on the couch in the front room of a condo, Sager leaned back with his right arm around Bonnie, cupping her right shoulder.

"You poor soul," she said, peering up into his eyes, "to almost get killed in a gunfight and then to save all those people. You are such a hero, a real hero. You must need some real connect time to come back to earth."

Inches from her face, Sager gazed into her eyes and could sense her lips coming to him. He met those lips with his, a first kiss. The tips of their tongues flickered and thrilled. His left hand massaged her right side, holding her close. He could feel her left breast pushing against his chest. A sweet perfume was in the air.

"Does this make you feel better?" she asked.

In a fluid motion with his left hand, Sager cupped her right breast, then massaged and squeezed it.

"It's better," Bonnie advised, "if you tease, not squeeze."

Sager, following instructions, found an erect nipple through the fabric of her shirt and bra.

"Now you're getting me going," Bonnie said.

Sager repeated the maneuver with her right breast.

"You like my tits?" she said. "I've seen you looking at them."

Sager affirmed by nuzzling his face between them, massaging her breasts with his face, cupping them with each hand.

"Do you have a girlfriend?" Bonnie asked.

Sager, his face buried up to his ears, ignored the question. He settled into another long, deep kiss, snuck his hand beneath her shirt and found the mark. A moment later, he forced his hand inside her bra, around her right breast and took a nipple between thumb and forefinger.

"There's like an electric shock going straight from my nipple to down there."

Encouraged, Sager removed his left hand from inside her bra, and in a quick, deft move, surged his hand below her waist. Bonnie released a moan, held him with both arms for a moment, then grabbed Sager's hand by the wrist and pulled it away.

"I think that's enough therapy for right now," she said. She stole a look at his pants and saw that she had definitely had an effect on the young inspector.

Sager leaned back — that was as far as she was going to allow for right now — and let the moment stay with him. She seemed perfect, he thought, just what I want.

"To get more, you need to tell me that I'm only yours," Bonnie said. "That you want me more than anything. That I'm beautiful and you dream about me. That it makes you feel alive when you touch me. That you love my body. You like to see me smile. That you…"

Sager shook his head yes, but said nothing. In the next moment, his phone buzzed and broke off her speech. A message had just arrived:

"GPS Tracking a go. Klondike and Clearwater in La Honda. Corner them, if up for it. I'm off to IRS for juicy stuff."

He gave Bonnie a kiss. "Got to go."

"Think you'll find where Stephen went?"

"Something like that," and he was gone.

It had never dawned on her that Sager had scarcely said a word the entire visit.

17

Alone at his cabin in La Honda, Storm Clearwater, pained from the ordeal at the hospital. His old friend, Jeffrey Bridges, the band's bass player, floated in and out of coherence, and when asleep, looked dead. All from a stray bullet from a botched robbery.

"It was my idea to go to the Oasis," Clearwater pondered. "What if I hadn't called him? What if he hadn't answered? None of that would have happened."

With a can of Bud Light in one hand, a hunk of sourdough and a slab of Tillamook cheddar in the other, Clearwater, head down, plowed out of his kitchen and clipped the doorway with his right hip and elbow. The jolt knocked the bread and cheese out of his hand and to the floor. Beer spilled on his hand and wrist.

"Shit!" He hit flashpoint and kicked the piece of bread across the living room, 15 feet on the fly.

"Why is everything going wrong?" Bridges just about dead. Lorelei in somebody else's arms. No money. No band deal. Still hurting from the motorcycle accident.

Clearwater relived when he'd held Lorelei close, that one time in Las Vegas, the moment when he could feel her heart beating into his chest. Then he remembered how easily she slipped away into Johnson's arms, how with a grin and a wave, she had turned and walked away that night. He might have it out with Johnson, over the girl, over the band, over the money.

Then he thought of the way she smiled, the light in her eyes when she laughed. She was for him, he knew, and he'd prove it.

Clearwater, his teeth clenched, set the beer down on the nearest end table and charged over to the chunk of bread, on the floor next to the front door. It was open an inch to let the place air out a bit. Mold was a problem in his little cabin at Redwood Terrace, up in the Santa Cruz Mountains. Just as he reached down for the bread, the pointed toe of his low-cut left boot clipped the partially open front door. The jolt wrenched his injured knee and shot electrifying pain through his leg.

"Ahhhh!" Clearwater shouted, and in the next second, with another flash-point reaction, he kicked the back of the door with his sharp-toed boot and blasted a hole in the cheap pine. He saw the damage and lashed out again, and this time hammered the door with the side of his left hand. The door surface cracked 12 inches vertically with a half-inch cavity.

Sweating now, his heart jumping, he stopped the assault, retreated to his Bud Light, and took a long drink.

How could things have gone from so good to so bad, so fast?

Abruptly, there was a distinctive rap at the door. Clearwater's musical mind recognized it as a half note followed by a pause, two sixteenth notes and a quarter note. For the moment, the cadence cleared the black cloud.

Clearwater found himself staring straight into the badge of Inspector Sager.

The electrons in Clearwater's brain were firing too fast to sort things out. As if on automatic pilot, he welcomed the inspector to his home, and then picked up the bread and cheese.

Sager couldn't miss the sweat on Clearwater's forehead, the mishmash of food in one hand, beer in the other, wet streaks and sprinkles on his clothes.

Clearwater swung the door wide open. "The place needs airing out."

Sager, wearing suit, tie and sunglasses, surveyed the mess. It was more a cabin than a house, more a hideout than a home — small and dark, with a cave-like feel under a canopy of redwoods, about five miles from La Honda in the mountains of the San Francisco Peninsula. The rug, an ancient off-white, needed cleaning. An old 12-string Gibson acoustic was propped up in a stand next to a sofa chair, in front of a 42-inch HD flat screen. Klondike was nowhere to be seen, though the GPS locator placed him in the area.

"I don't do drugs," Clearwater said. "Never have. The place is clean. I'm clean."

Sager laughed, stashing his sunglasses. He didn't even have the slightest notion to ask about drugs; amazing how people live in a world that only exists in their minds and how their thoughts burble to the surface without being prodded.

"I don't do drugs," Clearwater repeated.

"Maybe you should," Sager said with a touch of sarcasm. He closed the door behind him, eyeing the damage.

Clearwater grunted, trying to calm himself. "Everything's going wrong."

The agent seated himself without asking permission. "Sorry for the surprise," Sager lied. "Wanted to meet you here, so you'd feel comfortable, to ask you a few questions."

"What about?"

"Let's get right to it. Your itinerary the evening of Wednesday, September 25th."

Clearwater wiped the moisture off his forehead with the back of his right sleeve.

"How am I supposed to know that? That was two weeks ago."

Sager noted the agitation in the young guitarist's voice. "Well, you could look at your calendar, but let me help your memory. That was the night before you left to go to New York with the band."

Clearwater squinted, gazing off to an empty corner of the room, as if scrolling through his memory tapes.

Faking it, like they all do, Sager wrote in his notebook.

Clearwater smiled. Still faking it, Sager wrote.

"Hell, that's easy. Like everybody in the band, I was packing for the trip."

"Here?"

"Of course, here. I helped the roadies get the stage gear together earlier that week, and they took off in a semi truck across the country ahead of us. I was working that afternoon with Landru in the studio trying to get a mix on a song we recorded."

Sager crept to the edge of his seat.

"Who was driving the semi to New York?"

"Deego. The rest of the road crew and the band could catch up, flying."

Sager made a note. Another confirmation. That cleared the missing Deego DeGenaro, the ex-con from New Jersey, just like Korg had predicted. So Deego was likely a victim, not an accomplice.

"Can anybody verify you spent the evening here? Girlfriend? A buddy? Maybe you went to Applejack's?" Sager was well aware of the only watering hole within 10 miles, the old, woodsy mountain community icon, "or maybe Alice's," the restaurant in Sky Londa.

"I was here by myself, probably like everybody else, getting ready for the trip. I got squeezed that day because Landru and me were working in the studio that afternoon. When I got done, I came home and packed."

"How long did that take?"

"I don't know. I had the Giants' game on TV in the background, drank a few beers, barbecued a steak, put my stuff together."

Sager noted it: Watched Giants game.

"Who were they playing?"

"What's this about?"

"This is about where you were that night."

Clearwater massaged the tip of his beard, dark and fine-trimmed.

"OK, the Giants were playing the Mets, I think."

Sager watched the young guitarist's every move, then asked, "What about the next morning?"

"Loaded and drove to the airport."

"Alone?"

"Yeah, I live alone. My life is intense. I need peace and quiet to lay low and recharge my energy."

Sager stood to leave.

"That's it?" Clearwater asked. "You never even asked me about Stephen Griffin."

Sager's eyes lit up.

"Who said this was about Stephen Griffin?"

"Well, I just figured..."

Sager went to the door, and with a nod, departed.

TEN MINUTES LATER, the same distinctive knock rapped at the door.

"Now what?"

Sager was back. This time he did not remove his sunglasses.

"I'd like you to come downtown this afternoon for a lie detector test."

"Me? Klondike's your guy."

"Klondike's my guy for what?"

Clearwater stammered.

"Your guy who made Stephen Griffin disappear."

Sager's mind whirled.

"So you agree?"

"To what?"

"To come down and take the test."

"Sure. Whatever."

"I'll call you shortly with the details."

Back in his car, Sager scribbled more notes.

The first time he had left Clearwater's cabin, Sager had stopped in La Honda on Highway 84, and made a call to check out a detail. He had called the sports desk at the San Francisco Chronicle and spoken to a Mark Dayton. After putting Sager on hold for a moment, Dayton had returned and had been curt.

"September 25th? A Wednesday. Giants played the Cubs. In Chicago. Day game. Morning start, our time."

Klondike parked his massive frame on a stool at the old mahogany bar at Applejack's, the small, woodsy hangout in La Honda. When he was short-timing it at San Quentin, he dreamed of a day just like this one, when he'd ride out on Highway 84 on his chopper and end up right here. He had a glass of beer in one hand and a half dozen peanuts, or goobers as he called them, in the other. The bartender, a 40ish-woman with about 20 extra pounds, eyed the tattoos on the inside of each of the biker's massive forearms.

When Klondike sauntered in and took a seat on a bar stool, three other bikers at the bar bailed for the door, leaving their beers unfinished. On the way out, one looked back and saw the gothic letters FTW tattooed to the base of Klondike's shaved skull. A local sat at the opposite corner of the bar, nursing a Budweiser, amused at the scene. A group of three guys at a nearby table, tourists from England, paid the event no mind.

"You're gonna be nice, right?" asked the bartender, a hopeful look in her eye.

Klondike turned and looked behind him, thinking she was talking to someone else. Seeing no one was there, he figured out she was talking to him, and muttered like an apology. "Oh, right, oh, yeah, right."

The bartender had a nervous smile, unconvinced, and kept her distance. This big guy was a time bomb. Sooner or later, he was going off. She'd been at the job a few years and seen all the signs before.

At one time, Klondike had a dream life ahead of him, drafted in the fourth round to play defensive end for the Pittsburgh Steelers. Then he failed the drug test, positive for both amphetamines and steroids, and was kicked out of training camp. In a downward spiral, he hooked up with a biker club, Heaven's Martyrs. One weekend, the bikers were hired to provide security at a summer outdoor concert at Clear Lake, and Klondike met Johnson backstage. Johnson was simultaneously curious, fearful and awed by Klondike's ominous presence.

After a rental truck full of Johnson's guitars and sound equipment had been stolen, Johnson tracked down Klondike, and found that he liked the big guy's honor code. Two weeks later, Klondike was hired. Except for his state-paid vacation at San Quentin, he'd stayed by Johnson's side ever since and was his most trusted compatriot.

The reward for the big man was the wind in his face, the smell of the woods, pockets of changing temperatures as he rode from forested canyons to open grasslands, from ridgelines to the ocean. He'd crown a perfect day by pulling up to Applejack's in La Honda with his 124-inch, S&S stroker, the custom hardtail with the upswept fishtail pipes.

Now Klondike overheard the Englishmen, well into their third pitcher of beer.

"These Yanks drive garbage scows for bikes," said one. "When the engine sounds like everything is broken inside, that's when these scows are running good."

The three laughed and toasted British technology.

Klondike could feel the tattooed letters FTW rising at the base of his skull, but did nothing.

"You know why these lads' custom bikes have no odometers?" asked another. "Because the wankers don't want anybody to know how few miles they actually put on their scows." There appeared no meanness in the comment, just light-hearted joking, and the three laughed and toasted the "Triumph Motorcycle Company of Great Britain."

Klondike turned to the local at the end of the bar. "I may have to do something about this."

"Wankers, a bunch of wankers," added the third with a guffaw.

"I'd never ride one of those Harley-Davidson cows."

Klondike pointed a finger at the local. "Go hold open the door."

A scow was one thing, and, in fact, he wasn't quite sure what a scow was, but nobody called his chopper a cow.

Klondike turned and took a giant step toward the table, and grabbed one of the Brits with his left paw on a neck collar, his right paw on the back of the jeans. The local opened the door and Klondike heaved the fellow out through the entrance and onto the wood porch. It looked as if 110 volts was shooting through Klondike's forehead.

"Don't hurt 'em," a voice said in the back of Klondike's mind. "You'll go back to prison."

But Klondike's button had been pushed. He stalked another.

The local holding the door open pointed at the two remaining Englishman. "Get out of here! Save yourself!" In a flash, they quickly scurried outside.

All three were sitting on the covered porch, and

when they saw that the big man did not follow them out, they relaxed. In minutes, sitting there, they laughed like hell about a brush with near catastrophe with a genuine American King Kong.

Klondike's face never broke. He simply returned to his seat, and again sipped his beer.

The bartender peered over the top of the mahogany bar and found she was looking straight into the eyes of the Neanderthal. Klondike noticed nothing unusual, held up an empty glass and raised his eyebrows, requesting a re-fill.

He watched the tiny bubbles rise from the bottom and pondered the sudden appearance of two homicide inspectors following him around. He gazed at his reflection on the mirror-backed wall, the image splintered by bottles of Jack Daniels, Johnny Walker Red and Jim Beam.

Klondike tried to retrace his steps, wondered if he'd left anything amiss. He took a long, slow head-back drink, and then again raised his empty glass, tilting it.

Without a word, the bartender again complied.

'Hard to say where we stand,' Klondike thought, still looking straight ahead, into the mirror. 'Not sure about Johnson, either.'

ACROSS THE ROAD from Applejack's, Sager was parked in his car at a small market. He watched the entire affair from a distance. He decided to move in and trap the big man on Applejack's porch as he left the small establishment.

Klondike peered down at the razor-thin agent. "Now what?"

Sager flashed the badge. It had no apparent effect.

"You here to see Clearwater?" Sager asked.

"Hell no," Klondike barked. "I'm here for me. This is one of the few times and places I can go where it's just about hunkering down and trying to enjoy myself for once in my goddamn life. Now you show up. Where's your boss?"

"At this moment, Inspector Korg is engaged with Jesse James Johnson."

Klondike crossed his mammoth arms, feeling a psychological net being thrown over him.

"Get on with it. But just so you know, I've already had three surprise piss checks and I'm clean. I'm doing a good job for Johnson. The last security guy was eating linguini and clams in Seattle when some asshole stole the equipment truck."

Sager already knew about that; Johnson's '60 Les Paul Goldtop, worth $20,000, was lost in the robbery.

"I want to double check something." Sager said. "Again, the night before you flew out to New York, where were you that evening and the next morning."

"I already told you that."

"Tell me again." It was an order.

"I was with Johnson most of the evening. We barbecued steaks. We ate together, outside, his place. And then I finished packing at my cottage. We left together in the morning for his jet."

Sager's eyes gleamed.

"So nobody else can vouch for you or Johnson for every single minute of that Wednesday evening, Wednesday night and Thursday morning. Only you for he, and he for you, correct?"

"We didn't go anywhere," the big man protested, holding his line. "We had a beer, ate dinner, packed, and the next day, took off."

Sager wrote it all down. Gaps in the timeline, he thought, gaps.

"Are you sure you're not here to see Clearwater? He lives right down the road, you know."

Klondike made a guttural sound that was a mix of roar, grumble and snarl. "You already asked me that," he bellowed. "Never doubt anything I say. I don't explain what you don't understand."

That's right, Sager reminded himself, this guy lives by honor alone. Guys like this don't take kindly to anyone questioning their integrity.

"When was the last time you saw Stephen Griffin?"

"Hell, you know that. He came over to our place that afternoon, the day before we took off for New York."

Sager hit the curves hard on Highway 84, heading east back to Redwood City. He could hardly wait to get the polygraph on Clearwater. After all, he had an eyewitness who had put Clearwater at Griffin's on the early evening of Wednesday, September 25th. As far as he could verify, Clearwater was the last person to see Griffin alive—and he was lying about it.

At that moment, Landru and McNabb, the guitar players, stepped out of the Oasis, their appetites satiated, their moods lightened. After visiting Bridges at nearby Stanford Hospital, they had ventured to the Oasis once again to relive, or as McNabb put it, "outlive" the event.

"See you at Johnson's," Landru said.

But McNabb's gaze had strayed to El Camino Real.

Driving down the center lane was a black '57 Chevy Bel Air, classic and polished.

Only one person had a car like that: T-Bone Robertson, the drummer. Sitting next to him, shoulder to shoulder, they saw Lorelei Aicona.

Landru gawked as the car pulled over on the road's shoulder about 100 yards south of them. With the car running and brake lights on, they watched Robertson turn and kiss the young starlet.

She did not resist.

18

"AM I SPEAKING to my present husband?"

By the sound in Emma's voice, Korg knew the risk level was in the Yellow Zone.

"Only if this is my present wife," he said as upbeat as possible.

She got right to it. "When are you coming home?"

Yep. Definitely. Yellow Zone.

"Dinner at Harry's tonight, yours and the kids' favorite, and then a show."

"The plot thickens," Emma said, her voice lightening a shade. "You must think you are in trouble. Flowers, too?"

Korg tried his best to play it straight. "Actually, sweetheart, it's a mini-concert. A band I've gotten to know is giving a concert for a music bigshot. They're trying to get a label deal."

"You mean like American Idol? The kids will love it, though you know they won't sit with us, right?" After a short pause, Emma added, "What do you mean, 'A band you've gotten to know?' Since when do you know bands? Kristopher, you aren't exactly a rock-and-roller. And by the way, how was Las Vegas without me?"

Korg relented.

"It was all work, no play and very little sleep," Korg answered. "Chasing this band around is keeping me up at night. I miss you a lot. It was terrible to be there without you."

"Oh right, I bet, you liar," she said, but her voice danced because those were the words she was waiting to hear.

"You busy?" Korg asked his wife.

"Overwhelmed as usual."

"Kids OK?"

"As deranged as ever, so everything is normal. You?"

He laughed. "On the trail and on my way to the IRS office in Foster City to check out a few tax returns for this case," Korg explained. "If you're curious, you could turn on that computer sitting on my desk and scan those corporate shell accounts I told you about. Perhaps with your brilliant business mind, you will find something I missed."

"When will you be home?"

"I'll call. Love you."

WHEN KORG TURNED into the small parking lot in Foster City, he stopped for a moment and surveyed the office building. From the outside, it appeared like any other mid-rent office space on the outskirts of suburbia on the San Francisco Peninsula. It was outlined in faded gray paint with white trim. People came and went quietly, most dressed in suits. Well hidden were the pounding hearts and racing brain patterns, where electrons fired faster and with more voltage, as each step took them closer to the entry door.

This, Korg knew, was where IRS investigations took place on the Peninsula.

He opened the door and walked through a hallway to a second door, which led to a square room painted white, open in the center, with numbered telephones on all four walls, and plastic chairs near each. Korg picked up phone No. 6 and listened. Instantly, the line started ringing and then a woman answered on the second ring.

Korg surveyed the stages of anguish by the IRS respondents in the room, the worst being a squat contractor type whining to anybody who would listen. Three minutes passed and the door on the far side of the room opened. In walked David Toescher.

"I'm from the IRS and I'm here to help," Toescher joked.

Korg's face cracked into lines, the wrinkles tightening along the outer edges of his eyes.

"I'm from Homicide and you're innocent until proven guilty. Hah."

"Hey, Kris," Toescher cut in with a wink, "you're up for early retirement, aren't you?"

"Yeah, I'm out after this week. Going fishing. You want to go any time, great."

Toescher also wore a dark suit and tie. Like Korg, the suit didn't quite match the face; he'd look more at home in a t-shirt in a bar on a Friday night, waiting for a game of pool.

"Yeah I don't really fit in here anymore with all the young hot-shot MBAs they're bringing in. Hell, they work here, make a mark, and in five years they can write their own ticket on the outside with a corporation and make a fortune. These young geniuses: First I train them, and then in five years, I have to face them on the other side. Man, why didn't I think of that 20 years ago?"

Korg was sympathetic. "You could never represent some corporation trying to cheat the United States of America. That'd be like me trying to freelance out as a private investigator to protect a child kidnapper."

Toescher extended a hand and led the way. He unlocked the door and the pair entered a tiny room with nothing inside but another door and a telephone. The first door locked shut behind them. Toescher picked up the phone, and, following IRS protocol, announced his presence. The door buzzed, unlocked electronically, and Toescher led Korg through into a large office space with several dozen cubicles. They quickly arrived at Toescher's.

"I wish we had this much security at Homicide," Korg said. "Man, two firewalls?"

"You don't see somebody walking out of here after an audit rushing to put an American flag sticker on their car."

Toescher took his seat in his office.

"Well, Kris, your intuition looks like it's right on the mark."

"With Griffin? Or Johnson?"

Toescher held out a folder labeled "Stephen Griffin."

"Griffin got into a little tax trouble, but I wouldn't call him a cheat. We've been working with him for about 10 months. He went from poor to rich real fast. The guy didn't set up any investments as tax shelters. Like a lot of guys who come into money fast, they spend it on stuff they've always wanted."

Korg and Toescher both knew the story well. It

happened frequently with independent contractors, the self-employed and entrepreneurs. After years of counting pennies, goodies can be bought. Come time for quarterlies, there's no money left over for the IRS.

A natural chemistry emerged between the men. They were both Old School amid an era of young, fast-moving superstars who looked to the future, not the present.

"In terms of negotiation, Griffin's case was settled," explained Toescher. "Two months ago, we reached a deal with a payment schedule."

That remark brought Korg to life. So this is why Griffin could buy a Corvette. Because he'd settled with the IRS and could set a new budget to work from, and to celebrate, along with the promises of fresh income, he'd bought a new Corvette with all the goodies.

"What? He's clean now?"

"No, not completely," Toescher said. "He missed a payment, so we red-flagged him. Haven't heard a word. It's like he dropped off the edge of the world."

Korg didn't know whether to cheer or cry.

"I think he did."

"What? Drop off the edge of the world?"

"Yep."

"Dead? Nobody told us."

For a moment, Toescher noticed that Korg looked like a wise old sage; well, old at least.

"It ended up in my lap as a missing person's case," Korg said. "We were told he might run because of IRS trouble."

"Nope. All solved."

Korg wasn't done. "What about Johnson."

"You mean Jesse James Johnson, Incorporated?"

"Tell me more."

"We've got problems, or I should say, concerns."

Toescher pointed to several binders and folders on his desk.

"The guy pays almost no taxes."

Korg, though exhausted, ignited at the news. Toescher was entertained. He'd never seen Korg with this much energy.

"How can a gazillionaire like that pay no taxes?" Korg wondered.

Toescher held up one of the binders packed with documents.

"Hey, my first look, everything is in order," Toescher started. "The guy pays a ton of overhead, like we've got stacks of corporate deductions, and all of it appears legal. It's just suspicious as hell without independent confirmation, you know, line-by-line forensic accounting."

Korg shook his head and then pulled out a small envelope. "Look at this."

Korg passed over a packet of photographs. Inside was a series of photos of Johnson's place. The first showed the entry road, the ornate entry gate with arrow-tipped spikes edged by brick columns on each side, the mind-blowing remote camera security system.

"This is where he lives. Woodside. Incredible acreage in the redwoods, oaks and madrones. 10 acres. All fenced. Security system. Unbelievable home. Gorgeous caretaker's cottage. Recording studio and office building. All of it pristine."

One by one, Toescher examined the prints: lush landscaping with hundreds of freshly planted flowers, red maples and tall evergreens rising like towers; the driveway circled a fine-trimmed lawn, edged by a curving walkway. The house itself was stunning, a modern Victorian with porch and massive custom oak front door with hand-cut beveled glass.

"Let me tell you, the inside is even more impressive. The best of everything. Handwork everywhere. He told me the staircase railing alone cost him $100,000. I think the place covers about 8,000 square feet, all of it filled with one-of-a-kind stuff. It's unbelievable."

There were additional pictures of the Sound Factory, the state-of-the art 32-track mixing board and sound room, Klondike's bungalow, and a 10-port garage.

"Who knows what's in there," Korg said. "The amount of money it would take to finance this place is unbelievable."

Toescher looked at his watch. "Well, the guy's a rock star."

Korg's eyebrows crowned together. "Oh yeah? Well, how much has he claimed in earnings after expenses?"

Toescher regained full interest. He scrambled through massive folders that represented tax filings for the past three years.

Korg waited in silence, studying Toescher's face. The features changed with the seconds of time. First quizzical. Then earnest. Surprise followed by shock. A mutter of laughter. Then annoyance. When he finally looked up, his face was set in rock.

"According to these returns, he can't afford any of this stuff."

"That's how you get him," Korg said.

Toescher stood with his fingertips on top of a page of a return.

"According to this, Jesse James Johnson grossed $7.4 million, and then, after expenses, claimed a net of $2.6 million, and paid $1.04 million in taxes."

"That's a lot of money, but not enough to pay for all this stuff." Korg wrinkled up his eyes and nose in a crazy smile that looked like he'd just won the lottery.

"There's more," Korg said. His eyes gleamed.

Toescher was willing to forget that he had another appointment.

In a sweeping motion, Korg handed Toescher a piece of folded paper. In that cubicle, amid the library-like silence, the roar in Toescher's mind was deafening as he spread the sheet of paper before him:

Prychene Corporation, Bahamas, $12.7 million
Synchro Corporation, Jersey Island, $7.1 million
Zagorski Inc., Carson City, $250,000
Total: $20 Million

"What's this?" Toescher asked.

"Cash holdings. Almost all of it hidden in offshore accounts. And guess who controls all of them?"

Toescher's eyes begged for the answer.

Korg provided it.

"Johnson and his CPA attorney, Justin Goldberg." After waiting a moment to digest the implications, Korg added, "There's more."

Korg handed over another folded piece of paper. Toescher opened it, even more entranced.

Zagorski Inc., Carson City: 8 properties, $27.4 million
Morkul, Reno: 3 properties, $2.4 million

Smythwyck: Las Vegas, 1 property, $1.9 million
Prychene, Bahamas: 6 properties, $28.9 million
Synchro, Jersey Island: 4 properties, $18.2 million
Total property value: 22 properties, $68.8 million

Total value, cash & properties: $88.8 million

"What's this," Toescher asked again, but this time electrified.

"These are the real estate holdings of shell corporations held by Johnson."

Toescher let a noise out that sounded like all the air had just been sucked out of him.

Korg redirected the conversation.

"But let's get back to my guy, Griffin, who turned up missing, and the circumstances sure as hell fit a murder and complex cover-up."

Toescher tried to absorb the information as fast as it was being delivered.

"Griffin's checkbook receipts, electronic debits and credit card reports show he had $18,000 going out every month in payments," Korg continued.

"I get where you're going," Toescher said.

"Agents get a 15 percent fee. So if Griffin claims he earned $18,000 a month, well, that figures to $216,000 a year. If you project it further, it means Johnson was claiming an income of $1.44 million to Griffin. You know what this means?"

Korg was quick on his feet.

"Of course. Johnson was cheating Griffin, or maybe Griffin was getting money under the table, too."

Toescher noted it.

"There's a story in People Magazine that says Johnson made $15 million last year," Korg said.

"They could have just made that up," Toescher responded.

For a moment, Korg actually did look sage. "Or they could be low." He paused for effect: "Johnson's giveaway is the oldest trick in the IRS book."

"Right," Toescher responded, holding up a photo of Johnson's Woodside property.

"The stated earnings on the tax returns don't match up with the purchases. After all, where'd he get the money to pay for all of this stuff?"

Korg raised a finger.

"Man, this could be the motive I've been looking for. It confirms everything."

Toescher grinned.

"You're saying Griffin was getting shorted by Johnson. So when Griffin complained about it, somebody made him disappear. But why would Johnson risk shorting Griffin in the first place? You thought of that?"

Korg smiled. Maybe he was a sage after all, Pritchett be damned.

"CD sales are in the tank," Korg said. "In the music business, income is down 70 percent industry-wide. So despite everything you might think, the guy thinks he needs more money."

"You'd think, based what you've got here, he has enough money," Toescher suggested.

"That's what he'd say in court in a murder trial," Korg noted, "but you know how these money scumbags are. They never have enough. They get addicted to money, like a drug. He's got a cash register for a heart."

"I'll have to get the FBI and U.S. Attorneys office involved," Toescher said. "We've got conspiracy, tax evasion, money laundering, and lots of counts."

"They may have to stand in line behind me," Korg said. "Plus, we don't really know how it works, where the money comes from and how they launder it."

As Korg drove off, his phone chimed "Sweet Dream Woman" and he felt his heart leap. Even after all these years of marriage, Emma still could make his motor thump.

"The scam is worse than you think," Emma said. "I knew it was bad, but when you see the numbers, the level of this scam is staggering."

"I stumbled right into it," her husband said.

"Well, so did I," Emma replied.

"What?" Korg urged her on.

"I found another file and this one is full of dirt." Emma could not contain her excitement. "It was embedded inside a file called 'Goodies.'"

"I think I remember that," Korg answered. "Isn't 'Goodies' the listing of the sales of swag at concerts, like t-shirts, hats, jewelry, songbooks, that kind of stuff?"

"Right, but there's another folder in there called Bread Express," she answered, animated.

"Just a second, let me pull over." Korg guided his county-issue Ford into a Burger King parking lot. This he had to hear without distractions. "Go."

"Bread Express totals the sale of swag at each concert. You've got to see this. According to Griffin's numbers in his computer, the big weekend shows often grossed

$100,000-and-up in swag sales. But there's more."

"Yes, my brilliant wife."

"We're talking about all cash sales at the concert for the swag," she said. "Somehow they piped all that money into offshore accounts and didn't pay taxes on it."

"Whoa, that's good."

"There's more, a lot more."

Korg could sense Emma gathering herself.

"That cash apparently got funneled into the shell corporations," she said. "Then the shell corporations laundered it back into the United States, tax free, in real estate deals."

As Korg sat there in the Burger King parking lot, he felt his theories clicking. "The Bread Express. That's a good one."

"There's more, and this is even worse."

Korg turned his engine off. "Go."

"Did you see the folder named 'Rainbow?'"

"Rainbow? Don't remember that one."

"Well inside Rainbow is another folder named, 'The Pot.'"

Korg tried to follow along. "You mean like 'pot of gold?'"

"Exactly," Emma said. Her voice was edgy now.

"What Johnson did was require a big cash deposit for his concerts, $100,000 on weekends, $40,000 on week nights. That money was also somehow transferred into the offshore accounts."

"That's stunning," Korg said. "Are you saying the promoters were in on it?"

"Oh yeah, and you can see why," Emma explained. "The rest of the concert fee would be paid by check. That was the amount both Johnson and the promoter reported to the IRS as gross income. Meanwhile, the cash was all under the table, undeclared to the IRS.

They've been cooking the books like this for years."

Korg ruffled a palm over his cropped hair.

"So that's how they've done it," he said. "They run the cash from the advance deposits from concerts and sales of swag out of the country into an offshore account without declaring it or paying taxes on it. Then they run it through a shell corporation to buy real estate to launder the money back into America. When they sell the real estate, they have the cash to use any way they wish."

"And never pay and state or federal income tax on it," Emma said, completing the thought.

The line was silent for a moment before Korg broke in.

"Sweetheart, did I ever tell you that you are brilliant?"

"Not enough," Emma answered with a lilt, "just that you want my body."

"That is true. The brilliant part is a nice bonus."

Korg was invigorated by the information. "I'm going straight to Johnson's right now."

"Sweetie, there's one more thing you need to know."

"What's that?" Korg asked. "You're wearing your black lace for tonight?"

Emma laughed. "No, you one-track mind. Did you read any of Griffin's e-mails?"

"Sounds like I'm married to someone who might have?"

"Yes," Emma said. "I couldn't resist. But get this: Some people are very mad at him. Songwriters. Some of these songwriters wrote Griffin and accused him and Johnson of ripping off their songs. By the answers, Griffin apparently did pay for some of them, and invited them to send more songs in to him."

Korg noted it. "I'll ask Mr. Johnson about that shortly. See you tonight."

19

PRITCHETT'S ABSENCE FROM headquarters let Sager run with a hunch.

Never one to miss being in front of a television camera, she was at a political function with the press to unveil a wing to the new juvenile detention facility on Skyline. The previous week, a teenage gang leader, guilty of multiple armed robberies, had escaped jail with the help of two other inmates and a getaway driver. It was the lead story on TV news in the Bay Area. Residents were outraged, pointing out that before it was built, the county had assured them the place would be airtight. Now with her gleaming smile and business suit, Pritchett was out for damage control, to blame the previous administration, demonstrate that she was now in control, that she'd ordered a shakedown, and win at least a pyrrhic victory.

With Pritchett away, Sager had time to play. He seated Storm Clearwater in the county sheriff's interrogation room and then turned his attention to Kerwin Nakamura, the resident polygraph master.

Clearwater had tried to appear nonchalant, "Can

you believe this great late summer weather"..."Enjoy the show in Vegas?"... and with an attempt at a smile, poured himself into the cheap plastic chair with chromed legs, and folded his hands atop an 8-foot table.

Sager ignored the attempted banter. He focused instead on the technician, who affixed a series of five clasps, one on each finger of Clearwater's right hand. Then came a blood-pressure style band wrapped around his right bicep. A wire from each clasp led to the seismometer-like graph, whose scroll paper would record Clearwater's physical responses.

The clasps were tight. Clearwater became serious. He turned rigid, staring straight ahead. Under the clasps, his fingers began to sweat and his heart started to beat harder, exactly what the machine was tuned to record, and for Nakamura to examine and interpret.

"Hey, take it easy," Clearwater said. "These fingers are my tools."

Sager had the air of power. The technician, Nakamura, turned to ice. Behind one-way mirrored glass, a video camera was already running. Inspector Nelson, as a favor, positioned himself next to the camera as an observer.

"What's the reliability of this lie-detector stuff?" Clearwater asked.

Sager deferred to the technician.

Nakamura did not smile. "I've done this for 14 years. I've only missed on one guy. In my opinion, the way we administer the tests, it's near 100 percent."

After a silence, Clearwater blurted: "I didn't do it!"

Sager laughed. "Do what?"

"Kill Griffin!"

Sager cast an accusatory eye. "Now, why would you even bring up Stephen Griffin? We didn't ask you anything about him. We haven't told you why you are here. In fact, we didn't even ask you a question yet."

"Isn't that why I'm here? Because somebody killed Stephen Griffin and hid the body? What about Deego?"

Sager laughed. "My you're full of surprises."

Nakamura pointed his finger like a gun and pulled his thumb like the hammer on a .44 magnum.

"We're ready."

Sager phrased the questions so they were direct and charged with voltage.

"Is your name Storm Clearwater?

"No."

Sager held his face.

"What is your name?

"It's Frank. But I'd rather not say my last name."

"Why not?"

"A lot of us in show business change our names. I don't see how that's important. I don't want people to know my old name. It's not me. That's in the past, and it's not important. I want it to stay private."

"This is private."

"I don't care. I'm sure Johnson would feel the same. It's not relevant to anything you want to know."

Sager paused, surprised at the confrontational stance, but Clearwater filled the vacuum. "Besides, I didn't do it. I didn't kill Griffin."

"There you go. I didn't ask you anything about Griffin. Do you think Griffin is the reason you're sitting here?"

"Of course."

Nakamura pretended to monitor his polygraph unit. Sager and he had set up a series of questions as warm-ups, decoys, to later catch Clearwater off guard and perhaps trap him when the Q&A started.

"Griffin wasn't the kind of guy to run off and disappear, everybody knows that. I know it looks like he went to Las Vegas and disappeared. But somebody killed him."

"Do you own a firearm?"

"Yes. Several."

"Any handguns"

"Yes. Several. A .357 Smith & Wesson, and two antiques, a pair of chromed Colt .32s from the 1890s, and an old .44-40 that I can't get ammunition for."

"No kidding. I'd like to see those antiques. I'm a fan of firearms myself. Have you fired any of them recently?"

"Just the .357. I keep a target of Bin Laden in the woods behind my house. I go out and shoot him every once in a while. I'm afraid to fire the old .32s. Afraid they'll blow up with modern ammo."

Sager paused, then tried to warm up to the suspect. Of course, he failed. "OK, Clearwater, from here on out, we'll stick to yes-and-no answers, black-and-white. Say nothing else."

Nakamura pointed a finger in the air, indicating that he was ready to go.

"Did you kill Stephen Griffin?"

"See! I knew this is what this was about!"

Nakamura became aggravated. He rarely spoke, and never spoke out of turn, but now interjected: "Sager, get this guy under control!"

Sager stood. He glared at Clearwater, and then tried to relax.

"Listen, Clearwater, you're here because you lied to me earlier today. This is a way to clear things up so we can get on with our investigation. So confine your answers to the questions, yes or no, that's all."

Clearwater, nervous, pledged he would — after all, he repeated again that he hadn't killed anybody, especially not Griffin. The atmosphere in the room, already edgy, grew tense.

"I know I don't have to go along with this," Clearwater said. "I'm here because I want to clear my name. I want to straighten this out."

Sager started firing questions like rapid-fire bullets. The answers came just as fast.

"Did you want more money out of the band's success?"

"Yes."

"Did everybody want more money?"

"Yes."

"A lot more money?"

"Yes."

"Did you want it the most?"

"Probably."

"Were you angry because it appeared Johnson and Griffin were getting rich and you were getting nothing?"

"Yes."

Nakamura smiled. Now I'm getting some results I can read, he thought.

Sager pressed on.

"Did Griffin want more money?"

"Yes."

"Did Griffin need more money?"

"No."

Sager sipped from a bottle of water.

"Is your real name Franklin Finkelbaum?"

"Yes."

"The same Frank Finkelbaum who was convicted of assault for hitting a guy and knocking him out with one punch?"

"He was kissing my girlfriend."

Sager eyes fired darts. "Yes or no."

"Yes."

"Did she get a restraining order against you?"

"Yes."

"Were you ordered by the court to take anger management classes?"

"Yes."

"Did they work?"

"No."

Nakamura rubbed his chin. He was getting a good read on this guy now.

Sager paused for another sip, and then continued.

"So Johnson and Griffin are getting rich, and the band figures 'Why not us, too?'"

"Yes."

"Do you know, according to a story in a magazine, that Johnson grossed $15 million in performance fees alone last year?"

"Yes."

"Does it bother you that after you paid expenses last year, you had zero net cash to convert into savings?"

"Yes."

"Were you angry at Griffin?"

"Yes."

Sager smiled, trying to lighten the moment.

"You have quite a temper, don't you?"

"Kind of. Not very often. Sometimes."

"Would you call it a flash-point temper, where you can suddenly lash out if your button is pushed?"

"Yes."

"When I visited you at your cabin, did you bash a hole in that door because you were angry?"

"Yes."

"Were you angry about money?"

"No. Well, maybe a little. A lot things were building up inside and it exploded."

Sager folded his hands and stared directly into Clearwater's eyes. He noticed a few light spots of sweat on the guitarist's T-shirt, and reminded Clearwater again, "Only yes or no answers."

"Have you been convicted of assault?"

"Yes."

"Was your dad a bank robber?"

"Yes."

"Have you ever felt like robbing a bank?"

"Yes."

"When you shoot at the Bin Laden poster, have you ever imagined that it is somebody else?"

"Yes."

"Johnson."

"No."

"Did you ever imagine it was Griffin?"

A pause.

"Griffin?" Sager repeated.

"Yes." It was a soft mutter.

"Did you kill Griffin?

"No, I didn't do it."

"You didn't pump some bullets into him from your .357?"

"No."

"Didn't it feel good to pull the trigger and shoot the person who was holding you back, keeping you from success?"

"No."

"How long does it take for you to drive from your cabin to Griffin's beach house?"

"About 45 minutes."

"So you had time to go to Griffin's on the early evening of September 25th, a Wednesday, the day before your trip to New York."

"No."

It was time for Sager to spring his surprises.

"You were lying when you told me you watched a Giants game on TV as you got ready for your trip, weren't you?"

"No."

"Clearwater, the Giants played a day game in Chicago that day. There was no game that night. So you lied to me when you said you watched a baseball game that night."

"No."

"And if I told you that you were at Griffin's beach house on the late afternoon of Wednesday, September 25th, would you say that is a lie?"

Clearwater flushed and looked down at the table.

"Do I need a lawyer?"

"I'm the one asking the questions," Sager countered, and then added with a softer tone, "I'm just trying to figure out what happened that night so answer the questions, if you want."

"You went to Stephen's beach house, correct."

"No."

Sager toned down his volume. He spoke in a calm, direct manner.

"Did you kill him?"

Now it was Clearwater who was agitated.

"No!"

For no apparent reason, Clearwater looked over his shoulder, as if he was being shadowed. Sager drew him back into the moment.

"Did you go back the next day, Thursday morning?"

"No. I flew to New York."

Sager grew even more serious.

"Do you know where the body is?

"No!"

"If we checked your .357, would we find that it has been fired recently?"

"Yes."

"The last time you saw Stephen Griffin, was he alive?"

"Yes."

"Did he have any bullet holes in him?"

"No."

Out of the blue, Sager switched tactics.

"Is your name Frank."

"Yes."

"Is your real name Clearwater?"

"No."

"Did you murder Stephen Griffin?

"No."

"Do you feel that you are the reason Johnson and Griffin have made so much money?"

"Yes."

"Did you murder Stephen Griffin because all this money was pouring in and you felt you weren't getting the share you deserved?"

"No."

"Did you murder him because he was keeping you from getting your own label deal?"

"No."

"Did it feel good to shoot him or do you regret it?"

"I didn't do it. I didn't shoot anybody."

"We're done, Mr. Finkelbaum," Sager said.

"It's Storm Clearwater," the guitarist said and slinked out, hunched at the shoulders, headed for home.

SAGER AND NAKAMURA huddled, reviewing the lie-detector test results. Nakamura examined the polygraph read-out like a Grand Master pondering a move in the finals of a chess tournament.

"The guy is a liar," Nakamura said. "He failed the test."

"When I asked him point blank, "Did you kill Griffin?' and he said, 'No,' was that a lie?"

"I can't say 100 percent," Nakamura said. "He was one of the most nervous guys I've ever hooked up and that slightly skews the reads."

"Yes or no?"

"He could have done it," Nakamura said. "I have a read on the guy, but not a clear read on that single question if he committed the murder. We definitely caught him lying."

In some areas of the interrogation, Nakamura pointed out, the guy was steady and rattled off truthful answers in succession, then had blatantly lied repeatedly.

In the span of a few minutes, Sager calculated, Clearwater had established that he owned several handguns, including a .357 Smith & Wesson that had recently been fired, had a flash-point temper, verified he'd severely damaged a door out of anger, had been convicted of assault, and had a motive for the murder; that he'd saved no money despite a year of dramatic success for the band, and blamed Griffin for not getting a label deal or a fair share of the earnings.

"He clearly lied about not going to the beach house," Nakamura said. "He was there."

"Are you sure?" Sager countered.

"Absolutely."

"Then my witness has it right," Sager said. "Yeah, but with no body, no physical evidence, that doesn't make him a murderer."

"Yeah-but, yeah-but, yeah-but," Nakamura answered. "Keep it up and I'm going to start calling you 'Yeah-but."

Sager paid no attention. "Yeah, but the guy is inflamed about everything," Sager said.

"I've seen it before," Nakamura said. "A thermonuclear warhead with a hair-trigger detonation button."

"Korg was right," Sager recounted, "'Light the fuse and stand back.' "

After a pause, Sager gave Nakamura a dry grimace.

"We may have to lock his ass up for a couple days. He knows more. Maybe tonight. See how he likes it in County. Shake the tree and see what falls out."

20

"YOU'VE GOT A packet on your desk."

The words crackled over Korg's cell phone earpiece and they sent his blood pumping. It had to be what he'd been waiting for, he figured.

"Open it," Korg commanded. He was in his car, on his way to question Johnson again, but for this news, he pulled over under the shade of an oak.

Inside the courier packet, Sager announced, was a 10x14 envelope marked "Inspector Kristopher Korg."

"Who's it from?" Korg asked.

In the upper left corner, it was marked "Anders, SFPD."

"That's it," Korg announced. "Remember this, young man. This is what happens when you call in old favors from old friends. Never burn your bridges with your running mates. Anders and me go way back. Otherwise he'd never give this up to another agency."

"What's this have to do with us?"

"Maybe nothing." Korg could feel his heart thumping. "Open it up and tell me what's inside."

Sager broke for a moment to open the envelope.

"There's a note on top," Sager started, "It says, "Here's

the report on that roadie shot and thrown off the ballpark arcade. No suspects.' A few persons of interest."

"What's this have to do with us?" Sager asked again.

"That kid, Spoogs, what's his real name?"

Sager flipped a driver's license-style photo of the kid over on its face and scanned the back.

"His real name," Sager read, "is Stevie Griffith."

For Korg, sitting in his car on the shoulder of the road, the moment felt as if he was being cleansed by cool, fresh water.

"More," Korg urged, "more."

"They found a note," Sager said. "There's a copy of it here. It says: 'Meet me in a half hour at the Upper Deck arcade, right behind Section 307, to share a great view.' It's signed with a heart."

"So the kid was lured up there, probably by a woman. Find out if this Spoogs kid is gay. Just a loose end. But I'm betting not."

Sager scribbled a note, then continued.

"They found a small amount of cocaine in a bag in a pocket."

"No matter. More."

"He was shot by a small caliber handgun, but no casing was found, so it was probably from a revolver. But that's not what killed him. He was killed from the fall."

Korg tried to digest the information. "Anything else about the note?"

"Anders has a little stick-on memo here. He says Forensics tested the note for indented writing." After a momentary silence, Sager asked, "What's that, indented writing?"

"That's where impressions from what was written on

a previous page leave an imprint on the paper you're looking at," Korg explained. "But why," he asked. "What was imprinted on the note?"

"It doesn't seem to mean anything."

"What is it? Everything means something."

"On the note that apparently lured the kid to the arcade, there is indented writing that the lab deciphered as 'MSP, 2424.' What the hell does that mean?"

Korg ignored the question. "You know where you're going, like right now, right, Inspector Sager?"

"I'm already there."

Korg quickly added. "Make yourself invisible. We don't want Pritchett knowing you're on it. You'd just get yourself in more trouble with her."

"She's not even here. She's out at a TV op."

"Figures."

Sager had tracked Joan Day to the Palo Alto office of Benchmark, a subsidiary of Franklin, where she worked as a junior accountant. He felt some pangs as he drove down Sand Hill Road, just west of the Stanford Shopping Center. This was only a few miles away from where he had shot and killed two men. Maybe Pritchett was right. He did need some time away. But staying busy, like Korg said, seemed to give him direction.

Now in Benchmark's lobby, he placed six mug-shot style photos on a low glass table.

Joan Day first scanned the pictures with one sweep and then zoomed in on each for a more careful look.

"Do you see the man who was sitting next to you on the flight to Vegas?" Sager asked.

Day did not hesitate. "This one," she answered.

"Any doubt?"

"None. I'm absolutely certain."

She had pointed to the photo of Stevie Griffith, the young roadie.

Sager opened his phone and punched a text message to Korg: "Poz ID on Spoogs."

In another minute, he followed that up with another text: "How'd you know?"

Back in his car, Sager scrutinized the case file. What are we missing?

Korg's advice echoed in his thoughts: Don't think yourself into a world that only exists in your mind. Let the evidence paint the picture. Connect the verified facts and follow them where they lead.

Korg, no midget, felt dwarfed by the Neanderthal.

"Now is not good," Klondike woofed like a guard dog.

After Yamani had buzzed open the gate, Korg ran into Klondike while hunting down Johnson. Klondike was polishing an exotic black sports car.

Korg ignored the comment and countered. "What's with the car?"

Klondike appeared peeved. "I don't explain what people don't understand."

"Try."

Klondike looked like a steamroller. "OK, let's get this over with. It's Johnson's new Friday car. He wanted a new Friday car, and now he's got one."

Korg looked confused. "A Friday car? He shook his head, arms raised.

Klondike acquiesced.

"Hell, he's got a car for every day of the week, plus a few bonuses. This new one is for Fridays."

"What others?"

Klondike relaxed a bit, glad they were talking about cars and Johnson, and not about him.

"Hell, I can't keep 'em all straight, what car for what day. My favorite is the 1918 Stutz Bearcat, but he seems to like the 1931 Deusenberg and the 1944 Cadillac Roadster better, and a 1963 Corvette convertible, perfect condition, red-and-white. There's an old Daytona Spyder Ferrari in here, too."

"No kidding," Korg noted, faking stupefaction; he already knew about that one.

"Oh yeah. We call it The Loaner. He lets a lot of us drive the Spyder to keep it in good-running shape, stretch its legs. When honchos come in to visit, instead of them getting rental cars, Johnson always loans them the vintage Ferrari. Rock Winston's had it lately."

"Any new stuff," Korg asked.

"Oh yeah, a Cadillac Escalade, loaded, and there's a Hummer, the big one, in like-new shape."

A hint of a smile cracked the biker's Rock-of-Gibraltar face.

"You're not going to believe this, but he's got an old Volkswagen van in here, a beater, I mean it's junk. He takes it out when he wants to roam around incognito."

"I'm impressed," Korg said. "You know what 'incognito' means." After a pause, he added, "I've been counting. "That leaves one more garage empty."

"I'm impressed, too," Klondike responded. "You can count."

Korg smiled. "Got me here."

"The other garage, he's got some bikes stashed. Almost never drives them. A couple times a year he'll ride out with Clearwater and me to Applejack's. A Yamaha V-Max, a new Honda Interceptor, and then a chopper I built for him, with the S&S 145-inch tribute engine — 186 horsepower — 250 rear tire, right side drive, set up on a Ness frame, chromed, and a paint job with a mural of a Fender Stratocaster on the tank. I think it has about 200 miles on it, that's all. What a fuckin' waste."

Korg had no idea what Klondike was talking about, but it sounded impressive.

Then, out of the blue, Korg hit him low.

"You hated Stephen Griffin for making you drive the bus, didn't you?"

"How'd you know about that?"

"So you did hate driving the bus. Is that why you despised him?"

"He didn't like me, not the other way around," Klondike charged. "From Day 1, he didn't want me here, but Johnson hired me anyway. My security record is 100 percent. Griffin tried to run me off, late-paying my salary and then cheap-shorting me on overtime, acting like he didn't know what was going on. When that didn't work, he made me drive the fucking bus."

Korg went for the bulls-eye.

"When you were setting up that big show at AT&T Park, when Spoogs took off for that blonde, you took off after him. Where'd you go for the next 30 minutes?"

Klondike froze. "Do I need a lawyer?"

"Only if you want to face a grand jury."

Klondike again hesitated and looked off to the side. After five seconds, he spoke.

"I went off to look for him. First the Gator told me that Spoogs had complained about stomach problems. When I pressed him, he confessed that Spoogs said he was going to the upper deck arcade to meet that blondie. I went up to track him down. Never found him. I told all this stuff to the police. You know that."

Korg studied the big man and stared into the biker's mottled eyes. The story matched up with Anders' report.

"Fred, if I hooked you up to a lie detector, would you pass?"

"First, it's Klondike, and second, you're damn right I'd pass." It was practically a shout. "If I lied to you, that'd be a parole violation and they'd run my ass back to San Quentin."

"You didn't toss that kid off the arcade?"

"I felt like it. But he'd already gone over the side."

Korg appeared satisfied for the moment.

"We may have to hook you to the truth meter, my friend."

Korg motioned to the Sound Factory.

"Same with your friends inside." And Korg marched off to face Johnson and Winston.

21

THEY WERE INSIDE the Sound Factory. Zachary Cole, Johnson's booking agent and owner of Star Talent Booking Agency, held a pen. Rock Winston sat nearby.

"Before I sign," Cole said to Johnson, "let me double-check a few things."

"Of course," Johnson said, "Let's make sure we have this thing right."

"What kind of performance contract do you have on them now?" Cole asked.

"Standard revolving 13-week artist contract." Johnson said. Winston silently listened and Johnson continued.

"Since the band members are under contract with me, I can claim that I am their manager. Cole is the booking agent for the live shows. So we sign this contract between us committing Lorelei, Clearwater and the band to Star Talent Bookings for the next three years. Clearwater and Lorelei will have to stay with us even if they sign a label deal with Rock Winston here and Diogenes Sound."

"That puts them in our control," Cole chortled. "Even if they create an independent act, and there is nothing they can do about it."

Johnson glowed.

"Right. And since I represent them, only you and me need to sign this contract."

He smiled again, his eyes sparkling.

"They'll be locked up."

"Free money for us."

"The genius in it is to keep the wording simple."

Winston sat in the background, his face unbroken. "If I sign them to a label deal, we can piggyback them to your act, both at live shows and the sales racks. There's all kinds of cross-marketing potential, provided I get a guarantee that they won't split off on their own."

Cole, who would book the live shows, smirked.

"This contract guarantees that. It may be illegal. If they hit it big, by the time it was ready to go court, we could just cave. But we'd already have collected a windfall."

Cole understood. If Lorelei and Clearwater signed a band deal with Winston and Diogenes Sound, "We can skim 33 percent of everything they earn for live shows."

Johnson picked it up. "I can force them to open for me on the road. I'll increase their pay and they'll think they've hit it big. Hah. But we'll double the ticket prices because we'll have a two-for-one show. Plus I'll get 100 percent of their publishing royalties. The extra money will flood in without doing anything. And they'll still be under my control to play on my recordings."

That's how you do it, Johnson mused. That's how you stay on top; always stay one step ahead of 'em.

Cole banged his fist on the table. "Let's do it."

From his desk, Johnson retrieved a sheet of letterhead. It was already backdated, and read:

> Wolf Eyes Management, Inc. and Star Booking, Inc., agree that the Johnson Gang, featuring Lorelei Aicona and Storm Clearwater, and under contract to Wolf Eyes Management, Inc., will contract with Star Booking, Inc., for all of its live shows, performances and paid appearances for 33 percent of the gross for three years from the date of this contract. Wolf Eyes management, Inc. will also promote, sell and contract songs in return for publishing royalties.
>
> Signed: Jesse James Johnson, Wolf Eyes Management
>
> Signed: Zachary Cole, Star Talent Booking

They both signed. Winston beamed.

"Dealing with rookies should be a crime," Johnson said.

Cole laughed. "Actually, it is."

In the office foyer, Lorelei greeted Korg. Office manager Rosemary Yamani shuttled him to a seat. The boss would be out in a minute.

Korg engaged the young talent.

"Got a boyfriend?"

Lorelei shined like a beam of light.

"Everybody wants to pin me down," Lorelei said, the magic glint in her blue eyes. "I'm a free agent. But everybody wants to put me on a short leash."

Korg was not immune to Lorelei's charm. He found

himself chatting away, even flirting, asking irrelevant questions, talking about himself. Her natural charisma seemed to cast magic over everybody her eyes touched, and he felt it, too.

"What does Lorelei mean? That's not your real name, right? Seems like everybody is the music business has a stage name."

"Yeah, that's true," she said with a lilt. "I just like the way it rings. Like a siren. You hear it and you remember it."

Korg tried to show his musical knowledge. "Isn't there a song about Lorelei?'"

Lorelei laughed. "It's called, 'When I Dream of Lorelei," she said. "Can't say it's one of my favorites."

"Then there's Sweet Lorelei."

"That's Sweet Caroline."

Korg sloughed off his miscast memory with a grin. "Think you'll get a label deal?"

"I dream," she answered, gleaming. "And the man who can make those dreams come true is here in the next room."

Korg let the conversation flow. "If you sign, where'll you get the material for your act?"

"Oh, I've written some songs and they're ready to go. Storm Clearwater is a song machine. Between us, we'll have plenty."

Korg cast his glance askance, as if sizing up the young singer.

"Ever get a song recorded?"

"Yes, I mean no, I mean..." she appeared flustered.

"What?"

"Well, yes, I've had songs done, but nothing has come

of them for me. Just like everybody. It seems everybody with a guitar has a song."

"True," Korg said, a bit abashed. "True."

Korg gave Lorelei his card with phone numbers for cell and office. In turn, Lorelei provided Korg her cell phone number. They'd stay in touch if anything came up. She nodded, punched the numbers into her cell phone and gave him back his card.

"Now I don't have to worry about losing your card," she said. "I have your number for keeps."

Korg was charmed. "You see or hear anything, call me. Be careful. This is a cutthroat business."

Korg's cell phone bleated the theme for "The Good, The Bad and The Ugly." That meant one thing: a new text message.

With a few quick clicks, he read Sager's message.

"Spoogs is Stevie Griffith."

A moment later, another popped in. "How'd you know?"

THE DOOR OPENED. Johnson appeared and Lorelei seemed to float to his side. Korg spotted Winston in the background.

"You guys look happy," Korg pointed out.

"Yeah, we just signed a three-year management deal for the band," Johnson said. "Now we'll try to get them a label deal. We hope they hit it big."

Then, with a start, Johnson remembered that Korg, after all, was a homicide inspector. "What is it?" Johnson asked. "Did you find something out about Stephen?"

"Nah. Sorry to bother you, but maybe you could just

help us with one little detail."

Johnson was irked. He didn't have time for this. "Now what? Your questions are getting ridiculous. What about Deego? He still hasn't turned up. Actually, when he does, I'm gonna fire his ass."

Korg gathered himself. "What do you know about Griffin's tax problems?"

Johnson's eyes flashed surprise. "Let the guy rest in peace. Don't give this to the press."

Korg kept on. "Look, the way our investigation works is very simple," he explained. "When there are no more questions, that means we have the answers, and the investigation is solved. The press does its own thing."

"OK, but keep this private, in respect to the man responsible for much of my success."

Korg tilted his head with a hint of a grin. "I only talk to the press when we break a case." Johnson appeared satisfied with the answer. Cole and Winston, watching closely, stayed quiet. Lorelei seemed invisible.

"Stephen told me he was buried in tax problems," Johnson said. "He was in a lot of trouble with the IRS."

When the inspector did not respond, Johnson filled the void.

"If I'd known how serious it was, that idea that he'd jump off the deep end and disappear, I would have done anything to help him."

Korg peered curiously at the rock star, as if expecting more, and in turn, Johnson continued his soliloquy.

"He was having other problems, too. He was bonking one of my old back-up singers, MaryLou Dietz, and she was pressing us for more money, and she got fired. Clearwater and the band were on his case for more money, too. So that makes a fair contingent of people that was pretty upset with him."

Korg showed no reaction, and Johnson continued the spiel.

"There were others he had to deal with. Our lawyer, Goldberg. People at Diogenes. New acts Stephen was scouting. Stephen had a way of leaning on a lot of people to get his way, and in time, it made them mad. His philosophy was, 'If I don't push, then who will?' But if you want to be in show business, that's the way it is."

When Johnson finally stopped, Korg dropped the bomb: "You remember the kid named Spoogs?"

"Of yeah. The roadie. Told you already he used to work for us. He was the poor kid that got killed at the ballpark when we were setting up our show."

Korg delayed the next question for a few seconds to set it up.

"Did you know his real name was Stevie Griffith?"

"No," Johnson answered. "So what?"

Korg studied the reaction of Johnson and Winston. They held their faces. But then, at Las Vegas the other night, Korg had seen poker players hold their faces, a calculated move, not a natural act, when foolishly bluff-raising with Queen-9 off-suit.

"All the evidence points to murder," Korg charged. "Yes. Stephen Griffin was murdered. So was Spoogs. Part of the cover-up for sure. Deego? We'll see. Hasn't even been listed as missing, to be honest."

Johnson leaned against the wall to support himself. "God damn."

"I asked you once before: Can I depend on your help?" Korg asked.

Korg studied Johnson's face as he answered. "Yes. Anything you need. I already told you that." Again, he held his face.

Korg looked over Johnson's shoulder at Winston, who was watching the show intently. "Can we talk privately?" he asked Winston.

"Use my office," Johnson volunteered.

KORG SHUT THE door with a loud click.

With Winston, there was no push to prove who was in charge, no edge of meanness. There was no smiley buddy-buddy stuff, either. Then again, he ran Diogenes Sound. He could make people. Or break them. He'd done both many times.

Winston unconsciously fingered the Special Forces button on his lapel. Korg noted it.

"So why am I here with you?" Winston asked.

Simple and direct. So Korg replied in kind.

"In your younger days, you spend any time in, say, Cambodia?"

Winston raised his eyebrows.

"You do your homework, don't you?"

Winston pointed at his button. "You know what this means, then, don't you?"

"Gotta admit, I do, I do." Korg was almost half laughing.

"Yeah, those were the wild days. I was in Phoenix, if that means anything to you."

"No kidding?" Korg tried to act surprised.

"So there's actually something you don't already know?"

Korg raised a single finger. He decided to play it

straight. After all, Winston certainly was. "Actually, I know about Phoenix. Omega, too."

Winston pointed a single finger back at the inspector. "Touché. So what's going on?"

"I need your help."

"What is it, inspector? Let's not bullshit each other. Start with what you want to know most."

Korg's right eyebrow twisted up in a crazy twitch. The entire power dynamic of the interview had somehow turned on him. Winston was in charge. Korg tried to regain the advantage.

"OK, do you have your calendar with you, you know, appointments book?"

"Of course."

"Where were you the evening of Wednesday, September 25th, and the next morning, Thursday, September 26th?"

From a shirt pocket, Winston pulled a DayTimer's Two Year Planner, opened it and flipped to the page.

"Let's see. Wednesday. I was right here, San Francisco, at a hotel at the airport, the Clarion, to catch a plane the next morning. I spent that afternoon at Johnson's studio, getting an early listen of a song and coordinated our production timelines. That night I previewed an act in San Francisco. Got in late. Next day. Thursday. I worked over details here with Schwartz, our producer, and flew out."

"What time did your flight leave for L.A.?"

"Around noon or so," Winston said. When Korg took a moment to respond, Winston added, "Is that good or bad?"

"Not good," Korg said. "Based on what we know about Stephen Griffin's timeline."

After a pause he looked at the agent, "Anybody able to vouch for your whereabouts on that Wednesday night?"

"Maybe. Maybe not. I keep a low profile. People figure out a label executive is around, and everybody suddenly wants to be a rock star. They think I create them."

Korg watched Winston's eyes as he asked the next question.

"What group were you checking out?

Winston laughed. "My you're good. Yes, you're good. It was some all-girl band. Let me check my book. Here it is. The Rock Lick Chicks at a club called Bottom of the Hill."

Korg took a drink from his bottled water. He intuitively knew that everything Winston said would check out.

"What else?" Winston asked. It was a signal to Korg that Winston was ready to depart.

"How about last Saturday afternoon and evening?"

Again Winston shuffled through his calendar booklet. "That's easy, too."

"What do you mean?"

"That was set-up time before the concert at AT&T Park in San Francisco. All the acts were Diogenes' acts. I was out there, checking in with everybody. The live shows jump-start sales, so we fronted the bands expense money to get them there."

Then Winston eyed Korg with a scowl. "You don't think, because of my stuff with Phoenix and Omega, that I did Griffin?"

"Well, just have to check all the details, you know. Is there someone else who can account for all of your time Saturday afternoon and early evening?"

"I'm kind of a lone wolf, Korg. I do things my own way, beholden to no one. You should know that. I don't need a chaperone when I'm on the job."

"So nobody else can account for all of your time Saturday?"

"You know that's a bullshit question, Inspector Korg."

"Why is that?"

"Because I was at the park, working. I'm sure lots of people saw me. But why the hell do you ask?" Winston was irritated.

"Because somebody at the park shot this roadie kid, Spoogs, and tossed him over the arcade. Sounds like your line of work."

"You're dreaming. Anything else?"

"If you leave town or are back in town, let me know where you are so I can get a hold of you if I need to."

On his cell phone, Korg texted Sager: "Rock Winston, no alibi."

22

BACK AT THE office, Korg and Sager huddled with Sturgeon from Forensics. Korg couldn't hide his excitement.

"What ya got?"

Sturgeon answered Korg with his typical aplomb.

"We luminoled the whole place, the beach house. Nothing. Not even one tiny drop of blood. Not one verifiable sign of violence. It looks like nothing happened there."

Korg countered. "What about that dent in the wall? What about the glass? You said that could have been somebody throwing a picture frame against the wall."

Sturgeon tried to placate the inspector. "I said it was possible, that's all. There's no physical evidence that proves anything at all happened. It's unlikely a murder took place there."

Sager appeared downcast and glanced over at Korg, but the senior inspector was upbeat.

"Exactly what I thought. Had to make sure."

"You need anything else, you let me know," Sturgeon replied, "I'll get our people right on it."

Sager was crisp and blunt.

"Clearwater is a liar."

Korg was fascinated with the young inspector. "What do you want to do about it?"

"I think we take him down after the show tonight, in front of everybody, put some real pressure on him, and see if he cracks. At the minimum, we get the truth."

Korg considered the plan. "What is your bottom line?"

"Hey, Clearwater was there. Clearwater was at the beach house the evening Griffin disappeared. We know that for a fact. Yet he denied it. He's caught in several lies about that night. He could have done it. He's crazy."

Korg was impressed with the energy of his young partner.

"Inspector Sager, that was the highest number of continuous words I've ever heard come out of your mouth."

"He's a liar. Liars have something to hide. Here we have a complicated case where the perp has hidden a lot. It fits. The guy has dark secrets."

Sager drove the point home: "We know that Clearwater was at Griffin's Miramar beach house the last day he was seen alive. We know that Clearwater was enraged at Griffin for blocking the band from trying to get a label deal. It was likely a long buildup leading to a moment of rage."

Korg cautioned the junior inspector. "That doesn't make Clearwater a murderer."

"It might."

"True."

"Where's the body?"

"Good question."

Korg stroked his chin and measured his understudy.

"There are lots of good theories. Wouldn't you bet on Johnson setting the whole thing up and Klondike doing the dirty work? There's so much money in play. If Griffin tried to leverage Johnson, I could see him getting eliminated. And then there's Winston. When you've killed, I'm told it gets easier, you get used to it, like it's imprinted in you. It doesn't go away. It becomes who you are."

Sager, who had killed, flinched.

"That's not necessarily true."

BEFORE KORG LEFT for home, he downloaded his e-mail, and then went to Google and typed in "Lorelei." He, like the others, was transfixed by her grace, beauty and apparent smarts. Where had she come from? Surely someone so talented had made a splash somewhere, right?

But instead of reading about a young starlet on the rise, he read this account from *GreatMyths.com:*

> *"In legend, Lorelei the siren is said to haunt men to their deaths. Her music hypnotizes all who hear it. Sailors on the Rhine River who hear Lorelei sing are pulled in and then drawn to their peril.*
>
> *"According to the legend, Lorelei was a beautiful girl betrayed who then threw herself into the Rhine. Men who sail these waters hear the song of Lorelei and are pulled to shipwreck at the echoing Lorelei Rock."*

Another stage name? Korg wondered. Just like Jesse James Johnson, Storm Clearwater, Klondike and who knows who else?

He searched through a few more internet pages of listings for Lorelei and found restaurants, handbags, books and few personal websites, but no rock-and-rollers. So she was who she said she was, a pre-law student who gigged the college coffee houses.

Korg knew he could get distracted, to go sideways, as Pritchett put it, and so it was here. At Google, he then typed "Griffin missing." To his surprise, the page filled with hits.

He opened one and read:

> *The Griffin, built in North America by French explorer Robert de La Salle, disappeared on its maiden voyage in 1679 in Lake Michigan. It was never found. The lake, it is said, never gives up her dead.*

As Korg was leaving the building, he suddenly turned and headed back inside. With Pritchett, you'd better not leave things to chance. He wanted to make certain he had clearance to invite Johnson in for interrogation, and maybe a polygraph. With a high-profile star like Johnson, he didn't want to create a public relation's nightmare for Pritchett and screw-up his send-off. Everything by the book.

As he approached Pritchett's secretary's desk, Korg spotted the backside of Sager, who was standing at the doorway of Pritchett's office.

The piercing wail emitted from the room was unmistakable; it was Roberta Pritchett. "You are on leave. Get counseling. Human Resources has set it up for you."

Her voice shimmered: "As for Korg, he was once

OK, I guess. But the guy's brain has short-circuited. Pays no attention to the rules. Stay away from him. Get counseling."

"I think he's on to something with this case," Sager said. "This isn't just a missing person's case."

Pritchett looked up at the ceiling in frustration. "We have a big-time music agent missing." Even from a distance, the sound of her voice gnashed Korg's ears. "I need to tell the press we're looking for him. But we both know that Korg couldn't find a lost dog."

Korg burned. He turned and didn't stop walking until he reached his car, fulminating.

Screw it, he thought. I'm outta here. For a moment, a vision came to him: foggy mornings, the taste of salt air. He'd push the throttle forward on his 24-footer and head out to sea for whatever the day would bring. He'd leave Pritchett and all politicians like her in his wake.

"Screw this," he muttered.

The kids were still out, but would soon be home for dinner and the show.

The house was quiet, except for the hum of the pump of the large aquarium in the corner. Korg wore his sweat pants, no socks or shoes, and a wrinkled T-shirt with the words, "Fish Fear Me, Women Want Me." His graying black hair, though short-cropped, was ruffled. He sat with a palm on his forehead, raking that hair.

Emma stood behind her husband, palms on the corners of his shoulders.

"Are you sure honey? Are you sure you're ready for this? To end it right now?"

At their kitchen table, Korg stared at the badge and ID he'd set before him, encased in a black leather foldout sheath. A Pacifico, three-quarters empty, and his cell phone sat nearby. Korg had been staring at the badge for 15 minutes. It would be tough to give up the badge and go out on a bitter note.

"Thanks Emma, you've always been there for me. I love you. I think it's time now. I've had enough. No sense delaying."

In one sudden sweeping motion, Korg grunted and knocked the badge off the table — it landed on the kitchen vinyl floor with a heavy clunk of leather and metal. Then he grabbed his cell phone.

Emma watched, lips pursed, her eyes sad.

He punched the auto-dial for Pritchett. He expected the secretary to answer, but instead Pritchett answered it directly.

"This is Roberta Pritchett."

She sounded rushed and official.

"It's me, Korg."

"Did you break the case?"

"No."

"Then why are you calling me?"

"This can't wait."

There was a long pause. Then Korg continued.

"I want out now. You don't want me around. You make me feel like a piece of crap."

Another silence followed.

"I'm just an addendum now. I see no reason to wait."

He had figured it would be simple and fast; offer made and offer accepted.

"You are calling me for this?"

Pritchett's reaction caught Korg off guard.

"Well, yeah, I…"

"No. First, you don't call me unless a case is breaking. Second, you know how protocol works, and that doesn't change for you or anybody else. Your retirement is resolved. Friday."

Korg was contrite.

"Hell, Roberta, you don't want me around. It's obvious."

Pritchett toughened.

"Don't call me Roberta. And you think it is an accident you've been assigned this case? Get over it."

Korg listened, silent.

"You really still want me around?"

"You owe me the full week and I'm going to make damn sure you give it to me."

Pritchett hung up abruptly.

Korg finished his Pacifico. He was quiet, alternating his gaze between his badge, still lying face-up on the floor, and the aquarium, where a school of cardinal tetras were swimming in and out of the bubbles from an aerator.

Without a word, Emma reached down, picked up the badge, and handed it to her husband. "You dropped this."

Korg held it in his hands for a long time, looking at it, then peered up at his wife.

"She still wants me," he said.

Emma kissed her husband high on the cheekbone. "Let's have some fun tonight."

With a sigh and a soft smile, her husband answered, "I'll try."

23

Tickets came easy for the show. Korg had no trouble snagging all he needed for his family, as well as extras for their friends. Zack and Rebecca quickly disappeared; after all, they wouldn't be seen out at a show with "old people," especially parents. Sager, meanwhile, arrived with Bonnie Griffin on his arm, which drew an arched left eyebrow and a subtle smirk from the senior inspector.

As Korg parked, he saw the Neanderthal, standing like a security officer along a cordoned section of street, reserved parking for the band.

"Fred, this is my wife, Emma." Korg grinned like a leprechaun as he added, "And by the way, what happened to Griffin?"

Klondike scarcely acknowledged their presence. "That's your job." His eyes wandered over Korg's shoulder.

Korg and his wife turned to see a caravan approaching, led by a white stretch limo. Klondike guided the vehicles to the curb, and then sauntered over to the limo. Before the big man could get there, the limo driver, an elegant young black woman in a tuxedo, popped out and opened the door.

Jesse James Johnson, all leather and black denim, stepped out.

"That's him, right?" asked Emma. "He looks like a star."

"Oh yeah, and the band's right behind him."

The band members popped out of their vehicles, eager to hit the stage.

Emma watched them closely. "They seem so young."

Korg lightly placed a palm on his wife's shoulder. "Or is it because we're getting old?"

"What would they do if they weren't in a band?"

"Put it this way, if they won the lottery, they'd run their own act until the money ran out."

It was a warm fall evening. The temperature had hit the 80s on the Peninsula at mid-afternoon. As the sun dropped, coastal fog advanced inland to the skyline ridge to the west, and a cool breeze shot eastward down slope toward the bay. A gust propelled a piece of litter down the street, and Korg, who had a thing about trash, reached down and picked it up. When he returned, Emma stroked her husband's right arm. She admired his sense of decency and aversion to coarse behavior, such as littering.

Korg looked for a trash can and seeing none, went to stuff the scrap in his pocket. Without a thought, he looked at the paper in his hand.

The numbers, written in pen, jumped at him like a jack-in-the-box: 2424.

He bored in on the document. It was a map of McNee Ranch State Park, a simple 9-by-11 tri-fold sheet of paper, scuffed and dirty. He knew that McNee was an undeveloped coastal park at Montara Mountain and was located less than 10 miles from Griffin's beach house. Korg opened the map so it was flat between his hands. On the slopes of Montara Mountain, a location was circled with the hand-written words, "bunker."

"C'mon, let's get our seats," Emma pleaded.

But Korg was in another world.

That gust of wind had blown the little map out of one of the band cars when the group arrived. Korg quickly scanned each member of the caravan:

There was Johnson in his limo. Clearwater and Lorelei arrived in an old Corvette. Winston and Cole showed up together in Johnson's vintage Ferrari. The rest of the band members, Robertson, McNabb and Landru, arrived solo.

Korg turned and confronted Klondike.

"You ever see this before?" He held the map out for the big man's scrutiny.

"I don't have time for this." Klondike stomped off for the back stage, the FTW at the base of his skull aimed at Korg as he left.

There wasn't a bad seat in the house. It was open seating and the inspector and his wife stole seats in the back corner. This way he'd have a perfect view of Winston. Sager and Bonnie Griffin were seated off to the left, mid-crowd. Korg's kids, meanwhile, were front and center, and continuing to act as if their parents did not exist and had perhaps taken a rocket ship to Mars.

The music hall was the Little Fox, a small house on Broadway in Redwood City with cabaret seating for 240. Zachary Cole, the honcho at Star Booking, had reserved the venue. The entire affair was designed to create a live sound stage for Rock Winston. To fill the place, 300 tickets had been handed out free on KFOG, San Francisco's top-draw FM radio station. Johnson paid for everything.

Clearwater had expected the opposite response from Johnson, a confrontation followed by a showdown. The support of his vision to form an independent act, fronted by Lorelei, must be a reward for all he had done to help create Johnson's success, he figured. 'After all,' Clearwater concluded, 'I deserve this.'

The curtain rose, Clearwater stung a ringing E chord, Robertson's drums snapped to life, and Landru and McNabb shifted into gear, driving forward with the hip-shaking, shoulder-shimmying double-time sound that Clearwater had perfected with his mates. In the center of the house, Rock Winston, seated next to Johnson, took in the performance. Yes, that was the sound he wanted. With Clearwater as conductor, the band powered ahead like a musical locomotive.

After 4 bars, Lorelei glided out to center stage. She blushed to the cheers and her face glowed under the stage lights. She wore a thin burgundy top, tight, contrasted by a short black skirt, accented by a touch of platinum, with the familiar wisp of a chain around an ankle; the footlights caught it in glimmers. In the dim purple light on stage, Winston caught the wobble of her breasts under burgundy, and when he stared closer, he could barely glimpse the twin darts. His heart quickened.

"We're here to showcase some new sounds," she announced over the top of the band's churning rhythms, "and maybe get a label deal."

The crowd, though unfamiliar with her, was enthusiastic in its support.

Clearwater spotted Rock Winston and Jesse James Johnson at the center of the crowd. Johnson seemed proud. In the adjoining seat, Winston was cool and still, as if shooting a game of pool rather than readying to plunk down a bet in one of the world's biggest horse races. Then, off in the deep left corner, he spotted Inspector Korg. Shocked, Clearwater dropped his guitar pick.

Clearwater plucked a back-up pick from the top of his pickguard and the band swept into "No Dress Rehearsal," a double-timed rocker. Lorelei returned to the front and let loose. If Winston liked the sound, there was no proof of it on his face.

The band played songs rapid-fire style, driving the show with the music, not showmanship, jokes and banter, like Johnson did in Vegas. That's what Rock Winston wanted. Focus on the music. Get it down and let it roar. The rest will come. One after another, they played the songs prepared for Jesse James Johnson's new CD, only with Lorelei's haunting vocals. The sound was tight, edgy and right.

After 20 minutes, Lorelei stepped out front near the edge of the stage.

"Well, here's a brand new one," Lorelei announced. After a pause she stretched a hand out to the lead guitarist. "Storm Clearwater here just wrote it this morning. So you're the first to hear it."

Johnson gritted his teeth, Korg noticed, but then tried to appear pleased.

The lights faded to black, except for two spotlights

aimed at Lorelei and Clearwater, both out front near the edge of the stage. The song started quiet and slow, Clearwater finger picking in D. He had clicked the Telecaster pick-up selector to the center position, so both bridge and neck pick-ups were set in series. His foot punched the button on a stomp box to activate a stereo chorus effect. The result was a resonant, vibrant tone, not too clean, yet still shimmering.

Lorelei's voice sounded like a priceless instrument. Her range scaled from alto through soprano, but it was the tone that set it apart, clean and pristine at low volume, then howling and piercing on high, with the lines capped off with ironic finishes. Lorelei, with Clearwater's guitar wrapped around her words, created magic:

I'd rather wake up with you in the damnedest desert.
Than open my eyes to a city all alone.
Lonely has a way of eatin' my mind.
And I thank the Lord you blast that hell aside.

Her voice, as silken as her black hair, melted the crowd. Rock felt an upwelling in his chest when Lorelei smiled at him in mid-phrase. It felt like she was singing to him alone. He looked closer and could see the outlines of her nipples clearly through thin cotton.

Together, on the center of the stage, Lorelei and Storm continued, while the rest of the band watched the duo in the dimmed background. It seemed as if they were watching a love waltz:

Love is climbing a mountain.
Not all the steps are easy to take.

But it ain't no problem to be alone.
That's always the easiest choice to make.
If you don't live for your friends,
You're just gonna be a stranger when you die.

Love is climbing a mountain.

And it's there for you to climb.

Clearwater grinned over at Landru, and then nodded. He flipped the pick-up selector to the Telecaster's bridge pick-up, a single-wound Texas Tele that transformed the sound to a stiletto knife, bright, loud and cutting. He chopped a phased riff on his Telecaster, still in D, the speed twice as fast as the slow, melodic finger picking that opened the song.

Landru felt the pace, and fed right in with his Stratocaster, hitting the strings hard on cut time. McNabb, on bass, and Robertson, on the drums, sparked to life with a crack, picked up the rhythm that Clearwater was searching for, and fed it into the layers of sound. The song was building to a crescendo, and Lorelei took it right over the top at the double-timed pace.

Get on your knees and fill your hands with earth.
Look up to the clouds and ask what is your worth.
Plant the seed and care for your wife.
Live so you can give back to life.

Lorelei wasn't a shouter, a shrieker or a howler, but the penetrating wail of her voice captured the place, one heart at a time.

Landru broke off on a short lead run, eight bars, and Clearwater caught it on the turnaround to finish with eight more. Then, with the crazed glare of a guy whose electric guitar played through him, not the amp, he switched to the key of E, filling with hammer-ons. The rest of the band followed, and then Lorelei took the song home.

Love is climbing a mountain.
And it's there for us to climb.

And it's there for us to climb.

It ended with a resounding double backbeat on the snare and toms by Robertson. Lorelei looked over at Clearwater. They were able to read each other's thoughts without a word: "We've really got something here."

The crowd roared at the finish, and amid the cacophony, Clearwater eyed the young beauty at the center of the stage and wondered who the "*us*" was in the last line of the song. Clearwater originally had written, "And it's there for *you* to climb." On her own, Lorelei had changed it to "*us*."

In the center of the room, Johnson was ecstatic. Rock Winston, though, was difficult to read.

Clearwater and Landru high-fived.

"Very sweet," Emma said. "I could learn to like this rock-and-roll thing in your retirement."

Korg looked over at Sager and caught the young inspector's eye.

He gave him a thumbs-up and mouthed the words, "tonight."

"It's not quite as sweet as you might think," Korg said to his wife.

Back stage, Lorelei cornered Clearwater. "What do you think?"

"Think gold. Think platinum. Think a Grammy."

Korg glared past her.

"Hello there, Storm Clearwater. Please turn around and face the wall."

"What's this all about?"

"Don't let this get messy, Storm," Korg warned. "Don't make it worse than it already is."

Clearwater turned to the wall.

"Now put your hands behind you, please."

As his band mates watched, Clearwater felt the hard, cold metal of handcuffs bite into his wrists. He knew this moment meant one thing: You did wrong and now you must pay.

"Sorry to have to do this in front of everybody," Korg said.

From the side, Klondike, Johnson and Winston stood together and watched Korg lead the handcuffed Clearwater out of the building.

"I knew the guy was dirty," Klondike said with a growl.

Lorelei approached Johnson. A velvet arm reached for him.

"I could use a hug right now," she said.

24

"WE CAN DO this easy," Korg explained to Clearwater, sitting next to the suspect in the back seat, "or we can do this hard."

"Could you loosen the cuffs a little?"

"Depends on you. A lot depends on you."

Sager was driving. Clearwater was cuffed and uncomfortable, his hands behind his back, just how Korg wanted it. Sager guided the car up El Camino Real to Woodside Road, and then worked his way on that winding expressway though the foothills to Interstate 280. Heading north on 280, traffic was light, most cars ripping past at 70 and 75 while Sager poked along at 55 in the slow lane.

In the back seat, Korg turned to his right, an elbow resting on the seat back, and faced Clearwater.

"You haven't been honest with us," Korg said.

Clearwater bit his lower lip, his head down, his face blank, staring at nothing.

Korg was a rock.

"I know you lied. I know some other things, a lot of other things. Now here is your choice. We can do it by the book... you don't talk, you stay cuffed, I take you to headquarters, you get booked, you get an attorney, you'll get locked up and we'll never give you the chance to talk to us again." After a pause to let the words sink in, he added, "Or you can talk now. It's your choice."

Clearwater shook his head, stifled, stunned by his predicament. What would Lorelei think? Would Rock pull the plug on the label deal? Would his best friends, Landru and McNabb, turn on him? Was Robertson laughing right now? Would Johnson fire him? He thought of Bridges, in critical condition at Stanford Hospital, how he always said, "There's no right way to be wrong." Even his mom and dad would doubt him. After all, these were homicide inspectors.

Finally he managed a meek, "What do you want to know?"

Korg laughed.

"Like I have to fill in the blanks for you?"

Clearwater shut his eyes. This was bad, he thought, real bad. They were going to nail him for the murder of Stephen Griffin.

"I didn't do it."

From the driver's seat, Sager snickered darkly.

"I remember you saying that before," Sager said. "I remember you saying a lot of things. Some of them when you were wired to the lie-detector."

"I know. I know."

The admission cracked what was left of Clearwater's armor.

Korg pointed at the overhead green freeway sign. The exit for Highway 92 was one mile away. Half Moon Bay was to the west, San Mateo to the east.

"So do you want to do it by the book, we turn right, drive straight to headquarters and I book you? You never get another chance with me. Or do we turn left and have a talk at Miramar in Half Moon Bay. A nice, honest chat."

Clearwater did not hesitate. "Half Moon Bay."

Sager guided the Ford through the Highway 92 West ramp. Slow and deliberate, he cruised over the causeway at Crystal Springs Reservoir, headed up the hill, passed Skylawn Memorial Gardens at the summit and then glided down the other side to Half Moon Bay. He turned right at Highway 1, where the line of traffic crawled at 30, even this late, and then headed north.

Clearwater knew where they were going.

At Miramar, Sager turned left, and a moment later, drove up to a pullout along the rock breakwater, looking out at the Pacific Ocean. They were parked next to Stephen Griffin's beach house.

"Here are the rules," Korg announced.

"You tell the truth, off come the handcuffs," Korg said. "You keep telling the truth, they stay off."

Korg cracked a window and continued.

"But you lie even once and we're outta here. We go to headquarters, you get booked and I'll never give you another chance. You won't see me again until you're staring at me at the other table in court. This is your only chance to make it easy on yourself."

Korg could see that the sea was calm. Light waves foamed at the beach; cormorants and pelicans were posted on the rocks like sentries. Just offshore, a commercial trawler was heading into Pillar Point Harbor, its lights piercing the night.

Clearwater was nervous and confused. Where was this going? And why?

Korg was clearly in charge.

"OK, Clearwater, you know why you're here, right? You tell me what happened, no bullshit this time, or we run you in."

Clearwater, blanched and thirsty, waited for a question.

"What do you want to know?"

"If I need to ask, this is over."

Clearwater's words were slow and broken by a nervous edge. "The evening before we took off to New York, it's true, I came here."

"Face the far window," Korg ordered. He unlocked the handcuffs, and then added, "keep going."

"It was that Wednesday evening after we'd worked all day at the studio." Clearwater stopped, gathered himself, and looked at Korg for affirmation, and maybe a specific question, like the Q&A from Sager at the polygraph test.

"You talk. We listen."

"Well, at the studio, we kept talking about how Griffin had blocked our chance at a label deal. I didn't want to go to New York without getting some resolution, you know, about the band, about getting our own deal, where we stood, where I stood. We'd reached a point where we needed some resolution. So I came over here about dinnertime."

Korg rolled his eyes at the beleaguered guitarist. "Details, man, details about exactly what happened."

"OK, I'm trying. Yeah. Well, we fought. I don't mean

physical, but there was a lot of shouting and gesturing."

Clearwater started getting his footing.

"OK, I said that I was doing all the work and they were getting all the money. I've got nothing to show for it."

Korg finally spoke.

"But Stephen Griffin didn't care about that, did he?"

"No! He called me an ungrateful jerk! He said if I wanted to try it on my own, to go on right ahead. That there were guitar players before me and guitar players that would come after me who would feel exactly the same, and at the end of the day, it's the star's name up there on the marquee. The guitar player can be substituted like tiny parts in a child's toy. A child's toy. That's what he called my band."

"And you didn't like that, did you?"

"Hell no. But you see… I can't sing."

Clearwater's eyes dropped at the admission.

"Nobody wants you if you can't sing," he said. "Hell, Lorelei shows up, and we suddenly get a deal because she can front us. I've been doing this for years and years. I've made them rich. But I've got nothing."

Korg steered Clearwater a new direction.

"Who wrote the songs, 'Straight Ahead' and 'Hearts Make Their Own Rules?'… I found the lyrics in Griffin's computer."

The question seemed to come out of nowhere. Clearwater appeared mystified, but answered.

"Griffin and Johnson. They've got the copyrights. Griffin worked out the lyrics, Johnson the rhythms. When they'd come up with something, Johnson would call me and introduce the song, and I'd take it over from there."

"Aren't those considered Johnson's trademark songs?"

"Well, yeah, Straight Ahead is a new one, but it's definitely happening. That one could become an anthem."

Korg lowered his gaze.

"What kind of songwriting royalties would they get for these songs?"

Clearwater was trying to relax.

"You author or co-author all the songs on a CD and you get 50, 60 cents every time the CD sells. Johnson was selling 250,000, 300,000 CDs every time out, on top of electronic rights."

Korg pulled a pocket calculator out of his interior vest pocket and quickly punched the numbers. "That's about $180,000 per CD for songwriting, over a half a million dollars for three CDs."

"Yeah, plus you double it for publishing royalties, since he's got his own publishing company. Then you get more if other bands record the song, and a lot more if it becomes a hit on the internet or a ring tone. You get paid over and over."

Korg, seeing that Clearwater was starting to speak in rhythm for the first time, raised the stakes and put him back on point.

"So how'd you end it here with Griffin?"

"Well, I wasn't going to back down, and neither was he. I've never seen Stephen so agitated, so aggressive. He was really pissed off. It threw me off. Finally, he said, 'We'll get together, talk over some possibilities,' but he made it very clear that it would be no deal as the band stood. On our own, we would have no appeal. No star power. I have to admit now that he was right. Since he made a concession, it gave me something to look forward to and I left after that."

It was quiet for a moment. Korg zipped the window down all the way, rested his left elbow on the open window and took a long deep draw of the fresh salt air.

"That's about it," Clearwater added.

"So you didn't kill him and sink his body in the ocean off the Pillar Point Harbor breakwater?"

"No!" It came out as a half-shout.

"It's a serious crime to lie to an investigating officer," Korg admonished.

Clearwater panicked. "Am I going to jail?"

"You're still here so far, right? Tell me more about what you did that night."

"That night, I went home, barbecued a steak, packed, had a baseball game on in the background. I don't really remember if it was the Giants or not. I'm not a huge baseball guy."

"It wasn't," Sager interjected.

Clearwater nodded: "The next day we all flew out to New York."

Korg then withdrew a photograph.

It was a photograph of Griffin and his sister — the birthday party picture.

"Ever see this?"

Clearwater eyed it. "Nope. It's Stephen and Bonnie."

Korg relaxed his features, smiled gently, as if he had become Clearwater's best friend over the course of this talk.

"Now Storm, I want you to look at this very closely. See in the background, this large, framed photograph behind them on the wall?"

The agent pointed it out to Clearwater so there would

be no mistake.

"What about it? It's a picture of all of us, the band and management, together. We all got one. It was a present from Johnson."

Korg held his hands out, his thumbs and forefingers squared as to freeze-frame the moment.

"Now think very carefully, Storm. Remember back to that evening when you argued with Stephen Griffin."

Korg then pointed to the beach house, just a few yards distant from their parked car. Clearwater gritted his teeth. His face tightened as if his head was about to explode. This interview was starting to feel like a set-up. What was coming next, he wondered, again agitated, sure his next answer could determine his fate.

"Remember when you were inside… was this framed photograph on the wall?"

Clearwater laughed, the air powering out of him like an untied balloon blown up and let loose at a kid's birthday party.

"Of course. It was there. It's always there."

Korg raised his right eyebrow and squinted his left eye for effect. "OK, now we're getting somewhere."

Clearwater stared ahead, confused.

Korg noted it. 'Perfect.'

"OK, we're done here with you," Korg told Clearwater.

"By the way, I was thinking of taking my wife to McNee State Park up the road. You know how steep the hikes are? A nice walk with ocean views would be good, but we're not really up for anything too steep."

"Sure, we've all been to McNee. The trailhead is at a yellow pipe gate on the right, just before Devil's Slide. At the gate, if you hike left at the entrance gate, it's not too bad. You get a view of Gray Whale Cove and the ocean. Real pretty. It gets steep higher up."

"I've heard there's an old bunker up there. Hard to find."

"Some of the locals know it. Kind of cool. It's an old military radar site, I think."

After 15 seconds of silence, Sager turned his head toward Korg.

"You want to book him now?"

It was past midnight when Sager knocked on the door of the condo. He detected footsteps on the other side, faint at first, then louder. His pulse quickened at the sound. The porch light lit him up, and a moment later, the door opened a crack. Another pause. Then it opened wide. Sager stood there, his head at a slight angle, a jaunty edge to his eyes, electricity in his veins.

At the door, Bonnie Griffin, a bit drawn from the late hour, and soft, pliable and sensual in a red robe, stood in front of him. Her smile was warm and unrestrained. Her black hair fell loosely across the side of her face about her shoulders, and with a hand she swept it away.

"So Mr. Jeremy Sager, I thought you might find your way to my door tonight."

With the bright light behind her in the entryway, Sager could see through her robe and discern a perfect silhouette of her curvy body. His breath quickened. He loved the light in her brown eyes and soaked in her gaze, then snuck a peek below.

He reached down, parted the robe and cupped her breasts in his large hands. My God, he thought, perfection itself.

"Let's go inside," Bonnie said. "We don't want to give anyone a free late night show in the doorway."

She led him to her bedroom, lit a candle, and then lay on the bed. The robe fastened to her waist, but her knees fell open, and in the candlelight, Sager thought he spotted a glistening reflection. Bonnie, a devilish smile, looked into the eyes of the young inspector.

"Take off your pants," she ordered.

He complied in seconds. She reached up, grabbed him with her left hand and pulled him down beside her. He still wore his shirt, tie and coat.

"Mr. Jeremy Sager, you don't say much, do you?"

"No," he said, as his hands roamed across her landscape from mountain peaks to the deep canyons.

"If you want to keep going, you have to say you want me more than anything in the world."

He stopped for a moment, then cupped her face.

"I want you more than anything in the world."

"Really?"

Sager nodded as Bonnie loosened his tie.

"Then show me," she said.

25

THURSDAY

GUITARIST TARGETED IN MISSING PERSON PUZZLE

By Emmett Anderson
Chronicle Staff Writer

San Mateo County homicide inspectors questioned the leader of a renowned Bay Area rock band Wednesday night regarding the missing manager of rock star Jesse James Johnson.

Storm Clearwater, the leader of Johnson's band, was handcuffed and taken into custody by inspectors after a small showcase-style concert at the Fox Theater Redwood City.

Clearwater was questioned regarding the disappearance in late September of Johnson's manager, Stephen Griffin, according to San Mateo County Deputy District Attorney Joseph Roper.

"Storm Clearwater is a person of interest and inspectors decided to formalize our questioning," Roper said.

Those close to the situation said that Clearwater had several run-ins with Griffin in the past year over Clearwater's attempt to obtain a separate label deal for his band.

Clearwater is known for a mercurial and volatile personality and is largely credited for developing the sound that has helped Johnson to commercial success, according to those familiar with the band. Some call him an angry hermit who hides from the public in a small cabin in the Santa Cruz Mountains. He owns a collection of guns and loves to shoot them. Clearwater was once convicted of assault, according to court records.

Griffin was reported missing in late September when he failed to return phone calls to business partners during a trip he reortedly had scheduled to Las Vegas to scout talent, Roper said. His new Corvette was found at Long Term Parking in San Francisco, according to Roper, and a faxed itinerary of his trip was found at his Miramar home.

"We found that the flight ticket to Las Vegas was used by somebody else," Roper said. No records exist of Griffin staying in Las Vegas and his credit card and phone activity ceased, according to Roper.

According to reports, Clearwater lives in a comparative shack, Griffin in a dramatic oceanfront beach house in Miramar, and Johnson on a Woodside estate, where he operates a recording studio and keeps a collection of vintage cars.

"Storm Clearwater is a genius, whether it is on stage with a guitar in his hands, in the studio in front of the mixing board, or with a pen sitting down to write a song," Johnson said in a statement released by his office staff. "He is a dynamic force in the music business, a long-time friend. I believe he will be cleared of all wrongdoing."

Missing person cases involving wealthy, successful executives, such as Griffin, are extremely rare. About 100,000 people are listed as missing in

America, according to the FBI, nearly all of them are children taken by a divorced parent or runaways. Less than 1 percent of missing person cases involves adult males.

The folded newspaper was slammed down on the counter like a hammer on brick. The half dozen other patrons in the small Portola Valley café turned in shock.

"Sorry about that," muttered Johnson.

"Always keep your cool," advised Winston, taking a bite of his shrimp, cheese and avocado omelet. "Never let them know what you're thinking."

Jesse James Johnson and Rock Winston were eating breakfast, reviewing the Clearwater-Griffin story.

"Will this kill our sales and screw up the new CD?" Johnson asked.

Winston appeared unaffected.

"Fame is like a volleyball game. As long as the ball keeps getting batted back and forth over the net, you're in the game. It doesn't matter what anybody says. But if the ball hits the ground and nobody picks it up, you're dead."

"You're saying you think this could actually help?"

"Hell, man, this could keep you in the news all the way through to the release of the CD. It could be a blessing. We should fast-track the CD to get a maximum bounce out of this. There'll be a lot of low-hanging fruit."

Winston gazed off and visualized the riches at hand.

"I'll definitely have to sign Lorelei now and get something done fast. We'll double our money with a tour and publishing rights."

Johnson sipped his tea; good for the voice.

"Lorelei is a beauty, eh?"

"You get her yet?" asked Winston.

"Yeah, last night. Incredible. After all the adrenalin from her show, and then Clearwater getting handcuffed and carted off, she said she needed comforting."

"I bet you comforted her, eh?" Winston said with a grin. "You mind if I try for her tomorrow night?"

"'Course not." Johnson paused from his breakfast. "Nothing gets to you, does it? Is that why they call you Rock?"

Winston made a fist and smiled like a champion prizefighter.

"In the big picture, this Clearwater thing is nothing, even if he did Griffin. Maybe you should write two new songs for the CD, one called, "Now That You're Gone," a eulogy to Griffin, and then stack it with that sure hit, "Straight Ahead." Then end the CD with another song you can write called "How Could You Do It?" Make it a requiem for a murder."

Winston fantasized about the money pouring in.

"We could promote the CD as your personal communiqué to Griffin and Clearwater, Griffin in heaven, Clearwater in prison. That would get you on all the network talk shows, Jon Stewart to Piers Morgan. That kind of publicity would provide a launch for a new national tour. Every city you visit would want an interview before the show. We'd pack 'em in and sell platinum. You get my drift?"

At first, Johnson found this grand forecast difficult to believe, but from Winston's even-handed manner, he knew it must be the truth.

"How serious do you think this is?"

"When homicide cops get involved, there's always something there. Exactly what? You never know."

Johnson looked over Winston's shoulder to make sure no one was eavesdropping, and then spoke in a whisper barely audible.

"Was doing Spoogs really necessary?"

"From where I've been and what I've seen, it makes complete sense."

Johnson looked off to the left for a moment, appearing disengaged, surveyed the café again, and then returned to Winston.

"What about the blondie? Has anybody got a lead on her?"

Winston appeared more interested in surveying the scarce shrimp in his omelet.

"Sounds a lot like that blond MaryLou Dietz to me."

LOW, THIN FOG hung over the coast. A bright glow over the ridge to the east pledged that the sun would make an appearance by mid-morning. Korg, driving solo, cruised north on Highway 1 past Miramar, Moss Beach and Montara, to an obscure dirt pull-out at the foot of Montara Mountain. He stopped abruptly where a ranch-style road was blocked by a yellow pipe gate with a small golden sign that said, "State Park Property." There was space for only a few cars and Korg pulled to the far right and came to a stop on the shoulder.

Korg locked up his car, walked around the gate and wandered up the road about 50 yards to a dirt driveway on the left. He saw that it led through the woods to a rustic house set under a towering cypress. Then Korg spotted the sign: "Ranger's residence." He walked to the door and knocked.

The door opened and Ranger Brandon Simms appeared. In uniform, he had the classic outdoorsy ranger look, a rugged but warm face, mustache trimmed to code, a bit puffy at the belt.

Korg pointed at Simms' sidearm with an innocent smile. "You ever have to pull that thing?"

"Just this morning," Simms answered. "Another ranger was grabbing for the last doughnut."

Korg knew this was a fellow he could talk to. He pulled out the sheet map of McNee State Park that he'd picked up as litter the evening before, apparently blown out of one of the band's cars arriving for the show at the Fox Theater.

"For a state park, not much of a place," Korg noted. "Not much parking, no camping."

"That's right," Simms explained. "It's a primitive park for hiking, biking and horseback riding."

"What's that dirt road that runs up the mountain from the gate? Any public access?"

"Nope. That's just a service road for technicians to drive up to the Montara Mountain summit, you know, whenever they need to work on a transmitter or antenna up there. People show up, park at the gate during the week or down Highway 1 a bit at Montara State Beach, and head into the parkland and hike or bike around a bit. Some nice ocean views. The summit is a pretty cool spot."

Korg held the small map out to Simms. "What's this?" the inspector asked, pointing to the circled area on the map and labeled, "bunker."

Simms, in his easy, deliberate style, analyzed the map for only an instant. "I circled that myself."

"Explain," Korg asked.

"A lot of people want to see the bunkers. Back in the day, the military set up concrete bunkers and radar stations on the west slopes of this mountain," Simms said. "Same thing in Marin, on Mount Tamalpais. Bunkers, radar, Nike missile systems, tracking any invasion coming in on the Pacific. They've been on local TV shows lots of times. You want to go up there and take a look?"

Korg had a momentary look of anguish. "Do we have to walk?"

"I'll take you up there in my truck right now if you bring me a box of doughnuts."

Simms drove his state park pick-up truck at the pace of a fast walk about two miles up to a sub-ridge where the road split, the main stem turning sharply to the right. To the left, a set of power lines ran down along the ridge, east to west toward the ocean. Korg scanned below, across the sea, and saw the wispy puff-of-smoke spout of a passing whale. He returned to the issue at hand.

"See this deer trail?" Simms pointed.

Korg identified a faint channel through thigh-high chaparral that was routed down the ridge.

"You walk down this path about 50 yards and you'll find the bunker that's circled on your map," Simms said.

"Can I make it with these shoes?" Korg asked. "Will my suit get scuffed up?"

"Probably yes, on both counts."

"Hell, I'm here. Lead the way."

Simms worked slowly down the path, with Korg trailing behind. "Short steps, weight over your shoes, never lead with your head going downhill, you'll be OK."

Korg followed his guide. In a few minutes, they arrived at an old concrete bunker set into the side of the mountain. From here, the view of the ocean was fantastic, and it reminded Korg that soon he'd be retired. He'd come to places like this, hopefully with Emma, and maybe his kids, Zack and Rebecca, if they'd have him, and enjoy nature.

"How many people know about this?"

"All the locals who have heard about the bunker usually find it sooner or later. And like I said, it's been on TV. So we get a lot of people who make it like a treasure hunt. But I'll circle the spot on the map for anybody who asks, and tell them, 'Just turn left at the power lines.' So I'd have to say there's hundreds of people, maybe thousands, who know about this bunker. But it can go weeks without anybody coming down here."

Korg narrowed his questioning. "Ever had any trouble up here?"

Simms laughed. "Not too bad. Every once in a while, some high school guy will bring his young honey up here. There's some drug use, alcohol, mainly kids with a 6-pack. A few bums camped out in the bunker once. But nothing serious. 'Course, we don't have signs that show the way, and that keeps problems down. And since you have to walk, that keeps the riff-raff out."

Korg heard the sound of a nearby vehicle passing above them. "What's that?"

"One of the technicians driving up to the summit to work on the transmitters or something."

A thought hit Korg. From his inside coat pocket he retrieved the little map he'd picked up. Korg held it open to Simms, then pointed to the numbers jotted on the map: 2424.

"Does this mean anything to you?" Korg asked.

The ranger hesitated.

"Where'd you get that?" Simms asked.

"What does it mean?" Korg countered.

"What San Mateo County department did you say you were from?"

"Homicide."

Simms turned away. He scanned across the west facing slopes of Montara Mountain above him, then turned to his left and took in San Pedro Ridge and beyond across miles of Pacific Ocean. A few wisps of fog remained. The morning sun flickered silvers across the sea.

"Yeah, that 2424 means something," Simms admitted.

Korg waited in silence for more. The ranger provided it.

"That's the combination for the tumbler lock on that yellow pipe gate at the park entrance."

The tumblers in Korg's mind clicked into alignment.

"How many people have this?"

Simms was quick to rebound. "All the technicians. And who knows who they tell, right? I've told a few people. Parking is limited at the entrance, you know. Some people come here with real nice cars. I don't want to see their cars vandalized along the highway, so I let them drive in and park at my residence."

Korg flashed on the Anders' forensics report: The indented writing. The impression of "MSP 2424," now made sense. "McNee State Park" and the combination, "2424."

"Give me a list of everybody you can think of who knows this combination," Korg said

"I don't want my supervisor to see that list."

"It will just be between us."

When Korg returned to his car he pulled out a folder from beneath the front seat, and then reversed course and returned to the ranger's home.

Simms answered the door, only partly surprised at the reappearance. "You got my doughnuts already?"

Korg got right to it. On Simms' kitchen table, he spread out a series of photos. "You recognize anybody here?"

Korg watched the ranger's face. Like Morse Code, once trained, you could always read it. In Simms' eyes, he saw recognition, and perhaps a little fear.

"Will you tell anybody that I've given the combination out? Like I said, I might get in trouble with my boss."

"C'mon, Brandon, now I'm up to two boxes of doughnuts at the least. I'm just trying to trace down where this map I have came from."

Simms took a deep breath. "It's more like who don't I recognize?" With a pause, he pulled the photos of Klondike and Deego DeGenaro off to the side. "OK, I haven't seen any of these guys. I'd remember them."

He then pointed at Spoogs. "Don't recognize him, either. But on weekends, there's a ton of young guys just like this who roll through on mountain bikes."

"The rest?"

The remaining photos were of Griffin, Johnson, Winston, Clearwater, Lorelei and the former back-up singer, MaryLou Dietz.

Simms blushed. "At some point or another, I've seen all of them."

"I specifically gave the combination to Griffin. I knew him. Local guy. Came up here many times and would bring these other people along with him." Simms pointed at the photos of Johnson, Winston, Clearwater, MaryLou and Lorelei. "Don't know their names. Griffin would drive in at sunset a lot, usually with one of them. He'd go up the ridge a bit and watch the sun go down, and then head out."

Simms stopped as if he was done.

Korg quickly reined him in. He pointed at the photo of Marylou, the blond. "What about her?"

Simms took a depth breath. Apparently, Korg read in the ranger's face, there was something there.

"Yeah, MaryLou came down from San Francisco. She'd pick up dogs at the pound as part of their adopt-a-dog-for-a-day program, and hike around with them. I always thought that was sweet of her. I let her park inside. I was hoping to go out with her but we never quite connected."

He paused for a moment as he pointed out Lorelei. "Every once in a while, MaryLou would bring this other real pretty one." Simms said. "Not too often. Just now and then. Sometime MaryLou wanted to go up on the mountain with me. Just never quite connected with her. I think Griffin liked her, too."

Korg sat at the table and faced the ranger.

"Now think hard, Brandon. Did any of these people ever ask you how to find the bunker?"

Simms did not hesitate. "Sure," he said, "Griffin. Showed it to him myself, just like with you. We were friends. He gave me CDs all the time. Free tickets to concerts. Just as long as I let him drive in so he didn't have to leave his car out along the highway."

Korg's first call went straight to Sager. He caught the junior inspector as he was searching for a parking spot in San Francisco near 850 Bryant, headquarters for SFPD's homicide department.

"Remember," Korg barked, "Anders doesn't know you, has no reason to trust you. You're an outsider. He won't give up anything unless you have something to trade him."

"I'm ready for this," Sager responded.

"Not as ready as you think," Korg answered. In the next breath, Korg explained his discovery of the code numbers — MSP 2424 — discovered both on the map for McNee State Park and in the indented writing on the note that had led Spoogs to the arcade at AT&T Park.

"Don't give this info up too quickly," Korg cautioned. "Anders always knows more than he's telling."

"Just like you?"

"Learned it from him."

Korg, still parked at the gate, next punched the auto-dial for Roper.

There was no need for introductions. "I need the

'Daver Dogs," Korg told his old friend. "But do you have to tell Pritchett?"

26

ANDERS, KORG'S OLD partner at San Francisco Homicide, was more effervescent and talkative than most detectives. He enjoyed engaging in the hunt, step-by-step. As a result, the young Sager, with an academic pedigree, fast-paced appointments, lack of verbal skills and quick trigger, did not much impress Anders, except for one fact: "The word is, you saved my old partner's life in that botched robbery."

"No, I was just first to fire. I'm sure he'd have covered if I'd missed."

That answer worked for Anders.

"You must not know Inspector Korg too well," Anders said with a grin. "He couldn't hit water if he fell out of a boat."

After a pause, Anders asked, "So, what have you got for me?"

Sager was slow to answer. Korg's admonition was fresh in his mind. "That kid people call Spoogs – gotten anywhere on it?"

"Hold on there, not so fast, young man," Anders lectured. "I heard you had something good for me. Now here you are pumping me."

"I might have something."

"Plus, Spoogs is my case. You think he has something to do with your guy Griffin?"

Sager played one of his cards face up. "They're linked," Sager said. "We've determined that for a fact."

Anders was both chagrined and fascinated.

"This sounds like classic Korg. He's taught you well. Well, son, screw the cat-and-mouse. Give it up."

"What can you tell me about Spoogs?"

Anders noted that although both he and Sager were black, they couldn't have been more dissimilar. Anders figured the young inspector was in over his head, and yet if Korg was right, and the two cases were linked, he would eventually have to reveal everything he'd discovered. Sooner would be better than later.

ANDERS OPENED HIS cell and punched the auto-dial.

"Hey you old cowboy, what the hell are you doing sending your hunting dog to flush out the quail?"

Korg, driving down Highway 1, had been expecting the call from his old pal. "Remember the indented writing on the note?"

"Yeah."

"Inspector Sager can explain that to you."

"Did he figure it out? Or did you?"

"He did," Korg lied in the hope of facilitating Sager's mission to extract information out of Anders. "He's a bright kid. Hell of a future. Catch a lot of bad guys."

ANDERS RETURNED HIS gaze to Sager.

"Korg says you somehow figured out what the MSP 2424 means."

Sager, first taken aback that Korg credited him with the find, placated Anders. "It was your Forensics people that found the indented writing in the first place on the note."

"So what's it mean?"

"Will you tell me about the girl who delivered the note? She could lead us right to where we want to go." Anders countered.

Sager balked for a moment to provide more information, then figured that he had to earn Anders' respect.

"MSN stands for McNee State Park at Montara Mountain. 2424 is the combination of the tumbler lock on the gate at the entrance."

Anders didn't twitch a micro-muscle. "So what?"

Sager's glare was deadly. "The same numbers showed up on a document in our murder investigation of Stephen Griffin. So the two cases could be tied by 2424. Someone who knew the combination to the gate is the link to the two murders."

"How so?"

"Stephen Griffin never went to Las Vegas. We're sure he was murdered first. Spoogs, whose real name is Stevie Griffith, got duped to use Griffin's electronic ticket to go to Las Vegas. It was a scheme to make the murder look like a missing persons case."

Anders rubbed his chin. It was somewhat plausible. But it also sounded like one of Korg's typical far-out fantasies.

"This 2424 you found. What kind of document was it printed on? Where did it come from?"

Sager felt he had let enough line out and it was time

to bring some back in. "Inspector Korg has not cleared me yet to reveal that, but I'm sure it will be forthcoming shortly. So instead, tell me about the blond that lured Spoogs up to the arcade? We can't account for her."

Anders finally relented. "I'll tell you what little we know."

Sager inched closer to Anders, notebook open.

"There were roughly 100 people in AT&T Park setting up for the show at the time of Spoogs' murder. You couldn't get in without a backstage pass. So that means someone on the pass list handed Spoogs that note. The list has about 80 males. That leaves roughly 20 females. Most of them were setting up booths around the concourse to sell t-shirts and concessions. Of those 20, 12 are what you might consider real pretty, and about half of those are blonds."

Sager took it all down.

"I personally met with all six," Anders said. "One of them is a possibility. Her name is Marylou Dietz. She is a person of interest. She was there, so she had the opportunity. She was angry, because Johnson had just fired her. She'd tried to leverage more money out of him to sing back-up in the band. But motive? Don't see it. She's just a cute girl out of her league."

"She's on our list, too."

"Of course, that's the excitement of homicide detail. Right. Chasing your tail. I talked to all of them. Every one checked out. Not one even remotely set off any suspicion. Hell, it's possible the murderer got the girl in, set her up to deliver the note, then she left and was long gone by the time Klondike shot the kid and threw him over the arcade wall."

The silence that followed provided an awkward moment for Sager.

"Sir, that was a provocative statement you just made."

"Well, it makes the most sense. He was there. It was his style."

"It's true that he was mad. He has a penchant for violence."

"You know," Anders said, "a lot of this is not rocket science."

After another pause, Anders noted, "I just can't prove it." Anders then asked, "Do you think Klondike has an alibi for Griffin?"

"Actually, very thin."

"Figured." Anders stood. "Keep in touch. Anything else I can get for you?"

Sager was direct. "Can I get the pass list?"

"No problem," Anders said. "And take care of Korg. Keep him alive to the end of the week. It'd be nice if he made it that far."

Sager stalked his car, then stopped for a moment to text Korg: "Marylou Dietz. Alibi?" As he looked up, his eye caught a disheveled form 50 yards down the sidewalk, talking to a panhandler. An intuitive familiarity compelled him to take a closer look. The fellow was wearing an old Army coat, torn jeans, boots, and an old Giants cap. He stared closer: Beneath the bill of the cap was the face of Jesse James Johnson.

Sager stopped in his tracks, then partially hid himself in the entrance of a small market. As traffic poured past, cars, taxis, buses and bicyclists, he spied on Johnson.

For two minutes, Johnson engaged a male panhandler, unshaven, wearing dirty torn clothes, with mismatched shoes. The two talked as if the outside world did not exist. Then Johnson reached into his pocket and handed the man several bills. The panhandler shook Johnson's hand, grabbing it with two hands and pumping it, and then walked off, a hop to his step.

A few moments later, 30 feet down the street, Johnson addressed another panhandler, this one a black woman, middle-aged, her precise age impossible to gauge in her broken appearance. Sager jaywalked in traffic to approach.

An iron hand on his forearm stopped him. Sager turned. Out of the shadows, Klondike had grabbed him. "Stop," Klondike ordered.

"Since when do you tell a homicide inspector what to do?" Sager growled.

"Stop and watch."

The young black woman peered up into Johnson's eyes.

"If you could get some money, what would you do with it?" Johnson asked her.

"Are you puttin' me on," she asked.

Johnson repeated the question.

"Hell, I'd head back home to Mobile where my family is. I never shoulda left my momma and all my kin. It seems so long ago, likes another lifetime."

"Hard luck?"

"All I got is regrets. I left everything back home. Came out to California with Melvin, drove out in his old, piece-of-shit Cadillac. California was supposed to be my dream-come-true. Then Melvin gets his ass into crack, and then starts dealin', and next thing I know, he's going off to prison. I'm on the street. Can't get no work, not no way. Things been goin' downhill."

"How old are you?" Johnson asked.

"28."

My God, Sager thought, 'about my age.' Up close she looked about 50.

"What would you say if I could get you back to Mobile?" Johnson asked.

"This ain't no Wizard of Oz and magic balloon ride."

Johnson looked her straight in the eye. "Do you do drugs?"

"Maybe a little, but not much. Don't got no money for it anyway."

Johnson pulled a cluster of $20 bills from his wallet. "This is to get you back to Mobile," he started, and handed the woman $300. "Bus fare."

"Is this some kinda joke?"

"No joke. Now here's $100. For food."

"$100 for food?" She gazed at the bills.

"And another $200 to get some fresh clothes at Goodwill."

She grabbed the bills. $600. More money than she could imagine.

Johnson wasn't done. He turned to Klondike, shocked at the unexpected sight of Sager, but gathered himself to speak again to the woman.

"My friend here, this big fella, is going to make sure that you eat, get some clothes, and get your bus ticket to Mobile, OK?"

The woman was guarded and dubious. "What do I have to do for him?"

"Relax, relax," Johnson said, consciously easing his

shoulders, trying to soothe her. "Just consider the big fella your guardian angel, to make sure nobody on the street tries to rip you off. He'll make sure you get on that bus to Mobile."

Klondike turned to Sager. "See, man. See what's happening here?"

Sager was beyond stunned.

Klondike hit the auto-dial on his cell phone for Yellow Cab, and when he heard the computer voice, hit the button to order a cab. The GPS in the telephone automatically provided his location to dispatch, and a cab was on its way.

Johnson, dressed like a bum, turned to confront Sager, dressed like a homicide inspector.

"This is our little secret, OK, detective? I don't want the press to know about this. I don't want this getting on TV. I don't want to read about this in People magazine or anywhere else."

"Do you do this often?"

"Every couple of months. A lot of people are down on their luck. They have nothing."

"Don't a lot of them just want money for booze and drugs?"

"What you find, more than anything, is most of these people just want to go home. I buy more bus tickets than anything."

Sager was riveted. "How much do you give out?"

"About $10,000 a year, different spots in San Francisco, San Jose. Not that much, but it makes me feel good all over. I have Klondike with me for security and make sure the people get fed, get some clean clothes, even second-hand, and get them on a bus headed for home."

Johnson waved at the scenario.

"I'm discreet about it. I don't go to the Western Addition, 6th and Mission, Bayview and Hunter's Point out by Candlestick, or to west Oakland or east San Jose, Richmond. A few other spots. Too damn dangerous."

Johnson explained: "I show up, get a few people on their feet, and they're gone, on the bus and not around to tell anybody about it."

Then Johnson waved a hand. "If Stephen Griffin hadn't given me my break, I could be right here, on this corner, playing my guitar with the case open, hoping you would throw in a quarter. Who knows? Luck of the draw?"

Korg's cell phone chimed The Bitch Is Back. He knew who that was.

"Korg," answered the inspector, urgency in his voice. It must be about his order for the cadaver dogs.

"You still around, or are you out on your boat?" It sounded like Pritchett's fangs were out.

"I'm not on any boat. I'm on my case. In fact, right now I'm driving in to headquarters."

"Good. Get your ass in my office as soon as you walk in." Click.

Pritchett wore a trimmed suit, brown with light lines, set off by a brown silk scarf. Her brown steel eyes harpooned everything she chanced to gaze upon.

"How goes the case?"

"Good, good. Several things we're moving on."

Pritchett swiveled her leather chair and beamed. Korg made a mental note. This occurred about as often as a press conference.

"No body?"

"No body."

"No murder weapon?"

"No murder weapon."

"Lot of suspects?"

"Five suspects."

"No crime scene?"

"No crime scene."

"Any forensics or physical evidence tying anybody to a violent crime?"

Korg dropped his head. "No."

"Do you know where the murder took place?"

"No." Korg's voice had softened.

Pritchett swiveled again, adjusted a pile of neatly stacked papers on a corner of her polished desk, and then smiled again. That made it twice, Korg noted. Two smiles by Pritchett at Korg in a day was a record on the Pritchett Smile Meter. Having occurred in the same meeting, this sent the PSM into the red zone. This was beyond Sager's record of 1.5 smiles in 10 hours.

"Well, Kris, I know this case hasn't been easy, but I appreciate how far you've taken it, especially the tip to White Collar."

Kris? Korg couldn't remember Pritchett ever calling him Kris.

"I know your last day is tomorrow, and in light of that, I've decided to let you have the rest of the week off. Go fishing.

Enjoy your boat. Enjoy your retirement. Congratulations. Your outstanding career as a homicide inspector is over. I'm proud of the way you chose to go out. As of this moment, you are free. Enjoy yourself. Congratulations."

Korg sat there, his arms crossed, silent.

"What's wrong, Korg?"

"I think I can break this case," Korg answered. "I could break it this afternoon, maybe tomorrow."

Pritchett rolled her head in a mock gaze around the room. "What?"

"I want to bring a few more people in for lie-detector tests."

"Forget it. It's over. You're out. Retired. Enjoy it."

"No!" Korg howled, half shouting. "I've got until Friday to nail this case."

Pritchett leaned back in her chair, frustrated.

"Last night, you say you want to go fishing, I say go to work. Today I say go fishing and you say you want to go to work."

They looked at each other, neither eager to speak next.

Pritchett stood up, circled her desk and gazed out of her office window.

"What have you got?"

"A lot of little stuff," Korg said. "Things that don't make sense. But I can clear this up. Nail this case. I feel like I'm close."

Pritchett didn't answer. So with a bob of the head, Korg turned and left. He felt dizzy.

Overwhelmed by a matrix of emotion, Korg returned to his base, his giant desk in the small cubicle, his inner sanctum.

He sat down, not sure what to do next. Wendy Au, the mail clerk, sailed past behind him with a bin of the latest. She stopped and tossed an envelope on Korg's desk.

"This was on top of today's incoming," she said, explaining why she didn't bother taking it to the mail files with the rest.

Without much thought, Korg picked it up. The envelope was thin and very light, he noticed. He opened it and pulled out a single, folded sheet. He opened it and read it carefully:

You only get so much rope.

This made twice. Somebody was taunting him. Who? Why?

Who could be so twisted?

He swept out the door in hopes of the chance to face him.

He sat in his car, took a deep breath. Time was running out.

Korg, at a loss, texted Sager: "Know anything about MaryLou?"

27

KORG TURNED THE key in his county-issue Ford, but before he could move, his phone stopped him cold. He answered with a snarl.

"Yeah?"

It was Anders from SFPD Homicide. "My, are we not happy today?"

"Politicians," Korg said. "They don't understand."

Anders snorted. "Like anybody understands you?"

"You kinda do, right?" Korg suggested.

"I will never understand how you eat anchovies on pizzas," Anders said. "There are a few other things, too."

"A few? Well, that's not too bad." And then, cutting to the chase: "How'd my soon-to-be replacement do?"

"The kid?" Anders responded. "Very serious, that young man. 'Course, he just gunned down a couple of guys the other day, so I guess I'd be serious, too. Why's he working anyway? Shouldn't he be out on leave?"

"He knows I only have to tomorrow to figure this thing out. Plus he's better off keeping busy. Hell, he actually sounded happy when I talked to him this morning."

Anders put the conversation on track. "Well, he didn't ask something obvious, so I want to pass it along."

"You found something?"

"More like what we didn't find."

"My favorite."

Korg could hear some papers rustling as Anders opened his case file.

"Here it is," Anders started. "Up on the arcade, where the kid was shot, we didn't find any shell casings."

To Korg, that meant the murder weapon was a revolver, or the shooter took the time to hunt down the ejected casings from an autoloader and pick them up, a rare event in the hyper-stressed moment of a murder.

"Any idea of the caliber?" Korg asked.

"Small," Anders said. "The autopsy found two small holes in Spoog's back, real small like from a .22, .38 or .357, but we'd bet on the .38, since the bullet didn't go through but did a fair amount of internal damage." Korg knew, of course, that .38 and .357 cartridges use the same diameter bullets.

"You know why I'm giving you this, right?" Anders asked.

"If your shooter is my shooter, we're looking for the same gun, probably a small caliber revolver."

"I trained you well," Anders said with a snigger. After a pause, he added, "Actually, I had another reason for calling."

Korg waited.

"Did Sager really figure out what the 2424 meant? That sounded like a Korg to me."

"He's a bright young man, Inspector Anders. Gotta go. Got a gun to track down."

Intuition and years of friendship told Anders that Korg knew more than he was telling. "Do you know where to look? Or is this another famous Korg fishing expedition?"

"My man Sager is already on it."

Korg's mood had been lightened a bit by the call from his old friend. He clicked on his cell phone; it showed three calls during his meeting with Pritchett: Bonnie Griffin, Emma, and Sager. Hoping for karmic bonus points, he punched 1 on his auto dial. Emma answered mid-point of the second ring.

"Lunch at Café Viola," Emma said with a burst, half-request, half-order. But the excitement and kindness in her voice was unmistakable.

"You sound like you have something to tell me."

"I do," she said. "I was poking around Griffin's computer, like you asked me to, and found some hidden goodies. How about 1?"

"Might be a tad later, got something to do first. I'm on my way to Johnson's for a surprise visit."

Emma cautioned him. "Be careful with these guys, honey. Before you go over there, you might want to hear what I have to tell you."

"Lunch, sweetheart."

Korg clicked on his Bluetooth for hands-free dialing, and with voice command, rang up Sager, and intercepted him driving south on the 280 near San Bruno.

"Go to Clearwater's," Korg ordered. "You're looking for a small caliber revolver, probably a .38, something easy to conceal, like a Smith & Wesson P model, but maybe even a .357 or .22."

"You get a tip?" Sager asked.

"Yes. No. Maybe. You know, just doing detective work."

"You got a search warrant for me?"

"Don't have one of those either. No time. But you know that Clearwater is not going to be there."

Korg wasn't done.

"And check out all the Super Shuttles from the airport. Bring all your pictures for the drivers. We know that somebody drove Griffin's Corvette to Long Term Parking at San Francisco Airport. We can put a time on it from the parking ticket. If they acted alone, they had to get a ride out of there."

"And if they didn't act alone," Sager filled in, "somebody could have just picked them up. So two people could be involved."

"Right," Korg answered with a laugh. "What two people come to mind?"

"You already know that."

After taking in the moment, Korg added: "So while you're at it, check everybody's credit cards and see if anybody has a parking charge from the airport. And if you want, you're invited to a late lunch at Viola with my wife and Roper."

"Thanks."

"Inspector Sager, are you feeling OK? You actually sound happy.

"I am. Something good finally happened."

"Tell me about it at lunch, if you can make it."

SAGER POWERED SOUTH on the 280, weaving through a line of slower cars as if on a slalom course. His phone chimed, and on the cell phone display, he read "Bonnie Griffin." He was reluctant to answer; he didn't have time to hear War & Peace, Volume II.

But she was special, he realized, so he slipped on his earpiece and clicked it. "Hi there."

She was quick to answer, quicker to talk. "That was great, you were great, honey. But get this: I found something at Stephen's, something real important."

This was the first time Bonnie had called him "Honey." She was solidifying last night's gains. He smiled. She actually liked him, he was discovering, just the way he was.

Yet it was difficult for Sager to believe that Bonnie Griffin, of all people, had found something that he, Korg, Roper and Forensics had somehow overlooked at Griffin's beach house.

"What is it?"

"You have to see for yourself. I guarantee it will be worth your time."

That brought Sager to life. "Where are you?"

"I'm here in Miramar right now," Bonnie answered. "I'll wait for you."

Sager looked at his watch. He couldn't afford the time to go sideways on a straight-ahead investigation. But who knows? Maybe she had the missing piece.

"OK, I'll get there as fast as I can."

SAGER WAS EXASPERATED by the time he reached Griffin's Miramar beach house. He should have stalled her, especially with Korg's voice still ringing in his ears.

As he drove up to the beach house, he spotted Bonnie, leaning against her car, parked out front. She was staring up the road for the first sign of the inspector.

To his surprise, Bonnie was silent, melancholy. Her eyes were red, the centers moist.

"I got here as fast as I could," Sager started. "Show the way."

Instead she hugged him. A full-on body hug where she melded herself to the young detective.

Without a word, a first, Bonnie walked into the beach house. At the foyer, she pointed at a corner. Unopened mail was piled here along with a triangular box about 31/2 feet long.

This was nothing new. "What?" Sager asked.

Bonnie, silent and sullen, picked up the box and held it out.

Sager analyzed the return address: MG Golf. Apparently the box contained a specialized golf club that Griffin had ordered.

He scrutinized it further. Bonnie then pointed to the UPS label: The UPS driver had filled out the delivery form that the package had been dropped off on Thursday, September 26th.

Bonnie looked up at the inspector. Tears emerged from the corner of each eye and then slid down her cheek. Her heart was breaking. Sager reached over with his right arm. She relented in full sob.

They both knew what this meant.

If UPS had delivered a package on Thursday the 26th, a package that had been brought inside, it meant somebody had been here that day.

"If Stephen was here, he would have opened this

package for sure," Bonnie gurgled, her voice choked and broken. "He would have wanted to feel that golf club in his hands as soon as he got it. That's how he was."

Yet somebody had brought the package inside, maybe even signed for it with UPS.

That was the same day that somebody had changed the password for Expedia.com and booked a flight to Las Vegas — a flight that Sager now knew was taken by Spoogs, aka, Stevie Griffith.

"I'm sorry," Sager said, his soft heart leaking through the armor shield.

"I guess he's really gone," Bonnie said. "I guess I have to face that now."

Sager reached for her once again and felt her mesh with him, while her tears dripped on his cheeks.

When Sager arrived at Redwood Terrace outside of La Honda, the towering conifers were still dripping from the morning's bath of coastal fog. He pulled into Clearwater's meager carport, brown paint peeling off its beams, and eyed the shack. It was a small place with old plywood siding, and Sager could see that it too had the same decrepit peeling brown paint. Crooked steps at the entryway led to a small deck where a railing appeared likely to topple if a sparrow landed on it.

Nobody around, Sager noted. No neighbors. No barking dogs. It appeared to be all his. He hustled around the back. After all, he knew where Clearwater was, and it wasn't here.

As Sager pushed up a creaky bedroom window, he stopped with a cringe.

Maybe Pritchett was right. Korg was corrupting him. Up to now in his career, he'd done everything by the book. Whether anybody was watching or not, he'd followed protocol. That was one reason Pritchett fast-tracked him into Homicide, because she knew — right? — that Sager would never violate the black-white line of right and wrong faced by every cop.

As Sager slipped through the window into Clearwater's bedroom, he felt a strange sensation, light-headed and a bit woozy. His heart thumped, as if he were in a movie playing fast-forward where events proceeded too quickly to digest. So this is how a burglar feels. And in the next thought, he envisioned his plight if he were caught — a young, wiry and ferocious-looking black man caught sneaking into a rock star's home. The locals might string him up.

The shades were already drawn, so there was an added degree of secrecy. He quickly surveyed the residence. It was so small, 1,200 square feet, tops, with a living room, kitchen, bedroom and small mudroom. The smell of mold permeated every room. Kitchen? Nothing there. Living room? Everything out in the open. A TV, three guitars propped up in stands, beat-up sofa and comfort chair. That was it. Back to the bedroom. Pants, shirts and socks strewn around the floor. The bed was unmade, with an open sleeping bag strewn across the top. Sager quickly went to the closet.

Behind a jacket, leaned against a corner, he found a shotgun, a Mossberg .12 gauge pump shotgun, and a pioneer-style muzzleloader. Sager searched the top shelf and, in a shoebox, found several boxes of ammunition. He sat on a corner of the bed to inspect its contents:

Three boxes of shotgun shells, a small yellow plastic box of .50-caliber round balls, and beneath that, a small, slim box.

He grabbed the box, held it up to the light and read the end cap: .38, 125 grain, hollow point. So Storm Clearwater owned a .38, after all, here was the ammo. Sager opened the box. Inside, about half of the 20 cartridges were gone.

Inspired, Sager shrugged off the fact that this was an illegal search and began to scour the place. Under the mattress. In the cupboard. In the dresser drawers. Under the sink in the bathroom. As Sager checked under the sofa cushion in the small living room, he noticed again the guitars propped up in floor stands. One of them was a vintage acoustic Gibson 12-string. He practically leapt to it. When he picked up the guitar, he expected to hear a rattle inside its hollow body, but instead, it was empty.

Disappointed as he set it down, he admired Clearwater's two adjacent electric guitars. One was a gorgeous Telecaster with a body covered in hand-tooled leather, black with a white floral pattern. Next to that was a Stratocaster, black with a white pickguard. Sager laughed. Clearwater probably had more money tied up in these three guitars than in everything else in the house put together.

Sager picked up the Telecaster and noticed how good it felt in his hands. Perfect balance, polished neck. This was probably Clearwater's favorite, Sager figured, following the cord to the Fender amplifier. Sager gently placed the Telecaster back in its stand, and, with the sleeve of his jacket, wiped his prints off the neck.

He turned to the amplifier against the wall, and

turned it so he could see behind it. Inside, he saw a pair of speakers, wires and a mass of tubes and circuitry. With his right hand, he reached inside, half expecting his fingers to get snapped by a mousetrap.

Instead, he touched a textured, fabric container of some kind, about the size of his hand, with a solid, weighted feel to it. As he lifted it out of the back of the amplifier, he felt the hard handle in his palm.

Sager looked down and saw a small revolver in a lightweight holster. The handle was knurled soft plastic, the kind from which you can't lift fingerprints. He placed his left thumb and forefinger on each side of the knurled handle and pulled the pistol from its small holster. On its right side, the gun was stamped "S&W" on its stock, "Airweight" lasered in script above the trigger, and the name "Smith & Wesson" on its 1-inch barrel. Sager turned the weapon over and repeated the survey. On its tiny barrel, the gun was stamped ".38 S&W SPL P."

A firearms guru, Sager knew this model well. It was a high-quality hammerless .38 that weighed only 14 ounces. The gun was designed so it could fire when concealed, such as from inside a pocket. With no exposed hammer, there was no chance it would cock and fire by accident. This was the perfect concealed weapon.

He put the gun back in its sheath, tucked it back in the corner of the amplifier, and carefully shoved the amplifier back against the wall.

They would be waiting in Redwood City.

28

SAGER WAS THE last to arrive. He hustled through the front door, past the dining area and the small bar, en route to the patio and its outdoor seating. In a corner, at a table under an umbrella shade, he found Korg, Emma and Roper, all nibbling on garlic bread. A folder, closed but stuffed with documents, sat in front of Emma. For years, this small restaurant was where Roper held court with Korg and other inspectors and deputy DAs.

"The young superstar arrives," Roper said.

Korg put his hand on his wife's shoulder and returned her gaze.

Sager noted, the two had said their "I love yous" without a word being spoken. He'd never known what that felt like. For a moment, he felt a pang for Bonnie Griffin. He still felt her imprint from the hug they had shared at Miramar.

"How long does it take," Sager asked Emma, "to have that, the way you guys connect. How long does it take to really know somebody?"

Emma sipped her ice tea and then eyed the

young inspector. "It takes about ten years to really know somebody."

"Really?"

"That's right," interjected Korg. "Ten years. Then you really know them."

"Or kill them," Emma added.

The setting was the courtyard of Café Viola, a little Italian place on Broadway, within walking distance of county headquarters in downtown Redwood City. Viola's interior was a near duplicate of the little New York restaurant where a young Michael Corleone made his first kills in the movie *The Godfather.*

Sager noted this, then looked at Korg and said, "Whatever you do, don't tell me the veal is the best in the city."

And whatever you do," Korg answered, "Don't tell me you need to go to the bathroom."

"Actually, I do need to go to the bathroom."

Korg took a long drink, glad to be away from the center of attention. Since last Saturday, he'd had virtually no down time and had been working with a major sleep deficit.

Roper took over. "Are you close?"

"I think we've nailed Johnson and Goldberg," Korg said.

Sager almost choked on his ice tea. He'd figured on Clearwater or Klondike, maybe in tandem with the blond, MaryLou.

Roper leaned forward, waiting to hear more.

KORG ENJOYED THE audience.

"The short version is that Johnson, Goldberg and the

late Mr. Griffin devised a scheme to ship millions in cash earnings out of the country without paying taxes on it," Korg explained. "They'd bring the money back in and launder it through real estate deals."

Emma opened her folder and brought out a sheet of paper. "This is a cash flow chart," she explained.

She'd placed the name Jesse James Johnson twice in square boxes, both on top and on the bottom of the chart. With a red-tipped felt marking pen, she had drawn a series of boxes connected with lines, with a name in each box. Some boxes were corporations, some were offshore bank accounts.

"Emma is the smartest person I know and a genius at real estate," Korg said, "so I asked her to take a look at the files."

"For the record," Roper asked, "even smarter than you?"

"Like way smarter," Korg said. "I married up. But you already know that."

Sager felt a sudden rise of appreciation for Korg and the way he honored his wife. In this week, he'd learned that Korg was nowhere the gasbag that Pritchett had characterized. Then he thought of Griffin and the money scam. That must have been the motive for murder. That's why Korg called this lunch meeting, to get Roper, the assistant D.A., to move on it.

Roper sat with his hands clasped on the table, absorbing every word, ready to hear more.

"Each of these guys, Griffin, Goldberg and Johnson, has a key role, best as I can figure," Korg said. He glanced at Emma and she took over.

"This morning," Emma explained, "I was going

through Griffin's computer files and I found that he had set up a system to get large cash advances from show promoters. They would under-report by more than half the actual income from concerts. They would also clear huge amounts of money by the cash sale of band swag."

"That means the promoters are up for indictment, too," Roper said. "Conspiracy and tax evasion."

Emma glowed. "That's not even the half of it." After a nibble of garlic bread, she held up the piece of paper on which she had diagrammed the cash flow chart.

"Johnson would mix the cash from advances with additional cash from the concessions sales at concerts," she explained. "They would smuggle the cash out of the country and into offshore bank accounts."

Emma pointed to the cash-flow chart.

"Goldberg set up the offshore accounts and shell corporations in Nevada. The shell corporations are fronts for Johnson. They don't actually create products or do anything. The shell corporations exist simply as containers to transfer money. You establish them in Nevada because no state income taxes are charged there."

Korg made a point.

"These shell corporations in Nevada are the key. Without their names, nobody can trace how the funds are moved."

"How did you ever get all this?" Sager asked. "Don't investigations like this usually take the feds a couple of years?"

"It's all in Griffin's computer," Emma said. "All the puzzle pieces are right there. The key is knowing the names of the shell corportions. Without those, you can't trace the cash. Given all the details like this on a silver platter, any banker, CPA or real estate broker who is good with money could figure it out."

Roper grinned at his old buddy. "This will go straight to the U.S Attorney's office, FBI and IRS," Roper said. "Roberta Pritchett will love you."

"I'm already taken," Korg said. "But it will give her an excuse to have a TV press conference."

Roper shook his head at his old buddy. "You hear stories about this kind of fraud, but you never think it's going on right in your backyard," Roper said. "It's true that the hard part in breaking up these rings is getting the names of the shell corporations. There are so many phony Nevada corporations that you'd need a tip with the names and account numbers to prove how the money is being passed. Otherwise, the money vanishes into an abyss. To the IRS, it's as if it never existed."

Korg laughed and wiped his mouth with a napkin.

Emma took over again.

"The way it worked is that the money was transferred from corporation to corporation until it eventually ended up in an offshore account. That part is easy to pull off."

She paused. "I know I'm giving you the simplified version, but bear with me."

After a sip of her iced tea, she continued. "The difficult part is not getting the money out of the country," she said. "The tough part is getting it back in and spending it without paying taxes on it."

"You have to launder it back in," Roper said. "That's usually how the FBI nails 'em."

"Right," Korg said. "All that money sitting in the Bahamas was dirty. But as far as the IRS knew, it didn't exist. Johnson had to figure out a way to get it back in, undetected and untaxed. Go ahead, Emma, explain it."

Emma pointed again to the cash flow chart.

"Johnson orchestrated a real estate scheme using the shell corporations to bring the money into the country."

"The corporations again?" Sager asked.

"Right," she answered.

Roper jumped back in. "There are few better ways to launder money than through high-dollar real estate deals. But damn hard to prove."

Emma detailed it.

"Using the corporations, Johnson and Goldberg would buy luxury houses and plow in renovation money that they wired in from cash stashed in the offshore accounts. Then they would sell the house to a valid buyer. Johnson just pulled one off the other day for $3.7 million. There appears to be no profit, so hence, no capital gains taxes. The money from the sale goes into his pocket, via a shell corporation, to spend any way he pleases."

Korg, content to listen up to now, broke his silence. "That explains how Johnson, even with his CD sales and royalties in the tank, just bought an Enzo Ferrari for about $800,000."

"That's how the guy buys all kinds of stuff," Emma countered. "It was set up so he'd get most of the money back for his personal use, clean from being laundered in the real estate deals. He does it over and over."

Korg rapped the table twice.

"The final result is a continual stream of money, millions of dollars, to spend any way he wishes. Pays some taxes to make his business look legitimate to the IRS. Proceeds from real estate ventures are almost never questioned, especially not with someone of his prominence. Someone who is supposed to be loaded."

Roper laughed and turned to Sager. "At SFPD, we called Korg 'The Bulldog' because of the way he'd grab onto the most complex cases and not let go."

Emma provided the final synopsis of the operation. "They've laundered about $175 million through real estate purchases, renovations and sales, all of it through the shell corporations," she said. "The music business is like a Trojan Horse for him. Concerts provide millions in seed money. The big laundered profits come from these real estate deals. He's lucky that one of the few places in America where real estate hasn't crashed is here on the Peninsula, in Woodside, Portola Valley and Hillsborough."

She shook her head in a moment of derision.

"The money he makes from CD and electronic sales is hardly a factor. His albums are more like promotional tools to get people to the concerts."

Lunch was served. Korg plowed into a crisp Caesar. Roper raised a single finger.

"Can I ask a question?"

"Go."

"How can you eat those anchovies? Don't they taste like fish bait?"

"They are fish bait," Korg answered with a grin.

Emma nudged Sager in the biceps with a gentle elbow. "He's always been like this. Whatever you do, do not laugh or tell him he's funny."

"Then he gets out of control," Roper affirmed.

Sager appeared perplexed.

"I have a question of my own."

"Go."

"What about Griffin's murder? That's what I thought this lunch was about."

"Maybe it is," Korg explained.

"May I suggest," Sager continued, "we request a search warrant for Clearwater's cabin. I've got a very reliable tip that he's got the perfect concealed weapon, a hammerless Smith & Wesson .38, hidden in the back of an amplifier cabinet."

"Are you saying that could be the murder weapon?" Roper asked.

"Absolutely."

"How do you know Griffin was shot?"

Sager did not pause for the explanation.

"We don't. But we know for a fact that this kid, Stevie Griffith used Stephen Griffin's ticket to Las Vegas. We also know that Stevie Griffith, the one person who could testify as to who set him up with that ticket, was shot in the back at the arcade before the concert at AT&T Park in San Francisco."

"SFPD has the slug," Sager continued. "We could match it up."

Roper listened in silence, staring at his ravioli.

Korg cut in.

"It's a reasonable assertion that the perp who shot the kid also shot Griffin with the same gun."

Roper eyed Korg. "Man, this sounds like you. 'A reasonable assertion.' You don't even have a crime scene. Have you talked to San Francisco Homicide? Any ballistics on the gun in that San Francisco shooting?"

"Oh yeah, we've working with Anders and I've got the report. They didn't find a single shell casing on the arcade," Korg answered.

"No shell casings," Sager affirmed. "This makes it likely the firearm had to be a revolver, not an automatic, which ejects the casings. According to this very reliable tip we got, Clearwater's gun is a revolver. It fits."

Roper relented. "OK, young man, let's get that gun in our possession." He nodded at Korg. "I'll get moving on the paperwork to make it happen."

Sager, mollified, provided a further explanation.

"For my money, this case is not so complicated. It starts with a crime of rage and then a skilled cover-up. Clearwater's personality's a fit. He's got flash-point anger, is anti-social, with genius talent. Most murders are simple, like this. Then it gets complicated when they try to cover it up."

The group munched as Sager made his case. Korg was entertained to hear the young inspector talk so freely.

"It starts for Clearwater when the anger builds over months, knowing he created the sound that was making Johnson and Griffin millions, and yet he was getting nothing out of it. He admits that. He goes nuts when Griffin blocks him from his own label deal. He said so himself. A witness puts him on the scene at Griffin's beach house on the night Griffin disappeared. Clearwater lies to us when first interviewed, and keeps lying during the polygraph, and then finally admits he was there when we put the handcuffs on last night."

Sager scanned the trio, looking for a response. With

none forthcoming, he kept on.

"To get vengeance, he kills Griffin and hides the body. He pulls off the cover-up, sets up Spoogs to make it look like a missing person case, and then flies to New York. Then, at AT&T, to cover the only loose end, he does Spoogs, the one guy who could finger him, and the crime is complete."

"Nice theory," Roper noted.

"It makes sense."

"You could get the Grand Jury to indict, Murder One, easy."

Korg looked at Sager. "Did something good suddenly happen to you? Never seen you so effusive."

"Well, yes."

"It's a girl," Emma said. "All the signs."

"Good," Korg said. "Good. You deserve some good. You've had a tough week. As for getting the Grand Jury to indict, well, you might as well order a ham sandwich for Roper here. The key is, could our reputable Deputy District Attorney Roper convince a jury to convict?"

"All of it is circumstantial, and it could be argued, coincidental," Roper said.

"Not if the forensics on the slug match up," Sager countered.

Emma was a bit hesitant to enter the discussion.

"We're among friends, right?" she asked. "Can I make a suggestion?"

"You usually end up being right," Korg said.

"Check that," Roper acknowledged. "She's always right."

"I like the blackmail theory better," she said. "Griffin tries to leverage more money out of Johnson.

Johnson explodes. The night before leaving for New York, he has Klondike make Griffin disappear. Then he orchestrates the cover-up. Then at AT&T, they finish the job with Spoogs. Somewhere along the way, that road manager, Deego DeGenaro, who is also missing, somehow gets mixed up in this and he disappears, too."

She paused for effect.

"If Johnson is clever enough to orchestrate this money scam, he's got the mind to scheme the cover-up."

Korg took it in with a raised left eyebrow. "I'll take it under consideration, sweetheart."

Roper held court. "You've got a hell of a problem with no body, no crime scene, no murder weapon."

"Pritchett already explained that rather clearly to me."

"Sorry about that. Know that's a sore spot."

Sager interrupted.

"Make this simple. Get Clearwater's .38. Match up ballistics with the slug they took out of Spoogs. End of story."

Roper moved to part lunch on an upbeat note.

"Oh, we'll get all these guys. We'll work with the U.S Attorney's office. With Griffin's computer in hand, the FBI will do the groundwork. The U.S. Attorney will convene the federal grand jury, make the case, and they'll indict. Tax evasion. Conspiracy. Money laundering. Probably wire fraud. Maybe in a few years, they'll actually make the case."

"That's not what I care about," Korg said.

"The rest," Roper said as he stood to leave, "is up to

you, old friend," and then with a kind wave at Sager and Emma, "and maybe your partners."

"Time is short," Korg said to Sager. "You've got to go back to SFO."

"At the airport, go to the pick-up area for the Super Shuttles. Show the drivers all of our pictures. Somebody drove Stephen Griffin's Corvette to long term parking. To get back home or to their own vehicle, they likely took a Super Shuttle."

"Why not a taxi?"

"Taxi drivers remember their rides. No, it would be a Super Shuttle all right. That will be a lot easier to check than the taxi guys."

Sager was still unconvinced. "What if two people were involved? One drives Griffin's Corvette, the other follows, then picks up the driver and they're outta there."

"Remember, they all flew off to New York in the early afternoon. They'd need time to pull it off. That's why you trace everybody's credit cards and correlate the parking receipts. Check the times when they logged in to SFO on Thursday, September 26th. That's when the cover-up occurred."

"Got it," Sager said. He was learning to admire Korg's ability to distill complex thought. Pritchett knew nothing of this skill.

Then another thought crossed Sager's mind. "Guess what I found with Bonnie over at Griffin's beach house?"

"Oh, it's Bonnie now," Emma said. She never missed a thing.

Korg raised a hand. "Let me guess. Your zipper?"

Sager deflected the remark.

"A UPS package was delivered and placed inside Johnson's beach house on the morning of the 26th," Sager detailed. "It was not opened. The package was a special golf club of some kind. Bonnie said that her brother would have opened something so special to him immediately."

"That means somebody was there Thursday morning and placed the package inside the house. We have a timeline. The murder took place some time Wednesday evening. The cover-up, the next morning."

"That's right," Korg agreed. "Because there would not have been time to work the cover-up and still make the flight out of San Francisco International by early afternoon."

Emma put a gentle arm around her husband's shoulder. She prayed he would solve the case. The IRS scam was a gimme, she knew, delivered on a platter by the files in Griffin's computer, supported by the accidental discovery of financial documents at Johnson's, and the real estate records at the county assessor's office. The homicide, on the other hand, was his private torment. He'd be disgusted in the short term and devastated in the long-term if Pritchett forced him out before nailing the killer, she knew.

"I'm off straight to Johnson's," Korg announced. "Confront him with the tax stuff. See if he cracks on Griffin."

"Wouldn't it follow protocol to bring him into the office?" Sager said. "Maybe wire him to the bullshit detector?"

"He's too big. Pritchett would smell it a mile away. She'd never allow it. No, I don't want her anywhere close to being involved. And you sir, are not supposed to be working or anywhere close to headquarters."

"Why don't you enjoy some downtime with your Bonnie?" Emma asked.

"Is it that obvious?" Sager asked.

"Duh," Korg answered. "Why don't you make yourself useful as well as ornamental. After you hit SFO, how about you get the lowdown on that blond, MaryLou Dietz?"

"How much you want on her?"

"Everything you can get."

29

When Korg arrived at Johnson's, he found Lorelei and Landru chatting lightly in front of the Sound Factory, waiting for the rest of the crew. They looked at him as if he were, well, a homicide inspector.

"How's your friend doing?" Korg asked, trying to lighten the moment.

"You should know," Lorelei responded, the sweet lilt gone from her voice. "Last we saw, Storm Clearwater was with you, right? With handcuffs on?"

To appear as affable as possible, Korg tried to soften his face and warm his voice. "No, I mean the poor guy who got shot at the Oasis."

"That's Jeffrey Bridges, my best friend," Landru said. "He's not doing too well. In and out of it. But we're praying for him. Thanks for asking."

Lorelei ran her left hand through her silken black hair. "What's up with Storm Clearwater?"

Before Korg could answer, they both turned at the sound of the entrance gate opening. A vintage Daytona Spyder Ferrari, deep blue and polished, rumbled in and stopped nearby.

Even the affable Landru bit his lower lip. "There's a point where this becomes ridiculous," he said. "What is this, a new car for Thursdays?"

Jesse James Johnson did not emerge from the vehicle. The car door swung open and Clearwater stepped out, a trifle of a smile on his face, trying to appear as if he had driven up in a Ferrari countless times.

"What is this?" hooted Landru. "Clearwater! Give me a break! How'd you swing this?"

Lorelei chimed right in. "What about last night? Last we saw you were in handcuffs."

Clearwater looked at Korg and broke into a Felix-The-Cat grin. "The inspector here just wanted to throw a little scare into me and then talk a little," Clearwater said with a laugh. "So we did that."

Landru pointed at the Ferrari. "What about that?"

"Got my settlement money from the insurance company for the motorcycle accident, over the guy that left-turned me. It made a nice down payment. These old ones don't cost as much as you might think. Plus, I think good times are ahead."

Lorelei appeared about as warm as the South Pole.

A minute later, as Landru examined the interior of Clearwater's new ride, yet another vintage Ferrari Daytona Spyder roared up, this one jet black, glimmering under bright sun. Again, they turned to greet Johnson. Instead, Rock Winston appeared. The car was a loaner from Johnson, the one Johnson often provided to executives making trips to the Bay Area. "Give me 10 minutes with Johnson, then we're on," Winston said, bypassing a greeting.

Clearwater was sizing up Winston when he felt

a feather-light stroke across his shoulder and side. It made him tingle. Only one person had ever touched him like that.

"Well, at least I like the color," Lorelei said, the warmth back in her voice. "But I must say it's going to take awhile to get used to. You're more a pick-up truck-and-motorcycle kind of guy."

"It's the color of your eyes," he said. "Did you notice?"

She looked down and shook her head. "What am I gonna do with you?" Then with a sideways glance, shot him a pirate smile.

He eyed her. There was something there. He felt it. Something in the air between them.

Winston stomped inside, scarcely acknowledged Korg's presence, and then took charge. All stood, as if a judge had entered Superior Court. Winston, already briefed by Johnson on Clearwater's release, shook hands with the guitarist and bandleader.

"Glad to see you seem to have sorted out your personal issues," Winston said. He then turned to Lorelei, shook her hand lightly in a more formal greeting, and bowed his head a few inches.

The five band mates headed in to the meeting room.

"Mind if I tag along?" Korg asked.

There was no response and he sidled in and took a seat to the side.

Clearwater and Lorelei sat next to each other, both quizzical and intrigued at the possibilities.

"I just met with Johnson and he blessed the deal," Winston started, "so you're on your way." He paused to enjoy the transfixed gazes of the band mates in front of him. "I'll mention a few details and then be open to questions."

Korg, too, was fixated on every word. Truth was, back in the day, he too wanted to be a rock-and-roller. Now he was seeing how it worked. At the same time, he was searching for that one nugget clue that could break his case.

Winston waved his hand in the air. "I'll develop a contract with Henry Goldberg, your lawyer."

Clearwater beamed, yet Lorelei frowned.

"Our lawyer?" she said. "I didn't know he was our lawyer."

Clearwater pulled out a notebook and started jotting. Lorelei smiled, encouraged that the bandleader was taking notes.

Winston again took over. "Jesse is loaning his lawyer to you, to get you off on the right foot. You're lucky to have him."

Lorelei made a mental note. After all, she had signed nothing with Goldberg about personal representation. She had signed only the standard 13-week personal services contract to work for Jesse James Johnson.

Winston again addressed the band.

"A lot of bands spend a lot of time dickering with labels over percentages," Winston said. "This is usually an ego thing, not a money thing. That is not where the focus should be. The focus should be on creating music that we can market effectively to the radio slot, and then you guys get out on the road, play the songs on the album and promote the hell out of it. The fast money for the artist is in the live show. If you can integrate a tour with the rollout of a new album, hit it big, then you can make millions. That's how Johnson has done it, with the live shows. That's what we want for you."

Winston then shifted gears.

"If you keep the recording costs down, you have a better chance of making some money on the CD and electronic sales," Winston said. "If you write your own songs, you can make money right out of the gate with the release. If you have a hit, then you can get rich."

Lorelei waved a hand at Winston. "What kind of royalty points for the band are we talking?"

Winston noted that many legends in the business were paid royalty rates of 10 and 12 percent. "But we are willing to offer 14 percent, which I really had to fight for with our Board. But we want to provide the incentive for you to do your best work."

Lorelei countered.

"I heard Shania Twain got 40 percent for a deal at Mercury."

Winston responded to her challenge.

"That's true. In the history of the music business, there's never been a deal like that." He paused to assess Lorelei. "The music companies deal in quarterly reports. Mercury was having a down quarter, and was looking for a fast boost. So to salvage a bad quarter, Mercury offered her 40 percent if she could get the next CD done quickly to pick up the company. She saved Mercury's ass for quarterlies. That's how she made an extra $10 million."

Winston stopped for effect.

"An extra $10 million. Let me tell you, Lorelei, that's

what we want for you, too. If you make the big money, we make the big money. Everybody wins."

He stood. "I'll have a contract to Goldberg for you very soon."

To the side, Korg tracked the numbers. Emma, with her mind for business, would love this inside dirt.

Landru, consumed about the quality of the recording sessions, brought up an urgent point. "Will you pay for our recording sessions?"

Winston was quick to answer.

"I'm glad you asked that," he said. "The answer is yes. And let me explain why."

As Korg watched and listened, he saw the dynamic mental side of Winston. Back in the day, Winston's psychological power, coupled with physical strength and the instincts of an athlete, made him a paragon of might in Special Forces, and now, years later, as an executive.

"Diogenes will pay an advance of $25,000 for your time, typical for a project like this, along with another $115,000 in recording costs," Winston explained. "We'll also pay for a video, but to keep costs down, we're hoping to record it live at a show, do a sound stage, or knit together out-takes from your recording sessions."

The way Winston talked and carried himself was a message he was in charge and that he had an edge.

Lorelei raised her hand. Winston recognized her.

"What are the odds of us making any money at all out of this?"

"That's up to you," Winston said.

Lorelei laughed. Clearwater motioned for her to 'let it go,' worried she might blow the imminent deal. Instead she countered Winston: "Is it up to us? Isn't it true that very few CDs make money?"

"The fast money and the big money for you are in the live shows," Winston said. "But you need a hit song and a CD to jump-start the lucrative tours." There was authority in his words. "That is why I'm interested in you." He waved at hand at the band. "Lorelei has the voice, looks and magnetism to front an act. Clearwater, if he can stay out of jail, and Landru, together know how to create a sound and cut a CD quickly to keep the overhead down."

Impressive, Korg surmised. Here was a man who could make or kill dreams.

"You get perpetual income streams from electronic rights."

Lorelei wanted to hear more, Winston guessed, and he complied. "If you have a hit, you can add 10 percent on top of everything by selling a piece of the song as a cell phone ring tone. More if it hits on the internet as a downloaded favorite. On the big sellers, this can mean a significant bonus. You go to your mailbox and get these surprise checks."

Winston raised a fist for effect.

"There's also extra money for songwriting. Say Clearwater here writes your songs, or you two combine to co-write all the songs. You make the standard 75 percent mechanical rate per song, say for 11 songs on a CD, and you get an extra 60 cents per album. If we sell 200,000 units, that's an extra $120,000, clean, and you get paid from Day 1."

Winston paused to let that sink in.

"Think gold," he said. "Think platinum. That's what we want."

Winston understood negotiations, the fact that too much talk leads to doubt, and so he moved quickly to close.

"Congratulations," he finished. "You now have what millions of Americans dream of: a recording contract with Diogenes Sound. Goldberg will be in touch with you for the contracts, a formality at this point."

He smiled without showing teeth, and then with a quick nod to Korg, turned and walked out the door.

Lorelei turned to Clearwater, and saw that he was writing, studious yet sensitive, and she smiled warmly at her band mate, appreciative of his attention to detail.

McNabb and Robertson, each grinning like jack-o-lanterns — hey, they had a label deal — left to check out Clearwater's new ride. That left Korg in the room with Lorelei and Clearwater.

Clearwater glowed: "I like what he said, 'Think gold. Think platinum.'"

"Don't be too quick to spend any more money," Lorelei countered.

Korg enjoyed the interplay and the pair quickly surmised that.

"What do you think?" Lorelei asked the inspector.

"I think you better crunch the numbers," Korg answered. "That's what's my wife would do."

"Exactly," Lorelei said. "Let's crunch some numbers."

On a blank sheet of paper, she started working out the calculations. Her razor mind began to slice:

"A new CD that sells for $16.98 is probably wholesaled out for about $10. At 14 points, we'd make $1.40 per CD. If we sell 100,000, we'd make $140,000. Split five ways, that's only $28,000 apiece."

Korg tried to placate the young woman with his tone, but honesty prevailed in his words.

"It's actually worse than that," he said. "If Diogenes pays an advance of $25,000 for your time, like Winston said, along with another $115,000 in recording costs, that money would have to be paid back before royalty payments kicked in."

Clearwater appeared to give these facts no care, but Lorelei's gaze sunk to the floor.

"That would leave no profit," she said. "We could have a hit and sell 100,000 CDs and make no money."

"What's worse," Korg said, "today's kids do not buy the whole CD. They just download the one song they like on your album. So for a CD with 14 songs, the royalties are actually about seven percent of what you'd get compared to someone downloading the entire album."

Korg already knew the numbers. He had found them on Griffin's computer.

"More than 30,000 new titles were released last year," Korg said. "Ninety percent lost money and only about 100 sold more than a half a million copies. So even with a label deal and a CD, your odds of actually making some real money are less than 1 percent."

Korg paused, making sure the long-shot financial reality was sinking in. Despite the bleakness, Lorelei felt that the inspector was on her side.

"The cruddy thing is, even though we don't make any money if 100,000 CDs sell, Diogenes would still make $10 a pop and gross $1 million," she said.

Korg picked up the ball. "My wife says the labels

average a 20 percent profit. So they'd clear $200,000 on your little deal, even though they pay you nothing. They might get even more after their CPAs cook the books."

Lorelei touched Clearwater's arm. "The only way for this to have any chance to work for us is to cut recording costs down to rock-bottom," she explained. "We'll have to record live in the studio and limit dubs and studio time."

Clearwater finally showed some emotion.

"I don't understand," he said. "Look at all the money that Johnson is making. It seems to me we're getting ripped off from every direction. What about song pirating? What about on-line rip-offs. Kids passing songs around. Just about all my money comes from songwriting royalties. Those asshole kids are stealing from me."

"That's why the whole industry is down 50, 60 percent the past few years, and down 75 percent from the old days," Korg pointed out.

"It's true what Rock Winston said," Korg added. "The money for you is playing live."

Clearwater was frustrated. "We already do that and Johnson gets about everything."

Korg stood, shaking his head, commiserating with Clearwater and Lorelei over the long shot at success in the music business. He thanked them for their time — he got a piece of what he had come for — and headed out to call Sager.

Lorelei cornered Clearwater. She tilted her head and melted him with a smile and a stroke across his arm. "I liked that you were taking notes. It shows you're always thinking, planning for the future."

Clearwater beamed. "I can't turn it off." He pulled the notebook out of his back pocket, opened it, and handed the notebook to Lorelei.

She read:

The mirror sets off an alarm of mortality.
A shock of surprise, the tiredness in my eyes.
At night I submerge in your rhythmic breathing.
The scent of your neck, the warmth of your lullaby.

It is my feelings for you, in and out of the land of the dreaming,
That pours God's symmetry and the love for my bride.
The days go on, changes everywhere, wrinkled and gray.
Yet brightened by the shadow: I will love you 'til I die.

Her eyes caught fire in anger. "Incredible! This is what you were writing?"

Lorelei closed the pocket notebook, curtly handed it back to Clearwater, turned and marched out the door with an off-hand wave.

She ran headlong into Winston. "Want to join me for coffee?"

He had that look in his eye, Lorelei saw. This was getting tricky, and fast.

Korg's phone buzzed. A message. Sager.

"MaryLou Dietz. The blond. No alibi."

30

SAGER'S BLANK GLARE resembled the face of the Sphinx. Korg sat alongside. From behind the wheel of his detective-mobile, as Sager called it, his eyes locked on a line of what appeared to be miles of cars on northbound U.S. 101. The traffic jam was rolled up from another accident, this one at the perpetually gummed-up section of Bayshore Freeway south of San Mateo.

His trip to San Francisco Airport had been a failure. At the Super Shuttle pick-up area, he'd stopped each driver, asked if they were on the job for Thursday morning, September 26th, when Griffin's Corvette had been left at Long Term Parking. If so, he worked them through his pack of suspect photos. The process went quickly, with a steady procession of drivers arriving for pick-ups, but the response of each one was a zero. Sager even had time to hit up a dozen taxi drivers, but these attempts also came up blanks.

When Bonnie phoned again, he was quick to answer. "I found something else at Stephen's," Bonnie said, "and this time I think you should bring Inspector Korg with you."

"What?"

"You have to see it to believe it."

Sager said he'd call back and clicked off his phone. They had other business. Back to Johnson's first.

Korg was desperate for a break, but grim at the prospects. He broke the silence between them. "How you doin', you know, after the shooting? You OK?"

"Every day a bit better," Sager answered. "It pops into my head at the strangest times. I'll be getting gas, wondering why it costs so much, washing the window on the car, and out of the blue, I'll see those guys pulling those chrome automatics, and my training kicks in. But I guess I'm doin' OK, generally, with it."

"Good thing they both went down. That would have been a real mess any other way."

"This girl, Bonnie, she's been great. She showed up at just the right time."

Korg's cell phone sounded "The Bitch is Back." Nightmare time. "It's Pritchett. I'm not answering."

Sager gave no indication he heard the comment. The Sphinx. A nickname Korg had tagged that might stick.

A moment later, Sager's beeper went off.

"Damn traffic," he growled, and eyed the display. "Pritchett. Hey, she called you first, you call her. I'm supposed to be on leave."

"She beeped you. You call her."

"No. You."

Neither moved. Neither did the car, stuck in traffic. Finally, Korg's conscience got the better of him. He hit the auto-dial. The phone was in its first ring when Pritchett answered and started roaring.

"Korg! Where are you? We've got a body! Washed

up on the beach at Half Moon Bay. Looks like Griffin."

Korg sprung to life, shouting at Sager.

"Griffin washed up on the beach," he shouted.

Sager's eyes punched up, reflecting the afternoon light. "Where? Where?"

Korg motioned for quiet.

"Here's the lowdown," Pritchett continued. "A body just washed up with the high tide at the beach at Miramar in Half Moon Bay. That's right. Right near Griffin's place. A dog walker found it. They put it on a stretcher, covered it up, and moved it 150 yards inside the guest room at the Miramar Beach House. Forensics is en route."

"That's incredible. We're on our way."

"Get here fast. We'll give you the honor of looking inside the pockets of his clothes, confirm identity, and see if you find anything you can use. Forensics will supervise, then take over. It looks like your man."

"Looks like our guy!" Korg cried out to Sager.

"Korg, just get here fast," Pritchett ordered. "Miramar Beach House. You know the spot."

"Know it well." The phone clicked.

Korg turned to Sager and hooted, "Put out the light and catch the next train out of Dodge."

Sager transformed to Mr. Viper. He ripped the window down in a flash and whipped the flashing light onto the roof of the Ford. Korg lowered his passenger side window, displayed his badge, and other drivers in the right lanes acquiesced, allowing Sager to veer the car through traffic and to the road's shoulder on the far right, where he plowed his way to the exit for Highway 92 West. In minutes, he was racing at 80 mph.

"Can you believe this?" Korg asked, not requiring an answer. "Right as I'm running out of time, Griffin washes up on the beach."

"Bonnie tried to tell me something had happened over there and I cut her off."

The inspectors pulled into the parking area adjacent to the Miramar Beach House, filled with black-and-whites and unmarked sedans, right across the street from Stephen Griffin's home. At least the TV crews weren't here yet.

To the south, extended beach stretched for miles. To the north was the rock jetty of Pillar Point Harbor, with the shore curving around to Pillar Point and its giant tennis-ball like radar scope. The air carried the scent of algae from nearby rocks and the view spanned for miles across open water.

At the Beach House, Pritchett waited at the door.

"What kind of shape is the body in?" Korg asked.

"See for yourself."

For some unknown reason, Korg shook hands with Pritchett, and then added in a formal style, "Thank you for letting me have first shot." He then turned to Sager and nodded a "Let's go."

The energy was high between them, tense and edgy. Korg entered the Beach House foyer, set against rich mahogany walls finished to simulate the interior of a vintage yacht.

"The body is in the room on the right," Pritchett said, pointing with an open hand.

Korg turned through the doorway.

"SURPRISE!" The shout was thunderous and unified.

The room was filled with police officers, detectives, prosecutors, associates and sheriff's employees.

Korg was stunned.

"Congratulations on your retirement," said Pritchett as she shook Korg's hand. Sharp-eyed inspectors claimed they discerned glimmers of smiles from both Pritchett and Sager, but they would not swear to it.

It was a surprise retirement party. Korg had been lured, hooked and reeled in; everything but filleted and barbecued, but there was still a chance of that.

Sager broke into a full grin. "The idea of the body washing up was mine."

Korg was handed an Anchor Steam, wet from a tub of ice. His wife, Emma, walked up — another shocker — and gave him a huge kiss on the cheek, and whispered, "It's your day. Just for you."

Pritchett took the microphone. "Ladies and gentleman, I give you Inspector Kristopher Korg."

Again, a thunderous ovation filled the room. Korg had no idea he was so loved. Some of the force, he thought, had privately mocked him. But here they were, smiling, honoring him, with a warm fuzzy buzz in the room. On the side, standing with a quiet glow of appreciation, was his old partner from his San Francisco days, Leroy Anders. Nearby, Roper beamed in appreciation. But in the same scan, he noticed that Sturgeon, his pal from Forensics, wasn't there.

In command as usual, Pritchett recited the highlights of Korg's career, how he had graduated from San Jose State, majoring in police science, and his years with SFPD, how he had climbed the ladder to Homicide, broke the big Jacoby case and was nicknamed "The Bulldog." That inspired a roar of approval and a few woofs. Pritchett never mentioned the occasional leaks in the bucket in the latter years, and instead chose to talk about his skills as a boater, fishermen, navigator and man of many talents, inventor, "even building his own high-end computers."

Korg appeared in shock.

"It's time to join the human race, Kristopher Korg," Pritchett prodded.

"Even with the prospects of retirement and his boat, 4-Play, waiting just a short distance from where we stand, this man, Inspector Korg, chose to nail a few more bad guys rather than bail out early," she said.

"While on a missing person's case this month, Inspector Korg infiltrated a huge financial fraud scheme," Pritchett said. "This is an extremely complex web constructed to defraud the United States of America and its citizens with money laundering, offshore accounts, tax evasion and conspiracy. So Inspector Korg is going out on top. As our white collar crime division nails down the details and works with the FBI and U.S. Attorney's Office for the federal grand jury indictments, this will turn into a colossal fraud case — involving roughly $175 million — perpetrated by individuals who will learn that no person is above the law."

Again, a thunderous ovation filled the room. In the Sheriffs Department, such cases were rare landmarks.

"Remember," Pritchett concluded, quoting King Solomon, "Justice will only be achieved when those who are not injured by crime feel as indignant as those who are."

Korg took the microphone, as stiff as a wooden cigar store Indian. He looked across the crowd of his peers and tried to talk, but no sound came. He tried again, managed to croak "Thank," and choked off the "you."

The agents cheered and clapped, but there was a different sound to the applause, a sound that Korg had never heard. It was not a roar, it was not muted, but a deep, sustained resonance that said "Thank you for being here."

Korg looked down at his open pocket notebook. Finally, he found a strained, cracked voice.

"First I want to thank Emma, my beautiful, wonderful wife. I love her with all my heart, and her being here means the world to me." The words came out partly gurgled, but he managed to continue.

"As Roberta was introducing me, I wrote an outline here of what I would say."

The room grew quiet and Korg croaked on.

"I wrote, '1. Tell Joke. 2. Thank yous. 3. A good story of an arrest. 4. Tell joke on self. 5. Future.'"

Korg again choked off the words for a few seconds.

"None of that matters right now. I'm overwhelmed. Thank you so much. You've made a broken-down guy from the old school very proud to be among you."

Early that evening, after the ceremony and dinner, instead of driving straight home, Korg and his wife meandered along the beach to the harbor's rock jetty. They each sat on a rock along the breakwater, the scent of algae in the air, and watched the water, passing boats, distant freighters and pelicans, cormorants and gulls.

He put his arm around Emma's waist and felt the familiar sensation of her body fitting to his. Korg looked out to sea and took in the infinity of green.

"You know, the hard thing about this is that I didn't make the arrest, dammit. As of right now, Emma, that son-of-a-bitch is getting away with murder."

Emma ran her fingers through her husband's salt-and-pepper flecked hair.

"You did good, Kris," she said. "I love you. Now it's just us. No more Inspector Korg. Just Kris Korg. You're a free man."

"You're a good wife." He stopped to kiss her. "How'd I ever get so lucky?"

Emma tilted her head with a grin. "Cause I nabbed you when you thought you were nabbing me."

He smiled and watched an old anchovy trawler emerge from the harbor and head out to the open sea.

"You're right, that's what it comes down to," he said. "Just us. A life of love and the love of life."

They walked along the breakwater, arm in arm, as gentle waves lapped at the rocks.

Korg's phone rang the song, "I'm Just A Workin' Man." That was the coded ring for Mel Sturgeon from Forensics.

"Who's that," asked Emma.

"Sturgeon," Korg said. "He probably wants to apologize for missing the party. I should give him the chance, I guess."

"Go ahead, sweetheart," Emma prodded.

Korg punched the cell phone and didn't wait for a hello.

"Biggest party of my life and my pal doesn't even show up," Korg said with an affected mock anger. "See if I take you fishing Saturday."

"Hell, the fish never bite on your boat anyway," Sturgeon responded with a similar simulated ridicule.

"Go ahead and apologize," Korg ordered.

"Actually, it's you who should apologize."

"Oh yeah," Korg laughed, "and why is that?"

Sturgeon paused for moment to make sure the gravity of the words would have full effect.

"While you were partying, the 'daver dogs found your guy."

"You had the dogs looking for the body?"

IT TOOK KORG and Sager less than 10 minutes to reach the entrance at McNee State Park along Highway 1. Ranger Simms was waiting for them at the gate and waved them through on the park's service road. On the way up, Korg explained to Sager that Sturgeon had led a team of dogs trained to sniff out cadavers, and that the dogs and their masters had worked over the bunker area that afternoon and found the burial site.

Sturgeon was at the head of the spur trail that led down to the bunkers.

"How'd you know where to look?" Sager asked Korg.

"Old Indian trick," Korg said with a wink.

Korg and Sager quickly worked their way down the faint trail. Well below, they could see the heads of members of the search team and forensic crew bobbing above the chaparral. A cool breeze sailed off the ocean and up the slopes of Montara Mountain. From 30 yards out, Korg spotted tarps covering two body-sized humps.

One of the dogs on the K-9 team, a rapscallion-like golden retriever named Buddy, was still tugging at his leash at the edge of one of the bodies.

As Korg took the final steps to one of the tarps, a complex mix of emotions reverberated within him.

"You don't want to see this," Sturgeon warned.

Korg reached down to pull the tarp away, but Sturgeon tugged at his right sleeve and blocked him. "This is what you're looking for," Sturgeon said as he handed the inspector a billfold. "The rest is for me."

Sager loomed overhead in vulture mode.

Korg opened the billfold. Griffin's driver's license, with a beaming smile of a photo, jumped out at him.

"It's him," Korg said to Sager. "It's Stephen Griffin."

"It was in his pocket, right where it should be," Sturgeon said.

Korg quickly examined the contents.

"It's not here!" he shouted. "It's not here!"

"What? Sager asked.

Sturgeon looked on in fascination.

"Griffin's American Express Card," Korg exclaimed. "Perfect!"

They were both here. Stephen Griffin. Deego DeGenaro.

Sager tried to take in the crime scene and then stopped for moment to absorb the ocean view. It seemed to extend to forever. His cell phone vibrated in his pocket. He grabbed and stared at the caller ID: Roper.

"Inspector Sager, you've got your search warrants,"

Roper said. "Consider this a huge favor from the judge, considering we've got no body."

In response, Sager's voice was calm, low and steady. "Sir, you can tell the judge that we've got a body. In fact, two of them."

31

IT TOOK KORG an hour to track down Jesse James Johnson.

"They're all at the hospital," said Rosemary Yamani, the office manager. "I'm heading over there myself right now."

At Stanford Hospital, Jeffrey Bridges' health had crashed again. Vital signs were weak and he'd slipped in and out of consciousness for hours, often incoherent, and doctors ordered him back to intensive care.

Korg found the group in the waiting room. Bridges' parents, Jim and Andrea, had requested some time alone and were already with their son at bedside.

Before anybody spotted him, Korg withdrew to the hallway and text-messaged Sager: "No Klondike. No Winston. No MaryLou Dietz. Everybody else here."

Korg's surprise arrival startled Johnson.

"What are you doing here?" Johnson demanded. There was no disguising the anger in his words.

Korg, with the composure of an undertaker, took a seat, leaned forward, surveyed the group and stayed silent. Apprehension filled the air. All members of the band were there, with Johnson and Lorelei clearly bonded. To the side, Yamani and Winston waited for Korg to answer the question.

"Can't you see we're in a crisis here?" Johnson warned. "Can't this wait?"

"Sorry," Korg apologized, and it was genuine. "I'm afraid I have some bad news."

There was a sense among them of resignation, not surprise.

"Stephen Griffin, I'm afraid, is dead," Korg said. "We found his body this afternoon."

Korg eyed the players. Except for Lorelei, the newcomer of the group, no one held their face. Johnson had the most dramatic reaction. As the flash of reality cascaded over him, his eyes, mouth and shoulders wilted. He put his right palm over his eyes, dipped his head forward and down, and Korg heard the heavy breathing, scarcely audible, of a cry cut short.

Lorelei set a small hand on Johnson's arm and squeezed gently. "I'm here for you now," she said softly.

"Where? How?" Johnson sputtered to Korg.

Korg surveyed the room, making sure he missed nothing in the reactions on the faces before him. "We found him up on Montara Mountain at McNee Ranch State Park," Korg explained.

The inspector stopped to let the information sink in. Except for Johnson, who appeared crushed by every word, the others waited for more. But Korg, like a poker player looking for a tell, remained silent after pushing in his chips.

Johnson finally broke this silence, but as the boss, the band would have naturally deferred to him, Korg knew.

"He must have been murdered," Johnson mumbled.

"Why would you say that?" Korg asked.

Johnson hesitated for a moment, as if confused, then mumbled, "Because he couldn't have buried himself, you asshole."

"That thought did cross my mind," Korg said, appearing to commiserate with the rock star. He then added, "How did you know he was buried? I never mentioned that."

Johnson ignored the question.

Korg watched the rock star's face for any emotion as he added: "The body of Deego DeGenaro was in the same hole."

Johnson appeared in shock. No discernable inflections.

After a moment, Johnson broke.

"Do you know anything, you know, how it happened, anything at all?"

Korg stood and addressed the group. "I'd like to meet with you all tomorrow, 11 a.m., at Johnson's place and we'll try to sort it out and see if it doesn't lead somewhere."

"I'd like that very much." It was Landru, the first time he'd spoken. If Johnson was the heart of the band, Clearwater the brains, Robertson the guts, and McNabb the fabric, then Landru was the soul.

"Make sure you're all there," Korg said. It was a clear order. "We need the whole gang, Klondike, Winston, everybody. See what we come up with."

All said they would attend.

Korg felt the collective gaze of the group shift, cast over his shoulder. He turned to see a doctor who waited silently for his chance. When it came, the doctor said,

"You can all go in now. But don't put him on overload or you'll have to leave. If he's awake, talk one at a time. He's largely sedated and may appear confused. But his friends are maybe what he needs right now."

Landru took a gentle fist and beat it softly into his chest. "What he needs is our love."

The group filed in and Korg tagged along in the background.

Two days before, while sipping chicken soup, Bridges had lost consciousness. A moment later, his heart stopped beating. Doctors rushed in. Nearly a minute had passed when, without medical explanation, his heart started beating again. Before he stabilized, both lungs collapsed and his blood pressure dropped to 85 over 47.

"Terrible sore throat," Bridges had told the doctor in a muted voice. That was the result of a plastic oxygen pipe that had been jammed down his esophagus.

He was in the far bed with no other patients in the room. A sheet hanging from the ceiling on a runner created a wall for privacy. His eyes were half open. Bandages covered his torso, with wires and tubes connected to a battery of electronic monitors. On the far side of the bed, a print of two blue grouse, male and female perched on a Jeffrey pine, leaned against the wall; Landru had given it to him, a Native American image of the sacred spiral.

Landru grabbed Bridges' hand.

Bridges tried to talk, but his words were slurred and halting.

"I'm fine. No pain at all. I'll be fine."

Apparently, when his heart stopped, there had been some residual brain damage as well, and it short-circuited many of his thoughts. The big bass player floated in and out of consciousness, at times aware, at times not. There were moments of clarity and this was one of them.

With Johnson on the far end and Robertson on the other, they formed a half circle like a broken halo. Bridges' parents remained seated at bedside. Korg, trying to be invisible, stayed in the background.

"I've lived my life as hard as I could," Bridges whispered to the small group. "I just seemed to do a lot of things the hard way, and now I find again, I'm just trying to hold my own."

It seemed difficult to believe that a man so strong and vibrant, spiritually and physically, was shattered.

Lorelei was the only one perplexed. She didn't know this enigmatic, sensitive giant of a man. She hadn't planned to be here, to share in his pain. But as a member of the band, and to support Johnson, she'd come along.

For a few minutes, Bridges tried to listen to the light talk, but found it impossible to follow. Then, in a moment of clarity, he said: "You're either on the way up or you're on the way down. That's all there is to it. There ain't no balance point 'til you die."

Landru shifted around to the side of the bed. He rested a hand on Bridges' forearm and they stared into each other's eyes, as if searching for something. From the look in his eyes alone, Landru realized they had shared the marrow of life from the days in the band, on the road, creating music together.

Then it appeared that Bridges was trying to lift his arms, but was so weak he could only raise them an inch or two.

"Be still, Jeff," Landru commanded gently.

"I'm trying to reach those people," Bridges answered. The words came one breath at a time, his voice a thin whisper.

Lorelei eyed Clearwater. Her eyes were question marks.

"What people are those?" Clearwater asked softly.

Landru's right hand still comforted Bridges' forearm.

"The people right there," Jeff said.

"Where are they?"

"They're next to that staircase."

Landru and Clearwater smiled bleakly. There was no staircase. Johnson's eyes found Bridges' parents. Lorelei, with a Mona Lisa smile, clasped her hands.

The group was quiet as Bridges tried to lift an outreached hand, managing only enough strength to clear the bed sheet. Bridges moved his hand forward two or three inches. He appeared to be trying to grasp something. His eyes remained half-open.

Lorelei appeared to sense what was occurring. At the back of the room, Korg watched sadly. Jim and Andrea, as only parents can know, held each other in silent prayer. Lorelei moved forward, took Bridges' hand and squeezed it.

"Would you like us to help you reach them?" Lorelei asked with a soft smile full of love.

"Yes," Bridges whispered, his voice faint. "I want to go with them up the staircase."

Landru nodded at Clearwater. The group drew closer,

as if parting a curtain and gaining a glimpse into a secret world.

With Clearwater on one side and Landru on the other, they helped Bridges lift his arms an inch or two. He appeared to grasp something, his hands and fingers moving ever so lightly.

Bridges then lapsed into a coma-like state, a quixotic smile on his face.

Moments later, with his friends holding his arms, Jeffrey Brides died.

Clearwater cried softly and put his arms around Jim and Andrea. When he broke, Lorelei, too, put her arms around Bridges' parents.

"Those were angels he was seeing," Lorelei told them. "They took him up those stairs to heaven."

From his shirt pocket, Korg heard the muffled note of his cell phone announcing that a text message had just arrived. He quickly checked his phone, punched the buttons and read the note from Sager: "Got it, chief. Just as you figured."

Korg punched back.

"Make sure MaryLou Dietz is at the meeting tomorrow. I've got the rest of them covered."

32

FRIDAY

Kris Korg woke up unofficially retired, but found that his body clock was on the same schedule as when he was an inspector. Emma, sitting on a corner of their bed and brushing her hair, remained quiet, aware of the significance of the morning. He gave her a kiss on the cheek and a one-armed hug. "I'm going for a drive, hand the case over to Sager, and then maybe to the boat."

"It's time, honey," Emma said, "You can go to your boat any day you want. That is, on the days I haven't given you things to do."

He laughed. A romantic, Korg counted his blessings for a wife who had patience with the quirks of a homicide inspector and a fisherman. He had always been attracted to her natural brilliance. She was someone with whom he could match wits, and he admired her independence. He gave her shoulder another squeeze and she responded with a light pat on his chest over his heart. The magic was still there.

From their home in the Redwood City foothills, Korg drove the family car, the hybrid Escape, up 84, then turned right on Kings Mountain Road. He took his time, climbing up the twisty two-laner into the redwoods, past the entrance to Huddart County Park and eventually to Skyline Ridge. He turned right and drove north as the road burrowed a hole beneath the redwood canopy. At a sign for Purisima Creek Redwoods Open Space Preserve, Korg turned left and parked. There were two other cars there, one with a rack for a mountain bike. For the first time in years, Korg felt a sense of freedom that he'd never felt even on his boat.

Korg was wearing a denim long-sleeve shirt, his old blue jeans and athletic shoes, and with a deep breath at the trailhead, he walked out a bit on the North Ridge Trail. He descended for 15 minutes on a sub ridge, and then at a faint cut-off, climbed up a hilltop. He took a seat, pulled out a Romana Corona Deluxe, "best cigar for the money in the world," lit up, took a long draw, savored the cool, rich tobacco, and absorbed the sweeping view across the ocean before him.

From this lookout, it seemed he could sense the curvature of the earth on the distant water-edged horizon. To the northwest, he could make out the pinnacle of the Southeast Farallon Island, 27 miles off San Francisco. To his left, he could see the canyon rim of Whittemore Gulch and below it, a sea of redwoods. To his right, 10 miles of coastal foothills stretched to Half Moon Bay and Pillar Point Harbor, where his boat was moored, waiting for him. He smiled at the thought.

Korg let his gaze wander over to Miramar. He took a long draw on the Romana, his teeth biting into it. He turned his head, pivoting like an owl, and took in the distant west slope of Montara Mountain. He felt his jaw clench, eyes narrow into a squint and his face tighten. Korg leaned over and snubbed out his Romana. "I'm not done yet."

By 10 a.m. he was back at his car. He tossed the old cigar in a trash can, retrieved a soft carrying case from the Escape, and then entered a small restroom at the trailhead. Five minutes later, he was out, wearing a black suit with light pinstripes and a rich burgundy tie. The athletic shoes looked a bit foolish, but at the Escape he quickly pulled out black dress shoes he'd stashed in the SUV.

Korg drove out of the parking lot, turned south on Skyline, steady and deliberate. Pritchett may have retired me, he thought wistfully, but there is one last thing I must do.

WHEN HE REACHED Johnson's estate in the Woodside hills, the gate was already open. About 40 yards down the road, an unmarked patrol car was parked in the shade of a madrone on the side of the road, where an officer monitored anybody who might decide to drive off.

Klondike, whom Johnson had posted as his own sentry, waved Korg in, but the inspector stopped and lowered his driver window.

"Glad to see you here, big man," Korg said.

Klondike just stared at the inspector; he wasn't one for small talk.

Despite the spurn, Korg smiled gently at Johnson's enforcer.

"You know, Fred, I won't be seeing you again, probably, after today," Korg said. "But I want you to know that there is a lot about you I admire, even though you have broken the law. I like that you live by an honor code. Things are black-and-white with you. You have integrity. I like that."

"My name is Klondike."

"Sure. Right. Klondike."

Johnson's enforcer stood there like El Capitan, silent as the largest single piece of granite in the world. Korg started to drive off.

"Wait!" Klondike shouted. Korg stopped his car. The biker ambled up. He looked behind him to make sure no one else could hear the comment. "You too."

The parking area adjacent to the Sound Factory was jammed with cars. Sager lurked outside, holding a brown paper bag in one hand.

"Everybody here?" Korg asked.

"No Winston. No Johnson," Sager replied, and then added, "That lawyer, what's his name? Goldberg. He's waiting for you inside."

Across the grounds, the front door opened at the estate home and Johnson and Winston appeared, rigid and unsmiling, and then marched toward Korg. Johnson took the lead and Korg detected a nearly imperceptible lump in Winston's light sport coat. He was packing.

"What's this about?" Johnson charged.

"I have a little story to tell," Korg said. "I think you will both find it riveting."

They converged on the Sound Factory and entered the recording studio. Inside, the rest of the actors in this movie were already there. In one area, the band members, Clearwater, Landru, McNabb and Robertson sat huddled, in shock over Bridges' death and the news of finding the bodies of Stephen Griffin and Deego DeGenaro. Nearby, MaryLou, Lorelei and Talia traded small talk while trying to make sense of the urgent call for this meeting. Yamani, silent, sat nearby.

On the other side of the room, Johnson, Winston and Goldberg formed a triangle. Schwartz, the producer, was nearby in the glass-cased control room; he'd set up a microphone and would record the whole thing. A moment later, Klondike ambled in and took a seat.

Sager and Bonnie Griffin positioned themselves at the back of the room, in the center. Roper, the deputy District Attorney, regal and silent, sat on their immediate left. The lawyer, Goldberg, pulled Korg aside. "Who's in the lead here?"

Korg moved forward and raised a hand. "Relax." Then with a wave at the rest of the room, he added, "You're all here by invitation to hear a story about Stephen Griffin and the music business."

Goldberg's sidewalls were slicked back. It fit, Korg figured. This guy was a real grease ball. "I'll be watching closely," countered Goldberg, who then looked over at his client, Johnson. "I don't know what this is all about, Jesse, but don't say a damn thing."

Johnson remained confused. "I got nothing to say anyway. I don't know what this is about."

From the back of the room, Roper addressed the group. "Before you start, Kris, let me remind everybody here that you don't have to talk to us, don't have to answer any questions or tell us any stories. You have the right to remain silent, and have the right of an attorney to advise you..."

and he completed reciting Miranda. "Do you understand?"

"The D.A. just Mirandized us," Clearwater whispered to his mates. "Not good."

Landru appeared to have no response, sullen, apparently devastated from the death of Bridges, and now this. He didn't care. He'd come only because the police had told him to.

Korg stood in front of the group. The room had become his stage.

"This story starts," Korg explained, "early on the evening of Wednesday, September 25th, when a visitor arrived at Stephen Griffin's Miramar beach house. Later that night, this visitor killed Stephen. That person is here today."

Gasps were emitted all around, followed by a tomb-like silence as if the air had been sucked out of the room. Only Johnson, Klondike and Goldberg showed no emotion. Even Sager and Roper had perceptible rises as their gazes swept the room.

Korg, sensing his control of the room, kept up the momentum.

"If you let me use a little poetic license in my story, I believe they exchanged a familiar greeting. Clearly, they were not strangers."

Korg stopped for a moment, relaxed now, and broke into a grin. "For the purpose of the story, I will call this visitor 'Janus.' "

Korg paused again.

"In Roman mythology Janus was the god of gates, doors, beginnings and endings in time," Korg explained.

"Janus is described as having two heads that face the opposite directions. One looks back at the past and the other looks forward to the future. It's like Janus was two people."

Clearwater felt the gaze of a lot of eyes on him and the need for a defense. "That sounds like everybody in the music business," he said.

Korg chuckled. He liked his audience edgy and defenseless.

"Yeah, it's true that this unusual personality type is found in a lot of people in the arts." Korg gazed around the room. "A lot of geniuses have it. They have periods of complete irreverence, both daring and outgoing, and will stop at nothing to achieve their goals. During this period, they are capable of creative greatness. We're talking off-the-chart levels of achievement."

The room remained quiet.

"This cycles with periods of depression," Korg continued. "They withdraw from society, dark and isolated, self-absorbed in despair and loneliness. They feel victimized and see no way out of the darkness. That is when they are dangerous. Set this person off and you might as well detonate a nuclear bomb."

Off to the side, Landru found himself moving his chair a few inches away from Clearwater.

33

THE RECORDING STUDIO had become a performance hall, and the small audience, alive with whispers and murmurs, was entranced by the play unfolding before them.

Korg waved his right hand, asking for silence, and continued his story.

"We know that Stephen Griffin was murdered between the late afternoon of Wednesday, September, 25th and Thursday mid-morning, September 26th. The cover-up was carried out Thursday morning and was so elaborate that the time of death was probably Wednesday evening. That's what we're going with."

Korg issued this edict in matter-of-fact style. Even Sager was surprised at the inspector's power and clarity.

"The cover-up was a piece of work," Korg said. "On Thursday morning, Janus started early, perhaps even after a sleepless night, and plotted the day's events…

It was the morning after. Bleary-eyed, Janus stared into the bathroom mirror, heart racing. "No mistakes."

It was early, Janus knew, but there was no use

trying to sleep any longer, head spinning with ideas. An hour later, Janus pulled into the parking lot at the Miramar Beach House Restaurant & Bar. The coast was overcast, the first cold day of early fall. The smell of salt was in the ocean mist.

Janus examined Griffin's key ring. So many keys. One by one, keys were tested in the front door. The fifth was a match. Janus turned the knob and was in.

In the living room, Janus glimpsed at a framed photograph of Griffin, the band and all the players, on the far wall. Janus flamed, snatched it and hurled it against the wall. The glass smashed into bits.

It took a few minutes for Janus to gather a semblance of wits, but then began picking up the glass, first the big pieces, then the smaller ones. There were still glass crystals in the rug. Janus scurried to where Stephen kept his vacuum cleaner. Panting now, Janus charged back into the living room with it.

At that moment, there was a sharp knock on the door.

"Do nothing," Janus thought. "Nobody else has a key."

Nobody, that is, except for Bonnie Griffin. She watered Griffin's plants when he was on the road. This could be Bonnie, stopping in. Maybe Janus would be forced to do something about Bonnie, too. Janus scampered into the kitchen, and from a butcher block, pulled out a 12-inch carving knife. Janus then crept back into the living room and into the foyer, then waited near the door's hinges. If the door opened, Janus would be concealed behind it, ready to strike.

Another knock. Janus waited five minutes. Nothing. The booming cannon shots were jackhammer heartbeats.

Janus peered through the glass peephole at the top of the front door. Nobody there. Nobody at all. Janus unlocked the dead bolt, and then slowly opened the door a few inches.

Sitting there in the doorway was a long, narrow box, apparently delivered by UPS.

"What luck," Janus whooped, quickly nabbed the box, and set it inside.

Grinning, Janus returned to the living room and vacuumed up the remaining glass bits. "What am I to worry about a knock on the door anyway," Janus laughed.

Janus examined the box, long and narrow. Perfect. It would look as if Stephen had taken delivery of it that morning. It would throw the timeline off for the cops, Janus figured.

Janus rummaged through the bedroom closet, and on the top shelf, found Griffin's large leather travel bag. Janus then grabbed a couple of T-shirts, a few long sleeve shirts, blue jeans, socks — leaving the sock drawer slightly ajar, as if Griffin had been in a rush when packing, like guys always are, and had left at the last minute. Reaching into the fanny pack, Janus pulled out a plastic garbage bag, one of the big heavy-duty black ones, and tossed in the travel bag and Griffin's boots, the ones he always wore on his road trips.

"Now for the bathroom." Janus ran the shower, pulled out a fresh towel, held it in the stream of water for a moment, then tossed it on the floor. Janus then grabbed a toothbrush from the counter, opened a drawer and snatched the toothpaste, a razor, floss, deodorant. Janus swept the shower curtain aside and grabbed the

shampoo, pushing everything into the bag. After a few minutes, absorbed in the work, Janus became aware of the intense heart thumping again. "Relax. Relax. Everything is going to plan."

Now for the kitchen. Janus switched on the coffee maker, inserted a fresh filter and poured in some of Stephen's favorite Costa Rican blend. While it perked, Janus surveyed the sink. "Hah," Janus smiled. Janus knew Griffin liked soup for breakfast. Part of his new diet. After searching the pantry, Janus found three cans, turkey noodle. Janus pulled one out, opened it, dumped it in a small soup pot on the stove, and started to heat it.

In minutes, the aroma of the fresh-brewed coffee filled the house. Janus poured a cup and then dumped it and the rest down the drain; same with the soup, grinding it with the garbage disposer, rinsing the drain with hot water, letting the water run.

Now, acting more quickly, Janus piled the coffee pot, coffee cup, soup pot and soup bowl in the sink, and doused them with water. A quick rinse.

Korg paused for a moment. Each member of the audience was transfixed at where the tale would lead.

"Janus made it look like Stephen had taken delivery of a UPS package, ate breakfast and packed for a trip," Korg said.

After a pause, he picked up the narrative. "Janus went into Stephen's office and turned on his iMac..."

At the computer, Janus turned on the power, and while waiting for it to boot up, pulled out Griffin's American Express card. The computer uploaded Expedia.com. No password? No problem. In the next few minutes, Janus created a new account with a new password for Griffin, and quickly booked a ticket for the 1:18 p.m. AirWest flight from San Francisco to Las Vegas. With Griffin's American Express card, the purchase went through with a single click of the "purchase now" button. With another keystroke, the computer printed the flight itinerary. Janus placed it atop the desk for the cops to find.

Griffin kept a massive phone list affixed to the pullout tabletop from his desk. Janus plowed through it, and in seconds, hit the mark.

Janus punched the numbers for The Mirage Hotel in Las Vegas, and asked for Al "Little Mac" McKay, road manager for Tenaya.

"Hello." The voice sounded sleepy, incoherent.

"Hey Little Mac McKay," Janus started.

"Let me clear my head," McKay said. He needed two Excedrin to kill the start of a headache. He tried to wipe the sleep out of his eyes and clear the fog. "Who is this?"

"Did I wake you? Sorry about that. Jesse James Johnson's office calling."

"No, it's OK, what's up."

"We're calling you because Jesse's management contract with Stephen Griffin will be up this fall and he wants to discuss some possible options with you." Janus paused to let the words sink in. "He'll be playing Vegas. That'll be the best chance to connect."

"That sounds good, real good." The words were still blurred from sleep.

"In the meantime, Jesse has a request. He wants you to handle an extra roadie for Tenaya for a couple weeks."

Janus didn't wait for a response.

"This kid, Spoogs, he's a good kid. Work him into Tenaya's road crew. That would give you another hand, and he'd get to hang a bit with Tenaya."

McKay was trying to clear his brain fog and digest the request at the same time.

Then Janus closed the deal with the clincher. "Jesse says this is important to him. He wants this to happen starting tonight."

"Whatever," McKay said, still blurry, but the allure of easy money managing Johnson, maybe piggybacking his act to Tenaya's, was a clear vision. "Sure, I can handle that, now let me think..." there was a pause on the line, and then McKay continued: "Just have him check in with me here after the late show. I'll put him on the pass list for back stage. I'll take care of everything. We've got most of a floor at the hotel, like we always do. I'll have a room key for him under my name."

McKay, fully awake now, then addressed his self interest in the matter.

"Tell Jesse that I look forward to meeting with him in Las Vegas, work something out, and my management team could represent him."

Korg paused again. He saw the relief on Johnson's face, his shoulders relaxed, the hint of a smile. The way Korg told the tale, it seemed clear to everyone in the room that Johnson was not Janus.

"I wouldn't get too relaxed just yet," Korg said with a wry smile in Johnson's direction.

Johnson fidgeted and Goldberg stood. "What are you saying?" said the lawyer, agitated.

"Listen to the story and then make your play."

Still at Griffin's desk, Janus then punched in the next number. Spoogs, like McKay, was still in bed. It was part of the plan. Catch them off guard.

"Is this Spoogs?" Janus opened. "This is Jesse James Johnson's office calling."

Spoogs was shocked. The young roadie's voice accented dread and trepidation. "Do I still have a job?"

"Yes, but with some changes," Janus explained. "You're not going to New York this afternoon, like you planned. You're going to Las Vegas. Tenaya needs a spare hand for a couple weeks. Your name came up."

There was silence on the line from Stevie Griffith, still in shock, apprehensive and bleary-eyed. "Really?"

"When Tenaya's manager called and said they needed a good hand to fill in, we figured you were the guy. Don't screw it up."

"What? Tenaya? Really? Vegas? You're not kidding? This is incredible? Thank you, thank you, thank you."

Janus smiled.

"Cool it, Spoogs, you deserve it. Now listen, you'll have an e-ticket to get to Vegas, and this is how you get there. There'll be a back-stage pass after the show. Your contact is Al McKay. Stay out of Tenaya's way and don't blow it."

In the garage, Janus tossed the garbage bag in a corner, and in the next motion, pulled out Stephen's keys. With a turn of the ignition, the Corvette's engine rumbled to life in the enclosed garage. On the visor, Janus punched the remote button and the electric garage door raised with a clatter. Without waiting for the engine to warm, Janus drove the black sports car to the street, and then punched the remote switch to close the garage door.

In 25 minutes, Janus, heart still thumping and frazzled by time pressure, entered Long Term Parking for San Francisco International Airport. It was 11:17 a.m. Janus put the parking ticket on the Corvette's center console.

At nearly the same time, Spoogs arrived at the AirWest counter at San Francisco International Airport. Spoogs was wearing a Tenaya T-shirt, blue jeans with the holes in the knees, Air Jordan's and a Fender Custom Shop baseball hat. There wasn't much to his thin mustache and beard, just a hint of darkness. He checked his watch. It was 11:30 a.m.

"Stevie Griffith," he said to the attendant, identifying himself. "I have an electronic ticket on the 1:18 p.m. flight to Vegas."

The sales attendant looked up for a moment, then saw the line behind the young man had lengthened to about 60 people. She scanned the list. No Griffith. Oh wait, there it is, Griffin. Stephen Griffin."

The attendant paused to eye the lad.

"Could I see a photo ID?"

The roadie displayed his driver's license. She examined it: "Steven Griffith" and then checked the picture very carefully. Yes, the kid standing in front of her was definitely the guy in the picture, Steve Griffith.

Stevie grinned. "People call me Spoogs."

En route to boarding the jet, attendants checked

Stevie Griffith's photo ID at two different security checkpoints, each time taking care to match up his photograph with the individual standing in front of them.

From Long Term Parking, Janus took the shuttle bus to the terminal, and then with a quick switch, jumped on a courtesy van to the Marriott. From there, Janus tipped the bellhop to call a cab, a Yellow, driven by a Sikh wearing a turban, and in minutes, was being ferried back to Miramar. Janus was dropped at a house 200 yards from the beach house.

Janus unlocked the front door. Thunderous heartbeats again set off a pounding in the ears. The mind noise was deafening. Janus walked through the house, making certain nothing had been left amiss. Then, after retrieving the bag from the garage, Janus exited the house. A broad smile was impossible to hide.

The car started quickly, and in less than a minute, Janus turned north on Highway 1. At ease now, Janus eased past the traffic light at El Granada. A fog layer cast a muted tint over Montara Mountain. The air was dripping with mist, salty and wet. Janus zipped the window down, took a deep breath of the cool coastal air, and gazed across the faint horizon of the mountain's ridgeline.

In less than two minutes, Janus entered a small coastal town, Moss Beach, then turned left into a Chevron station with a small convenience store, and drove just behind it. Janus bounced out of the car with Griffin's travel bag and loaded garbage bag, the engine still running. Janus quickly tossed them in the dumpster.

The mission was complete. Janus checked the

clock: Still 94 minutes before the band's jet took off for New York.

Janus cruised down Highway 1 and sighed a long, deep breath, then pulled off at Venice Beach. For a moment, Janus watched the waves and reviewed all the details, making sure nothing had been overlooked. Then Janus tried to get back into the moment, starting with each breath. Content at perfection, Janus brought the car to life and left the coast. After all, there were places to be.

34

"ALL THE EVIDENCE points to a cover-up that happened just like this story," Korg said, and then, with a pause, "or at least very close,"

He enjoyed that those in front of him were fully engaged with every word. Nobody dared interrupt the inspector. No one, that is, except the inimitable Bonnie Griffin.

"Who did it?" she blurted out, "and how'd they do it?

Clearwater, always the square peg, again felt a lot of eyes aimed in his direction. Johnson picked up on that.

"Janus and Stephen clearly knew each other well," Korg said. "Clearly each wanted something from the other. There was a lot at stake. But they both acted to diffuse the tension. This is how I think it went down..."

On Wednesday evening, Griffin welcomed Janus at the front door. As each visitor does at Griffin's beach house, Janus stopped in front of the picture window and absorbed the panorama of the sea. Burnished sunrays poked holes through broken fog out to the west.

"Where to?" Griffin asked. "Here or somewhere else?"

Janus backed up a step. "Did you get the BBQ like I asked?"

"Yep."

"I know the perfect place. Let's go."

On their way out the door, Griffin caught a reflection of himself in a wall mirror in the foyer. Griffin stared, unmoved. His skin was white from living in the fog belt and from too much time inside. His body was soft. His forehead was balding.

The day was cooling off, pushed by a breeze off the Pacific. A heavy fog bank loomed just offshore, and as the temperature dropped, the fog migrated inshore in patches.

Griffin was disarmed by Janus' light-heartedness. He didn't know what to expect. A showdown? Maybe? Maybe not.

"You haven't even brought up the business," Stephen said. "To be honest, it's refreshing. But just so you know, I've been working on something special for you."

Janus drove the car toward Montara, five miles north of Miramar, and relaxed on the gas pedal when the Pacific Ocean stretched out before them. At the foot of Montara Mountain, Janus signaled right, then veered out of the line of traffic and onto a dirt spur road that led into McNee Ranch State Park. They stopped quickly at a yellow pipe gate that blocked access to the park's service road.

"Watch this." Janus jumped out, the engine still running, quickly aligned the four numbered tumblers on the lock, 2424, and opened the gate.

As they drove through, Stephen chuckled. "You

know Ranger Simms? He gave me the combination, too. Keeps me from having to park along the highway. All I had to do was give him some CDs."

The music business can have a strange effect on some people, Griffin noted.

Janus affirmed that. "Hah. Yeah, I know Brandon. He's aware of the problem of leaving my car out in front of the gate, within view of the highway, the danger of it being vandalized. So he gave me the combination for the lock and told me, 'Go ahead and just drive in anytime and park here. Safer for your car.' Yeah, he wants to talk about the music business." Then Janus added with a chuckle. "Says he wrote a song."

Stephen laughed. "Everybody's got a song."

It was about 7:30 p.m., a breezy, early fall evening. The fog bank had crept within a mile of shore, hovering there, waiting for the sun to fall and the temperature to drop a few degrees to dew point, when the fog would come rolling in and bury everything in sight.

"Nobody's ever up here this late," Janus said. "Not with the fog."

Janus drove at practically a walk, slowly climbing up the old dirt road.

Korg broke for a moment to take a drink from a bottle of water. "You know, we talked to everybody," he said to the group. "When I talked to MaryLou Dietz, she told me an amazing story about a hike on Montara Mountain."

Sitting next to Lorelei, MaryLou felt the stare of a lot of eyes.

"MaryLou used to borrow dogs from the shelter in San Francisco and take them for walks. So one day here, she was taking this dog for a walk and the dog flat out disappeared. After searching for 20 minutes, she thought she heard the dog panting, so she pulled back a bush and the dog was at the bottom of this hole, with a fawn sitting right next to him. It was an incredible sight. They were sitting there at the bottom of that hole, looking up.

"She had the ranger, Brandon Simms, get the dog and fawn out of there."

Korg laughed. "There's a reason why that's important."

He took another drink and continued.

"Did you hear the story how the ranger saved that dog in the hole?" Janus asked.

"Sure," Griffin answered with minimal interest. "Always wondered. Why was the hole there?"

"Turns out there are hidden holes like that all over the mountain. Back in the day, the military set up concrete bunkers and radar stations on the west slopes of this mountain in case the Japanese invaded the coast. They drilled dozens of holes where they were looking for water. Dry test wells, that's what they are. That's what the ranger told MaryLou.

"You know, I've always loved this place," Janus continued. "I think this is where I'll have my ashes scattered. What about you? Or do you want to be buried?"

Griffin didn't answer, so Janus continued.

"I want to go back there and show you where that happened."

"Where?"

"Back where the ranger rescued the dog and the fawn out of that hole. Nice view, too. Have a picnic and get everything taken care of, leave with everything done."

Janus grew quiet now, distant, brain spinning like a gyroscope. As they climbed, the coastal views were enhanced with each passing minute. That fog bank was prowling offshore, but below the cloud deck, the air was crystal, a stellar night with a beautiful sunset imminent.

Janus led the way down a faint trail. The route was almost invisible amid thigh-high chaparral. They figured their position by nearby power lines.

"Nice view, eh," Janus said, looking south, scanning the coastline.

Stephen took a seat on a boulder, opened his bag and peered in. "Ribs or chicken?"

Looking down at Griffin, Janus unzipped a small daypack.

"Stephen, there's something I want to ask you."

"Go ahead."

Janus took a deep breath.

"You know those hit songs on Johnson's CDs, 'No Dress Rehearsal,' 'What You Got I Need,' and the new one you told me about, 'Straight Ahead?'"

"Sure, what about them?"

"I saw on the disc jacket that you and Jesse James Johnson wrote "No Dress Rehearsal." Tell me, did you write the words or the music?"

Griffin peered up, his eyes a smile.

"Mainly me, the words, and Jesse, the music, but we work well together. Sometimes we'll get an idea

the other guy can put into the song. We've done it lots of times."

"I see," Janus said, "and tell me, who came up with the ideas for the songs in the first place."

"Me," he beamed. "I came up with all of them."

"That's what I thought." Then with a grin, Janus added, "How does that one verse go in the song?

"I need a night full of stars and some wide-open space. Room to stretch my toes and slow my pace."

Griffin confused, hesitated for a moment, then added the next line to the song:

"You know I don't want to be dead, c'mon and help me clear my head."

"Wrong!" Janus shouted, eyes turning to razor blades. "It goes like this."

"Lord you know I've got to clear my head.
Don't let the devil get me and make me dead."

Janus pulled a lightweight titanium .38 Smith & Wesson revolver out of the pack, raised it quickly and pulled the trigger. In the next quarter-second, the blast propelled an 80-grain lead slug at 800 feet per second into Stephen's chest.

Griffin staggered on his knees, took a half step, and then fell sideways, still conscious and semicoherent. He stared up into Janus' eyes.

"Those were my songs," Janus howled. "I wrote them all and you stole them from me. All those songs came from inside me."

Janus stood over him and fired again into Stephen's chest. The lead mushroomed upon impact and exploded the left ventricle artery of his heart.

"You took what I had inside me and left me with nothing."

The sun was just beginning to set, that orange fireball dropping below the fog layer. It appeared to hover for a moment in a clear range, below the clouds and yet above the ocean, and then dipped into the sea, piece by piece. A brilliant scheme of oranges and yellows refracted for miles. The air had cooled a bit, and Janus' arms, although covered with goose pimples, felt the flood of a warm, buzzing sensation.

Janus reached into Stephen's pants pocket and pulled out his keys, cell phone and billfold, and then rummaged through the billfold to find his American Express card. Then Janus dragged Griffin a few feet and dumped him into the dry well shaft and tossed his billfold on top of the body. "All you care about is money, so enjoy taking your billfold with you," Janus said to the body.

It took only a few minutes for Janus to return to the car, pull out a small shovel, and then return to the scene and cave in the sides of the hole. The dirt fell easily, covering Stephen in seconds.

Deego DeGenaro would go soon. Deego had been a part of the rip-off, too, a go-between for the songs, and was also the firewall that blocked contact with Griffin.

Yes, it would be easy to lure Deego up here and put him in the same hole. Nowhere as complicated. After all, nobody would miss Deego DeGenaro.

The sun completed its course past the horizon, and the fog turned from yellow to orange, and from orange to red, and finally to gray. Just as Janus cast the last shovel of dirt, it turned black up there on that mountain, and in the darkness, Janus traced the route back to the car. Stephen was 12 feet down, beneath four feet of dirt, too deep for animals to dig up and all of it camouflaged by chaparral. Nobody would ever find him. Soon, Deego would be right on top of him.

The temperature dropped to the mid-50s, nearing dew point, and the fog layer moved from sea toward land. By the time Janus reached the entrance gate, the night was as black as the eyeholes of a skull and the headlight beams refracted in the mist.

The windshield was covered in drops from the mist. It wasn't like rain. More like it was crying.

As they listened to Korg's tale, not a word had been spoken among them.

"Who is this Janus?" Johnson asked. "It sounds like Storm Clearwater?"

"It's not me," Clearwater urged, his voice charged with voltage. "I was over there that evening and met Griffin, but I left. Maybe it's MaryLou. Or you, Jesse."

"Shut up if you still want a job," Johnson threatened.

Korg raised a hand.

"When all this is done, there may not be many jobs to go around," Korg explained, calm and sure of himself.

"What do you mean by that?" Johnson flamed.

Korg waved with his right hand, motioning for silence.

35

KORG EYED JOHNSON with grim scorn. Landru, McNabb, MaryLou and Lorelei appeared hypnotized.

"Are you done?" Goldberg asked.

Korg's smile in response meant trouble for Goldberg. "As of this morning, the feds have put a hold on all of Johnson's bank accounts, corporate accounts and real estate holdings. As we speak, FBI agents are searching the main house for documents."

Voltage surged through Johnson's eyes.

"Your passport has been pulled," Korg said. "Your jet is being seized. No more trips to Bermuda."

"Do something," Johnson ordered his attorney.

Goldberg stood and ran his right palm across a greased-over sidewall. "I'll have your badge for this, Inspector Korg."

Korg laughed out loud. "A little late for that." Off to the side, both Sager and Roper stifled a chuckle.

"The feds are pulling your chain, too," Korg said to Goldberg. "You set up the entire scam."

"I have no idea what you are talking about," Goldberg responded.

"Let me help your memory."

The room was so quiet that they could have heard a flower bloom.

"The music industry is in severe decline, with income way down as the CD dies," Korg pointed out. "So just where has Johnson gotten the money for all the goodies he's been buying?"

Lorelei, her brain working fast, tried to decipher Korg's riddle. Clearwater, who had felt cheated by Johnson, leaned forward, validated, hoping for an answer. Korg provided it.

"Ever since Johnson's label income declined, he has been skimming cash from concerts," Korg explained. "Cash from advances and sales of T-shirts and other swag. That money has been taken to the Bahamas, and then laundered back into the U.S. tax-free through shell corporations and real estate deals."

A gasp swept through the room. But the comments appeared to have no effect on Johnson or his lawyer.

"The federal grand jury will indict you for tax evasion, filing false tax returns, money laundering and conspiracy," Korg said.

Klondike stood. "Does this violate my parole?" He blurted out.

Korg engaged the big man warmly. "We've got nothing on you my friend."

Then Korg again grew serious.

"One working theory was that Stephen Griffin, who was getting a cut from this scam, tried to blackmail Johnson for a bigger piece." Korg then turned to Johnson. "So you had Klondike kill him."

Jaws dropped throughout the room. Klondike again

stood, his face aflame. "Bullshit!" The words came out in a half shout. "Clearwater did it."

"It wasn't me!" Clearwater barked in return.

All eyes again turned to Johnson. He felt a need to defend himself, but was too stunned to find the words.

Goldberg jumped in. "Say nothing, Jesse. In fact, we can kick them all out of here right now."

"No, I want to hear this," Johnson said.

Korg's features softened as he turned to Klondike. "Relax, big man. We know you didn't do it."

Then Korg looked up and scanned across to the back of the room to Sager. "Bring it up."

Sager held up a brown paper bag. Korg signaled thumbs-up and Sager came to the front of the room and handed the bag over. Korg, alert for any change in the audience, spotted Winston as he ran his hand over the bulge in his jacket.

"You see that?" Korg whispered to Sager.

"I'm on it. Plus outside, we've got the place surrounded with uniforms." Sager then returned to the back of the room. His hand rested on his .40 Glock, concealed and holstered inside his jacket.

Korg was holding court again, in charge of the room. "On Thursday morning, the morning of the murder cover-up, UPS delivered a package. The driver told us that nobody responded to his knocks on the door so he left the package outside, on the porch. So it had to be either Griffin or the killer who brought it inside. That puts Clearwater out of the picture at the beach house. We know that, because Clearwater was there Wednesday evening, but not Thursday morning. So Clearwater is innocent, or worked the scheme with another person. We think Janus set him up as the patsy to take the fall. That UPS delivery clears Storm Clearwater doing this solo."

Clearwater put two fists in the air. He turned to his dream girl, Lorelei, and spoke in a half shout, "See! I told you. I didn't do anything!"

"Settle down, young man," Korg ordered. The senior inspector was on a roll now.

"When the killer tried to make it look like Griffin had flown off to Las Vegas, Janus messed up then, too. In the kitchen sink, Janus forgot to place a spoon or fork with the soup. In his closet, Janus overlooked taking Griffin's travel toiletries bag, and yet there was all the missing stuff in the bathroom. That didn't make sense."

Korg bit his lower lip, shook his head and continued.

"Stephen Griffin was a diabetic. Yet we found his medicine, his insulin kit, and there's no way a diabetic goes on a trip without it."

Every face in the audience seemed to ask a question, Korg saw.

"Then Janus blew it by changing the password in order to purchase the ticket through Expedia.com on his computer. Griffin traveled so much that he'd never forget his password and need to create a new account."

Korg paused for effect.

"So we knew right away this was no missing person's case. No, we knew it was murder, right from the start."

A collective gasp filled the room.

"And then there was Spoogs. His real name is Stevie Griffith. He was duped into using Griffin's ticket to Las Vegas and was able to take the flight because of the similarity in names, so it looked like Griffin flew to Vegas and disappeared. That's why Spoogs was killed.

To complete the cover-up."

Korg reached into the bag and pulled out a small piece of broken glass.

"I found this little piece of glass under the sofa, from a missing picture on the wall at Griffin's house. Forensics found the glass crystals on top of the lint in the vacuum cleaner bag. So once we figured out what the missing picture was, we figured that someone was enraged by Griffin and the entire Johnson music machine, so that started to hint at a motive."

Korg surveyed the group.

"Anybody got anything to say?"

Everyone stayed silent, tense and expectant.

Korg again reached into the bag. "With a search warrant, Sager found these."

The inspector clutched a stack of yellow sheets of lined legal paper, covered in a handwritten scrawl.

"What is that?" Johnson barked.

"You don't know?" Korg asked. "You should."

The senior agent held up the yellow sheets of paper in a 20-page clump.

"These are the original documents," Korg said to the group. "These are the songs that Janus wrote and that Griffin and Johnson stole."

This time Rock Winston appeared shocked. He looked ready to launch out of the room.

"And then there's this." Korg again reached into the bag. He pulled out two Zip-Loc bags. Each contained a single piece of paper, documents of some kind. Korg held up what appeared a blood-stained note card.

"SFPD found the note that baited the kid Spoogs up to the arcade at AT&T during the set-up for the concert," he said. "When graphologists compared the handwriting of the note to the stolen songs, they say it's a match.

In the back, Sager, hard-faced and sour, nodded at Korg that he was ready.

Korg waved across the room. "The killer calculated that the only one who could connect the dots was Spoogs, so he had to go."

The senior inspector straightened his tie and again reached into the bag.

"You see this?" Korg asked his audience, holding up a document.

He held it out to audience. "Let me read it for you."

Korg paused, unsmiling, then spoke in monotone:

"You only get so much rope."

Korg thumbed through the stack of songs. "Here it is." He held out a sheet of the yellow-lined paper.

"The name of this song is, well, what a surprise," Korg waived the document. "The name of this song is," pausing for inflection, *"You Only Get So Much Rope."*

The inspector dropped his gaze. "Guess that was one that never got recorded."

His words were deliberate and steady. "Spoogs, that poor kid. That one was a real sloppy job. The Griffin case was a lot tougher with no body for awhile, but it was so sophisticated, only one person could have pulled it off. But some mistakes were made there, too."

MaryLou Dietz felt the burn from laser stares. Clearwater, in particular, targeted her.

"Hey, don't look at me like that," she said. "I didn't do anything."

Korg relaxed his shoulders.

"The killer is actually two people," he said.

Another huff went through the room.

"What two?" shouted Clearwater. "It's Johnson and Winston, right? I knew it was them!"

Off to the side, Sager studied every detail. He knew that Winston could try to clean out the room if provoked.

Korg tilted his head with a glare, and Clearwater quickly piped down.

"What we have here is what is called dissociative identity disorder," Korg said. "Janus is two people. Janus swings back and forth between two completely different people, with two distinct identities and personalities."

Korg paused to let the words sink in with no apparent response from the audience.

"That's right, multiple personalities. Each has its own perception, and in this case, does not recognize the other."

Every one in the room gawked. Then, in a swift motion, Korg reached the inside the bag and pulled out a blond wig.

"This explains the mysterious blondie, Kristina," Korg explained, "the woman who had a date with Griffin on the evening of Wednesday, September 25th, the woman who lured Spoogs up to the arcade at AT&T Park."

Korg squared up to Lorelei.

"Turns out that everything you did was for nothing. You were going to get your own label deal anyway."

"I don't know what you're talking about," Lorelei said. "I didn't do anything. I have a label deal now. Just ask Rock Winston and Jesse James Johnson. Everything is fine. I hardly knew Stephen Griffin, met him once or twice with MaryLou."

Sager, standing well back in the room, was ferret-eyed, dark and scowling, his black eyebrows curving down in frowns.

Korg again addressed Lorelei. "We found your DNA in a hair strand on the inside of the wig. If you have nothing to hide, would you mind putting the wig on now?"

"Of course I don't mind," Lorelei answered. "I have nothing to hide. I didn't kill anybody. I'm a singer."

Korg handed the wig to the young woman. In an effortless maneuver, she massaged the wig into place. A perfect fit.

From the bag, Korg pulled a mirror out and held it up to her.

"Kristina, wasn't it you who wrote all those songs, not Lorelei?"

Kristina stood. Her face seemed to change, edged by roughness. Her eyes were daggers.

"I did it all," said Kristina, a crying howl in her voice.

"I wrote all those songs. I fed my songs through MaryLou to Deego and Stephen Griffin. Those songs came from inside me. Every time I heard them on the radio it was like my soul was raped, again and again. Stephen Griffin and Deego had to be punished."

"Was it easy to get Stephen and Deego up to bunker at the park?" Korg asked.

"Those idiots! All I had to do is make them think they had a chance to fuck me, and they'd do anything I said! They deserved to die and I gave them what they deserved."

"What about Spoogs?"

"Same thing. He was hoping I'd blow him. He's

no different."

Korg reached over and removed the blond wig and placed it on the open seat next to her, then again, held up the mirror.

"What's going on?" Lorelei asked. "Why are you looking at me like that? I want to go home now. I want to pet my cat."

She looked at Jesse with urgent eyes. "Take me home now, Jesse."

With no response, she smiled sweetly at Clearwater. "I know, Storm, that you'll help me now, right? We've had something between us, I know that. Will you help me?" Her voice sounded like a little girl, an 8-year-old hoping for a favor.

The response was silence.

Suddenly, her eyes flared. Lorelei reached over, picked up the wig and jammed it on her head, slightly astray.

"OK, you assholes, you're all a part of it, you're all against me," Kristina shouted. Her face agitated, eyes wide, a cry in her voice. "I'll take you all down."

In the next instant, Kristina stood and in one motion, pulled a .38 Smith & Wesson from her purse and jumped back, waving it across the room.

"Anybody move and they die," Kristina wailed. Then she turned to Johnson. "You were next, for stealing my songs. You pig. Just like Griffin. You deserve this. You get it now and my mission is complete."

Kristina had a deranged grin as she swung her gun toward Johnson.

"You took all I had inside me. I have nothing left to lose. But vengeance will be mine and I will have that forever."

From Kristina's blind side, Winston dove in a flying leap. In a synchronized movement, honed from years of action in Special Forces, he swept up with his right hand and knocked Kristina's gun hand skyward. A shot exploded through the ceiling. In the same motion, Winston barreled into Kristina's side, knocking her down. The band members leapt for whatever cover they could find. In the swiftness of the action, Korg was frozen.

On the floor, Winston had a hand on Kristina's left shoulder, then saw, in her right hand, that she still had the gun. He thrust forward and clenched a grip on her forearm and another shot fired. The slug slammed into the wall.

From the side, a sizzling sound zapped through the air.

Kristina let out a sick howl that pierced the room. But she still clutched the small firearm.

Sager pulled the trigger a second time on the Taser gun. A dart had embedded in her neck with his first shot: 50,000 volts went coursing through her body, paralyzing her for the moment. She contorted in spasms.

Winston whacked her wrist with a karate chop and the gun fell free. He pounced on it.

In seconds, Sager had Kristina in handcuffs.

Korg stood over her.

"Listen to me real close," he said. *"You only get so much rope."*

Uniformed officers, who had secured the property and

been waiting outside for the arrest, stormed the room.

But it was already over. Sager was reading Kristina her rights.

She ignored the young inspector and turned to Korg: "I'll have somebody get you," she wailed. "I know people. I'm connected. Never forget. I'll get you for this."

From the side, Bonnie Griffin sprinted toward Kristina. From her angle she had a clear line, and with an outstretched palm, rammed Kristina in the temple and knocked her down. The collision knocked the wig off.

Sager pounced, pulling Bonnie away. "You did it, you bitch," Bonnie cried. "You killed my brother."

Korg held up the mirror once again to the wigless suspect.

"What's going on?" Lorelei said. "Why am I in handcuffs? Why are you hurting me?" She started to cry, then sob, lost in confusion, disarray and pain.

Korg set a gentle hand on her shoulder. He spoke with a touch of emotion in his voice.

"I actually get it, Lorelei, that it wasn't you who killed Stephen Griffin, Spoogs and Deego. I'll try to help you the best I can."

36

THAT EVENING, THE Korg family celebrated with a trip to Harry's Hofbrau. At the buffet line, the retired inspector chose the roast turkey dinner.

"Big surprise," criticized Zack. "You always get the same thing."

"I know what I like," Korg confirmed, then looked over at Emma. "You want anything at the bar? I'm heading up."

"My favorite, please."

At the bar, Korg ordered a glass of chilled pinot grigio for his wife and an ice-cold Pacifico for himself.

His cell phone chimed. A message. He clicked his Smartphone. Roper.

"Daver dogs found another mass gravesite by accident on Montara Mountain. You wouldn't want to unretire, would you?"

Korg punched back. "Not a chance."

"You sure?" came the response.

With a grin, he pounded. "At Harry's, about to get my first retirement Pacifico. Have one too, in spirit with me, right now."

"Got it, bud."

Waiting, he noticed a TV in the upper right corner of the bar, behind the bartender. It was the 6 o'clock news, and his gaze settled on the screen at random, not paying close attention.

Suddenly, a photo of Sager, the official police mug shot, appeared on the screen. Korg straightened. The clip then switched to a shot of Sager and Pritchett, standing on the steps of the courthouse.

"Hey," Korg shouted to the bartender while simultaneously planting a $20 bill on the bar, "turn up the volume, quick, just for a second, and keep the twenty."

The bartender danced over to comply with the request.

Korg listened in. On the bottom of the screen, a subhead flashed "Rock-and-Roller Gone Bad."

"In a gun battle today in Woodside, San Mateo County Homicide Inspector Jeremy Sager subdued and arrested the suspect police believe is responsible for three murders. The victims include the missing agent for rock star Jesse James Johnson, Stephen Griffin. In the arrest, the suspect fired at Sager, according to police, but the inspector then captured Kristina Aicona without injury when he subdued her with a Taser."

The screen flashed a photo of Lorelei. At the bar, Korg walled out everything but the newscast. "Kristina Aicona has the stage name of Lorelei. She was a back-up singer for Jesse James Johnson. When arrested, she claimed the band had stolen songs from her."

The picture switched back to Pritchett. Korg winced at the sound of her piercing voice.

"In the past week, Inspector Sager broke up an armed

robbery in Menlo Park in which he returned fire from two suspects, ending their lives. In the process, he saved the life of a fellow agent and many bystanders."

The news anchor again took over.

"According to San Francisco Homicide, the suspect will also be charged in the murder of a young stagehand who was shot and thrown off the arcade at AT&T Park before the recent Fall Festival Concert. The suspect is also accused of killing the rock band's road manager. San Francisco Police credit Sager for tying the cases together."

The bartender turned to Korg as he placed a Pacifico in front of him. "Looks like we have a new hero in town," he said, pointing a finger at the television, and then with a wink, added, "It's good to see that new D.A. cracking down on crime."

The news anchor took over the screen. "More at 11 about what police call the murder suspect's split personality."

Korg took a long draw on the Pacifico, shook his head and walked back to his family.

On the drive home, Emma punched the radio. The digital readout popped up for KSAN-FM.

Korg immediately recognized the guitar riff. Storm Clearwater. Nobody else could get that sound out of a guitar.

"Quiet," he ordered his family. He turned up the volume and listened:

Looked at the stars and they had gone away.
Soon to come is our judgment day.

Thomas F. Stienstra

No longer can we leave our thoughts unsaid.
Time has come for all to look straight ahead.

Lookin', lookin' straight ahead.
Lookin' lookin' straight ahead.

37

SATURDAY

From Korg's right, the muzzle blast exploded in a volley of shots. They sizzled over his head. He ducked behind a cement wall next to a trash can.

"Automatics!" he shouted, probably an AK-47. With only a handgun, he was outgunned.

He tried to assess his chances and his options. Chances? He was cornered in the garbage stall, with chest-high cement walls on three sides. In the far corner, Roper was holed up in a small wood fort he'd built for his kids long ago. Their one hope was that the assassins did not know the lay-out of Roper's backyard. It appeared there were three gunmen.

Options? Not many.

The assailants had apparently tailed Korg. Roper was showing off fresh brickwork around a new barbecue area when they were waylaid by gunfire. As shots sprayed around them, both dove behind the brickwork, and then during a pause in the gunfire, scampered to separate hiding places.

Korg hoped that his old friend could read his mind.

He remembered Kristina shouting at him when Sager had taken her away: *I'll have somebody get you. I know people. I'm connected. Never forget. I'll get you for this.*

Here it was his first day of retirement and he was in a showdown.

The guns blazed again. They riddled the wood fort. He listened for any sound from Roper, but there was none. No return shots were fired.

He prayed his friend was OK, just lying prone to avoid the shots. 'Read my mind, Joe, read my mind.'

In the far corner of his hiding place, Korg placed his baseball cap on the top of the concrete ledge.

Machine gun fire instantly drilled it. In seconds, the cap was blasted beyond recognition. Korg was glad he wasn't still in it.

That gave him a few seconds to creep to the edge of the opening of the concrete walls, and lie prone, so he could fire from the ground. Maybe the assassins wouldn't expect that. Maybe they'd look for him to burst over the top of the wall in an explosion of fire, from where his hat had been. In his distant memory, he remembered from his training so long ago, to never fire over the top of wall.

Roper opened up. From a rifle slot in the fort, he fired a series of shots.

The assassins, apparently unhurt, again riddled the fort. Quiet followed.

Then Korg saw them. A pair of shooters, one shorter than the other, dressed in black with masks, carrying AK-47s. Working in tandem, without a word and motioning with hand signs, they approached the fort and split up to cover each side. It appeared they were moving in to finish off Roper.

"Not my best friend," Korg muttered under his breath.

Korg rose to a knee, left hand steadying his right, clutching and aiming his gun, and pulled the trigger. His first shot struck the shorter assassin, in the left kidney. Down he went.

The taller assassin turned to fire, but Korg squeezed off a single shot first that drilled the attacker in the chest. He, too, went down.

Korg emerged, and tentatively, he approached the fallen gunmen.

To his surprise, a third assailant appeared to the right and pointed his gun barrel at Korg.

"Prepare to die," he shouted.

Korg had no time to react.

From behind, a single shot drilled the shooter in the back of the head. Roper emerged, his own gun leading the way. He fired another into the shooter, splayed wide, face down.

"Not my best friend," Roper said.

"Thanks," Korg said.

"No, thank you," Roper said. "They had me. You saved my life."

Korg, still tense, answered, "No, you saved my life."

He reached down and turned the first shooter over face up, then removed his mask. He gazed down into the eyes of his son, Zack, paintball gun at his side.

"We finally won," dad said to son.

A few feet away, Rebecca shed her mask. "No you didn't," she claimed. "You cheated."

Korg laughed a winner's laugh.

"Now just how did I cheat?"

"We hit your hat. Your hat is part of your body. So we actually got you."

"Sweetheart, I didn't have it on my head."

Nearby, Roper's son, Robert, shed his mask with a defeated look.

Roper put his arm around Korg's shoulder.

"Ah, you've got to love it," he said with a warm smile.

Korg looked over at his best friend and son Robert with appreciation. He took in the plight of his son and daughter, one pleading the case, the other sheepish. Then, at the brick barbecue, he saw Roper's wife, Cynthia, and next to her, Emma, taking in the scene.

Yes, Korg thought, these are the people I love.

And he felt the day wash over him.

Acknowledgments

Many people had a direct influence shaping this book and I owe them my appreciation and gratitude.

My wife Stephani helped transform the story line and inspired me to get the thing done as best I could.

On a canoe trip, Steve Griffin of Michigan, a muse, writing coach and all-around genius, helped work out two key conflicts in the story line and edited the book. I'd trust my life with him, just as I did this book. That's why I named a lead character after him.

I'm indebted to Suzanne Finney, who line-edited the book and also provided several valuable suggestions, all which I used. John Beath also read the manuscript and I also incorporated his ideas.

It looked like the book was going to take a year or two to get published through traditional channels, but Michael Furniss of Wild Earth Press took my catalog and suggested we put *The Sweet Redemption* out front in the process, and I am greatly appreciative. He came up with the great line, "You only get so much rope." Plus he might just be the greatest guy and best friend on the planet.

John Lescroart, the novelist and my fishing buddy, provided priceless advice, especially one late night in his limo heading out of San Francisco after a book signing. John then introduced me to Al Giannini, the nonpareil prosecutor out of San Mateo County. In turn, Giannini arranged a meeting with Homicide Inspector Joseph J. Toomey of the San Francisco Police Department, Detective Gregg Oglesby of the Daly City Police Department, and inspectors Thomas J. Paulin and Ivan Grosshauser of San Mateo County's Bureau of Investigations. That meeting, amid cigars and fermented spirits, solved the sticking points of the story line.

Readers of the draft who provided additional input were: Jim McDaniel, Shelly and Lance Lewis, Kerima Furniss, Robert Stienstra, Jr., David Zimmer, Ed Rice, Doug Laughlin, Tom Hedtke and Il Ling New. Thank you, all.

Kris Keyston, my younger son, helped pick many character names from his classmates, mixing and matching first names and last. His older brother, Jeremy Keyston, helped work out the gunplay scenes.

Robert and Eleanor Stienstra, my parents, instilled my sense of ethics, basic right-and wrong, love, faith and loyalty that runs through the book.

Reyna Patty told me the deathbed story of the angels on the staircase. My poker buddies, the late John Korb, and Rick Sager, inspired the names for the inspectors. Bob Warren and Rusty Ballinger trusted me with their stories about Delta Force, Phoenix and Omega. Liam Furniss was an early sounding board and provided the nickname, "Spoogs." Clyde Gibbs told me stories about giving money away to panhandlers.

In the world of law, lawyers and enforcement, thank you to Mark Danari and Charles Walker of San Francisco International Airport Security; Lt. Judie Pursell, supervisor of homicide detail at the San Francisco Police Department; Rick Speier, chief of IRS criminal investigations; the Solano County polygraph unit; the late Dan Furniss, an attorney with Townsend & Townsend; attorneys Eric Bergstrom, Chuck Bourdon and Kamran Meyer. Thank you.

From the world of music, I owe great thanks to the late Waylon Jennings, Tom Coster and Elvin Bishop. I am greatly appreciative to Waylon, whose guitar I keep next to my writing desk as a reminder of his inspiration, the success he earned against great odds in a tough business, and the stories he told me about how it all works. Thank you to the late John R. Cash, Hank Williams, Jr., Jessi Colter, Lisa McDowell, Jerry "Jigger" Bridges and Thomas Mattola.

From the San Francisco Chronicle, I owe appreciation about writing skills, the creative process and support in a tough business: Dave Dayton ("Please, not you too"), Steve Proctor ("Don't go sideways on me"), Mark Smoyer, Larry Yant, Al Saracevic, Glenn Schwarz, Ward Bushee, Bruce Jenkins, Joan Ryan and Gwen Knapp.

From radio: Bob Simms of KBFK-Sacramento, John Hamilton of KGO-San Francisco, Ed Cavagnaro of KCBS-San Francisco, and Dave Morey and Peter Finch of KFOG-San Francisco.

From television: Doug Laughlin of ABC; Jim Schlosser, Chris Turner and Celso Bulgatti from Barbary Coast Productions.

Rich Renouf of MacShasta was the computer

technician who oversaw the project and salvaged the manuscript after a hard-drive crash. Scary stuff.

Jim Klinger, the late Ed Dunckel, the late Jeffrey Patty, Craig Chaquico, Dusty Baker, George Seifert, Keith Fraser, Bill Powell, Patty Sakuma and Buzz Eggleston had an effect at various points while I was writing the book.

Thank you for your guidance and inspiration.

—Tom Stienstra

Thomas F. Stienstra

Thomas F. Stienstra is the national award winning outdoors columnist for the San Francisco Chronicle and for *sfgate.com*. His books have sold more than 1 million copies, his weekly radio feature is broadcast from KCBS-San Francisco, and he has hosted his own television show on CBS. He lives with his wife, Stephani, in Northern California.

Thomas F. Stienstra can be reached at his website:
www.TomStienstra.com

Publisher's Note

If you enjoyed this book, be sure to check out two recently published eBooks by Tom Stienstra. They are: the photo-adventure story *Sierra Crossing: The Epic Trek You Can Do In A Week,* and, *Sunday Drive Getaways: 120 Outdoor Adventures in the San Francisco Bay Area and Beyond.* To read more about them, see the slides show and to order the books, go to:

www.wildearthpress.com

You may also get on our mailing list to be notified of upcoming titles as they are published.

We love hearing from you...

Send your feedback to *wildearthpress@gmail.com.* If you see anything that needs updating, clarification, or correction, please drop us a line. Personal comments for Tom Stienstra can be sent to: *tstienstra@sfchronicle.com.*

For more information go to:
www.wildearthpress.com
Find us on Facebook (Wild Earth Press)